STRANGERS ON A TRAIN

Patricia Highsmith was born in Fort Worth, Texas, in 1921. Her parents moved to New York when she was six, and she attended the Julia Richmond High School and Barnard College. In her senior year she edited the college magazine, having decided at the age of sixteen to become a writer. Her first novel, *Strangers on a Train*, was made into the famous film by Alfred Hitchcock in 1951. *The Talented Mr Ripley*, published in 1955, was awarded the Edgar Allan Poe Scroll by the Mystery Writers of America and introduced the fascinating anti-hero Tom Ripley, who was to appear in many of her later crime novels. Patricia Highsmith died in Locarno, Switzerland, in February 1995. Her last novel, *Small g: A Summer Idyll*, was published posthumously just over a month later.

ALSO BY PATRICIA HIGHSMITH

Patricia Highsmith

STRANGERS ON A TRAIN

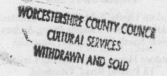
V
V I N T A G E

Published by Vintage 1999

8 10 9 7

'Leaden-Eyed' from *The Congo and Other Poems* by
Vachel Lindsay, copyright 1914, 1942, by The Macmillan
Company and used with their permission

First published in Great Britain by Cresset Press 1950

This edition first published in Great Britain by
William Heinemann 1966

A CIP catalogue record for this book
is available from the British Library

ISBN 0 09 928307 7

Papers used by Random House are natural,
recyclable products made from wood grown in sustainable forests;
the manufacturing processes conform to the environmental
regulations of the country of origin

Printed and bound in Great Britain by
Bookmarque Ltd, Croydon, Surrey

To all the Virginias

I

The train tore along with an angry, irregular rhythm. It was having to stop at smaller and more frequent stations, where it would wait impatiently for a moment, then attack the prairie again. But progress was imperceptible. The prairie only undulated, like a vast, pink-tan blanket being casually shaken. The faster the train went, the more buoyant and taunting the undulations.

Guy took his eyes from the window and hitched himself back against the seat.

Miriam would delay the divorce at best, he thought. She might not even want a divorce, only money. Would there really ever be a divorce from her?

Hate had begun to paralyse his thinking, he realized, to make little blind alleys of the roads that logic had pointed out to him in New York. He could sense Miriam ahead of him, not much farther now, pink and tan-freckled, and radiating a kind of unhealthful heat, like the prairie out the window. Sullen and cruel.

Automatically, he reached for a cigarette, remembered for the tenth time that he couldn't smoke in the Pullman car, then took one anyway. He tapped it twice on the face of his wristwatch, read the time, 5.12, as if it meant anything today, and fitted the cigarette into the corner of his mouth before he brought the cupped match up. The cigarette replaced the match inside his hand, and he smoked in slow, steady pulls. Again and again his brown eyes dropped to the stubborn, fascinating ground out the window. A tab of his soft shirt collar began to ride up. In the reflection the dusk had started to create in the window's glass, the peak of white collar along his jaw suggested a style of the last century, like his black hair that grew high and loose on top and lay close in back. The rise of hair and the slope of his long nose gave him a look of intense purpose and somehow of forward motion, though from the front, his heavy, horizontal brows and mouth imposed a stillness and reserve. He wore flannel trousers that needed pressing, a dark jacket that slacked over his slight body and showed faintly purple where the light struck it, and a tomato-coloured woollen tie, carelessly knotted.

He did not think Miriam would be having a child unless she wanted it. Which should mean the lover intended to marry her. But why had she sent for him? She didn't need him to get a divorce. And why did he go over the same dull ground he had four days ago when he had got her letter? The five or six lines in Miriam's round handwriting had said only that she was going to have a child and wanted to see him. That she was pregnant guaranteed the divorce, he reasoned, so why was he nervous? A suspicion that he might, in some unreachable depth of himself, be jealous because she was going to bear another man's child and had once aborted his own tormented him above all. No, it was nothing but shame that nettled him, he told himself, shame that he had once loved such a person as Miriam. He mashed his cigarette on the heater's grilled cover. The stub rolled out at his feet, and he kicked it back under the heater.

There was so much to look forward to now. His divorce, the work in Florida – it was practically certain the board would pass on his drawings, and he would learn this week – and Anne. He and Anne could begin to plan now. For over a year he had been waiting, fretting, for something – *this* – to happen so he would be free. He felt a pleasant explosion of happiness inside him, and relaxed in the corner of the plush seat. For the last three years, really, he had been waiting for this to happen. He could have bought a divorce, of course, but he hadn't ever amassed that much spare money. Starting a career as an architect, without benefit of a job with a firm, had not been easy and still wasn't. Miriam had never asked for an income, but she plagued him in other ways, by talking of him in Metcalf as if they were still on the best of terms, as if he were up in New York only to establish himself and eventually send for her. Occasionally she wrote him for money, small but irritating amounts which he let her have because it would be so easy for her, so natural to her, to start a campaign in Metcalf against him, and his mother was in Metcalf.

A tall blond young man in a rust-brown suit dropped into the empty seat opposite Guy and, smiling with a vague friendliness, slid over into the corner. Guy glanced at his pallid, undersized face. There was a huge pimple in the exact centre of his forehead. Guy looked out the window again.

The young man opposite him seemed to debate whether to start a conversation or take a nap. His elbow kept sliding along the window-sill, and whenever the stubby lashes came open, the grey bloodshot eyes were looking at him and the soft smile came back. He might have been slightly drunk.

Guy opened his book, but his mind wandered after half a page. He looked up as the row of white fluorescent lights flickered on down the ceiling of the car, let his eyes wander to the unlighted cigar that still gyrated conversationally in a bony hand behind one of the seat backs, and to the monogram that trembled on a thin gold chain across the tie of the young man opposite him. The monogram was C A B, and the tie was of green silk, hand-painted with offensively orange-coloured palm trees. The long rust-brown body was sprawled vulnerably now, the head thrown back so that the big pimple or boil on the forehead might have been a topmost point that had erupted. It was an interesting face, though Guy did not know why. It looked neither young nor old, neither intelligent nor entirely stupid. Between the narrow bulging forehead and the lantern jaw, it scooped degenerately, deep where the mouth lay in a fine line, deepest in the blue hollows that held the small scallops of the lids. The skin was smooth as a girl's, even waxenly clear, as if all its impurities had been drained to feed the pimple's outburst.

For a few moments, Guy read again. The words made sense to him and began to lift his anxiety. But what good will Plato do you with Miriam, an inner voice asked him. It had asked him that in New York, but he had brought the book anyway, an old text from a high school philosophy course, an indulgence to compensate him, perhaps, for having to make the trip to Miriam. He looked out the window and, seeing his own image, straightened his curling collar. Anne was always doing that for him. Suddenly he felt helpless without her. He shifted his position, accidentally touched the outstretched foot of the young man asleep, and watched fascinatedly as the lashes twitched and came open. The bloodshot eyes might have been focused on him all the while through the lids.

'Sorry,' Guy murmured.

' 'S all right,' the other said. He sat up and shook his head sharply. 'Where are we?'

'Getting into Texas.'

The blond young man brought a gold flask from his inside pocket, opened it, and extended it amiably.

'No, thanks,' Guy said. The woman across the aisle, Guy noticed, who had not looked up from her knitting since St Louis, glanced over just as the flask upended with a metallic splash.

'Where you bound?' The smile was a thin wet crescent now.

'Metcalf,' Guy said.

'Oh. Nice town, Metcalf. Down on business?' He blinked his sore-looking eyes politely.

'Yes.'

'What business?'

Guy looked up reluctantly from his book. 'Architect.'

'Oh,' with wistful interest. 'Build houses and things?'

'Yes.'

'I don't think I've introduced myself.' He half stood up. 'Bruno. Charles Anthony Bruno.'

Guy shook his hand briefly. 'Guy Haines.'

'Glad to meet you. You live in New York?' The hoarse baritone voice sounded false, as if he were talking to wake himself up.

'Yes.'

'I live in Long Island. Going to Santa Fe for a little vacation. Ever been to Santa Fe?'

Guy shook his head.

'Great town to relax in.' He smiled, showing poor teeth. 'Mostly Indian architecture there, I guess.'

A conductor stopped in the aisle, thumbing through tickets. 'That your seat?' he asked Bruno.

Bruno leaned possessively into his corner. 'Drawing-room next car.'

'Number Three?'

'I guess. Yeah.'

The conductor went on.

'Those guys!' Bruno murmured. He leaned forward and gazed out the window amusedly.

Guy went back to his book, but the other's obtrusive boredom, a feeling he was about to say something in another instant, kept him from concentrating. Guy contemplated going to the diner, but for some reason sat on. The train was slowing again. When Bruno looked as if he were going to speak, Guy got up, retreated into the next car, and leapt the steps to the crunchy ground before the train had quite stopped.

The more organic air, weighted with nightfall, struck him like a smothering pillow. There was a smell of dusty, sun-warm gravel, of oil and hot metal. He was hungry and lingered near the diner, pacing in slow strides with his hands in his pockets, breathing the air deeply, though he disliked it. A constellation of red and green and white lights hummed southward in the sky. Yesterday, Anne might have come this route, he thought, on her way to Mexico. He might have been with her. She had wanted him to come with her as far as Metcalf. He might have asked her to stay over a day and meet his mother, if it had not been for Miriam. Or even regardless of Miriam, if he had been another sort of person, if he could be simply unconcerned. He had told Anne about Miriam, about almost all of it, but he could not bear the thought of their meeting. He had wanted to travel alone on the train in order to think. And what had he thought so far? What good had thinking or logic ever been where Miriam was concerned?

The conductor's voice shouted a warning, but Guy paced till the last moment, then swung himself aboard the car behind the diner.

The waiter had just taken his order when the blond young man appeared in the doorway of the car, swaying, looking a little truculent with a short cigarette in his mouth. Guy had put him quite out of mind and now his tall rust-brown figure was like a vaguely unpleasant memory. Guy saw him smile as he sighted him.

'Thought you might have missed the train,' Bruno said cheerfully, pulling out a chair.

'If you don't mind, Mr Bruno, I'd like privacy for a while. I have some things to think over.'

Bruno stabbed out the cigarette that was burning his fingers and looked at him blankly. He was drunker than before. His face seemed smeared and fuzzy at the edges. 'We could have privacy in my place. We could have dinner there. How about it?'

'Thanks, I'd rather stay here.'

'Oh, but I insist. Waiter!' Bruno clapped his hands. 'Would you have this gentleman's order sent to Drawing-Room Three and bring me a steak medium rare with French fries and apple pie? And two Scotch and sodas fast as you can, huh?' He looked at Guy and smiled, the soft wistful smile. 'Okay?'

Guy debated, then got up and came with him. What did it matter after all? And wasn't he utterly sick of himself?

There was no need of the Scotches except to provide glasses and ice. The four yellow-labelled bottles of Scotch lined up on an alligator suitcase were the one neat unit of the little room. Suitcases and wardrobe trunks blocked passage everywhere except for a small labyrinthine area in the centre of the floor, and on top of them were strewn sports clothes and equipment, tennis rackets, a bag of golf clubs, a couple of cameras, a wicker basket of fruit and wine bedded in fuchsia paper. A splay of current magazines, comic books and novels covered the seat by the window. There was also a box of candy with a red ribbon across the lid.

'Looks kind of athletic, I guess,' Bruno said, suddenly apologetic.

'It's fine.' Guy smiled slowly. The room amused him and gave him a welcome sense of seclusion. With the smile his dark brows relaxed, transforming his whole expression. His eyes looked outward now. He stepped lithely in the alleys between suitcases, examining things like a curious cat.

'Brand-new. Never felt a ball,' Bruno informed him, holding out a tennis racket for him to feel. 'My mother makes me take all this stuff, hoping it'll keep me out of bars. Good to hock if I run out, anyway. I like to drink when I travel. It enhances things, don't you think?' The highballs arrived, and Bruno strengthened them from one of his bottles. 'Sit down. Take off your coat.'

But neither of them sat down or removed his coat. There was an awkward several minutes when they had nothing to say to each other. Guy took a swallow of the highball that seemed to be all Scotch, and looked down at the littered floor. Bruno had odd feet, Guy noticed, or maybe it was the shoes. Small, light tan shoes with a long plain toecap shaped like Bruno's lantern chin. Somehow old-fashioned-looking feet. And Bruno was not so slender as he had thought. His long legs were heavy and his body rounded.

'I hope you weren't annoyed,' Bruno said cautiously, 'when I came in the diner.'

'Oh, no.'

'I felt lonely. You know.'

Guy said something about its being lonely travelling in a drawing-room alone, then nearly tripped on something: the strap of a Rolleiflex camera. There was a new white scratch deep down the side of its leather case. He was conscious of Bruno's shy stare. He was going to be bored, of course. Why had he come? A pang of conscience made him want to return to the diner. Then the waiter arrived with a pewter-covered tray, and snapped up a table. The smell of charcoal-broiled meat cheered him. Bruno insisted so desperately on paying the check that Guy gave it up. Bruno had a big mushroom-covered steak. Guy had hamburger.

'What're you building in Metcalf?'

'Nothing,' Guy said. 'My mother lives there.'

'Oh,' Bruno said interestedly. 'Visiting her? Is that where you're from?'

'Yes. Born there.'

'You don't look much like a Texan.' Bruno shot ketchup all over his steak and French fries, then delicately picked up the parsley and held it poised. 'How long since you been home?'

'About two years.'

'Your father there, too?'

'My father's dead.'

'Oh. Get along with your mother okay?'

Guy said he did. The taste of Scotch, though Guy didn't much care for it, was pleasant because it reminded him of Anne. She drank Scotch, when she drank. It was like her, golden, full of light, made with careful art. 'Where do you live in Long Island?'

'Great Neck.'

Anne lived much farther out on Long Island.

'In a house I call the Doghouse,' Bruno went on. 'There's dogwood all around it and everybody in it's in some kind of doghouse, down to the chauffeur.' He laughed suddenly with real pleasure, and bent again over his food.

Looking at him now, Guy saw only the top of his narrow thin-haired head and the protruding pimple. He had not been conscious of the pimple since he had seen him asleep, but now that he noticed it again, it seemed a monstrous, shocking thing and he saw it alone. 'Why?' Guy asked.

'Account of my father. Bastard. I get on okay with my mother, too. My mother's coming out to Santa Fe in a couple days.'

'That's nice.'

'It is,' Bruno said as if contradicting him. 'We have a lot of fun together – sitting around, playing golf. We even go to parties together.' He laughed, half ashamed, half proud, and suddenly uncertain and young. 'You think that's funny?'

'No,' said Guy.

'I just wish I had my own dough. See, my income was supposed to start this year, only my father won't let me have it. He's deflecting it into his own exchequer. You might not think so, but I haven't got any more money now than I had when I was in school with everything paid for. I have to ask for a hundred dollars now and then from my mother.' He smiled, pluckily.

'I wish you had let me pay the check.'

'A-aw, now!' Bruno protested. 'I just mean it's a hell of a thing, isn't it, when your own father robs you. It isn't even his money, it's my mother's family's money.' He waited for Guy to comment.

'Hasn't your mother any say about it?'

'My father got his name put on it when I was a kid!' Bruno shouted hoarsely.

'Oh.' Guy wondered how many people Bruno had met, bought dinners for, and told the same story about his father. 'Why did he do that?'

Bruno brought his hands up in a hopeless shrug, then hid them fast in his pockets. 'I said he was a bastard, didn't I? He robs everyone he can. Now he says he won't give it to me because I won't work, but that's a lie. He thinks my mother and I have too good a time as it is. He's always scheming up ways to cut in.'

Guy could see him and his mother, a youngish Long Island society woman who used too much mascara and occasionally, like her son, enjoyed tough company. 'Where'd you go to college?'

'Harvard. Busted out sophomore year. Drinking and gambling.' He shrugged with a writhing movement of his narrow shoulders. 'Not like you, huh? Okay, I'm a bum, so what?' He poured more Scotch for both of them.

'Who said you were?'

'My father says so. He should've had a nice quiet son like you, then everybody would've been happy.'

'What makes you think I'm nice and quiet?'

'I mean you're serious and you choose a profession. Like architecture. Me, I don't feel like working. I don't have to work, see? I'm not a writer or a painter or a musician. Is there any reason a person should work if they don't have to? I'll get my ulcers the easy way. My father has ulcers. Hah! He still has hopes I'll enter his hardware business. I tell him his business, all business, is legalized throat-cutting, like marriage is legalized fornication. Am I right?'

Guy looked at him wryly and sprinkled salt on the French fried potato on his fork. He was eating slowly, enjoying his meal, even vaguely enjoying Bruno, as he might have enjoyed an entertainment on a distant stage. Actually, he was thinking of Anne. Sometimes the faint continuous dream he had of her seemed more real than the outside world that penetrated only in sharp fragments, occasional images, like the scratch on the Rolleiflex case, the long cigarette Bruno had plunged into his pat of butter, the shattered glass of the photograph of the father

15

Bruno had thrown out in the hall in the story he was telling now. It had just occurred to Guy he might have time to see Anne in Mexico, between seeing Miriam and going to Florida. If he got through with Miriam quickly, he could fly to Mexico and fly to Palm Beach. It hadn't occurred to him before because he couldn't afford it. But if the Palm Beach contract came through, he could.

'Can you imagine anything more insulting? Locking the garage where my own car is?' Bruno's voice had cracked and was stuck at a shrieking pitch.

'Why?' Guy asked.

'Just because he knew I needed it bad that night! My friends picked me up finally, so what does he get out of it?'

Guy didn't know what to say. 'He keeps the keys?'

'He took *my keys*! Took them out of my room! That's why he was scared of me. He left the house that night, he was so scared.' Bruno was turned in his chair, breathing hard, chewing a fingernail. Some wisps of hair, darkened brown with sweat, bobbed like antennae over his forehead. 'My mother wasn't home, or it never could have happened, of course.'

'Of course,' Guy echoed involuntarily. Their whole conversation had been leading to this story, he supposed, that he had heard only half of. Back of the bloodshot eyes that had opened on him in the Pullman car, back of the wistful smile, another story of hatred and injustice. 'So you threw his picture out in the hall?' Guy asked meaninglessly.

'I threw it out of my mother's room,' Bruno said, emphasizing the last three words. 'My father put it in my mother's room. She doesn't like the Captain any better than I do. The Captain! – *I* don't call him anything, brother!'

'But what's he got against you?'

'Against me and my mother, too! He's different from us or any other *human*! He doesn't like anybody. He doesn't like anything but money. He cut enough throats to make a lot of money, that's all. Sure he's smart! Okay! But his conscience is sure eating him now! That's why he wants me to go into his business, so I'll cut throats and feel as lousy as he does!' Bruno's stiff hand closed, then his mouth, then his eyes.

Guy thought he was about to cry, when the puffy lids lifted and the smile staggered back.

'Boring, huh? I was just explaining why I left town so soon, ahead of my mother. You don't know what a cheerful guy I am really! Honest!'

'Can't you leave home if you want to?'

Bruno didn't seem to understand his question at first, then he answered calmly, 'Sure, only I like to be with my mother.'

And his mother stayed because of the money, Guy supposed. 'Cigarette?'

Bruno took one, smiling. 'You know, the night he left the house was the first time in maybe ten years he'd gone out. I wonder where the hell he even went. I was sore enough that night to kill him and he knew it. Ever feel like murdering somebody?'

'No.'

'I do. I'm sure sometimes I could kill my father.' He looked down at his plate with a bemused smile. 'You know what my father does for a hobby? Guess.'

Guy didn't want to guess. He felt suddenly bored and wanted to be alone.

'He collects cookie cutters!' Bruno exploded with a snickering laugh. 'Cookie cutters, honest! He's got all kinds – Pennsylvania Dutch, Bavarian, English, French, a lot of Hungarian, all around the room. Animal-cracker cookie cutters framed over his desk – you know, the things kids eat in boxes? He wrote the president of the company and they sent him a whole set. The machine age!' Bruno laughed and ducked his head.

Guy stared at him. Bruno himself was funnier than what he said. 'Does he ever use them?'

'Huh?'

'Does he ever make cookies?'

Bruno whooped. With a wriggle, he removed his jacket and flung it at a suitcase. For a moment he seemed too excited to say anything, then remarked with sudden quiet, 'My mother's always telling him to go back to his cookie cutters.' A film of sweat covered his smooth face like thin oil. He thrust his smile solicitously half across the table. 'Enjoy your dinner?'

'Very much,' Guy said heartily.

'Ever hear of the Bruno Transforming Company of Long Island? Makes AC-DC gadgets?'

'I don't think so.'

'Well, why should you? Makes plenty of dough though. You interested in making money?'

'Not awfully.'

'Mind if I ask how old you are?'

'Twenty-nine.'

'Yeah? I would've said older. How old you think I look?'

Guy studied him politely. 'Maybe twenty-four or five,' he answered, intending to flatter him, for he looked younger.

'Yeah, I am. Twenty-five. You mean I do look twenty-five with this — this *thing* right in the centre of my head?' Bruno caught his underlip between his teeth. A glint of wariness came in his eyes, and suddenly he cupped his hand over his forehead in intense and bitter shame. He sprang up and went to the mirror. 'I meant to put something over it.'

Guy said something reassuring, but Bruno kept looking at himself this way and that in the mirror, in an agony of self-torture. 'It *couldn't* be a pimple,' he said nasally. 'It's a boil. It's everything I *hate* boiling up in me. It's a plague of Job!'

'Oh, now!' Guy laughed.

'It started coming Monday night after that fight. It's getting worse. I bet it leaves a scar.'

'No, it won't.'

'Yes, it will. A fine thing to get to Santa Fe with!' He was sitting in his chair now with his fists clenched and one heavy leg trailing, in a pose of brooding tragedy.

Guy went over and opened one of the books on the seat by the window. It was a detective novel. They were all detective novels. When he tried to read a few lines, the print swam and he closed the book. He must have drunk a lot, he thought. He didn't really care, tonight.

'In Santa Fe,' Bruno said, 'I want everything there is. Wine, women, and song. Hah!'

'What do you want?'

'Something.' Bruno's mouth turned down in an ugly grimace of unconcern. 'Everything. I got a theory a person ought to do everything it's possible to do before he dies, and maybe die trying to do something that's really impossible.'

Something in Guy responded with a leap, then cautiously drew back. He asked softly, 'Like what?'

'Like a trip to the moon in a rocket. Setting a speed record in a car – blindfolded. I did that once. Didn't set a record, but I went up to a hundred sixty.'

'Blindfolded?'

'And I did a robbery.' Bruno stared at Guy rigidly. 'Good one. Out of an apartment.'

An incredulous smile started on Guy's lips, though actually he believed Bruno. Bruno could be violent. He could be insane, too. Despair, Guy thought, not insanity. The desperate boredom of the wealthy, that he often spoke of to Anne. It tended to destroy rather than create. And it could lead to crime as easily as privation.

'Not to get anything,' Bruno went on. 'I didn't want what I took. I especially took what I didn't want.'

'What did you take?'

Bruno shrugged. 'Cigarette lighter. Table model. And a statue off the mantel. Coloured glass. And something else.' Another shrug. 'You're the only one knows about it. I don't talk much. Guess you think I do.' He smiled.

Guy drew on his cigarette. 'How'd you go about it?'

'Watched an apartment house in Astoria till I got the time right, then just walked in the window. Down the fire escape. Sort of easy. One of the things I cross off my list, thinking thank God.'

'Why "thank God"?'

Bruno grinned shyly. 'I don't know why I said that.' He refilled his glass, then Guy's.

Guy looked at the stiff, shaky hands that had stolen, at the nails bitten below the quick. The hands played clumsily with a match cover and dropped it, like a baby's hands, on to the ash-sprinkled steak. How boring it was really, Guy thought, crime. How motiveless often. A certain type turned to crime. And who would know from Bruno's hands, or his room, or his ugly wistful face that he had stolen? Guy dropped into his chair again.

'Tell me about you,' Bruno invited pleasantly.

'Nothing to tell.' Guy took a pipe from his jacket pocket, banged it on his heel, looked down at the ashes on the carpet, and then forgot them. The tingling of the alcohol sank deeper into his flesh. He thought, if the Palm Beach contract came through, the two weeks before work began would pass quickly. A divorce needn't take long. The pattern of the low white buildings on the green lawn in his finished drawing swam familiarly in his mind, in detail, without his trying to evoke them. He felt subtly flattered, immensely secure suddenly, and blessed.

'What kind of houses you build?' Bruno asked.

'Oh – what's known as modern. I've done a couple of stores and a small office building.' Guy smiled, feeling none of the reticence, the faint vexation he generally did when people asked him about his work.

'You married?'

'No. Well, I am, yes. Separated.'

'Oh. Why?'

'Incompatible,' Guy replied.

'How long you been separated?'

'Three years.'

'You don't want a divorce?'

Guy hesitated, frowning.

'Is she in Texas, too?'

'Yes.'

'Going to see her?'

'I'll see her. We're going to arrange the divorce now.' His teeth set. Why had he said it?

Bruno sneered. 'What kind of girls you find to marry down there?'

'Very pretty,' Guy replied. 'Some of them.'

'Mostly dumb though, huh?'

'They can be.' He smiled to himself. Miriam was the kind of Southern girl Bruno probably meant.

'What kind of girl's your wife?'

'Rather pretty,' Guy said cautiously. 'Red hair. A little plump.'

'What's her name?'

'Miriam. Miriam Joyce.'

'Hm-m. Smart or dumb?'

'She's not an intellectual. I didn't want to marry an intellectual.'

'And you loved her like hell, huh?'

Why? Did he show it? Bruno's eyes were fixed on him, missing nothing, unblinking, as if their exhaustion had passed the point where sleep is imperative. Guy had a feeling those grey eyes had been searching him for hours and hours. 'Why do you say that?'

'You're a nice guy. You take everything serious. You take women the hard way, too, don't you?'

'What's the hard way?' he retorted. But he felt a rush of affection for Bruno because Bruno had said what he thought about him. Most people, Guy knew, didn't say what they thought about him.

Bruno made little scallops in the air with his hands, and sighed.

'What's the hard way?' Guy repeated.

'All out, with a lot of high hopes. Then you get kicked in the teeth, right?'

'Not entirely.' A throb of self-pity piqued him, however, and he got up, taking his drink with him. There was no place to move in the room. The swaying of the train made it difficult even to stand upright.

And Bruno kept staring at him, one old-fashioned foot dangling at the end of the crossed leg, flicking his finger again and again on the cigarette he held over his plate. The unfinished pink and black steak was slowly being covered by the rain of ashes. Bruno looked less friendly, Guy suspected, since he had told him he was married. And more curious.

'What happened with your wife? She start sleeping around?'

That irritated him, too, Bruno's accuracy. 'No. That's all past anyway.'

'But you're still married to her. Couldn't you get a divorce before now?'

Guy felt instantaneous shame. 'I haven't been much concerned about a divorce.'

'What's happened now?'

'She just decided she wanted one. I think she's going to have a child.'

'Oh. Fine time to decide, huh? She's been sleeping around for three years and finally landed somebody?'

Just what had happened, of course, and probably it had taken the baby to do it. How did Bruno know? Guy felt that Bruno was superimposing upon Miriam the knowledge and hatred of someone else he knew. Guy turned to the window. The window gave him nothing but his own image. He could feel his heartbeats shaking his body, deeper than the train's vibrations. Perhaps, he thought, his heart was beating because he had never told anyone so much about Miriam. He had never told Anne as much as Bruno knew already. Except that Miriam had once been different – sweet, loyal, lonely, terribly in need of him and of freedom from her family. He would see Miriam tomorrow, be able to touch her by putting out his hand. He could not bear the thought of touching her oversoft flesh that once he had loved. Failure overwhelmed him suddenly.

'What happened with your marriage?' Bruno's voice asked gently, right behind him. 'I'm really very interested, as a friend. How old was she?'

'Eighteen.'

'She start sleeping around right away?'

Guy turned reflexively, as if to shoulder Miriam's guilt. 'That's not the only thing women do, you know.'

'But she did, didn't she?'

Guy looked away, annoyed and fascinated at the same time. 'Yes.' How ugly the little word sounded, hissing in his ears!

'I know that Southern redhead type,' Bruno said, poking at his apple pie.

Guy was conscious again of an acute and absolutely useless shame. Useless, because nothing Miriam had done or said would embarrass or surprise Bruno. Bruno seemed incapable of surprise, only of a whetting of interest.

Bruno looked down at his plate with coy amusement. His

eyes widened, bright as they could be with the bloodshot and the blue circles. 'Marriage,' he sighed.

The word 'marriage' lingered in Guy's ears, too. It was a solemn word to him. It had the primordial solemnity of *holy, love, sin*. It was Miriam's round terracotta-coloured mouth saying, 'Why should I put myself out for *you*?' and it was Anne's eyes as she pushed her hair back and looked up at him on the lawn of her house where she planted crocuses. It was Miriam turning from the tall thin window in the room in Chicago, lifting her freckled, shield-shaped face directly up to his as she always did before she told a lie, and Steve's long dark head, insolently smiling. Memories began to crowd in, and he wanted to put his hands up and push them back. The room in Chicago where it had all happened . . . He could smell the room, Miriam's perfume, and the heat from painted radiators. He stood passively, for the first time in years not thrusting Miriam's face back to a pink blur. What would it do to him if he let it all flood him again, now? Arm him against her or undermine him?

'I mean it,' Bruno's voice said distantly. 'What happened? You don't mind telling me, do you? I'm interested.'

Steve happened. Guy picked up his drink. He saw the afternoon in Chicago, framed by the doorway of the room, the image grey and black now like a photograph. The afternoon he had found them in the apartment, like no other afternoon, with its own colour, taste, and sound, its own world, like a horrible little work of art. Like a date in history fixed in time. Or wasn't it just the opposite, that it travelled with him always? For here it was now, as clear as it had ever been. And, worst of all, he was aware of an impulse to tell Bruno everything, the stranger on the train who would listen, commiserate, and forget. The idea of telling Bruno began to comfort him. Bruno was not the ordinary stranger on the train by any means. He was cruel and corrupt enough himself to appreciate a story like that of his first love. And Steve was only the surprise ending that made the rest fall into place. Steve wasn't the first betrayal. It was only his twenty-six-year-old pride that had exploded in his face that afternoon. He had told the story to himself a thousand times, a classic story, dramatic for all his stupidity. His stupidity only lent it humour.

23

'I expected too much of her,' Guy said casually, 'without any right to. She happened to like attention. She'll probably flirt all her life, no matter whom she's with.'

'I know, the eternal high school type.' Bruno waved his hand. 'Can't even pretend to belong to one guy, ever.'

Guy looked at him. Miriam had, of course, once.

Abruptly he abandoned his idea of telling Bruno, ashamed that he had nearly begun. Bruno seemed unconcerned now, in fact, whether he told it or not. Slumped, Bruno was drawing with a match in the gravy of his plate. The down-turned half of his mouth, in profile, was sunken between nose and chin like the mouth of an old man. The mouth seemed to say, whatever the story, it was really beneath his contempt to listen.

'Women like that draw men,' Bruno mumbled, 'like garbage draws flies.'

2

The shock of Bruno's words detached him from himself. 'You must have had some unpleasant experiences yourself,' he remarked. But Bruno troubled by women was hard to imagine.

'Oh, my father had one like that. Redhead, too. Named Carlotta.' He looked up, and the hatred for his father penetrated his fuzziness like a barb. 'Fine, isn't it? It's men like my father keep 'em in business.'

Carlotta. Guy felt he understood now why Bruno loathed Miriam. It seemed the key to Bruno's whole personality, to the hatred of his father and to his retarded adolescence.

'There's two kinds of guys!' Bruno announced in a roaring voice, and stopped.

Guy caught a glimpse of himself in a narrow panel mirror on the wall. His eyes looked frightened, he thought, his mouth grim, and deliberately he relaxed. A golf club nudged him in the back. He ran his fingertips over its cool varnished surface. The inlaid metal in the dark wood recalled the binnacle on Anne's sailboat.

'And essentially one kind of women!' Bruno went on. 'Two-timers. At one end it's two-timing and the other end it's a whore! Take your choice!'

'What about women like your mother?'

'I never seen another woman like my mother,' Bruno declared. 'I never seen a woman take so much. She's good-looking, too, lots of men friends, but she doesn't fool around with them.'

Silence.

Guy tapped another cigarette on his watch and saw it was 10.30. He must go in a moment.

'How'd you find out about your wife?' Bruno peered up at him.

Guy took his time with his cigarette.

'How many'd she have?'

'Quite a few. Before I found out.' And just as he assured himself it made no difference at all now to admit it, a sensation as of a tiny whirlpool inside him began to confuse him. Tiny, but realer than the memories somehow, because he had uttered it. Pride? Hatred? Or merely impatience with himself, because all that he kept feeling now was so useless? He turned the conversation from himself. 'Tell me what else you want to do before you die?'

'Die? Who said anything about dying? I got a few crack-proof rackets doped out. Could start one some day in Chicago or New York, or I might just sell my ideas. And I got a lot of ideas for perfect murders.' Bruno looked up again with that fixity that seemed to invite challenge.

'I hope your asking me here isn't part of one of your plans.' Guy sat down.

'Jesus Christ, I *like* you, Guy! I really do!'

The wistful face pled with Guy to say he liked him, too. The loneliness in those tiny, tortured eyes! Guy looked down embarrassedly at his hands. 'Do all your ideas run to crime?'

'Certainly not! Just things I want to do, like – I want to give a guy a thousand dollars some day. A beggar. When I get my own dough, that's one of the first things I'm gonna do. But didn't you ever feel you wanted to steal something? Or kill somebody?

You must have. Everybody feels those things. Don't you think some people get quite a kick out of killing people in wars?'

'No,' Guy said.

Bruno hesitated. 'Oh, they'd never admit it, of course, they're afraid! But you've had people in your life you'd have liked out of the way, haven't you?'

'No.' Steve, he remembered suddenly. Once he had even thought of murdering him.

Bruno cocked his head. 'Sure you have. I see it. Why don't you admit it?'

'I may have had fleeting ideas, but I'd never have done anything about them. I'm not that kind of person.'

'That's exactly where you're wrong! Any kind of person can murder. Purely circumstances and not a thing to do with temperament! People get so far – and it takes just the least little thing to push them over the brink. Anybody. Even your grandmother. I know.'

'I don't happen to agree,' Guy said tersely.

'I tell you I came near murdering my father a thousand times! Who'd you ever feel like murdering? The guys with your wife?'

'One of them,' Guy murmured.

'How near did you come?'

'Not near at all. I merely thought of it.' He remembered the sleepless nights, hundreds of them, and the despair of peace unless he avenged himself. Could something have pushed him over the line then? He heard Bruno's voice mumbling, 'You were a hell of a lot nearer than you think, that's all I can say.' Guy gazed at him puzzledly. His figure had the sickly, nocturnal look of a croupier's, hunched on shirt-sleeved forearms over the table, thin head hanging. 'You read too many detective stories,' Guy said, and having heard himself, did not know where the words had come from.

'They're good. They show all kinds of people can murder.'

'I've always thought that's exactly why they're bad.'

'Wrong again!' Bruno said indignantly. 'Do you know what percentage of murders get put in the papers?'

'I don't know and I don't care.'

'One twelfth. One twelfth! Just imagine! Who do you think

the other eleven twelfths are? A lot of little people that don't matter. All the people the cops know they'll never catch.' He started to pour more Scotch, found the bottle empty, and dragged himself up. A gold penknife flashed out of his trousers pocket on a gold chain fine as a string. It pleased Guy aesthetically, as a beautiful piece of jewellery might have. And he found himself thinking, as he watched Bruno slash round the top of a Scotch bottle, that Bruno might murder one day with the little penknife, that he would probably go quite free, simply because he wouldn't much care whether he were caught or not.

Bruno turned, grinning, with the new bottle of Scotch. 'Come to Santa Fe with me, huh? Relax for a couple of days.'

'Thanks, I can't.'

'I got plenty of dough. Be my guest, huh?' He spilled Scotch on the table.

'Thanks,' Guy said. From his clothes, he supposed, Bruno thought he hadn't much money. They were his favourite trousers, these grey flannels. He was going to wear them in Metcalf and in Palm Beach, too, if it wasn't too hot. Leaning back, he put his hands in his pockets and felt a hole at the bottom of the right one.

'Why not?' Bruno handed him his drink. 'I like you a lot, Guy.'

'Why?'

'Because you're a good guy. Decent, I mean. I meet a lot of guys – no pun – but not many like you. I admire you,' he blurted, and sank his lip into his glass.

'I like you, too,' said Guy.

'Come with me, huh? I got nothing to do for two or three days till my mother comes. We could have a swell time.'

'Pick up somebody else.'

'Cheeses, Guy, what d'you think I do, go around picking up travelling companions? I like you, so I ask you to come with me. One day even. I'll cut right over from Metcalf and not even go to El Paso. I'm supposed to see the Canyon.'

'Thanks, I've got a job as soon as I finish in Metcalf.'

'Oh.' The wistful, admiring smile again. 'Building something?'

'Yes, a country club.' It still sounded strange and unlike himself, the last thing he would have thought he'd be building, two months ago. 'The new Palmyra in Palm Beach.'

'Yeah?'

Bruno had heard of the Palmyra Club, of course. It was the biggest in Palm Beach. He had even heard they were going to build a new one. He had been to the old one a couple of times.

'You designed it?' He looked down at Guy like a hero-worshipping little boy. 'Can you draw me a picture of it?'

Guy drew a quick sketch of the buildings in the back of Bruno's address book and signed his name, as Bruno wanted. He explained the wall that would drop to make the lower floor one great ballroom extending on to the terrace, the louvre windows he hoped to get permission for that would eliminate air-conditioning. He grew happy as he talked, and tears of excitement came in his eyes, though he kept his voice low. How could he talk so intimately to Bruno, he wondered, reveal the very best of himself? Who was less likely to understand than Bruno?

'Sounds terrific,' Bruno said. 'You mean, you tell them how it's gonna look?'

'No. One has to please quite a lot of people.' Guy put his head back suddenly and laughed.

'You're gonna be famous, huh? Maybe you're famous now.'

There would be photographs in the news magazines, perhaps something in the newsreels. They hadn't passed on his sketches yet, he reminded himself, but he was so sure they would. Myers, the architect he shared an office with in New York was sure. Anne was positive. And so was Mr Brillhart. The biggest commission of his life. 'I might be famous after this. It's the kind of thing they publicize.'

Bruno began to tell him a long story about his life in college, how he would have become a photographer if something hadn't happened at a certain time with his father. Guy didn't listen. He sipped his drink absently, and thought of the commissions that would come after Palm Beach. Soon, perhaps, an office building in New York. He had an idea for an office building in New York, and he longed to see it come into being. Guy Daniel Haines. *A name*. No longer the irksome, never quite banished awareness that he had less money than Anne.

'Wouldn't it, Guy?' Bruno repeated.

'What?'

Bruno took a deep breath. 'If your wife made a stink now about the divorce. Say she fought about it while you were in Palm Beach and made them fire you, wouldn't that be motive enough for murder?'

'Of Miriam?'

'Sure.'

'No,' Guy said. But the question disturbed him. He was afraid Miriam had heard of the Palmyra job through his mother, that she might try to interfere for the sheer pleasure of hurting him.

'When she was two-timing you, didn't you feel like murdering her?'

'No. Can't you get off the subject?' For an instant, Guy saw both halves of his life, his marriage and his career, side by side as he felt he had never seen them before. His brain swam sickeningly, trying to understand how he could be so stupid and helpless in one and so capable in the other. He glanced at Bruno, who still stared at him, and feeling slightly befuddled, set his glass on the table and pushed it fingers' length away.

'You must have wanted to once,' Bruno said with gentle, drunken persistence.

'No.' Guy wanted to get out and take a walk, but the train kept on and on in a straight line, like something that would never stop. Suppose Miriam did lose him the commission. He was going to live there several months, and he would be expected to keep on a social par with the directors. Bruno understood such things very well. He passed his hand across his moist forehead. The difficulty was, of course, that he wouldn't know what was in Miriam's mind until he saw her. He was tired, and when he was tired, Miriam could invade him like an army. It had happened so often in the two years it had taken him to turn loose of his love for her. It was happening now. He felt sick of Bruno. Bruno was smiling.

'Shall I tell you one of my ideas for murdering my father?'

'No,' Guy said. He put his hand over the glass Bruno was about to refill.

'Which do you want, the busted light socket in the bathroom or the carbon monoxide garage?'

'Do it and stop talking about it!'

'I'll do it, don't think I won't! Know what else I'll do some day? Commit suicide if I happen to feel like committing suicide, and fix it so it looks like my worst enemy murdered me.'

Guy looked at him in disgust. Bruno seemed to be growing indefinite at the edges, as if by some process of deliquescence. He seemed only a voice and a spirit now, the spirit of evil. All he despised, Guy thought, Bruno represented. All the things he would not want to be, Bruno was, or would become.

'Want me to dope out a perfect murder of your wife for you? You might want to use it some time.' Bruno squirmed with self-consciousness under Guy's scrutiny.

Guy stood up. 'I want to take a walk.'

Bruno slammed·his palms together. 'Hey! Cheeses, what an idea! We murder for each other, see? I kill your wife and you kill my father! We meet on the train, see, and nobody knows we know each other! Perfect alibis! Catch?'

The wall before his eyes pulsed rhythmically, as if it were about to spring apart. *Murder*. The word sickened him, terrified him. He wanted to break away from Bruno, get out of the room, but a nightmarish heaviness held him. He tried to steady himself by straightening out the wall, by understanding what Bruno was saying, because he could feel there was logic in it somewhere, like a problem or a puzzle to be solved.

Bruno's tobacco-stained hands jumped and trembled on his knees. 'Air-tight alibis!' he shrieked. 'It's the idea of my life! Don't you get it? I could do it some time when you're out of town and you could do it when I was out of town.'

Guy understood. No one could ever, possibly, find out.

'It would give me a great pleasure to stop a career like Miriam's and to further a career like yours.' Bruno giggled. 'Don't you agree she ought to be stopped before she ruins a lot of other people? Sit down, Guy!'

She hasn't ruined me, Guy wanted to remind him, but Bruno gave him no time.

'I mean, just supposing the set-up was that. Could you do it?

You could tell me all about where she lived, you know, and I could do the same for you, as good as if you lived there. We could leave fingerprints all over the place and only drive the dicks batty!' He snickered. 'Months apart, of course, and strictly no communication. Christ, it's a cinch!' He stood up and nearly toppled, getting his drink. Then he was saying, right in Guy's face, with suffocating confidence: 'You could do it, huh, Guy? Wouldn't be any hitches, I swear. I'd fix everything, I swear, Guy.'

Guy thrust him away, harder than he had intended. Bruno rose resiliently from the window seat. Guy glanced about for air, but the walls presented an unbroken surface. The room had become a little hell. What was he doing here? How and when had he drunk so much?

'I'm positive you *could*!' Bruno frowned.

Shut up with your damned theories, Guy wanted to shout back, but instead his voice came like a whisper: 'I'm sick of this.'

He saw Bruno's narrow face twist then in a queer way – in a smirk of surprise, a look that was eerily omniscient and hideous. Bruno shrugged affably.

'Okay. I still say it's a good idea and we got the absolutely perfect set-up right here. It's the idea I'll use. With somebody else, of course. Where are you going?'

Guy had at last thought of the door. He went out and opened another door on to the platform where the cooler air smashed him like a reprimand and the train's voice rose to an upbraiding blare. He added his own curses of himself to the wind and the train, and longed to be sick.

'Guy?'

Turning, he saw Bruno slithering past the heavy door.

'Guy, I'm sorry.'

'That's all right,' Guy said at once, because Bruno's face shocked him. It was doglike in its self-abasement.

'Thanks, Guy.' Bruno bent his head, and at that instant the pound-pound-pound of the wheels began to die away, and Guy had to catch his balance.

He felt enormously grateful, because the train was stopping.

He slapped Bruno's shoulder. 'Let's get off and get some air!'

They stepped out into a world of silence and total blackness. 'The hell's the idea?' Bruno shouted. 'No lights!'

Guy looked up. There was no moon either. The chill made his body rigid and alert. He heard the homely slap of a wooden door somewhere. A spark grew into a lantern ahead of them, and a man ran with it towards the rear of the train where a box-car door unrolled a square of light. Guy walked slowly towards the light, and Bruno followed him.

Far away on the flat black prairie a locomotive wailed, on and on, and then again, farther away. It was a sound he remembered from childhood, beautiful, pure, lonely. Like a wild horse shaking a white man. In a burst of companionship, Guy linked his arm through Bruno's.

'I don't *wanna* walk!' Bruno yelled, wrenching away and stopping. The fresh air was wilting him like a fish.

The train was starting. Guy pushed Bruno's big loose body aboard.

'Nightcap?' Bruno said dispiritedly at his door, looking tired enough to drop.

'Thanks, I couldn't.'

Green curtains muffled their whispers.

'Don't forget to call me in the morning. I'll leave the door unlocked. If I don't answer, come on in, huh?'

Guy lurched against the walls of green curtains as he made his way to his berth.

Habit made him think of his book as he lay down. He had left it in Bruno's room. His Plato. He didn't like the idea of its spending the night in Bruno's room, or of Bruno's touching it and opening it.

3

He had called Miriam immediately, and she had arranged to meet him at the high school that lay between their houses.

Now he stood in a corner of the asphalt gamefield, waiting. She would be late, of course. Why had she chosen the high school, he wondered. Because it was her own ground? He had loved her when he had used to wait for her here.

Overhead, the sky was a clear strong blue. The sun poured down moltenly, not yellow but colourless, like something grown white with its own heat. Beyond the trees, he saw the top of a slim reddish building he did not know, that had gone up since he had been in Metcalf two years ago. He turned away. There was no human being in sight, as if the heat had caused everyone to abandon the school building and even the homes of the neighbourhood. He looked at the broad grey steps that spilled from the dark arch of the school doors. He could still remember the inky, faintly sweaty smell on the fuzzy edges of Miriam's algebra book. He could still see the MIRIAM pencilled on the edge of its pages, and the drawing of the girl with the Spencerian marcel wave on the flyleaf, when he opened the book to do her problems for her. Why had he thought Miriam any different from all the others?

He walked through the wide gate between the criss-cross wire fence and looked up College Avenue again. Then he saw her, under the yellow-green trees that bordered the sidewalk. His heart began to beat harder, but he blinked his eyes with deliberate casualness. She walked at her usual rather stolid pace, taking her time. Now her head came into view, haloed by a broad, light-coloured hat. Shadow and sun speckled her figure chaotically. She gave him a relaxed wave, and Guy pulled a hand out of his pocket, returned it, and went back into the gamefield, suddenly tense and shy as a boy. She knows about the Palm Beach job, he thought, that strange girl under the trees. His mother had told him, half an hour ago, that she had mentioned it to Miriam when Miriam last telephoned.

'Hello, Guy.' Miriam smiled and quickly closed her broad orangey-pink lips. Because of the space between her front teeth, Guy remembered.

'How are you, Miriam?' Involuntarily he glanced at her figure, plump, but not pregnant-looking, and it flashed through his mind she might have lied. She wore a brightly-flowered skirt and a white short-sleeved blouse. Her big white pocket-book was of woven patent leather.

She sat down primly on the one stone bench that was in the shade, and asked him dull questions about his trip. Her face had grown fuller where it had always been full, on the lower cheeks, so that her chin looked more pointed. There were little wrinkles under her eyes now, Guy noticed. She had lived a long time, for twenty-two.

'In January,' she answered him in a flat voice. 'In January the child's due.'

It was two months advanced then. 'I suppose you want to marry him.'

She turned her head slightly and looked down. On her short cheek, the sunlight picked out the largest freckles, and Guy saw a certain pattern he remembered and had not thought of since a time when he had been married to her. How sure he had once been that he possessed her, possessed her every frailest thought! Suddenly it seemed that all love was only a tantalizing, a horrible next-best to knowing. He knew not the smallest part of the new world in Miriam's mind now. Was it possible that the same thing could happen with Anne?

'Don't you, Miriam?' he prompted.

'Not *right* now. See, there're complications.'

'Like what?'

'Well, we might not be able to marry as soon as we'd like to.'

'Oh.' *We*. He knew what he would look like, tall and dark, with a long face, like Steve. The type Miriam had always been attracted to. The only type she would have a child by. And she did want this child, he could tell. Something had happened, that had nothing to do with the man, perhaps, that made her want a child. He could see it in the prim, stiff way she sat on the bench, in that self-abandoned trance he had always seen or imagined in pregnant women's faces. 'That needn't delay the divorce though, I suppose.'

'Well, I didn't think so – until a couple of days ago. I thought Owen would be free to marry this month.'

'Oh. He's married now?'

'Yeah, he's married,' she said with a little sigh, almost smiling.

Guy looked down in vague embarrassment and paced a slow step or two on the asphalt. He had known the man would be married. He had expected he would have no intention of marrying her unless he were forced to. 'Where is he? Here?'

'He's in Houston,' she replied. 'Don't you want to sit down?'

'No.'

'You never did like to sit down.'

He was silent.

'Still have your ring?'

'Yeah.' His class ring from Chicago, that Miriam had always admired because it meant he was a college man. She was staring at the ring with a self-conscious smile. He put his hands in his pockets. 'As long as I'm here, I'd like it settled. Can we do it this week?'

'I want to go away, Guy.'

'For the divorce?'

Her stubby hands opened in a limp ambiguous gesture and he thought suddenly of Bruno's hands. He had forgotten Bruno completely, getting off the train this morning. And his book.

'I'm sort of tired of staying here,' she said.

'We can get the divorce in Dallas if you like.' Her friends here knew, he thought, that was all.

'I want to wait, Guy. Would you mind? Just a while?'

'I should think you'd mind. Does he intend to marry you or not?'

'He could marry me in September. He'd be free then, but –'

'But what?' In her silence, in the childlike lick of her tongue on her upper lip, he saw the trap she was in. She wanted this child so much, she would sacrifice herself in Metcalf by waiting until four months before it was born to marry its father. In spite of himself, he felt a certain pity for her.

'I want to go away, Guy. With you.'

There was a real effort at sincerity in her face, so much that he almost forgot what she was asking, and why. 'What is it you want, Miriam? Money to go away somewhere?'

The dreaminess in her grey-green eyes was dispersing like a mist. 'Your mother said you were going to Palm Beach.'

'I might be going there. To work.' He thought of the Palmyra with a twinge of peril. It was slipping away already.

'Take me with you, Guy? It's the last thing I'll ask you. If I could stay with you till December and then get the divorce –'

'Oh,' he said quietly, but something throbbed in his chest, like the breaking of his heart. She disgusted him suddenly, she and all the people around her whom she knew and attracted. Another man's child. Go away with her, be her husband until she gave birth to another man's child.

'If you don't take me, I'll come anyway.'

'Miriam, I could get that divorce now. I don't have to wait to see the child. The law doesn't.' His voice shook.

'You wouldn't do that to me,' Miriam replied with that combination of threat and pleading that had played on both his anger and his love when he loved her, and baffled him.

He felt it baffling him now. And she was right. He wouldn't divorce her now. But it was not because he still loved her, not because she was still his wife and was therefore due his protection, but because he pitied her and because he remembered he had once loved her. He realized now he had pitied her even in New York, even when she wrote him for money. 'I won't take the job if you come out there. There'd be no use in taking it,' he said evenly, but it was gone already, he told himself, so why discuss it?

'I don't think you'd give up a job like that,' she challenged.

He turned away from her twisted smile of triumph. That was where she was wrong, he thought, but he was silent. He took two steps on the gritty asphalt and turned again, with his head high. Be calm, he told himself. What could anger accomplish? Miriam had used to hate him when he reacted like this, because she loved loud arguments. She would love one even this morning, he thought. She had hated him when he reacted like this, until she had learned that in the long run it hurt him more to react like this. He knew he played into her hands now, yet he felt he could react in no other way.

'I haven't even got the job yet, you know. I'll simply send them a telegram saying I don't want it.' Beyond the treetops, he noticed again the new reddish building he had seen before Miriam came.

'And then what?'

'A lot of things. But you won't know about them.'

'Running away?' she taunted. 'Cheapest way out.'

He walked again, and turned. There was Anne. With Anne, he could endure this, endure anything. And in fact, he felt strangely resigned. Because he was with Miriam now, the symbol of the failure of his youth? He bit the tip of his tongue. There was inside him, like a flaw in a jewel, not visible on the surface, a fear and anticipation of failure that he had never been able to mend. At times, failure was a possibility that fascinated him, as at times, in high school and college, when he had allowed himself to fail examinations he might have passed; as when he married Miriam, he thought, against the will of both their families and all their friends. Hadn't he known it couldn't succeed? And now he had given up his biggest commission, without a murmur. He would go to Mexico and have a few days with Anne. It would take all his money, but why not? Could he possibly go back to New York and work without having seen Anne first?

'Is there anything else?' he asked.

'I've said it,' she told him, out of her spaced front teeth.

4

He walked home slowly, approaching Ambrose Street, where he lived, through Travis Street, which was shaded and still. There was a small fruit shop now on the corner of Travis and Delancey Streets, sitting right on somebody's front lawn like a children's play store. Out of the great Washatorium building that marred the west end of Ambrose Street, girls and women in white uniforms were pouring, chattering, on their way to an early lunch. He was glad he did not meet anyone on the street he had to speak to. He felt slow and quiet and resigned, and even rather happy. Strange how remote – perhaps how foreign – Miriam seemed five minutes after talking with her, how unimportant, really, everything seemed. Now he felt ashamed of his anxiety on the train.

'Not bad, Mama,' he said with a smile when he came home.

His mother had greeted him with an anxious lift of her eyebrows. 'I'm glad to hear that.' She pulled a rocker around and sat down to listen. She was a small woman with light brown hair, with a pretty, rather fine straight-nosed profile still, and a physical energy that seemed to twinkle off in sparks now in the silver of her hair. And she was almost always cheerful. It was this fact that chiefly made Guy feel that he and she were quite different, that had estranged him from her somewhat since the time he had suffered from Miriam. Guy liked to nurse his griefs, discover all he could about them, while his mother counselled him to forget. 'What did she say? You certainly weren't gone very long. I thought you might have had lunch with her.'

'No, Mama.' He sighed and sank down on the brocade sofa. 'Everything's all right, but I'll probably not take the Palmyra job.'

'Oh, Guy. Why not? Is she –? Is it true she's going to have a child?'

His mother was disappointed, Guy thought, but so mildly disappointed, for what the job really meant. He was glad she didn't know what the job really meant. 'It's true,' he said, and let his head go back until he felt the cool of the sofa's wooden frame against the back of his neck. He thought of the gulf that separated his life from his mother's. He had told her very little of his life with Miriam. And his mother, who had known a comfortable, happy upbringing in Mississippi, who kept herself busy now with her big house and her garden and her pleasant, loyal friends in Metcalf – what could she understand of a total malice like Miriam's? Or, for instance, what could she understand of the precarious life he was willing to lead in New York for the sake of a simple idea or two about his work?

'Now what's Palm Beach got to do with Miriam?' she asked finally.

'Miriam wants to come with me there. Protection for a time. And I couldn't bear it.' Guy clenched his hands. He had a sudden vision of Miriam in Palm Beach, Miriam meeting Clarence Brillhart, the manager of the Palmyra Club. Yet it was not the vision of Brillhart's shock beneath his calm, unvarying courtesy, Guy knew, but simply his own revulsion that made it impossible. It was just that he couldn't bear having Miriam anywhere near him when he worked on a project like this one. 'I couldn't bear it,' he repeated.

'Oh,' was all she said, but her silence now was one of understanding. If she made any comment, Guy thought, it was bound to remind him of her old disapproval of their marriage. And she wouldn't remind him at this time. 'You couldn't bear it,' she added, 'for as long as it would take.'

'I couldn't bear it.' He got up and took her soft face in his hands. 'Mama, I don't care a bit,' he said, kissing her forehead. 'I really don't care a row of beans.'

'I don't believe you do care. Why don't you?'

He crossed the room to the upright piano. 'Because I'm going to Mexico to see Anne.'

'Oh, are you?' she smiled, and the gaiety of this first morning with him won out. 'Aren't you the gadabout!'

'Want to come to Mexico?' He smiled over his shoulder. He began to play a saraband that he had learned as a child.

'Mexico!' his mother said in mock horror. 'Wild horses wouldn't get me to Mexico. Maybe you can bring Anne to see me on your way back.'

'Maybe.'

She went over and laid her hands shyly on his shoulders. 'Sometimes, Guy, I feel you're happy again. At the funniest times.'

5

What has happened? Write *immediately*. Or better, telephone collect. We're here at the Ritz for another two weeks. Missed you so on the trip, seems a shame we couldn't have flown down together, but I understand. I wish you well every moment of the day, darling. This must be over soon and we'll get it over. Whatever happens, tell me and let's face it. I often feel you *don't*. Face things, I mean.

You're so close, it's absurd you can't come down for a day or so. I hope you'll be in the mood. I hope there'll be time. Would love to have *you* here, and you know the family would. Darling, I do love the drawings and I'm so terribly proud of you I can even stand the idea of your being away in the months ahead because you'll be building them. Dad most impressed, too. We talk about you all the time.

> All my love, and all that goes
> with it. Be happy, darling.
>
> A.

Guy wrote a telegram to Clarence Brillhart, the manager of the Palmyra Club: 'Owing to circumstances, impossible for me to take commission. My deepest regrets and thanks for your championing and constant encouragement. Letter following.'

Suddenly he thought of the sketches they would use in lieu of his – the imitation Frank Lloyd Wright of William Harkness Associates. Worse yet, he thought as he dictated the telegram over the phone, the board would probably ask Harkness to copy some of his ideas. And Harkness would, of course.

He telegraphed Anne that he would fly down Monday and that he was free for several days. And because there was Anne, he did not bother to wonder how many months it would be, how many years, perhaps, before another job as big as the Palmyra would come within his reach.

6

That evening, Charles Anthony Bruno was lying on his back in an El Paso room, trying to balance a gold fountain-pen across his rather delicate, dished-in nose. He was too restless to go to bed, not energetic enough to go down to one of the bars in the neighbourhood and look things over. He had looked things over all afternoon, and he did not think much of them in El Paso. He did not think much of the Grand Canyon either. He thought more of the idea that had come to him night before last on the train. A pity Guy hadn't awakened him that morning. Not that Guy was the kind of fellow to plan a murder with, but he liked him, as a person. Guy was somebody worth knowing. Besides, Guy had left his book, and he could have given it back.

The ceiling fan made a *wuz-wuz-wuz* sound because one of its four blades was missing. If the fourth had been there, he would have been just a little cooler, he thought. One of the taps in the john leaked, the clamp on the reading light over the bed was broken so it hung down, and there were fingerprints all over the closet door. And the best hotel in town, they told him! Why was there always something wrong, maybe only one thing, with every hotel room he had ever been in? Some day he was going to find the perfect hotel room and buy it, even if it was in South Africa.

He sat up on the edge of the bed and reached for the telephone. 'Gimme long-distance.' He looked blankly at a smudge of red dirt his shoe had put on the white counterpane. 'Great Neck 166J ... Great Neck, yeah.' He waited. 'Long Island ... In *New York*, lunk, ever hear of it?'

In less than a minute, he had his mother.

'Yeah, I'm here. You still leaving Sunday? You better ... Well, I took that muleback trip. Just about pooped me, too ... Yeah, I seen the canyon ... Okay, but the colours are kind of corny ... Anyhow, how's things with you?'

He began to laugh. He pushed off his shoes and rolled back on the bed with the telephone, laughing. She was telling him about coming home to find the Captain entertaining two of her friends – two men she had met the night before – who had dropped in, thought the Captain was her father, and proceeded to say all the wrong things.

7

Propped on his elbow in bed, Guy stared at the letter addressed to him in pencil.

'Guess I'll have only one more time to wake you for another good long while,' his mother said.

Guy picked up the letter from Palm Beach. 'Maybe not so long, Mama.'

'What time does your plane leave tomorrow?'

'One-twenty.'

She leaned over and superfluously tucked in the foot of his bed. 'I don't suppose you'll have time to run over and see Ethel?'

'Oh, certainly I will, Mama.' Ethel Peterson was one of his mother's oldest friends. She had given Guy his first piano lessons.

The letter from Palm Beach was from Mr Brillhart. He had been given the commission. Mr Brillhart had also persuaded the board about the louvre windows.

'I've got some good strong coffee this morning,' his mother said from the threshold. 'Like breakfast in bed?'

Guy smiled at her. 'Would I!'

He reread Mr Brillhart's letter carefully, put it back in its envelope, and slowly tore it up. Then he opened the other letter. It was one page, scrawled in pencil. The signature with the heavy flourish below it made him smile again: Charles A. Bruno.

Dear Guy:

This is your train friend, remember? You left your book in my room that night & I found a Texas address in it which I trust is still right. Am mailing book to you. Read some in it, myself, didn't know there was so much conversation in Plato.

A great pleasure dining with you that night & hope I may list you among my friends. It would be fine to see you in Santa Fe & if you possibly change your mind, address is: Hotel La Fonda, Santa Fe, New Mex. for next two weeks at least.

I keep thinking about that idea we had for a couple of murders. It could be done, I am sure. I cannot express to you my supremest confidence in the idea! Though I know subject does not interest you.

What's what with your wife as that was very interesting? Please write me soon. Outside of losing wallit in El Paso (stolen right off a bar in front of me) nothing has happened of note. Didn't like El Paso, with apologies to you.

Hoping to hear from you soon,

Your friend,
Charles A. Bruno

P.S. Very sorry for sleeping late and missing you that a.m.

C.A.B.

The letter pleased him somehow. It was pleasant to think of Bruno's freedom.

'Grits!' he said happily to his mother. 'Never get grits with my fried eggs up North!'

He put on a favourite old robe that was too hot for the weather, and sat back in bed with the *Metcalf Star* and the teetery-legged bed-tray that held his breakfast.

Afterwards, he showered and dressed as if there were something he had to do that day, but there wasn't. He had visited the Cartwrights yesterday. He might have seen Peter Wriggs, his boyhood friend, but Peter had a job in New Orleans now. What was Miriam doing, he wondered. Perhaps manicuring her nails on her back porch, or playing checkers with some little girl neighbour who adored her, who wanted to be just like her. Miriam was never one to brood when a plan went askew. Guy lighted a cigarette.

A soft, intermittent *chink* came from downstairs, where his mother or Ursline the cook was cleaning the silver and dropping it piece by piece on to a heap.

Why hadn't he left for Mexico today? The next idle twenty-four hours were going to be miserable, he knew. Tonight, his uncle again, and probably some friends of his mother's dropping over. They all wanted to see him. Since his last visit, the *Metcalf Star* had printed a column about him and his work, mentioning his scholarships, the Prix de Rome that he hadn't been able to use because of the war, the store he had designed in Pittsburg, and the little annexe infirmary of the hospital in Chicago. It read so impressively in a newspaper. It had almost made him feel important, he remembered, the lonely day in New York when the clipping had arrived in his mother's letter.

A sudden impulse to write Bruno made him sit down at his work table, but, with his pen in his hand, he realized he had nothing to say. He could see Bruno in his rust-brown suit, camera strap over his shoulder, plodding up some dry hill in Santa Fe, grinning with his bad teeth at something, lifting his camera unsteadily and clicking. Bruno with a thousand easy dollars in his pocket, sitting in a bar, waiting for his mother. What did he have to say to Bruno? He recapped his fountain-pen and tossed it back on the table.

'Mama?' he called. He ran downstairs. 'How about a movie this afternoon?'

His mother said she had already been to movies twice that week. 'You know you don't like movies,' she chided him.

'Mama, I really want to go!' he smiled, and insisted.

8

The telephone rang that night at about eleven. His mother answered it, then came in and called him from the living-room where he sat with his uncle and his uncle's wife and his two cousins, Ritchie and Ty.

'It's long-distance,' his mother said.

Guy nodded. It would be Brillhart, of course, asking for further explanations. Guy had answered his letter that day.

'Hello, Guy,' the voice said. 'Charley.'

'Charley who?'

'Charley Bruno.'

'Oh! – How are you? Thanks for the book.'

'I dint send it yet but I will,' Bruno said with the drunken cheer Guy remembered from the train. 'Coming out to Santa Fe?'

'I'm afraid I can't.'

'What about Palm Beach? Can I visit you there in a couple weeks? I'd like to see how it looks.'

'Sorry, that's all off.'

'Off? Why?'

'Complications. I've changed my mind.'

'Account of your wife?'

'N-no.' Guy felt vaguely irritated.

'She wants you to stay with her?'

'Yes. Sort of.'

'Miriam wants to come out to Palm Beach?'

Guy was surprised he remembered her name.

'You haven't got your divorce, huh?'

'Getting it,' Guy said tersely.

'*Yes, I'm paying for this call!*' Bruno shouted to someone. 'Cheeses!' disgustedly. 'Listen, Guy, you gave up that job account of her?'

'Not exactly. It doesn't matter. It's finished.'

'You have to wait till the child's born for a divorce?'

Guy said nothing.

'The other guy's not going to marry her, huh?'

'Oh, yes, he is –'

'Yeah?' Bruno interrupted cynically.

'I can't talk any longer. We've got guests here tonight. I wish you a pleasant trip, Charley.'

'When can we talk? Tomorrow?'

'I won't be here tomorrow.'

'Oh.' Bruno sounded lost now, and Guy hoped he was. Then the voice again, with sullen intimacy. 'Listen, Guy, if you want anything done, you know, all you have to do is give a sign.'

Guy frowned. A question took form in his mind, and immediately he knew the answer. He remembered Bruno's idea for a murder.

'What do you want, Guy?'

'Nothing. I'm very content. Understand?' But it was drunken bravado on Bruno's part, he thought. Why should he react seriously?

'Guy, I mean it,' the voice slurred, drunker than before.

'Good-bye, Charley,' Guy said. He waited for Bruno to hang up.

'Doesn't sound like everything's fine,' Bruno challenged.

'I don't see that it's any of your business.'

'Guy!' in a tearful whine.

Guy started to speak, but the line clicked and went dead. He had an impulse to ask the operator to trace the call. Then he thought, drunken bravado. And boredom. It annoyed him that Bruno had his address. Guy ran his hand hard across his hair, and went back into the living-room.

9

All of what he had just told her of Miriam, Guy thought, did not matter so much as the fact he and Anne were together on the gravel path. He took her hand as they walked, and gazed around him at the scene in which every object was foreign – a broad level avenue bordered with giant trees like the Champs-Elysées, military statues on pedestals, and beyond, buildings he did not know. The El Paso de la Reforma. Anne walked beside him with her head still lowered, nearly matching his slow paces. Their shoulders brushed, and he glanced at her to see if she were about to speak, to say he was right in what he had decided, but her lips were still thoughtful. Her pale yellow hair, held by a silver bar at the back of her neck, made lazy movements in the wind behind her. It was the second summer he had seen her when the sun had only begun to tan her face, so her skin about equalled in pigment the colour of her hair. Soon her face would be darker than her hair, but Guy liked her best the way she was now, like something made of white gold.

She turned to him with the faintest smile of self-consciousness on her lips because he had been staring at her. 'You couldn't have borne it, Guy?'

'No. Don't ask me why. I couldn't.' He saw that her smile stayed, tinged with perplexity, perhaps annoyance.

'It's such a big thing to give up.'

It vexed him now. He felt done with it. 'I simply loathe her,' he said quietly.

'But you shouldn't loathe anything.'

He made a nervous gesture. 'I loathe her because I've told you all this while we're walking here!'

'Guy, really!'

'She's everything that should be loathed,' he went on, staring in front of him. 'Sometimes I think I hate everything in the world. No decency, no conscience. She's what people mean when they say America never grows up, America rewards the corrupt. She's the type who goes to the bad movies, acts in them, reads the love-story magazines, lives in a bungalow, and whips her husband into earning more money this year so they can buy on the instalment plan next year, breaks up her neighbour's marriage –'

'Stop it, Guy! You talk so like a child!' She drew away from him.

'And the fact I once loved her,' Guy added, 'loved all of it, makes me ill.'

They stopped, looking at each other. He had had to say it, here and now, the ugliest thing he could say. He wanted to suffer also from Anne's disapproval, perhaps from her turning away and leaving him to finish the walk by himself. She had left him on one or two other occasions, when he had been unreasonable.

Anne said, in that distant, expressionless tone that terrified him, because he felt she might abandon him and never come back, 'Sometimes I can believe you're still in love with her.'

He smiled, and she softened. 'I'm sorry,' he said.

'Oh, Guy!' She put out her hand again, like a gesture of beseeching, and he took it. 'If you'd only grow up!'

'I read somewhere people don't grow emotionally.'

'I don't care what you read. They do. I'll prove it to you if it's the last thing I do.'

He felt secure suddenly. 'What else can I think about now?' he asked perversely, lowering his voice.

'That you were never closer to being free of her than now, Guy. What do you suppose you should think about?'

He lifted his head higher. There was a big pink sign on the top of a building: TOME XX, and all at once he was curious to know what it meant and wanted to ask Anne. He wanted to ask her why everything was so much easier and simpler when he was with her, but pride kept him from asking now, and the question would have been rhetorical anyway, unanswerable by Anne in words, because the answer was simply Anne. It had been so since the day he met her, in the dingy basement of the Art Institute in New York, the rainy day he had slogged in and addressed the only living thing he saw, the Chinese red raincoat and hood. The red raincoat and hood had turned and said: 'You get to 9A from the first floor. You didn't have to come all the way down here.' And then her quick, amused laugh that mysteriously, immediately, lifted his rage. He had learned to smile by quarter inches, frightened of her, a little contemptuous of her new dark green convertible. 'A car just makes more sense,' Anne said, 'when you live in Long Island.' The days when he was contemptuous of everything and courses taken here and there were no more than tests to make sure he knew all the instructor had to say, or to see how fast he could learn it and leave. 'How do you suppose anybody gets in if not through pull? They can still throw you out if they don't like you.' He had seen it her way finally, the right way, and gone to the exclusive Deems Architectural Academy in Brooklyn for a year, through her father's knowing a man on the board of directors.

'I know you have it in you, Guy,' Anne said suddenly at the end of a silence, 'the capacity to be terribly happy.'

Guy nodded quickly, though Anne was not looking at him. He felt somehow ashamed. Anne had the capacity to be happy. She was happy now, she had been happy before she met him, and it was only he, his problems, that ever seemed to daunt her happiness for an instant. He would be happy, too, when he lived with Anne. He had told her so, but he could not bear to tell her again now.

'What's that?' he asked.

A big round house of glass had come into view under the trees of Chapultepec Park.

'The botanical gardens,' Anne said.

There was no one inside the building, not even a caretaker. The air smelled of warm, fresh earth. They walked around, reading unpronounceable names of plants that might have come from another planet. Anne had a favourite plant. She had watched it grow for three years, she said, visiting it on successive summers with her father.

'Only I can't even remember these names,' she said.

'Why should you remember?'

They had lunch at Sanborn's with Anne's mother, then walked around in the store until it was time for Mrs Faulkner's afternoon nap. Mrs Faulkner was a thin, nervously energetic woman, tall as Anne, and for her age as attractive. Guy had come to be devoted to her, because she was devoted to him. At first, in his mind, he had built up the greatest handicaps for himself from Anne's wealthy parents, but not one of them had come true, and gradually he had shed them. That evening, the four of them went to a concert at the Bellas Artes, then had a late supper at the Lady Baltimore Restaurant across the street from the Ritz.

The Faulkners were sorry he wouldn't be able to stay the summer with them in Acapulco. Anne's father, an importer, intended to build a warehouse on the docks there.

'We can't expect to interest him in a warehouse if he's building a whole country club,' Mrs Faulkner said.

Guy said nothing. He couldn't look at Anne. He had asked her not to tell her parents about Palm Beach until after he left. Where would he go next week? He might go to Chicago and study for a couple of months. He had stored away his possessions in New York, and his landlady awaited his word as to whether to rent his apartment or not. If he went to Chicago, he might see the great Saarinen in Evanston and Tim O'Flaherty, a young architect who had had no recognition yet, but whom Guy believed in. There might be a job or two in Chicago. But New York was too dismal a prospect without Anne.

Mrs Faulkner laid her hand on his forearm and laughed. 'He

wouldn't smile if he got all New York to build over, would you, Guy?'

He hadn't been listening. He wanted Anne to take a walk with him later, but she insisted on his coming up to their suite at the Ritz to see the silk dressing-gown she had bought for her cousin Teddy, before she sent it off. And then, of course, it was too late for a walk.

He was staying at the Hotel Montecarlo, about ten blocks from the Hotel Ritz, a great shabby building that looked like the former residence of a military general. One entered it through a wide carriage drive, paved in black and white tile like a bathroom floor. This gave into a huge dark lobby, also tile floored. There was a grotto-like bar-room and a restaurant that was always empty. Stained marble stairs wound around the patio, and going up behind the bellhop yesterday, Guy had seen, through open doorways and windows, a Japanese couple playing cards, a woman kneeling at prayer, people writing letters at tables or merely standing with a strange air of captivity. A masculine gloom and an untraceable promise of the supernatural oppressed the whole place, and Guy had liked it instantly, though the Faulkners, including Anne, chaffed him about his choice.

His cheap little room in a back corner was crammed with pink and brown painted furniture, had a bed like a fallen cake, and a bath down the hall. Somewhere down in the patio, water dripped continuously, and the sporadic flush of toilets sounded torrential.

When he got back from the Ritz, Guy deposited his wristwatch, a present from Anne, on the pink bed table, and his billfold and keys on the scratched brown bureau, as he might have done at home. He felt very content as he got into bed with his Mexican newspaper and a book on English architecture that he had found at the Alameda book-store that afternoon. After a second plunge at the Spanish, he leaned his head back against the pillow and gazed at the offensive room, listened to the little ratlike sounds of human activity from all parts of the building. What was it that he liked, he wondered. To immerse himself in ugly, uncomfortable, undignified living so that he gained new power to fight it in his work? Or was it a sense of hiding from Miriam? He would be harder to find here than at the Ritz.

Anne telephoned him the next morning to say that a telegram had come for him. 'I just happened to hear them paging you,' she said. 'They were about to give you up.'

'Would you read it to me, Anne?'

Anne read: ' "Miriam suffered miscarriage yesterday. Upset and asking to see you. Can you come home? Mama." – Oh, Guy!'

He felt sick of it, all of it. 'She did it herself,' he murmured.

'You don't know, Guy.'

'I know.'

'Don't you think you'd better see her?'

His fingers tightened on the telephone. 'I'll get the Palmyra back anyway,' he said. 'When was the telegram sent?'

'The ninth. Tuesday, at 4 p.m.'

He sent a telegram off to Mr Brillhart, asking if he might be reconsidered for the job. Of course he would be, he thought, but how asinine it made him. Because of Miriam. He wrote to Miriam:

This changes both our plans, of course. Regardless of yours, I mean to get the divorce now. I shall be in Texas in a few days. I hope you will be well by then, but if not, I can manage whatever is necessary alone.

Again my wishes for your quick recovery.

Guy

Shall be at this address until Sunday.

He sent it airmail special delivery.

Then he called up Anne. He wanted to take her to the best restaurant in the city that night. He wanted the most exotic cocktails in the Ritz Bar to start with, all of them.

'You really feel happy?' Anne asked, laughing, as if she couldn't quite believe him.

'Happy and – strange. *Muy extranjero.*'

'Why?'

'Because I didn't think it was fated. I didn't think it was part of my destiny. The Palmyra, I mean.'

'I did.'

'Oh, you did!'

'Why do you think I was so mad at you yesterday?'

He really did not expect an answer from Miriam, but Friday morning when he and Anne were in Xochimilco, he felt prompted to call his hotel to see if a message had come. There was a telegram waiting. And after saying he would pick it up in a few minutes, he couldn't wait, once he was back in Mexico City, he telephoned the hotel again from a drugstore in the Socalo. The Montecarlo clerk read it to him: ' "Have to talk with you first. Please come soon. Love Miriam." '

'She'll make a bit of a fuss,' Guy said after he repeated it to Anne. 'I'm sure the other man doesn't want to marry her. He's got a wife now.'

'Oh.'

He glanced at her as they walked, wanting to say something to her about her patience with him, with Miriam, with all of it. 'Let's forget it,' he smiled, and began to walk faster.

'Do you want to go back now?'

'Certainly not! Maybe Monday or Tuesday. I want these few days with you. I'm not due in Florida for another week. That's if they keep to the first schedule.'

'Miriam won't follow you now, will she?'

'This time next week,' Guy said, 'she won't have a single claim on me.'

10

At her dressing-table in Hotel La Fonda, Santa Fe, Elsie Bruno sat removing the night's dry skin cream from her face with a cleansing tissue. Now and then, with wide, absent blue eyes, she leaned closer to the mirror to examine the little mesh of wrinkles below her lids and the laugh lines that curved from the base of her nose. Though her chin was somewhat recessive, the lower part of her face projected, thrusting her full lips forward in a manner quite different from Bruno's face. Santa Fe, she thought, was the only place she could see the laugh lines in the mirror when she sat all the way back at her dressing-table.

'This light around here – might as well be an X-ray,' she remarked to her son.

Bruno, slumped in his pyjamas in a rawhide chair, cast a puffy eye over at the window. He was too tired to go and pull the shade down. 'You look good, Mom,' he croaked. He lowered his pursed lips to the glass of water that rested on his hairless chest, and frowned thoughtfully.

Like an enormous walnut in feeble, jittery squirrel hands, an idea, bigger and closer than any idea he had ever known, had been revolving in his mind for several days. When his mother left town, he intended to crack open the idea and start thinking in earnest. His idea was to go and get Miriam. The time was ripe, and the time was now. Guy needed it now. In a few days, a week even, it might be too late for the Palm Beach thing, and he wouldn't.

Her face had grown fatter in these few days in Santa Fe, Elsie thought. She could tell by the plumpness of her cheeks compared to the small taut triangle of her nose. She hid the laugh lines with a smile at herself, tilted her curly blonde head, and blinked her eyes.

'Charley, should I pick up that silver belt this morning?' she asked casually, as if she spoke to herself. The belt was two hundred and fifty something, but Sam would send another thousand on to California. It was such a good-looking belt, like nothing in New York. What else was Santa Fe good for but silver?

'What else is he good for?' Bruno murmured.

Elsie picked up her shower cap and turned to him with her quick broad smile that had no variations. 'Darling,' coaxingly. 'Umm-m?'

'You won't do anything you shouldn't while I'm gone?'

'No, Ma.'

She left the shower cap perched on the crown of her head, looked at a long narrow red nail, then reached for a sandpaper stick. Of course, Fred Wiley would be only too happy to buy the silver belt for her – he'd probably turn up at the station with something atrocious and twice as expensive anyway – but she didn't want Fred on her neck in California. With the least encouragement, he would come to California with her. Better that he only swore eternal love at the station, wept a little, and went straight home to his wife.

'I must say last night was funny though,' Elsie went on. 'Fred saw it first.' She laughed, and the sandpaper stick flew in a blur.

Bruno said coolly, 'I had nothing to do with it.'

'All right, darling, you had nothing to do with it!'

Bruno's mouth twisted. His mother had awakened him at 4 in the morning, in hysterics, to tell him there was a dead bull in the Plaza. A bull sitting on a bench with a hat and coat on, reading a newspaper. Typical of Wilson's collegiate pranks. Wilson would be talking about it today, Bruno knew, elaborating on it till he thought of something dumber to do. Last night in La Placita, the hotel bar, he had planned a murder – while Wilson dressed a dead bull. Even in Wilson's tall stories about his war service, he had never claimed to have killed anybody, not even a Jap. Bruno closed his eyes, thinking contentedly of last night. Around ten o'clock, Fred Wiley and a lot of other baldheads had trooped into La Placita half crocked, like a musical comedy stagline, to take his mother to a party. He'd been invited too, but he had told his mother he had a date with Wilson, because he needed time to think. And last night he had decided yes. He had been thinking really since Saturday when he talked to Guy, and here it was Saturday again, and it was tomorrow or never, when his mother left for California. He was sick of the question, could he do it. How long had the question been with him? Longer than he could remember. He *felt* like he could do it. Something kept telling him that the time, the circumstances, the cause would never be better. A pure murder, without personal motives! He didn't consider the possibility of Guy's murdering his father a motive, because he didn't count on it. Maybe Guy could be persuaded, maybe not. The point was, now was the time to act, because the set-up was so perfect. He'd called Guy's house again last night to make sure he still wasn't back from Mexico. Guy had been in Mexico since Sunday, his mother said.

A sensation like a thumb pressing at the base of his throat

54

made him tear at his collar, but his pyjama jacket was open all the way down the front. Bruno began to button it dreamily.

'You won't change your mind and come with me?' his mother asked, getting up. 'If you did, I'd go up to Reno. Helen's there now and so's George Kennedy.'

'Only one reason I'd like to see you in Reno, Mom.'

'Charley –' She tipped her head to one side and back again. 'Have patience? If it weren't for Sam, we wouldn't be here, would we?'

'Sure, we would.'

She sighed. 'You won't change your mind?'

'I'm having fun here,' he said through a groan.

She looked at her nails again. 'All I've heard is how bored you are.'

'That's with Wilson. I'm not gonna see him again.'

'You're not going to run back to New York?'

'What'd I do in New York?'

'Grannie'd be so disappointed if you fell down again this year.'

'When did I ever fall down?' Bruno jested weakly, and suddenly felt sick enough to die, too sick even to throw up. He knew the feeling, it lasted only a minute, but God, he thought, let there not be time for breakfast before the train, don't let her say the word breakfast. He stiffened, not moving a muscle, barely breathing between his parted lips. With one eye shut, he watched her move towards him in her pale blue silk wrapper, a hand on her hip, looking as shrewd as she could which wasn't shrewd at all, because her eyes were so round. And she was smiling besides.

'What've you and Wilson got up your sleeves?'

'That punk?'

She sat down on the arm of his chair. 'Just because he steals your thunder,' she said, shaking him slightly by the shoulder. 'Don't do anything too awful, darling, because I haven't got the money just now to throw around cleaning up after you.'

'Stick him for some more. Get me a thousand, too.'

'Darling.' She laid the cool backs of her fingers against his forehead. 'I'll miss you.'

'I'll be there day after tomorrow probably.'

'Let's have fun in California.'

'Sure.'

'Why're you so serious this morning!'

'I'm not, Ma.'

She tweaked the thin dangling hair over his forehead, and went on into the bathroom.

Bruno jumped up and shouted against the roar of her running bath, 'Ma, I got money to pay my bill here!'

'What, angel?'

He went closer and repeated it, then sank back in the chair, exhausted with the effort. He did not want his mother to know about the long-distance calls to Metcalf. If she didn't, everything was working out fine. His mother hadn't minded very much his not staying on, hadn't really minded enough. Was she meeting this jerk Fred on the train or something? Bruno dragged himself up, feeling a slow animosity rising in him against Fred Wiley. He wanted to tell his mother he was staying on in Santa Fe for the biggest experience of his life. She wouldn't be running the water in there now, paying no attention to him, if she knew a fraction of what it meant. He wanted to say, Ma, life's going to be a lot better for both of us soon, because this is the beginning of getting rid of the Captain. Whether Guy came through with his part of the deal or not, if he was successful with Miriam, he would have proved a point. A perfect murder. Some day, another person he didn't know yet would turn up and some kind of a deal could be made. Bruno bent his chin down to his chest in sudden anguish. How could he tell his mother? Murder and his mother didn't go together. 'How gruesome!' she would say. He looked at the bathroom door with a hurt, distant expression. It had dawned on him that he couldn't tell anyone, ever. Except Guy. He sat down again.

'Sleepyhead!'

He blinked when she clapped her hands. Then he smiled. Dully, with a wistful realization that much would happen before he saw them again, he watched his mother's legs flex as she tightened her stockings. The slim lines of her legs always gave him a lift, made him proud. His mother had the best-looking legs he had ever seen on anyone, no matter what age. Ziegfeld had picked her, and hadn't Ziegfeld known his stuff? But she had married right back into the kind of life she had run away from. He was going to liberate her soon, and she didn't know it.

'Don't forget to mail *that*,' his mother said.

Bruno winced as the two rattlesnakes' heads tipped over towards him. It was a tie rack they had bought for the Captain, made of interlocking cowhorns and topped by two stuffed baby rattlers sticking their tongues out at each other over a mirror. The Captain hated tie racks, hated snakes, dogs, cats, birds – What didn't he hate? He would hate the corny tie rack, and that was why he had talked his mother into getting it for him. Bruno smiled affectionately at the tie rack. It hadn't been hard to talk his mother into getting it.

11

He stumbled on a goddamned cobblestone, then drew himself up pridefully and tried to straighten his shirt in his trousers. Good thing he had passed out in an alley and not on a street, or the cops might have picked him up and he'd have missed the train. He stopped and fumbled for his wallet, fumbled more wildly then he had earlier to see if the wallet was there. His hands shook so, he could hardly read the 10.20 a.m. on the railroad ticket. It was now 8.10 according to several clocks. If this was Sunday. Of course it was Sunday, all the Indians were in clean shirts. He kept an eye out for Wilson, though he hadn't seen him all day yesterday and it wasn't likely he would be out now. He didn't want Wilson to know he was leaving town.

The Plaza spread suddenly before him, full of chickens and kids and the usual old men eating piñones for breakfast. He stood still and counted the pillars of the Governor's palace to see if he could count seventeen, and he could. It was getting so the pillars weren't a good gauge any more. On top of a bad hangover, he ached now from sleeping on the goddamned cobblestones. Why'd he drunk so much, he wondered, almost tearfully. But he had been all alone, and he always drank more alone. Or was that true? And who cared anyway? He remembered one brilliant and powerful thought that had come to him last night watching a televised shuffleboard game: *the way to see the world was to see it drunk*. Everything was created to be seen drunk. Certainly this wasn't the way to see the world, with his head splitting every time he turned his eyes. Last night he'd wanted to celebrate his last night in Santa Fe. Today he'd be in Metcalf, and he'd have to be sharp. But had he ever known a hangover a few drinks couldn't fix? A hangover might even help, he thought: he had a habit of doing things slowly and cautiously with a hangover. Still, he hadn't planned anything, even yet. He could plan on the train.

'Any mail?' he asked mechanically at the desk, but there wasn't any.

He bathed solemnly and ordered hot tea and a raw egg sent up to make a prairie oyster, then went to the closet and stood a long while, wondering vaguely what to wear. He decided on the red-brown suit in honour of Guy. It was rather inconspicuous, too, he noticed when he had it on, and it pleased him that he might have chosen it unconsciously for this reason also. He gulped the prairie oyster and it stayed down, flexed his arms – but suddenly the room's Indian décor, the loony tin lamps, and the strips hanging down the walls were unbearable, and he began to shake all over again in his haste to get his things and leave. What things? He didn't need anything really. Just the paper on which he had written everything he knew about Miriam. He got it from the back pocket of his suitcase and stuck it into the inside pocket of his jacket. The gesture made him feel like a businessman. He put a white handkerchief into his breast pocket, then left the room and locked the door. He figured he could be back tomorrow night, sooner if he could possibly do it tonight and catch a sleeper back.

Tonight!

He could hardly believe it as he walked towards the bus station, where one caught the bus for Lamy, the railroad terminal. He had thought he would be so happy and excited – or maybe quiet and grim – and he wasn't at all. He frowned suddenly, and his pallid, shadowy-eyed face looked much younger. Was something going to take the fun out of it after all? What would take it out? But something always had taken the fun out of everything he had ever counted on. This time he wouldn't let it. He made himself smile. Maybe it was the hangover that had made him doubt. He went into a bar and bought a fifth from a barman he knew, filled his flask, and asked for an empty pint bottle to put the rest in. The barman looked, but he didn't have one.

At Lamy Bruno went on to the station, carrying nothing but the half empty bottle in a paper bag, not even a weapon. He hadn't planned yet, he kept reminding himself, but a lot of planning didn't always mean a murder was a success. Witness the –

'Hey, Charley! Where you going?'

It was Wilson, with a gang of people. Bruno forced himself to walk towards them, wagging his head boredly. They must have just got off a train, he thought. They looked tired and seedy.

'Where you been for two days?' Bruno asked Wilson.

'Las Vegas. Didn't know I was there until I was there, or I'd have asked you. Meet Joe Hanover. I told you about Joe.'

'H'lo, Joe.'

'What're you so mopey about?' Wilson asked with a friendly shove.

'Oh, Charley's hung over!' shrieked one of the girls, her voice like a bicycle bell right in his ear.

'Charley Hangover, meet Joe Hanover!' Joe Hanover said, convulsed.

'Haw haw.' Bruno tugged his arm away gently from a girl with a lei around her neck. 'Hell, I gotta catch this train.' His train was waiting.

'Where *you* going?' Wilson asked, frowning so his black eyebrows met.

'I hadda see someone in Tulsa,' Bruno mumbled, aware he mixed his tenses, thinking he must get away *now*. Frustration made him want to weep, lash out at Wilson's dirty red shirt with his fists.

Wilson made a movement as if he would wipe Bruno away like a chalk streak on a blackboard. 'Tulsa!'

Slowly, with a try at a grin, Bruno made a similar gesture and turned away. He walked on, expecting them to come after him, but they didn't. At the train, he looked back and saw the group moving like a rolling thing out of the sunlight into the darkness below the station roof. He frowned at them, feeling something conspiratorial in their closeness. Did they suspect something? Were they whispering about him? He boarded the train casually, and it began to move before he found his seat.

When he awakened from his nap, the world seemed quite changed. The train was speeding silkily through cool bluish mountainland. Dark green valleys were full of shadows. The sky was grey. The air-conditioned car and the cool look of things outside was as refreshing as an icepack. And he was hungry. In the diner he had a delicious lunch of lamb chops, French fries and salad, and fresh peach pie washed down with two Scotch and sodas, and strolled back to his seat feeling like a million dollars.

A sense of purpose, strange and sweet to him, carried him along in an irresistible current. Merely in gazing out the window, he felt a new co-ordination of mind and eye. He began to realize what he intended to do. He was on his way to do a murder which not only would fulfil a desire of years, but would benefit a friend. It made Bruno very happy to do things for his friends. And his victim deserved her fate. Think of all the other good guys he would save from ever knowing her! The realization of his importance dazzled his mind, and for a long moment he felt completely and happily drunk. His energies that had been dissipated, spread like a flooded river over land as flat and boring as the Llano Estacado he was crossing now, seemed gathered in a vortex whose point strove towards Metcalf like the aggressive thrust of the train. He sat on the edge of his seat and wished Guy were opposite him again. But Guy would try to stop him, he knew; Guy wouldn't understand how much he wanted to do it or how easy it was. But for Christ's sake, he ought to understand how useful! Bruno ground his smooth, hard rubberlike fist into his palm, wishing the train would go faster. All over his body, little muscles twitched and quivered.

He took out the paper about Miriam, laid it on the empty

seat opposite him, and studied it earnestly. *Miriam Joyce Haines, about twenty-two*, said his handwriting in precise, inked characters, for this was his third copy. *Rather pretty. Red hair. A little plump, not very tall. Pregnant so you could tell probably since a month. Noisy, social type. Probably flashy dressed. Maybe short curly hair, maybe a long permanent.* It wasn't very much, but it was the best he could do. A good thing she had red hair at least. Could he really do it tonight, he wondered. That depended on whether he could find her right away. He might have to go through the whole list of Joyces and Haineses. He thought she'd be living with her family probably. Once he saw her, he was sure he would recognize her. The little bitch! He hated her already. He thought of the instant he would see her and recognize her, and his feet gave an expectant jump on the floor. People came and went in the aisle, but Bruno did not look up from the paper.

She's going to have a child, Guy's voice said. The little floozy! Women who slept around made him furious, made him ill, like the mistresses his father used to have, that had turned all his school holidays into nightmares because he had not known if his mother knew and was only pretending to be happy, or if she did not know at all. He recreated every word he could of his and Guy's conversation on the train. It brought Guy close to him. Guy, he considered, was the most worthy fellow he had ever met. He had earned the Palm Beach job, and he deserved to keep it. Bruno wished he could be the one to tell Guy he still had it.

When Bruno finally replaced the paper in his pocket and sat back with one leg comfortably crossed, his hands folded on his knee, anyone seeing him would have judged him a young man of responsibility and character, probably with a promising future. He did not look in the pink of health, to be sure, but he did reflect poise and an inner happiness seen in few faces, and in Bruno's never before. His life up to now had been pathless, and seeking had known no direction, finding had revealed no meaning. There had been crises — he loved crises and created them sometimes among his acquaintances and between his father and mother — but he had always stepped out of them in time to avoid participation. This, and because he occasionally found it impossible to show sympathy even when it was his mother who was hurt by his father, had led his mother to think that a part of him was cruel, while his father and many other people believed him heartless. Yet an imagined coolness in a stranger, a friend he telephoned in a lonely dusk who was unable or unwilling to spend the evening with him, could plunge him into sulking, brooding melancholy. But only his mother knew this. He stepped out of crises because he found pleasure in depriving himself of excitement, too. So long had he been frustrated in his hunger for a meaning of his life, and in his amorphous desire to perform an act that would give it meaning, that he had come to prefer frustration, like some habitually unrequited lovers. The sweetness of fulfilment of anything he had felt he would never know. A quest with direction and hope he had always felt, from the start, too discouraged to attempt. Yet there had always been the energy to live one more day. Death held no terror at all, however. Death was only one more adventure untried. If it came on some perilous business, so much the better. Nearest, he thought, was the time he had driven a racing car blindfolded on a straight road with gas pedal on the floor. He never heard his friend's gunshot that meant stop, because he was lying unconscious in a ditch with a broken hip. At times he was so bored he contemplated the dramatic finality of suicide. It had never occurred to him that facing death unafraid might be brave, that his attitude was as resigned as that of the swamis of India, that to commit suicide required a particular kind of despondent nerve. Bruno had that kind of nerve always. He was actually a little ashamed of ever considering suicide, because it was so obvious and dull.

Now, on the train to Metcalf, he had direction. He had not felt so alive, so real and like other people since he had gone to Canada as a child with his mother and father – also on a train, he remembered. He had believed Quebec full of castles that he would be allowed to explore, but there had not been one castle, not even time to look for any, because his paternal grandmother had been dying, which was the only reason they had come anyway, and since then he had never placed full confidence in the purpose of any journey. But he did in this one.

In Metcalf, he went immediately to a telephone book and checked on the Haineses. He was barely conscious of Guy's address as he frowned down the list. No Miriam Haines, and he hadn't expected any. There were seven Joyces. Bruno scribbled a list of them on a piece of paper. Three were at the same address, 1235 Magnolia Street, and one of them there was Mrs M. J. Joyce. Bruno's pointed tongue curled speculatively over his upper lip. Certainly a good bet. Maybe her mother's name was Miriam, too. He should be able to tell a lot from the neighbourhood. He didn't think Miriam would live in a fancy neighbourhood. He hurried towards a yellow taxi parked at the kerb.

12

It was almost nine o'clock. The long dusk was sliding steeply into night, and the residential blocks of small flimsy-looking wooden houses were mostly dark, except for a glow here and there on a front porch where people sat in swings and on front steps.

'Lemme out here, this is okay,' Bruno said to the driver. Magnolia Street and College Avenue, and this was the one-thousand block. He began walking.

A little girl stood on the sidewalk, staring at him.

'Hyah,' Bruno said, like a nervous command for her to get out of the way.

'H'lo,' said the little girl.

Bruno glanced at the people on the lighted porch, a plump man fanning himself, a couple of women in the swing. Either he was tighter than he thought or luck was going to be with him, because he certainly had a hunch about 1235. He couldn't have dreamt up a neighbourhood more likely for Miriam to live in. If he was wrong, he'd just try the rest. He had the list in his pocket. The fan on the porch reminded him it was hot, apart from his own feverlike temperature that had been annoying him since late afternoon. He stopped and lighted a cigarette, pleased that his hands did not shake at all. The half bottle since lunch had fixed his hangover and put him in a slow mellow mood. Crickets chirruped everywhere around him. It was so quiet, he could hear a car shift gears two blocks away. Some young fellows came around a corner, and Bruno's heart jumped, thinking one might be Guy, but none of them was.

'You ol' jassack!' one said.

'Hell, I tol' her I ain't foolin' with no man don't give his brother an even break . . .'

Bruno looked after them haughtily. It sounded like another language. They didn't talk like Guy at all.

On some houses, Bruno couldn't find a number. Suppose he couldn't find 1235? But when he came to it, 1235 was very legible in tin numerals over the front porch. The sight of the house brought a slow pleasant thrill. Guy must have hopped up those steps very often, he thought, and it was this fact alone that really set it apart from the other houses. It was a small house like all the others on the block, only its yellow-tan clapboards were more in need of paint. It had a driveway at the side, a scraggly lawn, and an old Chevvy sedan sitting at the kerb. A light showed at a downstairs window and one in a back corner window upstairs that Bruno thought might be Miriam's room. But why didn't he *know*? Maybe Guy really hadn't told him enough!

Nervously, Bruno crossed the street and went back a little the way he had come. He stopped and turned and stared at the house, biting his lip. There was no one in sight, and no porch lighted except one down at the corner. He could not decide if the faint sound of a radio came from Miriam's house or the one next to it. The house next to it had two lighted windows downstairs. He might be able to walk up the driveway and take a look at the back of 1235.

Bruno's eyes slid alertly to the next-door front porch as the light came on. A man and woman came out, the woman sat down in the swing, and the man went down the walk. Bruno backed into the niche of a projecting garage front.

'Pistachio if they haven't got peach, Don,' Bruno heard the woman call.

'I'll take vanilla,' Bruno murmured, and drank some out of his flask.

He stared quizzically at the yellow-tan house, put a foot up

64

behind him to lean on, and felt something hard against his thigh: the knife he had bought in the station at Big Springs, a hunting knife with a six-inch blade in a sheath. He did not want to use a knife if he could avoid it. Knives sickened him in a funny way. And a gun made noise. How would he do it? Seeing her would suggest a way. Or would it? He had thought seeing the house would suggest something, and he still felt like this was the house, but it didn't suggest anything. Could that mean this wasn't the house? Suppose he got chased off for snooping before he even found out. Guy hadn't told him enough, he really hadn't! Quickly he took another drink. He mustn't start to worry, that would spoil everything! His knee buckled. He wiped his sweaty hands on his thighs and wet his lips with a shaky tongue. He pulled the paper with the Joyce addresses out of his breast pocket and slanted it towards the street light. He still couldn't see to read. Should he leave and try another address, maybe come back here?

He would wait fifteen minutes, maybe half an hour.

A preference for attacking her out of doors had taken root in his mind on the train, so all his ideas began from a simple physical approach to her. This street was almost dark enough, for instance, very dark there under the trees. He preferred to use his bare hands, or to hit her over the head with something. He did not realize how excited he was until he felt his body start now with his thoughts of jumping to right or left, as it might be, when he attacked her. Now and then it crossed his mind how happy Guy would be when it was done. Miriam had become an object, small and hard.

He heard a man's voice, and a laugh, he was sure from the lighted upstairs room in 1235, then a girl's smiling voice: 'Stop that? – Please? Plee-ee-ease?' Maybe Miriam's voice. Babyish and stringy, but somehow strong like a strong string, too.

The light blinked out and Bruno's eyes stayed at the dark window. Then the porch light flashed on and two men and a girl – *Miriam* – came out. Bruno held his breath and set his feet on the ground. He could see the red in her hair. The bigger fellow was redheaded, too – maybe her brother. Bruno's eyes caught a hundred details at once, the chunky compactness of her figure, the flat shoes, the easy way she swung around to look up at one of the men.

'Think we ought to call her, Dick?' she asked in that thin voice. 'It's kinda late.'

A corner of the shade in the front window lifted. 'Honey? Don't be out too long!'

'No, Mom.'

They were going to take the car at the kerb.

Bruno faded towards the corner, looking for a taxi. Fat chance in this dead burg! He ran. He hadn't run in months, and he felt fit as an athlete.

'Taxi!' He didn't even see a taxi, then he did and dove for it.

He made the driver circle and come into Magnolia Street in the direction the Chevvy had been pointed. The Chevvy was gone. Darkness had closed in tight. Far away he saw a red tail-light blinking under trees.

'Keep going!'

When the tail-light stopped for a red and the taxi closed some of the distance, Bruno saw it was the Chevvy and sank back with relief.

'Where do you want to go?' asked the driver.

'Keep going!' Then as the Chevvy swung into a big avenue, 'Turn right.' He sat up on the edge of his seat. Glancing at a kerb, he saw 'Crockett Boulevard' and smiled. He had heard of Crockett Boulevard in Metcalf, the widest longest street.

'Who're the people's names you want to go to?' the driver asked. 'Maybe I know 'em.'

'Just a minute, just a minute,' Bruno said, unconsciously assuming another personality, pretending to search through the papers he had dragged from his inside pocket, among them the paper about Miriam. He snickered suddenly, feeling very amused, very safe. Now he was pretending to be the dopey guy from out of town, who had even misplaced the address of where he wanted to go. He bent his head so the driver could not see him laughing, and reached automatically for his flask.

'Need a light?'

'Nope, nope, thank you.' He took a hot swallow. Then the

Chevvy backed into the avenue, and Bruno told the driver to keep going.

'Where?'

'Get going and shut up!' Bruno shouted, his voice falsetto with anxiety.

The driver shook his head and made a click with his tongue. Bruno fumed, but they had the Chevvy in sight. Bruno thought they would never stop driving and that Crockett Boulevard must cross the whole state of Texas. Twice Bruno lost and found the Chevvy. They passed roadstands and drive-in movies, then darkness put up a wall on either side. Bruno began to worry. He couldn't tail them out of town or down a country road. Then a big arch of lights appeared over the road. WELCOME TO LAKE METCALF'S KINGDOM OF FUN, it said, and the Chevvy drove under it and into a parking lot. There were all kinds of lights ahead in the woods and the jingle of merry-go-round music. An amusement park! Bruno was delighted.

'Four bucks,' said the driver sourly, and Bruno poked a five through the front window.

He hung back until Miriam and the two fellows and a new girl they had picked up had gone through the turnstile, then he followed them. He stretched his eyes wide for a good look at Miriam under the lights. She was cute in a plump college-girl sort of way, but definitely second-rate, Bruno judged. The red socks with the red sandals infuriated him. How could Guy have married such a thing? Then his feet scraped and he stood still: she wasn't pregnant! His eyes narrowed in intense perplexity. Why hadn't he noticed from the first? But maybe it wouldn't show yet. He bit his underlip hard. Considering how plump she was, her waist looked even flatter than it ought to. Maybe a sister of Miriam's. Or she had had an abortion or something. Or a miscarriage. Miss Carriage! How *do* you do? Swing it, sister! She had fat little hips under a tight grey skirt. He moved on as they did, following evenly, as if magnetized. Had Guy lied about her being pregnant? But Guy wouldn't lie. Bruno's mind swam in contradictions. He stared at Miriam with his head cocked. Then something made a connection in his mind before he was aware of looking for it: if something had happened to the child, then all the more reason why he should erase her, because Guy wouldn't be able to get his divorce. She could be walking around now if she had had an abortion, for instance.

She stood in front of a sideshow where a gypsy woman was dropping things into a big fish bowl. The other girl started laughing, leaning all over the redheaded fellow.

'Miriam!'

Bruno leapt off his feet.

'Oooh, yes!' Miriam went across to the frozen custard stand.

They all bought frozen custards. Bruno waited boredly smiling, looking up at the ferris wheel's arc of lights and the tiny people swinging in benches up there in the black sky. Far off through the trees, he saw lights twinkling on water. It was quite a park. He wanted to ride the ferris wheel. He felt wonderful. He was taking it easy, not getting excited. The merry-go-round played 'Casey would waltz with the strawberry blonde...' Grinning, he turned to Miriam's red hair, and their eyes met, but hers moved on and he was sure she hadn't noticed him, but he mustn't do that again. A rush of anxiety made him snicker. Miriam didn't look at all smart, he decided, which amused him, too. He could see why Guy would loathe her. He loathed her, too, with all his guts! Maybe she was lying to Guy about having a baby. And Guy was so honest himself, he believed her. Bitch!

When they moved on with their frozen custards, he released the swallow-tailed bird he had been fingering in the balloon seller's box, then wheeled around and bought one, a bright yellow one. It made him feel like a kid again, whipping the stick around, listening to the tail's *squee-wee-wee*!

A little boy walking by with his parents stretched his hand towards it, and Bruno had an impulse to give it to him, but he didn't.

Miriam and her friends entered a big lighted section where the bottom of the ferris wheel was and a lot of concessions and sideshows. The roller coaster made a *tat-tat-tat-tat-tat* like a machine-gun over their heads. There was a clang and a roar as someone sent the red arrow all the way to the top with a sledge-hammer. He wouldn't mind killing Miriam with a sledge-hammer, he thought. He examined Miriam and each of the three to see if any seemed aware of him, but he was sure they weren't. If he didn't do it tonight, he mustn't let any of them notice him. Yet somehow he was sure he would do it tonight. Something would happen that he could. This was his night. The cooler night air bathed him, like some liquid that he frolicked in. He waved the bird in wide circles. He liked Texas, Guy's state! Everybody looked happy and full of energy. He let Miriam's group blend into a crowd while he took a gulp from his flask. Then he loped after them.

They were looking at the ferris wheel, and he hoped they would decide to ride it. They really did things big in Texas, Bruno thought, looking up admiringly at the wheel. He had never seen a ferris wheel big as this. It had a five-pointed star in blue lights inside it.

'Ralph, how 'bout it?' Miriam squealed, poking the last of the frozen custard cone into her mouth with her hand against her face.

'Aw, 's ain't no fun. H'bout the merry-go-round?'

And they all went. The merry-go-round was like a lighted city in the dark woods, a forest of nickel-plated poles crammed with zebras, horses, giraffes, bulls, and camels all plunging down or upward, some with necks arched out over the platform, frozen in leaps and gallops as if they waited desperately for riders. Bruno stood still, unable to take his dazzled eyes from it even to watch Miriam, tingling to the music that promised movement at any instant. He felt he was about to experience again some ancient, delicious childhood moment that the steam calliope's sour hollowness, the stitching hurdy-gurdy accompaniment, and the drum-and-cymbal crash brought almost to the margin of his grasp.

People were choosing mounts. And Miriam and her friends were eating again, Miriam diving into a popcorn bag Dick held for her. The pigs! Bruno was hungry, too. He bought a frankfurter, and when he looked again, they were boarding the merry-go-round. He scrambled for coins and ran. He got the horse he had wanted, a royal blue one with an upreared head and an open mouth, and as luck would have it, Miriam and her friends kept weaving back through the poles towards him, and Miriam and Dick took the giraffe and the horse right in front of him. Luck was with him tonight ! Tonight he should be gambling !

> *Just like the strain – te-te-dum –*
> *Of a haunting refrain – te-te-dum –*
> *She'll start upon – BOOM! a marathon – BOOM!*

Bruno loved the song and so did his mother. The music made him suck in his belly and sit his horse like a ramrod. He swung his feet gaily in the stirrups. Something swatted him in the back of the head, he turned belligerently, but it was only some fellows rough-housing with one another.

They started off slowly and militantly to 'The Washington Post March'. Up, up, up he went and down, down, down went Miriam on her giraffe. The world beyond the merry-go-round vanished in a light-streaked blur. Bruno held the reins in one hand as he had been taught to do in his polo lessons, and ate the frankfurter with the other.

'Yeeee-hooo !' yelled the redheaded fellow.

'Yeeee-hooo !' Bruno yelled back. 'I'm a Texan !'

'Katie?' Miriam leaned forward on the giraffe's neck, and her grey skirt got round and tight. 'See the fellow over there in the check shirt?'

Bruno looked. He saw the fellow in the checked shirt. He looked a little like Guy, Bruno thought, and thinking of this, he missed what Miriam said about him. Under the bright lights, he saw that Miriam was covered with freckles. She looked increasingly loathsome, so he began not to want to put his hands on her soft sticky-warm flesh. Well, he still had the knife. A clean instrument.

'A clean instrument !' Bruno shouted jubilantly, for no one could possibly hear him. His was the outside horse, and next to him was a boxed double seat thing made out of swans, which was empty. He spat into it. He flung away the rest of the frankfurter and wiped the mustard off his fingers on the horse's mane.

'Casey would waltz with the strawberry blonde, while the band – played – aaaawn !' Miriam's date sang out with vehemence.

They all joined in and Bruno with them. The whole merry-go-round was singing. If they only had drinks! Everybody should be having a drink!

'His brain was so loaded, it nearly exploded,' sang Bruno at the cracking top of his lungs, 'the poor girl would shake with alaa-arm!'

'Hi, Casey!' Miriam cooed to Dick, opening her mouth to catch the popcorn he was trying to throw into it.

'Yak-yak!' Bruno shouted.

Miriam looked ugly and stupid with her mouth open, as if she were being strangled and had turned pink and bloated. He could not bear to look at her, and still grinning, turned his eyes away. The merry-go-round was slowing. He hoped they would stay for another ride, but they got off, linked arms, and began to walk towards the twinkling lights on the water.

Bruno paused under the trees for another little nip from the nearly empty flask.

They were taking a rowboat. The prospect of a cool row was delightful to Bruno. He engaged a boat, too. The lake looked big and black, except for the lightless twinkles, full of drifting boats with couples necking in them. Bruno got close enough to Miriam's boat to see that the redheaded fellow was doing the rowing, and that Miriam and Dick were squeezing each other and giggling in the back seat. Bruno bent for three deep strokes that carried him past their boat, then let his oars trail.

'Want to go to the island or loaf around?' the redheaded fellow asked.

Petulantly, Bruno slumped sideways on the seat, waiting for them to make up their minds. In the nooks along the shore, as if from little dark rooms, he heard murmurs, soft radios, laughter. He tipped his flask and drained it. What would happen if he shouted 'Guy!'? What would Guy think if he could see him now? Maybe Guy and Miriam had been out on dates on this lake, maybe in the same rowboat he sat in now. His hands and the lower part of his legs tingled cosily with the liquor. If he had Miriam here in the boat with him, he would hold her head under the water with pleasure. Here in the dark. Pitch dark and no moon. The water made quick licking sounds against his boat. Bruno writhed in sudden impatience. There was the sucking sound of a kiss from Miriam's boat, and Bruno gave it back to them with a pleasurable groan thrown in. *Smack, smack!* They must have heard him, because there was a burst of laughter.

He waited until they had paddled past, then followed leisurely. A black mass drew closer, pricked here and there with the spark of a match. The island. It looked like a neckers' paradise. Maybe Miriam would be at it again tonight, Bruno thought, giggling.

When Miriam's boat landed, he rowed a few yards to one side and climbed ashore, and set his boat's nose up on a little log so it would be easy to recognize from the others. The sense of purpose filled him once more, stronger and more imminent than on the train. In Metcalf hardly two hours, and here he was on an island with her! He pressed the knife against him through his trousers. If he could just get her alone and clap his hand over her mouth — or would she be able to bite? He squirmed with disgust at the thought of her wet mouth on his hand.

Slowly he followed their slow steps, up rough ground where the trees were close.

'We cain't sit here, the ground's wet,' whined the girl called Katie.

'Sit on mah coat if y'wanta,' a fellow said.

Christ, Bruno thought, those dumb Southern accents!

'When I'm walkin' with m'honey down honeymoon lane . . . ,' somebody sang, off in the bushes.

Night murmurs. Bugs. Crickets. And a mosquito at his ear. Bruno boxed his ear and the ear rang maddeningly, drowning out the voices.

'. . . shove off.'

'Why cain't we find a place?' Miriam yapped.

'Ain't no place an 'watch whatcha step in !'

'Watcha step-ins, gals !' laughed the redheaded fellow.

What the hell *were* they going to do? He was bored! The music of the merry-go-round sounded tired and very distant, only the *tings* coming through. Then they turned around right in his face, so he had to move off to one side as if he were going somewhere. He got tangled in some thorny underbrush and occupied himself getting free of it while they passed him. Then he followed, downward. He thought he could smell Miriam's perfume, if it wasn't the other girl's, a sweetness like a steamy bathroom that repelled him.

'. . . and now,' said a radio, 'coming in very cautiously . . . Leon . . . *Leon* . . . lands a hard right to the Babe's face *and-listentothecrowd*!' A roar.

Bruno saw a fellow and a girl wallowing down there in the bushes as if they were fighting, too.

Miriam stood on slightly higher ground, not three yards away from him now, and the others slid down the bank towards the water. Bruno inched closer. The lights on the water silhouetted her head and shoulders. Never had he been so close!

'Hey!' Bruno whispered, and saw her turn. 'Say, isn't your name Miriam?'

She faced him, but he knew she could barely see him. 'Yeah. Who're you?'

He came a step nearer. 'Haven't I met you somewhere before?' he asked cynically, smelling the perfume again. She was a warm ugly black spot. He sprang with such concentrated aim, the wrists of his spread hands touched.

'Say what d'you –?' —

His hands captured her throat on the last word, stifling its abortive uplift of surprise. He shook her. His body seemed to harden like rock, and he heard his teeth crack. She made a grating sound in her throat, but he had her too tight for a scream. With a leg behind her, he wrenched her backward, and they fell to the ground together with no sound but of a brush of leaves. He sunk his fingers deeper, enduring the distasteful pressure of her body under his so her writhing would not get them both up. Her throat felt hotter and fatter. Stop, stop, stop! He willed it! And the head stopped turning. He was sure he had held her long enough, but he did not lessen his grip. Glancing behind him, he saw nothing coming. When he relaxed his fingers, it felt as if he had made deep dents in her throat as in a piece of dough. Then she made a sound like an ordinary cough that terrified him like the rising dead, and he fell on her again, hitched himself on to his knees to do it, pressing her with a force he thought would break his thumbs. All the power in him he poured out through his hands. And if it was not enough? He heard himself whimper. She was still and limp now.

'Miriam?' called the girl's voice.

Bruno sprang up and stumbled straight away towards the centre of the island, then turned left to bring him out near his boat. He found himself scrubbing something off his hands with his pocket handkerchief. Miriam's spit. He threw the handkerchief down and swept it up again, because it was monogrammed. He was thinking! He felt great! It was done!

'Mi-ri-am!' with lazy impatience.

But what if he hadn't finished her, if she were sitting up and talking now? The thought shot him forward and he almost toppled down the bank. A firm breeze met him at the water's edge. He didn't see his boat. He started to take any boat, changed his mind, then a couple of yards farther to the left found it, perched on the little log.

'Hey, she's fainted!'

Bruno shoved off, quickly, but not hurrying.

'Help, somebody!' said the girl's half gasp, half scream.

'Gawd! – Huh-*help*!'

The panic in the voice panicked Bruno. He rowed for several choppy strokes, then abruptly stopped and let the boat glide over the dark water. What was he getting scared about, for Christ's sake? Not a sign of anyone chasing him.

'Hey!'

'F'God's sake, she's *dead*! Call somebody!'

A girl's scream was a long arc in silence and somehow the scream made it final. A beautiful scream, Bruno thought with a queer, serene admiration. He approached the dock easily, behind another boat. Slowly, as slowly as he had ever done anything, he paid the boatkeeper.

'On the island!' said another shocking, excited voice from a boat. 'Girl's dead, they said!'

'Dead?'

'Somebody call the cops!'

Feet ran on the wooden dock behind him.

Bruno idled towards the gates of the park. Thank God he was so tight or hung over or something he could move so slowly! But a fluttering, unfightable terror rose in him as he passed through the turnstile. Then it ebbed quickly. No one was even looking at him. To steady himself, he concentrated on wanting a drink. There was a place up the road with red lights that looked like a bar, and he went straight towards it.

'Cutty,' he said to the barman.

'Where you from, son?'

Bruno looked at him. The two men on the right were looking at him, too. 'I want a Scotch.'

'Can't get no hard liquor round here, man.'

'What is this, part of the park?' His voice cracked like the scream.

'Can't get no hard liquor in the state of Texas.'

'Gimme some of that!' Bruno pointed to the bottle of rye the men had on the counter.

'Here. Anybody wants a drink that bad.' One of the men poured some rye in a glass and pushed it over.

It was rough as Texas going down, but sweet when it got there. Bruno offered to pay him, but the man refused.

Police sirens sounded, coming closer.

A man came in the door.

'What happened? Accident?' somebody asked him.

'I didn't see anything,' the man said unconcernedly.

My brother! Bruno thought, looking the man over, but it didn't seem the thing to do to go over and talk to him.

He felt fine. The man kept insisting he have another drink, and Bruno had three fast. He noticed a streak on his hand as he lifted the glass, got out his handkerchief, and calmly wiped between his thumb and forefinger. It was a smear of Miriam's orangey lipstick. He could hardly see it in the bar's light. He thanked the man with the rye, and strolled out into the darkness, walking along the right side of the road, looking for a taxi. He had no desire to look back at the lighted park. He wasn't even thinking about it, he told himself. A streetcar passed, and he ran for it. He enjoyed its bright interior, and read all the placards. A wriggly little boy sat across the aisle, and Bruno began chatting with him. The thought of calling Guy and seeing him kept crossing his mind, but of course Guy wasn't here. He wanted some kind of celebration. He might call Guy's mother again, for the hell of it, but on second thought, it didn't seem wise. It was the one lousy note in the evening, the fact he couldn't see Guy, or even talk or write to him for a long while. Guy would be in for some questioning, of course. But he was free! It was done, done, done! In a burst of well-being, he ruffled the little boy's hair.

The little boy was taken aback for a moment, then in response to Bruno's friendly grin, he smiled, too.

At the Atchison, Topeka and Santa Fe Railroad terminal, he got an upper berth on a sleeper leaving at 1.30 a.m., which gave him an hour and a half to kill. Everything was perfect and he felt terribly happy. In a drugstore near the station, he bought a pint of Scotch to refill his flask. He thought of going by Guy's house to see what it looked like, debated it carefully, and decided he could. He was just heading for a man standing by the door, to ask directions – he knew he shouldn't go there in a taxi – when he realized he wanted a woman. He wanted a woman more than ever before in his life, and that he did pleased him prodigiously. He hadn't wanted one since he got to Santa Fe, though twice Wilson had got him into it. He veered away right in the man's face, thinking one of the taxi drivers outside would be better to ask. He had the shakes, he wanted a woman so badly! A different kind of shakes from liquor shakes.

'Ah don' know,' said the blank, freckle-faced driver leaning against the fender.

'What d'you mean, you don't know?'

'Don' know, that's all.'

Bruno left him in disgust.

Another driver down the sidewalk was more obliging. He wrote Bruno an address and a couple of names on the back of a company card, though it was so close by, he didn't even have to drive him there.

13

Guy leaned against the wall by his bed in the Montecarlo, watching Anne turn the pages of the family album he had brought from Metcalf. These had been wonderful days, his last two with Anne. Tomorrow he left for Metcalf. And then Florida. Mr Brillhart's telegram had come three days ago, saying the commission was still his. There was a stretch of six months' work ahead, and in December the commencement of their own house. He had the money to build it now. And the money for the divorce.

'You know,' he said quietly, 'if I didn't have Palm Beach, if I had to go back to New York tomorrow and work, I could, and take anything.' But almost as he said it, he realized that Palm Beach had given him his courage, his momentum, his will, or whatever he chose to call it, that without Palm Beach these days with Anne would give him only a sense of guilt.

'But you don't have to,' Anne said finally. She bent lower over the album.

He smiled. He knew she had hardly been listening to him. And, in fact, what he had said didn't matter, as Anne knew. He leaned over the album with her, identifying the people that she asked about, watching amusedly as she examined the double page of his pictures that his mother had collected, from baby-hood to about twenty. He was smiling in every one of them, a shock of black hair setting off a sturdier, more careless-looking face than he had now.

'Do I look happy enough there?' he asked.

She winked at him. 'And very handsome. Any of Miriam?' She let the remaining pages slip past her thumbnail.

'No,' Guy said.

'I'm awfully glad you brought this.'

'My mother would have my neck if she knew it was in Mexico.' He put the album back in his suitcase so he wouldn't possibly leave it behind. 'It's the most humane way of meeting families.'

'Guy, did I put you through much?'

He smiled at her plaintive tone. 'No! I never minded a bit!' He sat down on the bed and pulled her back with him. He had met all of Anne's relatives, by twos and threes, by dozens at the Faulkners' Sunday suppers and parties. It was a family joke how many Faulkners and Weddells and Morrisons there were, all living in New York State or in Long Island. Somehow he liked the fact she had so many relatives. The Christmas he had spent at the Faulkners' house last year had been the happiest of his life. He kissed both her cheeks, then her mouth. When he put his head down, he saw Anne's drawings on the Montecarlo stationery on the counterpane, and idly began to push them into a neat stack. They were ideas for designs that had come to her after their visit to the Museo Nacionale this afternoon. Their lines were black and definite, like his own rough sketches. 'I'm thinking about the house, Anne.'

'You want it big.'

He smiled. 'Yes.'

'Let's have it big.' She relaxed in his arms. They both sighed, like one person, and she laughed a little as he wrapped her closer.

It was the first time she had agreed to the size of the house. The house was to be Y-shaped, and the question had been whether to dispense with the front arm of it. But the idea sang in Guy's head only with both arms. It would cost much, much more than twenty thousand, but Palm Beach would bring a flock of private commissions, Guy expected, that would be fast, well-paid jobs. Anne had said her father would like nothing better than to make them a wedding present of the front wing, but to Guy that seemed as unthinkable as removing it. He could see the house shining white and sharp against the brown bureau across the room. It projected from a certain white rock he had seen near a town called Alton in lower Connecticut. The house was long, low, and flat-roofed, as if alchemy had created it from the rock itself, like a crystal.

'I might call it "The Crystal",' Guy said.

Anne stared up reflectively at the ceiling. 'I'm not so fond of naming houses – houses' names. Maybe I don't like "Crystal".'

Guy felt subtly hurt. 'It's a lot better than "Alton". Of all the insipid names! That's New England for you. Take Texas now –'

'All right, you take Texas and I'll take New England.' Anne smiled, stopping Guy in his tracks, because in reality she liked Texas and Guy liked New England.

Guy looked at the telephone, with a funny premonition it was going to ring. He felt rather giddy in his head, as if he had taken some mildly euphoric drug. It was the altitude, Anne said, that made people feel that way in Mexico City. 'I feel as if I could call up Miriam tonight and talk to her and everything would be all right,' Guy said slowly, 'as if I could say just the right thing.'

'There's the telephone,' Anne said, perfectly serious.

Seconds passed, and he heard Anne sigh.

'What time is it?' she asked, sitting up. 'I told Mother I'd be back by twelve.'

'Eleven-seven.'

'Aren't you sort of hungry?'

They ordered something from the restaurant downstairs. Their ham and eggs were an unrecognizable dish of vermilion colour, but quite good, they decided.

'I'm glad you got to Mexico,' Anne said. 'It's been like something I knew so well and you didn't, something I wanted you to know. Only Mexico City isn't like the rest.' She went on, eating slowly, 'It has a nostalgia like Paris or Vienna and you want to come back no matter what's happened to you here.'

Guy frowned. He had been to Paris and Vienna with Robert Treacher, a Canadian engineer, one summer when neither of them had any money. It hadn't been the Paris and Vienna Anne had known. He looked down at the buttered sweet roll she had given him. At times he wanted passionately to know the flavour of every experience Anne had ever known, what had happened to her in every hour of her childhood. 'What do you mean, no matter what's happened to me here?'

'I mean whether you've been sick. Or robbed.' She looked up at him and smiled. But the lamp's light that made a glow through her smoke-blue eyes, a crescent glow on their darker rims, lent a mysterious sadness to her face. 'I suppose it's contrasts that make it attractive. Like people with incredible contrasts.'

Guy stared at her, his finger crooked in the handle of his coffee cup. Somehow her mood, or perhaps what she said, made him feel inferior. 'I'm sorry I don't have any incredible contrasts.'

'Oh-ho-ho!' Then she burst out in a laugh, her familiar gay laugh that delighted him even when she laughed at him, even when she had no intention of explaining herself.

He sprang up. 'How about some cake. I'm going to produce a cake like a jinni. A wonderful cake!' He got the cookie tin out of the corner of his suitcase. He had not thought of the cake until that moment, the cake his mother had baked him with the blackberry jam he had praised at his breakfasts.

Anne telephoned the bar downstairs and ordered a very special liqueur that she knew of. The liqueur was a rich purple like the purple cake, in stemmed glasses hardly bigger around than a finger. The waiter had just gone, they were lifting the glasses, when the telephone rang, in nervous, iterant rings.

'Probably Mother,' Anne said.

Guy answered it. He heard a voice talking distantly to an operator. Then the voice came louder, anxious and shrill, his mother's voice:

'Hello?'

'Hello, Mama.'

'Guy, something's happened.'

'What's the matter?'

'It's Miriam.'

'What about her?' Guy pressed the receiver hard against his ear. He turned to Anne, and saw her face change as she looked at him.

'She's been killed, Guy. Last night –' She broke off.

'What, Mama?'

'It happened last night.' She spoke in the shrill, measured tones that Guy had heard only once or twice before in his life. 'Guy, she was murdered.'

'Murdered!'

'Guy, *what*?' Anne asked, getting up.

'Last night at the lake. They don't know anything.'

'You're —'

'Can you come home, Guy?'

'Yes, Mama. — How?' he asked stupidly, wringing the telephone as if he could wring information from its two old-fashioned parts. 'How?'

'Strangled.' The one word, then silence.

'Did you —?' he began. 'Is —?'

'Guy, what is it?' Anne held to his arm.

'I'll be home as fast as I can, Mama. Tonight. Don't worry. I'll see you very soon.' He hung up slowly and turned to Anne. 'It's Miriam. Miriam's been killed.'

Anne whispered, 'Murdered — did you say?'

Guy nodded, but it suddenly struck him there might be a mistake. If it were just a report —

'When?'

But it was last night. 'Last night, she said.'

'Do they know who?'

'No. I've got to go tonight.'

'My God.'

He looked at Anne, standing motionless in front of him. 'I've got to go tonight,' he said again, dazedly. Then he turned and went to the telephone to call for a plane reservation, but it was Anne who got the reservation for him, talking rapidly in Spanish.

He began to pack. It seemed to take hours getting his few possessions into his suitcase. He stared at the brown bureau, wondering if he had already looked through it to see if everything were out of its drawers. Now, where he had seen the vision of the white house, a laughing face appeared, first the crescent mouth, then the face — Bruno's face. The tongue curved lewdly over the upper lip, and then the silent convulsed laughter came again, shaking the stringy hair over the forehead. Guy frowned at Anne.

'What's the matter, Guy?'

'Nothing,' he said. How *did* he look now?

14

Supposing Bruno had done it? He couldn't have, of course, but just supposing he had? Had they caught him? Had Bruno told them the murder was a plan of theirs? Guy could easily imagine Bruno hysterical, saying anything. There was no predicting what a neurotic child like Bruno would say. Guy searched his hazy memory of their conversation on the train and tried to recall if in jest or anger or drunkenness he had said anything that might have been taken as a consent to Bruno's insane idea. He hadn't. Against this negative answer, he weighed Bruno's letter that he remembered word for word: *that idea we had for a couple of murders. It could be done, I am sure. I cannot express to you my supremest confidence –*

From the plane window, Guy looked down into total blackness. Why wasn't he more anxious than he was? Up the dim cylinder of the plane's body, a match glowed at someone's cigarette. The scent of Mexican tobacco was faint, bitter, and sickening. He looked at his watch: 4.25.

Towards dawn he fell asleep, yielding to the shaking roar of the motors that seemed bent on tearing the plane apart, tearing his mind apart, and scattering the pieces in the sky. He awakened to a grey overcast morning, and a new thought: Miriam's lover had killed her. It was so obvious, so likely. He had killed her in a quarrel. One read such cases so often in the newspapers, the victims so often women like Miriam. There was a front-page story about a girl's murder in the tabloid *El Grafico* he had bought at the airport – he hadn't been able to find an American paper, though he had almost missed the plane looking for one – and a picture of her grinning Mexican lover holding the knife with which he had killed her, and Guy started to read it, becoming bored in the second paragraph.

A plain-clothes man met him at the Metcalf airport and asked if he would mind answering a few questions. They got into a taxi together.

'Have they found the murderer?' Guy asked him.

'No.'

The plain-clothes man looked tired, as if he had been up all night, like the rest of the reporters and clerks and police in the old North Side courthouse. Guy glanced around the big wooden room, looking for Bruno before he was aware of doing so. When he lighted a cigarette, the man next to him asked him what kind it was, and accepted the one Guy offered him. They were Anne's Belmonts that he had pocketed when he was packing.

'Guy Daniel Haines, 717 Ambrose Street, Metcalf ... When did you leave Metcalf? ... And when did you get to Mexico City?'

Chairs scraped. A noiseless typewriter started bumping after them.

Another plain-clothes man with a badge, with his jacket open and a swagbelly protruding, strolled closer. 'Why did you go to Mexico?'

'To visit some friends.'

'Who?'

'The Faulkners. Alex Faulkner of New York.'

'Why didn't you tell your mother where you were going?'

'I did tell her.'

'She didn't know where you were staying in Mexico City,' the plain-clothes man informed him blandly, and referred to his notes. 'You sent your wife a letter Sunday asking for a divorce. What did she reply?'

'That she wanted to talk with me.'

'But you didn't care to talk with her any more, did you?' asked a clear tenor voice.

Guy looked at the young police officer, and said nothing.

'Was her child to be yours?'

He started to answer, but was interrupted.

'Why did you come to Texas last week to see your wife?'

'Didn't you want a divorce pretty badly, Mr Haines?'

'Are you in love with Anne Faulkner?'

Laughter.

'You know your wife had a lover, Mr Haines. Were you jealous?'

'You were depending on that child for your divorce, weren't you?'

'That's all!' someone said.

A photograph was thrust in front of him, and the image spun with his anger before it straightened to a long dark head, handsome and stupid brown eyes, a cleft, manly chin – a face that might have been a movie actor's, and no one had to tell him this was Miriam's lover, because this was the kind of face she had liked three years ago.

'No,' Guy said.

'Haven't you and he had some talks together?'

'That's all!'

A bitter smile pulled at the corner of his mouth, yet he felt he might have cried, too, like a child. He hailed a taxi in front of the courthouse. On the ride home, he read the double column on the front of the *Metcalf Star*:

QUEST CONTINUES FOR GIRL'S SLAYER

June 12 – The quest continues for the slayer of Mrs Miriam Joyce Haines of this city, victim of strangulation by an unknown assailant on Metcalf Island Sunday night.

Two fingerprint experts arrive today who will endeavour to establish classifications of fingerprints taken from several oars and rowboats of the Lake Metcalf rowboat docks. But police and detectives fear that obtainable fingerprints are hazy. Authorities yesterday afternoon expressed the opinion that the crime might have been the act of a maniac. Apart from dubious fingerprints and several heelprints around the scene of the attack, police officials have not yet uncovered any vital clue.

Most important testimony at the inquest, it is believed, will come from Owen Markman, 30, longshoreman of Houston, and a close friend of the murdered woman.

Interment of Mrs Haines's body will take place today at Remington Cemetery. The cortège departs from Howell Funeral Home on College Avenue at 2.00 p.m. this afternoon.

Guy lighted a cigarette from the end of another. His hands were still shaking, but he felt vaguely better. He hadn't thought of the possibility of a maniac. A maniac reduced it to a kind of horrible accident.

His mother sat in her rocker in the living-room with a handkerchief pressed to her temple, waiting for him, though she did not get up when he came in. Guy embraced her and kissed her cheek, relieved to see she hadn't been crying.

'I spent yesterday with Mrs Joyce,' she said, 'but I just can't go to the funeral.'

'There isn't any need to, Mama.' He glanced at his watch and saw it was already past 2. For an instant, he felt that Miriam might have been buried alive, that she might awaken and scream in protest. He turned, and passed his hand across his forehead.

'Mrs Joyce,' his mother said softly, 'asked me if you might know something.'

Guy faced her again. Mrs Joyce resented him, he knew. He hated her now for what she might have said to his mother. 'Don't see them again, Mama. You don't have to, do you?'

'No.'

'And thank you for going over.'

Upstairs on his bureau, he found three letters and a small square package with a Santa Fe store label. The package contained a narrow belt of braided lizard skin with a silver buckle formed like an H. A note enclosed said:

Lost your Plato book on way to post office. I hope this will help make up.

Charley

Guy picked up the pencilled envelope from the Santa Fe hotel. There was only a small card inside. On the card's back was printed:

NICK TOWN METCALF

Turning the card, he read mechanically:

24 HOUR
DONOVAN TAXI SERVICE
RAIN OR SHINE
Call 2-3333
SAFE FAST COURTEOUS

Something had been erased beneath the message on the back.

Guy held the card to the light and made out one word: Ginnie. It was a Metcalf taxi company's card, but it had been mailed from Santa Fe. It doesn't mean anything, doesn't prove anything, he thought. But he crushed the card and the envelope and the package wrappings into his waste-basket. He loathed Bruno, he realized. He opened the box in the waste-basket and put the belt in, too. It was a handsome belt, but he happened also to loathe lizard and snake skin.

Anne telephoned him that night from Mexico City. She wanted to know everything that had happened, and he told her what he knew.

'They don't have any suspicion who did it?' she asked.

'They don't seem to.'

'You don't sound well, Guy. Did you get any rest?'

'Not yet.' He couldn't tell her now about Bruno. His mother had said that a man had called twice, wanting to talk to him, and Guy had no doubt who it was. But he knew he could not tell Anne about Bruno until he was sure. He could not begin.

'We've just sent those affidavits, darling. You know, about your being here with us?'

He had wired her for them after talking to one of the police detectives. 'Everything'll be all right after the inquest,' he said.

But it troubled him the rest of the night that he had not told Anne about Bruno. It was not the horror that he wished to spare her. He felt it was some sense of personal guilt that he himself could not bear.

There was a report going about that Owen Markman had not wanted to marry Miriam after the loss of the child, and that she had started a breach-of-promise action against him. Miriam really had lost the child accidentally, Guy's mother said. Mrs Joyce had told her that Miriam had tripped on a black silk nightgown that she particularly liked, that Owen had given her, and had fallen downstairs in her house. Guy believed the story implicitly. A compassion and remorse he had never before felt for Miriam had entered his heart. Now she seemed pitiably ill-fated and entirely innocent.

15

'Not more than seven yards and not less than five,' the grave, self-assured young man in the chair replied. 'No, I did not see anyone.'

'I think about fifteen feet,' said the wide-eyed girl, Katherine Smith, who looked as frightened as if it had just happened. 'Maybe a little more,' she added softly.

'About thirty feet. I was the first one down at the boat,' said Ralph Joyce, Miriam's brother. His red hair was like Miriam's, and he had the same grey-green eyes, but his heavy square jaw took away the resemblance. 'I wouldn't say she had any enemy. Not enough to do something like this.'

'I didn't hear one thing,' Katherine Smith said earnestly, shaking her head.

Ralph Joyce said he hadn't heard anything, and Richard Schuyler's positive statement ended it:

'There weren't any sounds.'

The facts repeated and repeated lost their horror and even their drama for Guy. They were like dull blows of a hammer, nailing the story in his mind forever. The nearness of the three others was the unbelievable. Only a maniac would have dared come so near, Guy thought, that was certain.

'Were you the father of the child Mrs Haines lost?'

'Yes.' Owen Markman slouched forward over his locked fingers. A glum, hangdog manner spoilt the dashing good looks Guy had seen in the photograph. He wore grey buckskin shoes, as if he had just come from his job in Houston. Miriam would not have been proud of him today, Guy thought.

'Do you know anyone who might have wanted Mrs Haines to die?'

'Yes.' Markman pointed at Guy. 'Him.'

People turned to look at him. Guy sat tensely, frowning straight at Markman, for the first time really suspecting Markman.

'Why?'

Owen Markman hesitated a long while, mumbled something, then brought out one word: 'Jealousy.'

Markman could not give a single credible reason for jealousy, but after that accusation of jealousy came from all sides. Even Katherine Smith said, 'I guess so.'

Guy's lawyer chuckled. He had the affidavits from the Faulkners in his hand. Guy hated the chuckle. He had always hated legal procedure. It was like a vicious game in which the objective seemed not to disclose the truth but to enable one lawyer to tilt at another, and unseat him on a technicality.

'You gave up an important commission –' the coroner began.

'I did not give it up,' Guy said. 'I wrote them before I had the commission, saying I didn't want it.'

'You telegraphed. Because you didn't want your wife to follow you there. But when you learned in Mexico that your wife had lost her child, you sent another telegram to Palm Beach that you wished to be considered for the commission. Why?'

'Because I didn't believe she'd follow me there then. I suspected she'd want to delay the divorce indefinitely. But I intended to see her – this week to discuss the divorce.' Guy wiped the perspiration from his forehead, and saw his lawyer purse his lips ruefully. His lawyer hadn't wanted him to mention the divorce in connection with his change of mind about the commission. Guy didn't care. It was the truth, and they could make of it what they wished.

'In your opinion was her husband capable of arranging for such a murder, Mrs Joyce?'

'Yes,' said Mrs Joyce with the faintest quiver, her head high. The shrewd dark red lashes were almost closed, as Guy had so often seen them, so that one never knew where her eyes rested. 'He wanted his divorce.'

There was an objection that Mrs Joyce had said a few moments before that her daughter wanted the divorce and Guy Haines did not because he still loved her. 'If both wanted a divorce, and it has been proven Mr Haines did, why wasn't there a divorce?'

The court was amused. The fingerprint experts could not come to agreement on their classifications. A hardware dealer, into

88

whose store Miriam had come the day before her death, got tangled up as to whether her companion had been male or female, and more laughter camouflaged the fact he had been instructed to say a man. Guy's lawyer harangued on geographical fact, the inconsistences of the Joyce family, the affidavits in his hand, but Guy was sure that his own straightforwardness alone had absolved him from any suspicion.

The coroner suggested in his summation that the murder would seem to have been committed by a maniac unknown to the victim and the other parties. A verdict was brought in of 'person or persons unknown', and the case was turned over to the police.

A telegram arrived the next day, just as Guy was leaving his mother's house:

ALL GOOD WISHES FROM THE GOLDEN WEST.

UNSIGNED

'From the Faulkners,' he said quickly to his mother.

She smiled. 'Tell Anne to take good care of my boy.' She pulled him down gently by his ear and kissed his cheek.

Bruno's telegram was still wadded in his hand when he got to the airport. He tore it into tiny bits and dropped them into a wire trash-basket at the edge of the field. Every one of the pieces blew through the wire and went dancing out across the asphalt, gay as confetti in the windy sunlight.

16

Guy struggled to find a definite answer about Bruno – had he or hadn't he? – and then gave it up. There was too much incredible in the possibility that Bruno had done it. What weight did the Metcalf taxi company's card have? It would be like Bruno to find such a card in Santa Fe and mail it on to him. If it were not the act of a maniac, as the coroner and everyone else believed, wasn't it far more likely that Owen Markman had arranged it?

He closed his mind to Metcalf, to Miriam, and to Bruno, and

concentrated on the work for Palm Beach which, he saw from the first day, would demand all that he had in diplomacy, technical knowledge, and sheer physical strength. Except for Anne, he closed his mind to all his past that, for all his idealistic aims and the fighting for them, and the small success he had known, seemed miserable and grubbing compared to the magnificent main building of the country club. And the more he immersed himself in the new effort, the more he felt recreated also in a different and more perfect form.

Photographs from newspapers and news magazines took pictures of the main building, the swimming pool, the bathhouses, and the terracing in the early stages of construction. Members of the club were also photographed inspecting the grounds, and Guy knew that below their pictures would be printed the amount of money each had donated to the cause of princely recreation. Sometimes he wondered if part of his enthusiasm might be due to a consciousness of the money behind the project, to the lavishness of space and materials he had to work with, to the flattery of the wealthy people who continually invited him to their homes. Guy never accepted their invitations. He knew he might be losing himself the small commissions he would need next winter, but he also knew he could never force himself to the social responsibilities that most architects assumed as a matter of course. Evenings when he did not want to be alone, he caught a bus to Clarence Brillhart's house a few miles away, and they had dinner together, listened to phonograph records, and talked. Clarence Brillhart, the Palmyra Club manager, was a retired broker, a tall, white-haired old gentleman whom Guy often thought he would have liked as a father. Guy admired most of all his air of leisure, as imperturbable on the bustling, hectic construction grounds as in his own home. Guy hoped he might be like him in his own old age. But he felt he moved too fast, had always moved too fast. There was inevitably, he felt, a lack of dignity in moving fast.

Most evenings Guy read, wrote long letters to Anne, or merely went to bed, for he was always up by five and often worked all day with a blowtorch or mortar and trowel. He knew almost all the workmen by name. He liked to judge the temperament of each man, to know how it contributed or did not contribute to the spirit of his buildings. 'It is like directing a symphony,' he wrote to Anne. In the dusks, when he sat smoking his pipe in a thicket of the golf course, gazing down on the four white buildings, he felt that the Palmyra project was going to be perfect. He knew it when he saw the first horizontals laid across the spaced marble uprights of the main building. The Pittsburgh store had been marred at the last moment by the client's change of mind about the window area. The hospital annex in Chicago had been ruined, Guy thought, by the cornice that was of darker stone than he had intended. But Brillhart permitted no interference, the Palmyra was going to be as perfect as his original conception, and Guy had never created anything before that he felt would be perfect.

In August, he went North to see Anne. She was working in the design department of a textile company in Manhattan. In the autumn, she planned to go into partnership in a shop with another woman designer she had met. Neither of them mentioned Miriam until the fourth and last day of Guy's visit. They were standing by the brook behind Anne's house, in their last few minutes together before Anne drove him to the airport.

'Do you think it was Markman, Guy?' Anne asked him suddenly. And when Guy nodded: 'It's terrible – but I'm almost sure.'

Then one evening when he returned from Brillhart's house to the furnished room where he lived, a letter from Bruno awaited him with one from Anne. The letter was from Los Angeles, forwarded by his mother from Metcalf. It congratulated him on his work in Palm Beach, wished him success, and begged for just a word from him. The P.S. said:

Hope you are not annoyed at this letter. Have written many letters and not mailed them. Phoned your mother for your address, but she wouldn't give it to me. Guy, honestly there is nothing to worry about or I wouldn't have written. Don't you know I'd be the first one to be careful? Write soon. I may go to Haiti soon. Again your friend and admirer. C.A.B.

A slow ache fell through him to his feet. He could not bear to be alone in his room. He went out to a bar, and almost before he knew what he was doing, had two ryes and then a third. In the mirror behind the bar, he saw himself glance at his sunburnt face, and it struck him that his eyes looked dishonest and furtive. *Bruno had done it.* It came thundering down with a weight that left no possibility of doubt any longer, like a cataclysm that only a madman's unreason could have kept suspended all this while. He glanced about in the little bar as if he expected the walls to topple down on him. *Bruno had done it.* There was no mistaking Bruno's personal pride in his, Guy's, freedom now. Or the P.S. Or possibly even the trip to Haiti. But what did Bruno *mean?* Guy scowled at the face in the mirror and dropped his eyes, looked down at his hands, the front of his tweed jacket, his flannel trousers, and it flashed through his mind he had put these clothes on this morning as a certain person and that he would take them off tonight as another person, the person he would be from now on. He *knew* now. This was an instant — He could not say just what was happening, but he felt his entire life would be different, must be different, from now on.

If he knew Bruno had done it, why didn't he turn him in? What did he feel about Bruno besides hatred and disgust? Was he afraid? Guy didn't clearly know.

He resisted an impulse to telephone Anne until it was too late, and finally, at three in the morning, could resist no longer. Lying on his bed in the darkness, he talked to her very calmly, about commonplace matters, and once he even laughed. Even Anne did not notice anything wrong, he thought when he had hung up. He felt somehow slighted, and vaguely alarmed.

His mother wrote that the man who had called while he was in Mexico, and said his name was Phil, had called again to ask how he might reach him. She was worried that it might have something to do with Miriam, and wondered if she should tell the police.

Guy wrote back to her: 'I found out who the annoying telephoner was. Phil Johnson, a fellow I knew in Chicago.'

17

'Charley, what're all these clippings?'

'Friend of mine, Ma!' Bruno shouted through the bathroom door. He turned the water on harder, leaned on the basin, and concentrated on the bright nickel-plated drain-stop. After a moment, he reached for the Scotch bottle he kept under towels in the clothes hamper. He felt less shaky with the glass of Scotch and water in his hand, and spent a few seconds inspecting the silver braid on the sleeve of his new smoking jacket. He liked the jacket so much, he wore it as a bathrobe also. In the mirror, the oval lapels framed the portrait of a young man of leisure, of reckless and mysterious adventure, a young man of humour and depth, power and gentleness (witness the glass held delicately between thumb and forefinger with the air of an imperial toast) — a young man with two lives. He drank to himself.

'Charley?'

'Minute, Mom!'

He cast a wild eye about the bathroom. There was no window. Lately it happened about twice a week. Half an hour or so after he got up, he felt as if someone were kneeling on his chest and stifling him. He closed his eyes and dragged air in and out of his lungs as fast as he could. Then the liquor took. It bedded his leaping nerves like a hand passing down his body. He straightened and opened the door.

'Shaving,' he said.

His mother was in tennis shorts and a halter, bending over his unmade bed where the clippings were strewn. 'Who was she?'

'Wife of a fellow I met on the train coming down from New York. Guy Haines.' Bruno smiled. He liked to say Guy's name. 'Interesting, isn't it? They haven't caught the murderer yet.'

'Probably a maniac,' she sighed.

Bruno's face sobered. 'Oh, I doubt it. Circumstances are too complicated.'

Elsie stood up and slid her thumb inside her belt. The bulge just below her belt disappeared, and for a moment she looked as Bruno had seen her all her life until this last year, trim as a twenty-year-old down to her thin ankles. 'Your friend Guy's got a nice face.'

'Nicest fellow you ever saw. It's a shame he's dragged in on it. He told me on the train he hadn't seen his wife in a couple of years. Guy's no more a murderer than I am!' Bruno smiled at his inadvertent joke, and to cover it added, 'His wife was a round-heels anyway –'

'Darling.' She took him by the braid-edged lapels. 'Won't you watch your language a little for the duration? I know Grannie's horrified sometimes.'

'Grannie wouldn't know what a roundheels means,' Bruno said hoarsely.

Elsie threw her head back and shrieked.

'Ma, you're getting too much sun. I don't like your face that dark.'

'I don't like yours that pale.'

Bruno frowned. The leathery look of his mother's forehead offended him painfully. He kissed her suddenly on the cheek.

'Promise me you'll sit in the sun a half-hour today anyway. People come thousands of miles to get to California, and here you sit in the house!'

Bruno frowned down his nose. 'Ma, you're not interested in my friend!'

'I am interested in your friend. You haven't told me much about him.'

Bruno smiled shyly. No, he had been very good. He had let the clippings lie out in his room only today for the first time, because he was sure now both he and Guy were safe. If he talked a quarter of an hour about Guy now, his mother would probably forget, too. If it were even necessary that she forget. 'Did you read all that?' He nodded towards the bed.

'No, not all that. How many drinks this morning?'

'One.'

'I smell two.'

'All right, Mom, I had two.'

'Darling, won't you watch the morning drinks? Morning drinks are the end. I've seen alcoholic after alcoholic –'

'Alcoholic is a nasty word.' Bruno resumed his slow circuit of the room. 'I feel better since I drink a little more, Ma. You said yourself I'm more cheerful and my appetite's better. Scotch is a very pure drink. Some people it agrees with.'

'You drank too much last night, and Grannie knows it. Don't think she doesn't notice, you know.'

'About last night don't ask me.' Bruno grinned and waved his hand.

'Sammie's coming over this morning. Why don't you get dressed and come down and keep score for us?'

'Sammie gives me ulcers.'

She walked to the door as gaily as if she had not heard. 'Promise me you'll get some sun today anyway.'

He nodded and moistened his dry lips. He did not return her smile as she closed the door, because he felt as if a black lid had fallen on him suddenly, as if he had to escape something before it was too late. He had to see *Guy* before it was too late! He had to get rid of his father before it was too late! He had things to do! He did not want to be here, in his grandmother's house furnished just like his own house in Louis Quinze, eternal Louis Quinze! But he did not know where else he wanted to be. He was not happy if he were long away from his mother, was he? He bit his underlip and frowned, though his small grey eyes were quite blank. Why did she say he didn't need a drink in the mornings? He needed it more than any other drink of the day. He flexed his shoulders in a slow rotary movement. Why should he feel low? The clippings on the bed were about him. Week after week went by and the dumb police got nothing on him, nothing except the heelprints, and he had thrown his shoes away long ago! The party last week with Wilson in the San Francisco hotel was nothing to what he would do now if he had Guy to celebrate with. A perfect murder! How many people could do a perfect murder on an island with a couple of hundred other people around?

He was not like the dopes in the newspapers who killed 'to see what it felt like', and never had a bloody thing to report except sometimes a sick-making, 'It wasn't as good as I expected.' If he were interviewed, he would say, 'It was terrific! There's nothing in the world like it!' ('Would you ever do it again, Mr Bruno?') 'Well, I might,' reflectively, with caution, as an arctic explorer when asked if he will winter up north again next year might reply uncommittingly to a reporter. ('Can you tell us a little bit about your sensations?') He would tip the microphone towards him, look up, and muse, while the world awaited his first word. How had it felt? Well, there's only *it*, see, and nothing to compare it with. She was a rotten woman anyway, you understand. It was like killing a hot little rat, only she was a girl so it made it a murder. The very warmth of her had been disgusting, and he remembered thinking that before he took his fingers away, the heat would really have stopped coming, that after he left her, she would grow chill and hideous, like she really was. ('Hideous, Mr Bruno?') Yes, hideous. ('Do you think a corpse is hideous?') Bruno frowned. No, he did not really think he thought a corpse was hideous. If the victim was evil, like Miriam, people ought to be pretty glad to see the corpse, oughtn't they? ('Power, Mr Bruno?') Oh, yes, he had felt terrific power! That was it. He had taken away a life. Now, nobody knew what life was, everybody defended it, the most priceless possession, but he had taken one away. That night there had been the danger, the ache of his hands, the fear in case she made a sound, but the instant when he felt that life had left her, everything else had fallen away, and only the mysterious *fact* of the thing he did remained, the mystery and the miracle of stopping life. People talked about the mystery of birth, of beginning life, but how explainable that was! Out of two live germ cells! What about the mystery of stopping life? Why should life stop because he held a girl's throat too tightly? What was life anyway— What did Miriam feel after he took his hands away? Where was she? No, he didn't believe in a life after death. She was stopped, and that was just the miracle. Oh, he could say a great deal at his interview with the press! ('What significance did it have for you that your victim was female?') Where had that question come from? Bruno hesitated, then recovered his poise. Well, the fact she was a female had given him greater enjoyment. No, he did not therefore conclude that his pleasure had partaken of the sexual. No, he did not hate women either. Rather not! Hate is akin to love, you know. Who said that? He didn't believe it for a minute. No, all he would say was that he wouldn't have enjoyed it quite so much, he thought, if he had killed a man. Unless it was his father.

The telephone . . .

Bruno had been staring at it. Every telephone suggested Guy. He could reach Guy now with two well-placed calls, but a call might annoy Guy. Guy might still be nervous. He would wait for Guy to write. A letter should come any day now, because Guy must have got his letter the end of last week. The one thing Bruno needed to make his happiness complete was to hear Guy's voice, to have a word from him saying he was happy. The bond between Guy and him now was closer than brotherhood. How many brothers liked their brothers as much as he liked Guy?

Bruno threw a leg out the window and stood up on the wrought iron balcony. The morning sunshine did feel rather good. The lawn was broad and smooth as a golf course all the way to the ocean. Then he saw Sammie Franklin, dressed in white tennis clothes with his rackets under his arm, grinning his way towards his mother. Sammie was big and flabby, like a softened-up boxer. He reminded Bruno of another Hollywood stooge who had hung around his mother when they were here three years ago. Alexander Phipps. Why did he even remember their phony names? He heard Sammie's chuckle as he extended his hand to his mother, and an old antagonism fluttered up in Bruno and lay still again. *Merde*. Disdainfully he took his eyes from Sammie's broad flannel backsides, and examined the view from left to right. A couple of pelicans flew loggily over a hedge and plopped down on the grass. Far out on the pale water he saw a sailboat. Three years ago he had begged his grandmother to get a sailboat, and now that she had one, he never felt like using it.

The tennis balls *wokked* around the tan stucco corner of the house. Chimes sounded from downstairs, and Bruno went back into his room, so he would not know what time it was. He liked to see a clock by accident as late as possible in the day, and find it was later than he had thought. If there was no letter from Guy in the noon mail, he thought, he might catch a train to San Francisco. On the other hand, his last memory of San Francisco was not pleasant. Wilson had brought a couple of Italian fellows up to the hotel, and Bruno had bought all the dinners and several bottles of rye. They had called Chicago on his telephone. The hotel had chalked up two calls to Metcalf, and he couldn't remember the second at all. And the last day, he had been twenty dollars short on the bill. He didn't have a cheque account, so the hotel, the best hotel in town, had held his suitcase until his mother wired the money. No, he wouldn't go back to San Francisco.

'Charley?' called the high, sweet voice of his grandmother.

He saw the curved handle of the door start to move, made an involuntary lunge for the clippings on his bed, then circled back to the bathroom instead. He shook tooth powder into his mouth. His grandmother could smell liquor like a dry sourdough in the Klondike.

'Aren't you ready to have some breakfast with me?' his grandmother asked.

He came out combing his hair. 'Gee, you're all dressed up!' She turned her small unsteady figure around for him like a fashion model, and Bruno smiled. He liked the black lace dress with the pink satin showing through it. 'Looks like one of those balconies out there.'

'Thank you, Charley. I'm going into town the latter part of the morning. I thought you might like to come with me.'

'Could be. Yeah, I'd like that, Grannie,' he said good-naturedly.

'So it's *you've* been clipping my *Times*! I thought it was one of the servants. You must be getting up awfully early these mornings.'

'Yep,' Bruno said agreeably.

'When I was young, we used to get poems out of newspapers for our scrapbooks. We made scrapbooks out of everything under the sun. What're you going to do with these?'

'Oh, just keep 'em.'

'Don't you make scrapbooks?'

'Nope.' She was looking at him, and Bruno wanted her to look at the clippings.

'Oh, you're just a *ba-aby*!' She pinched his cheek. 'Hardly a bit of fuzz on your chin yet! I don't know why your mother's worried about you –'

'She's not worried.'

'– when you just need time to grow up. Come on down to breakfast with me. Yes, pyjamas and all.'

Bruno gave her his arm on the stairs.

'I've got the least bit of shopping to do,' said his grandmother as she poured his coffee, 'and then I thought we'd do something nice. Maybe a good movie – with a murder in it – or maybe the amusement park. I haven't been to an amusement park in *a-ages*!'

Bruno's eyes opened as wide as they could.

'Which would you like? Well, we can look over the movies when we get there.'

'I'd like the amusement park, Grannie.'

Bruno enjoyed the day, helping her in and out of the car, piloting her around the amusement park, though there was not much after all his grandmother could do or eat. But they rode the ferris wheel together. Bruno told his grandmother about the big ferris wheel in Metcalf, but she did not ask him when he had been there.

Sammie Franklin was still at the house when they came home, staying for dinner. Bruno's eyebrows drew together at the first sight of him. He knew his grandmother cared as little for Sammie as he did, and Bruno felt suddenly a great tenderness for her, because she accepted Sammie so uncomplainingly, accepted any mongrel his mother brought on the place. What had he and his mother been doing all day? They had been to a movie, they said, one of Sammie's movies. And there was a letter for him upstairs in his room.

Bruno ran upstairs. The letter was from Florida. He tore it open with his hands shaking like ten hangovers. He had never wanted a letter so badly, not even at camp, when he had waited for letters from his mother.

Dear Charles,

I do not understand your message to me, or for that matter your great interest in me. I know you very slightly, but enough to assure me that we have nothing in common on which to base a friendship. May I ask you please not to telephone my mother again or communicate with me?

Thank you for trying to return the book to me. Its loss is of no importance.

Guy Haines

Bruno brought it up closer and read it again, his eyes lingering incredulously on a word here and there. His pointed tongue stretched over his upper lip, then disappeared suddenly. He felt shorn. It was a feeling like grief, or like a death. Worse! He glanced about his room, hating the furniture, hating his possessions. Then the pain centred in his chest, and reflexively he began to cry.

After dinner, Sammie Franklin and he got into an argument about vermouths. Sammie said the drier the vermouth, the more one had to put into a martini, though he admitted he was not a martini drinker. Bruno said he was not a martini drinker either, but he knew better than that. The argument went on even after his grandmother said good night and left them. They were on the upstairs terrace in the dark, his mother in the glider and he and Sammie standing by the parapet. Bruno ran down to the bar for the ingredients to prove his point. They both made martinis and tasted them, and though it was clear Bruno was right, Sammie kept holding out, and chuckling as if he didn't quite mean what he said either, which Bruno found insufferable.

'Go to New York and learn something!' Bruno shouted. His mother had just left the terrace.

'How do you know what you're saying anyway?' Sammie retorted. The moonlight made his fat grinning face blue-green and yellow, like gorgonzola cheese. 'You're pickled all day. You –'

Bruno caught Sammie by the shirtfront and bent him backwards over the parapet. Sammie's feet rattled on the tiles. His shirt split. When he wriggled sideways to safety, the blue had left his face and it was a shadowless yellow-white.

'Th-the hell's the matter with you?' he bellowed. 'You'd a shoved me over, wouldn't you?'

'No, I wouldn't!' Bruno shrieked, louder than Sammie. Suddenly he couldn't breathe, like in the mornings. He took his stiff, sweaty hands down from his face. He had done a murder, hadn't he? Why should he do another? But he had seen Sammie squirming on the points of the iron fence right below, and he had wanted him there. He heard Sammie stirring a highball fast. Bruno stumbled over the threshold of the french window into the house.

'And *stay* out!' Sammie shouted after him.

The shaking passion in Sammie's voice sent a throb of fear through him. Bruno said nothing as he passed his mother in the hall. Going downstairs, he clung to the banister with both hands, cursing the ringing, aching, unmanageable mess in his head, cursing the martinis he had drunk with Sammie. He staggered into the living-room.

'Charley, what did you do to Sammie?' His mother had followed him in.

'Ah, whad I do to Sammie!' Bruno shoved his hand towards her blurred figure and sat down on the sofa with a bounce.

'Charley – come back and apologize.' The white blur of her evening dress came closer, one brown arm extended towards him.

'Are you sleeping with that guy? *Are you sleeping with that guy?*' He knew he had only to lie back on the sofa and he would pass out like a light, so he lay back, and never felt her arm at all.

18

In the month after Guy returned to New York, his restlessness, his dissatisfaction with himself, with his work, with Anne, had focused gradually on Bruno. It was Bruno who made him hate to look at pictures of the Palmyra now, Bruno who was the real cause of his anxiety that he had blamed on the dearth of commissions since he had come back from Palm Beach. Bruno who had made him argue so senselessly with Anne the other evening about not getting a better office, not buying new furniture and a rug for this one. Bruno who had made him tell Anne he did not consider himself a success, that the Palmyra meant nothing. Bruno who had made Anne turn quietly away from him that evening and walk out the door, who had made him wait until he heard the elevator door close, before he ran down the eight flights of stairs and begged her to forgive him.

And who knew? Perhaps it was Bruno who kept him from getting jobs now. The creation of a building was a spiritual act. So long as he harboured his knowledge of Bruno's guilt, he corrupted himself in a sense. Such a thing could be perceived in him, he felt. Consciously, he had made up his mind to let the police trap Bruno. But as the weeks went by and they didn't, he was plagued by a feeling that he should act himself. What stopped him was both an aversion to accusing a man of murder and a senseless but lingering doubt that Bruno might not be guilty. That Bruno had committed the crime struck him at times as so fantastic, all his previous conviction was momentarily wiped out. At times, he felt he would have doubted even if Bruno had sent him a written confession. And yet, he had to admit to himself that he was *sure* Bruno had done it. The weeks that went by without the police picking up any strong trail seemed to confirm it. As Bruno had said, how could they with no motivation? His letter to Bruno in September had silenced him all the autumn, but just before he left Florida, a sober note from Bruno had said he would be back in New York in December and he hoped to be able to have a talk with him. Guy was determined to have nothing to do with him.

Still he fretted, about everything and about nothing, but chiefly about his work. Anne told him to be patient. Anne reminded him that he had already proven himself in Florida. In greater measure than ever before, she offered him the tenderness and reassurance he needed so, yet he found that in his lowest, most stubborn moments he could not always accept it.

One morning in mid-December, the telephone rang as Guy sat idly studying his drawings of the Connecticut house.

'Hello, Guy. This is Charley.'

Guy recognized the voice, felt his muscles tensing for a fight. But Myers was within earshot across the room.

'How are you?' Bruno asked with smiling warmth. 'Merry Christmas.'

Slowly Guy put the telephone back in its cradle.

He glanced over at Myers, the architect with whom he shared the big one-room office. Myers was still bent over his drawing-board. Under the edge of the green window-shade, the bobbing pigeons still pecked at the grain he and Myers had sprinkled on the sill a few moments ago.

The telephone rang again.

'I'd like to see you, Guy,' Bruno said.

Guy stood up. 'Sorry. I don't care to see you.'

'What's the matter?' Bruno forced a little laugh. 'Are you nervous, Guy?'

'I just don't care to see you.'

'Oh. Okay,' said Bruno, hoarse with hurt.

Guy waited, determined not to retreat first, and finally Bruno hung up.

Guy's throat was dry, and he went to the drinking fountain in the corner of the room. Behind the fountain, sunlight lay in a precise diagonal across the big aerial photograph of the four nearly finished Palmyra buildings. He turned his back to it. He'd been asked to make a speech at his old school in Chicago, Anne would remind him. He was to write an article for a leading architectural magazine. But so far as commissions went, the Palmyra Club might have been a public declaration that he was to be boycotted. And why not? Didn't he owe the Palmyra to Bruno? Or at any rate to a murderer?

On a snowy evening a few days later, as he and Anne came down the brownstone steps of his West Fifty-third Street apartment house, Guy saw a tall bareheaded figure standing on the sidewalk gazing up at them. A tingle of alarm travelled to his shoulders, and involuntarily his hand tightened on Anne's arm.

'Hello,' Bruno said, his voice soft with melancholy. His face was barely visible in the dusk.

'Hello,' Guy replied, as if to a stranger, and walked on.

'Guy!'

Guy and Anne turned at the same time. Bruno came towards them, hands in the pockets of his overcoat.

'What is it?' Guy asked.

'Just wanted to say hello. Ask how you are.' Bruno stared at Anne with a kind of perplexed, smiling resentment.

'I'm fine,' Guy said quietly. He turned away, drawing Anne with him.

'Who is he?' Anne whispered.

Guy itched to look back. He knew Bruno would be standing where they had left him, knew he would be looking after them, weeping perhaps. 'He's a fellow who came around looking for work last week.'

'You can't do anything for him?'

'No. He's an alcoholic.'

Deliberately Guy began to talk about their house, because he knew there was nothing else he could talk about now and possibly sound normal. He had bought the land, and the foundations were being laid. After New Year's, he was going up to Alton and stay several days. During the movie, he speculated as to how he could shake Bruno off, terrify him so that he would be afraid to contact him.

What did Bruno want with him? Guy sat with his fists clenched at the movie. The *next* time, he would threaten Bruno with police investigation. And he would carry it through, too. What vast harm was there in suggesting he be investigated?

But what did Bruno want with him?

19

Bruno had not wanted to go to Haiti, but it offered escape. New York or Florida or anywhere in the American continent was torture so long as Guy was there, too, and would not see him. To blot out his pain and depression, he had drunk a great deal at home in Great Neck, and to occupy himself had measured the house and the grounds in paces, measured his father's room with tailor's tape, moving doggedly, stooping, measuring and remeasuring, like a tireless automaton that wavered only slightly off its track now and then, betraying the fact it was drunk and not deranged. Thus he spent ten days after seeing Guy, waiting for his mother and her friend Alice Leffingwell to get ready to go to Haiti.

There were moments when he felt his whole being in some as yet inscrutable stage of metamorphosis. There was the deed he had done, which in his hours alone in the house, in his room, he felt sat upon his head like a crown, but a crown that no one else could see. Very easily and quickly, he could break down in tears. There was the time he had wanted a caviar sandwich for lunch, because he deserved the finest, big black caviar, and when there had been only red in the house, had told Herbert to go out and get some black. He had eaten a quarter of the toasted sandwich, sipping a Scotch and water with it, then had almost fallen asleep staring at the triangle of toasted bread that finally had begun to lift at one corner. He had stared at it until it was no longer a sandwich, the glass with his drink no longer a glass, and only the golden liquid in it part of himself, and he had gulped it all. The empty glass and the curling toast had been live things that mocked him and challenged his right to use them. A butcher's truck had departed down the driveway just then and Bruno had frowned after it, because everything had suddenly come alive and was fleeing to escape him – the truck, the sandwich, and the glass, the trees that couldn't run away but were disdainful, like the house that imprisoned him. He had hit both his fists against the wall simultaneously, then seized the sandwich and broken its insolent triangular mouth and burnt it, piece by piece, in the empty fireplace, the caviar popping like little people, dying, each one a life.

Alice Leffingwell, his mother and he, and a crew of four including two Puerto Ricans left for Haiti in mid-January on the steam yacht, *Fairy Prince*, which Alice had spent all autumn and winter wresting from her former husband. The trip was a celebration of her third divorce, and she had invited Bruno and his mother months before. Bruno's delight in the voyage inspired him to a pretence of indifference and boredom during the first days. No one noticed. Alice and his mother spent whole afternoons and evenings chattering together in the cabin, and in the mornings they slept. To justify his happiness to himself at such a dull prospect as being cooped up on a ship for a month with an old bag like Alice, Bruno convinced himself he had been under quite a strain watching out the police didn't get on his trail, and that he needed leisure to dope out the details of how his father could be got rid of. He also reasoned that the more time elapsed, the more likely Guy would be to change his attitude.

On shipboard, he detailed two or three key plans for the murder of his father, of which any other plans laid on the estate would be mere variations. He was very proud of his plans – one with gun in his father's bedroom, one with knife and two choices of escape, and one with either gun or knife or strangulation in the garage where his father put his car every evening at 6.30. The disadvantage of the last plan was lack of darkness, but it had compensations in comparative simplicity. He could all but hear in his ears the efficient *click-click* of his plans' operations. Yet whenever he finished a careful drawing, he felt obliged to tear it up for safety. He was eternally making drawings and tearing them up. The sea from Bar Harbour to the southernmost of the Virgin Islands was strewn with the subdivided seeds of his ideas when the *Fairy Prince* rounded Cape Maisi bound for Port-au-Prince.

'A princely harbour for my *Prince*!' cried Alice, relaxing her mind in a lull of conversation with his mother.

Around the corner from them, in the shade, Bruno fumbled up the paper he had been drawing on and lifted his head. In the left quarter of the horizon, land was visible in a grey fuzzy line. Haiti. Seeing it made it seem more distant and foreign than when he had not seen it. He was going farther and farther away from Guy. He pulled himself from the deck-chair and went over to the port rail. They would spend days in Haiti before they moved on, and then they would move farther south. Bruno stood perfectly still, feeling frustration corrode him internally

a
le
by
the

the
Gera
how
moti
the tr
negoti
seen M

Som
never f
the seco

The s
worse, n
Citadelle
he stoppe
One of the
since the
drunk, roa
and the rest

Their figures were fuzzy but their laughs were s
coiled from Alice's fingers on his shoulder. He c
he knew what he wanted to say. What wer
room if they didn't have a message from G
'What? What guy?' asked his mothe
'G'way!' he shouted, and he mea
'Oh, he's out,' said his mot
hospital case nearly dead. 'P
Bruno jerked his hea
washcloth. He hated
killed for him, d
asked him to
didn't eve
Guy wa
Thr

...y Prince,
...ned Bruno a 'wite bum-m'
and a lot of ......ings Bruno could not understand but which
made everybody laugh. Bruno left the bar with dignity, too tired
and disgusted to fight, with a quiet determination to report it to
Alice and get the Puerto Rican fired and blacklisted. A block
away from the ship, the Puerto Rican caught up with him and
kept on talking. Then, crossing the gangplank, Bruno lurched
against the handrope and fell off into the filthy water. He
couldn't say the Puerto Rican had pushed him, because he
hadn't. The Puerto Rican and another sailor, also laughing,
fished him out and dragged him in to his bed. Bruno crawled
off the bed and got his bottle of rum. He drank some straight,
then flopped on the bed and fell asleep in his wet underwear.

Later, his mother and Alice came in and shook him awake.

'What happened?' they kept asking, giggling so they could
hardly talk. 'What happened, Charley?'

arp. He re-
uldn't talk, but
they doing in his
y?

t both of them.
er deploringly, as if he were a
or boy. Poor, poor boy.'

this way and that to avoid the cool
them both and he hated Guy! He had
odged police for him, kept quiet when he
fallen in the stinking water for him, and Guy
want to see him! Guy spent his time with a girl!
sn't scared or unhappy, just didn't have time for him!
times he had seen her around Guy's house in New York!
he had her here, he would kill her just like he had killed
Miriam!

'Charley, Charley, hush!'

Guy would get married again and never have time for him.
See what sympathy he'd get now when this girl played him for
a sucker! He'd been seeing her in Mexico, not just visiting
friends. No wonder he'd wanted Miriam out of the way! And
he hadn't even mentioned Anne Faulkner on the train! Guy had
used him. Maybe Guy would kill his father whether he liked it
or not. Anybody can do a murder. Guy hadn't believed it, Bruno
remembered.

20

'Have a drink with me,' Bruno said. He had appeared out of
nowhere, in the middle of the sidewalk.

'I don't care to see you. I'm not asking questions. I don't care
to see you.'

'I don't care if you ask questions,' Bruno said with a weak
smile. His eyes were wary. 'Come across the street. Ten minutes.'

Guy glanced around him. Here he is, Guy thought. Call the

police. Jump him, throw him down to the sidewalk. But Guy only stood rigidly. He saw that Bruno's hands were rammed in his pockets, as if he might have a gun.

'Ten minutes,' Bruno said, luring him with the tentative smile.

Guy hadn't heard a word from Bruno in weeks. He tried to summon back the anger of that last evening in the snow, of his decision to turn Bruno over to the police. This was the critical moment. Guy came with him. They walked into a bar on Sixth Avenue and took a back booth.

Bruno's smile grew wider. 'What're you scared about, Guy?'

'Not a thing.'

'Are you happy?'

Guy sat stiffly on the edge of his seat. He was sitting opposite a murderer, he thought. Those hands had crushed Miriam's throat.

'Listen, Guy, why didn't you tell me about Anne?'

'What about Anne?'

'I'd have liked to know about her, that's all. On the train, I mean.'

'This is our last meeting, Bruno.'

'Why? I just want to be friends, Guy.'

'I'm going to turn you over to the police.'

'Why didn't you do that in Metcalf?' Bruno asked with the lowest pink gleam in his eyes, as only he could have asked it, impersonally, sadly, yet with triumph. Oddly, Guy felt his inner voice had asked him the question in the same way.

'Because I wasn't sure enough.'

'What do I have to do, make a written statement?'

'I can still turn you over for investigation.'

'No, you can't. They've got more on you than on me.' Bruno shrugged.

'What're you talking about?'

'What do you think they'd get on me? Nothing.'

'I could tell them!' He was suddenly furious.

'If I wanted to say you paid me for it,' Bruno frowned self-righteously, 'the pieces would fit like hell!'

'I don't care about pieces.'

'Maybe you don't, but the law does.'

'What pieces?'

'That letter you wrote Miriam,' Bruno said slowly, 'the cover-up of that job cancelling. The whole convenient trip to Mexico.'

'You're insane!'

'Face it, Guy! You're not making any sense!' Bruno's voice rose hysterically over the jukebox that had started up near them. He pushed his hand flat across the table towards Guy, then closed it in a fist. 'I like you, Guy, I swear. We shouldn't be talking like this!'

Guy did not move. The edge of the bench cut against the back of his legs. 'I don't want to be liked by you.'

'Guy, if you say anything to the police, you'll only land us both in prison. Don't you see?'

Guy had thought of it, even before now. If Bruno clung to his lies, there could be a long trial, a case that might never be decided unless Bruno broke down, and Bruno wouldn't break down. Guy could see it in the monomaniacal intensity with which Bruno stared at him now. Ignore him, Guy thought. Keep away. Let the police catch him. He's insane enough to kill you if you make a move.

'You didn't turn me in in Metcalf because you like me, Guy. You like me in a way.'

'I don't like you in the least.'

'But you're not going to turn me in, are you?'

'No,' Guy said between his teeth. Bruno's calm amazed him. Bruno was not afraid of him at all. 'Don't order me another drink. I'm leaving.'

'Wait a minute.' Bruno got money from his wallet and gave it to the waiter.

Guy sat on, held by a sense of inconclusiveness.

'Good-looking suit.' Bruno smiled, nodding towards Guy's chest.

His new grey flannel chalk-stripe suit. Bought with the Palmyra money, Guy thought, like his new shoes and the new alligator briefcase beside him on the seat.

'Where do you have to go?'

'Downtown.' He was to meet a prospective client's representative at the Fifth Avenue Hotel at 7. Guy stared at Bruno's hard, wistful eyes, feeling sure Bruno thought he was on his way to meet Anne now. 'What's your game, Bruno?'

'You know,' Bruno said quietly. 'What we talked about on the train. The exchange of victims. You're going to kill my father.'

Guy made a sound of contempt. He had known it before Bruno said it, had suspected it since Miriam's death. He stared into Bruno's fixed, still wistful eyes, fascinated by their cool insanity. Once as a child he had stared at a mongoloid idiot on a streetcar, he remembered, like this, with a shameless curiosity that nothing could shake. Curiosity and fear.

'I told you I could arrange every detail.' Bruno smiled at the corner of his mouth, amusedly, apologetically. 'It'd be very simple.'

He hates me, Guy thought suddenly. He'd love to kill me, too.

'You know what I'll do if you don't.' Bruno made a gesture of snapping his fingers, but his hand on the table was carelessly limp. 'I'll just put the police on to you.'

Ignore him, Guy thought, ignore him! 'You don't frighten me in the least. It'd be the easiest thing in the world to prove you insane.'

'I'm no more insane than you are!'

It was Bruno who ended the interview a moment later. He had a 7 o'clock appointment with his mother, he said.

The next encounter, so much shorter, Guy felt he lost, too, though at the time he thought he had won. Bruno tried to intercept him one Friday afternoon as he was leaving his office on the way to Long Island to see Anne. Guy simply brushed past him and climbed into a taxi. Yet a feeling of having physically run away shamed him, began to undermine a certain dignity that had up to then been intact. He wished he had said something to Bruno. He wished he had faced him for an instant.

21

In the next days, there was hardly an evening when Bruno was not standing on the sidewalk across the street from his office building. Or if not there, standing across the street from where he lived, as if Bruno knew the evenings he would come straight home. There was never a word now, never a sign, only the tall figure with the hands in the pockets of the long, rather military overcoat that fit him closely, like a stovepipe. There was only the eyes following him, Guy knew, though he did not look back until he was out of sight. For two weeks. Then the first letter came.

It was two sheets of paper: the first a map of Bruno's house and the grounds and roads around it and the course Guy would take, neatly drawn with dotted and ruled ink lines, and the second a typed, closely written letter lucidly setting forth the plan for the murder of Bruno's father. Guy tore it up, then immediately regretted it. He should have kept it as evidence against Bruno. He kept the pieces.

But there was no need to have kept them. He received such a letter every two or three days. They were all mailed from Great Neck, as if Bruno stayed out there now – he had not seen Bruno since the letters began – writing perhaps on his father's typewriter the letters that must have taken him two or three hours to prepare. The letters were sometimes drunken. It showed in the typing mistakes and in the emotional bursts of the last paragraphs. If he were sober, the last paragraph was affectionate and reassuring as to the ease of the murder. If he were drunk, the paragraph was either a gush of brotherly love or a threat to haunt Guy all his life, ruin his career and his 'love affair', and a reminder that Bruno had the upper hand. All the necessary information might have been got from any one of the letters, as if Bruno anticipated he might tear most of them up unopened. But despite his determination to tear up the next, Guy would open it when it came, curious as to the variations in the last paragraph. Of Bruno's three plans, the one with a gun, using the back entrance of the house, came most often, though each letter invited him to take his choice.

The letters affected him in a perverse way. After the shock of the first, the next few bothered him hardly at all. Then as the tenth, twelfth, fifteenth appeared in his mailbox, he felt they hammered at his consciousness or his nerves in a manner that he could not analyse. Alone in his room he would spend quarter hours trying to isolate his injury and repair it. His anxiety was unreasonable, he told himself, unless he thought Bruno would turn on him and try to murder him. And he didn't really. Bruno had never threatened that. But reasoning could not alleviate the anxiety, or make it less exhausting.

The twenty-first letter mentioned Anne. 'You wouldn't like Anne to know your part in Miriam's murder, would you? What girl would marry a murderer? Certainly not Anne. The time is getting short. The first two weeks in March is my deadline. Until then it would be easy.'

Then the gun came. It was handed him by his landlady, a big package in brown paper. Guy gave a short laugh when the black gun toppled out. It was a big Luger, shiny and new-looking except for a chip off the cross-hatched handle.

Some impulse made Guy take his own little revolver from the back of his top drawer, made him heft his own beautiful pearl-handled gun over his bed where the Luger lay. He smiled at his action, then brought the Texas gun up closer to his eyes and studied it. He had seen it in a glutted pawnshop window on lower Main Street in Metcalf when he was about fifteen, and had bought it with money from his paper route, not because it was a gun but because it was beautiful. Its compactness, the economy of its short barrel had delighted him. The more he had learned of mechanical design, the more pleased he had been with his gun. He had kept it in various top drawers for fifteen years. He opened the chamber and removed the bullets, three of them, and turned the cylinder around with six pulls of the trigger, admiring the deep pitched clicks of its perfect machinery. Then he slipped the bullets back, put the gun into its lavender-coloured flannel bag, and replaced it in his drawer.

How should he get rid of the Luger? Drop it over an embankment into the river? Into some ashcan? Throw it out with his trash? Everything he thought of seemed either suspect or melodramatic. He decided to slip it under his socks and underwear in a bottom drawer until something better occurred to him. He thought suddenly of Samuel Bruno, for the first time as a person. The presence of the Luger brought the man and his potential death into juxtaposition in his mind. Here in his room was the complete picture of the man and his life, according to Bruno, the plan for his murder – a letter had been waiting in his box that morning, too, and lay on his bed now unopened – and the gun with which he was supposed to kill him. Guy got one of Bruno's recent letters from among a few in the bottom drawer.

Samuel Bruno [Bruno seldom referred to him as 'my father'] is the finest example of the worst that America produces. He comes of low-class peasants in Hungary, little better than animals. He picked a wife of good family, with his usual greed, once he could afford her. All this time my mother quietly bore his unfaithfulness, having some concept of the sacredness of marriage contract. Now in his old age he tries to act pius before it is too late, but it is too late. I wish I could kill him myself but I have explained to you due to Gerard, his private detective, it is impossible. If you ever had anything to do with him, he would be your personal enemy, too. He is the kind of man who thinks all your ideas about architecture as beauty and about adiquate houses for everyone are idiotic & doesn't care what kind of factory he has as long as the roof doesn't leak and ruin his machinery. It may interest you to know his employees are on strike now. See *N.Y Times* last Thurs. p. 31 bottom left. They are striking for a living wage. Samuel Bruno does not hesitate to rob his own son . . .

Who would believe such a story if he told it? Who would accept such fantasy? The letter, the map, the gun – They seemed like props of a play, objects arranged to give a verisimilitude to a story that wasn't real and never could be real. Guy burnt the letter. He burnt all the letters he had, then hurried to get ready for Long Island.

He and Anne were going to spend the day driving, walking in the woods, and tomorrow drive up to Alton. The house would be finished by the end of March, which would give them a leisurely two months before the wedding to furnish it. Guy smiled as he gazed out the train window. Anne had never said she wanted a June wedding; it was simply drifting that way. She had never said she wanted a formal wedding, only, 'Let's not have anything too slapdash.' Then when he had told her he wouldn't mind a formal wedding if she wouldn't, she had let out a long 'Oh-h!' and grabbed him and kissed him. No, he didn't want another three-minute wedding with a stranger for a witness. He began sketching on the back of an envelope the twenty-storey office building he had learned last week he had a good chance of being commissioned for, that he had been saving as a surprise for Anne. He felt the future had suddenly become the present. He had everything he wanted. Running down the platform steps, he saw Anne's leopard coat in the little crowd by the station door. Always he would remember the times she waited for him here, he thought, the shy dance of impatience she did when she caught sight of him, the way she smiled and half turned round, as if she wouldn't have waited half a minute longer.

'Anne!' He put his arm around her and kissed her cheek.

'You didn't wear a hat.'

He smiled because it was exactly what he had expected her to say. 'Well, neither did you.'

'I'm in the car. And it's snowing.' She took his hand and they ran across the crisp lane towards the cars. 'I've got a surprise!'

'So have I. What's yours?'

'Sold five designs yesterday on my own.'

Guy shook his head. 'I can't beat that. I've just got one office building. Maybe.'

She smiled and her eyebrows went up. 'Maybe? Yes!'

'Yes, yes, yes!' he said, and kissed her again.

That evening, standing on the little wooden bridge over the stream back of Anne's house, Guy started to say, 'Do you know what Bruno sent me today? A gun.' Then, not that he had come close to saying it, but the remoteness of Bruno and his connection with him from his and Anne's life shocked him with a terrible realization. He wanted no secrets from Anne, and here was one bigger than all he had told her. Bruno, the name that haunted him, would mean nothing to Anne.

'What is it, Guy?'

She knew there was something, he thought. She always knew. 'Nothing.'

He followed her as she turned and walked towards the house. The night had blackened the earth, made the snowy ground hardly distinguishable from woods and sky. And Guy felt it again – the sense of hostility in the clump of woods east of the house. Before him, the kitchen door spilled a warm yellow light some way on to the lawn. Guy turned again, letting his eyes rest on the blackness where the woods began. The feeling he had when he gazed there was discomforting and relieving at once, like biting on an ailing tooth.

'I'll walk around again,' he said.

Anne went in, and he turned back. He wanted to see if the sensation were stronger or weaker when Anne was not with him. He tried to feel rather than see. It was still there, faint and evasive, where the darkness deepened at the baseline of the woods. Nothing of course. What chance combination of shadow and sound and his own thoughts had created it?

He slipped his hands into his overcoat pockets and moved stubbornly closer.

The dull snap of a twig plummeted his consciousness to earth, focused it at a certain point. He sprinted towards it. A crackling of bushes now, and a moving black figure in the blackness. Guy released all his muscles in a long drive, caught it, and recognized the hoarse intake of breath as Bruno's. Bruno plunged in his arms like a great powerful fish underwater, twisted and hit him an agonizing blow on the cheekbone. Clasping each other, they both fell, fighting to free arms, fighting as if they both fought death. Bruno's fingers scratched frenziedly at his throat, though Guy kept his arm straight. Bruno's breath hissed in and out between his drawn-back lips. Guy hit the mouth again with his right fist that felt broken, that would no longer close.

'Guy!' Bruno burst out indignantly.

Guy caught him by the front of his collar. Suddenly they both stopped fighting.

'You knew it was me!' Bruno said in a fury. 'Dirty bastard!'

'What're you doing here?' Guy pulled him to his feet.

The bleeding mouth spread wider, as if he were going to cry. 'Lemme go!'

Guy shoved him. He fell like a sack to the ground and tottered up again.

'Okay, kill me if you want to! You can say it's self-defence!' Bruno whined.

Guy glanced towards the house. They had struggled a long way into the woods. 'I don't want to kill you. I'll kill you next time I find you here.'

Bruno laughed, the single victorious clap.

Guy advanced menacingly. He did not want to touch Bruno again. Yet a moment before, he had fought with 'Kill, kill!' in his mind. Guy knew there was nothing he could do to stop Bruno's smile, not even kill him. 'Clear out.'

'You ready to do that job in two weeks?'

'Ready to turn you over to the police.'

'Ready to turn yourself over?' Bruno jeered shrilly. 'Ready to tell Anne all about it, huh? Ready to spend the next twenty years in jail? Sure, I'm ready!' He brought his palms together gently. His eyes seemed to glow with a red light. His swaying figure was like that of an evil spirit's that might have stepped from the twisted black tree behind him.

'Get someone else for your dirty work,' Guy muttered.

'Look who's talking! I want you and I've got you! Okay!' A laugh. 'I'll start. I'll tell your girl friend all about it. I'll write her tonight.' He lurched away, tripped heavily, and staggered on, a loose and shapeless thing. He turned and shouted, 'unless I hear from *you* in a day or so.'

Guy told Anne he had fought with a prowler in the woods. He suffered only a reddened eye from the battle, but he saw no way to stay on at the house, not go to Alton tomorrow, except by feigning injury. He had been hit in the stomach, he said. He didn't feel well. Mr and Mrs Faulkner were alarmed, and insisted to the policeman who came to look over the grounds that they have a police guard for the next few nights. But a guard was not enough. If Bruno came back, Guy wanted to be there himself. Anne suggested that he stay on Monday, so he would have someone to look after him in case he were sick. Guy did stay on.

Nothing had ever shamed him so much, he thought, as the two days in the Faulkner house. He was ashamed that he felt the need to stay, ashamed that on Monday morning he went into Anne's room and looked on the writing-table where the maid put her mail to see if Bruno had written. He hadn't. Anne left each morning for her shop in New York before the mail was delivered. On Monday morning, Guy looked through the four or five letters on her writing-table, then hurried out like a thief, afraid the maid might see him. But he often came into her room when she was not there, he reminded himself. Sometimes when the house was filled with people, he would escape to Anne's room for a few moments. And she loved to find him there. At the threshold, he leaned his head back against the door jamb, picking out the disorder in the room – the unmade bed, the big art books that didn't fit in the bookshelves, her last designs thumbtacked to a strip of green cork down one wall, on the corner of the table a glass of bluish water that she had neglected to empty, the brown and yellow silk scarf over the chair back, that she had evidently changed her mind about. The gardenia scent of the cologne she had touched to her neck at the last moment still lingered in the air. He longed to merge his life with hers.

Guy stayed until Tuesday morning when there was no letter from Bruno either, and then went in to Manhattan. Work had piled up. A thousand things nettled him. The contract with the Shaw Realty Company for the new office building still had not been settled. He felt his life disorganized, without direction, more chaotic than when he had heard of Miriam's murder. There was no letter from Bruno that week except one that awaited him, that had arrived Monday. It was a short note saying thank God his mother was better today and he could leave the house. His mother had been dangerously ill for three weeks with pneumonia, he said, and he had stayed with her.

Thursday evening when Guy got back from a meeting of an architectural club, his landlady Mrs McCausland said he had had three calls. The telephone rang as they stood in the hall. It was Bruno, sullen and drunk. He asked if Guy was ready to talk sense.

'I didn't think so,' Bruno said. 'I've written Anne.' And he hung up.

Guy went upstairs and took a drink himself. He didn't believe Bruno had written or intended to write. He tried for an hour to read, called Anne to ask how she was, then restlessly went out and found a late movie.

On Saturday afternoon, he was supposed to meet Anne in Hempstead, Long Island, to see a dog show there. If Bruno had written the letter, Anne would have got it by Saturday morning, Guy thought. But obviously she hadn't. He could tell from her wave to him from the car where she sat waiting for him. He asked her if she had enjoyed the party last night at Teddy's. Her cousin Teddy had had a birthday.

'Wonderful party. Only no one wanted to go home. It got so late I stayed over. I haven't even changed my clothes yet.' And she shot the car through the narrow gate and into the road.

Guy closed his teeth. The letter might be waiting for her at home then. All at once, he felt sure the letter *would* be waiting for her, and the impossibility of stopping it now made him weak and speechless.

He tried desperately to think of something to say as they walked along the rows of dogs.

'Have you heard anything from the Shaw people?' Anne asked him.

'No.' He stared at a nervous dachshund and tried to listen as Anne said something about a dachshund that someone in her family had.

She didn't know yet, Guy thought, but if she didn't know by today, it would be only a matter of time, a matter of a few days more, perhaps, until she did know. Know what, he kept asking himself, and going over the same answer, whether for reassurance or self-torture, he did not know: that on the train last summer he had met the man who murdered his wife, that he had consented to the murder of his wife. That was what Bruno would tell her, with certain details to make it convincing. And in a courtroom, for that matter, if Bruno distorted only slightly their conversation on the train, couldn't it amount to an agreement between murderers? The hours in Bruno's compartment, that tiny hell, came back suddenly very clearly. It was hatred that had inspired him to say as much as he had, the same petty hatred that had made him rage against Miriam in Chapultepec Park last June. Anne had been angry then, not so much at what he had said as at his hatred. Hatred, too, was a sin. Christ had preached against hatred as against adultery and murder. Hatred was the very seed of evil. In a Christian court of justice, wouldn't he be at least partially guilty of Miriam's death? Wouldn't Anne say so?

'Anne,' he interrupted her. He had to prepare her, he thought. And he had to *know*. 'If someone were to accuse me of having had a part in Miriam's death, what would you –? Would you –?'

She stopped and looked at him. The whole world seemed to stop moving, and he and Anne stood at its still centre.

'Had a part? What do you mean, Guy?'

Someone jostled him. They were in the middle of the walk. 'Just that. Accused me, nothing more.'

She seemed to search for words.

'Just accused me,' Guy kept on. 'I just want to know. Accused me for no reason. It wouldn't matter, would it?' Would she still marry him, he wanted to ask, but it was such a pitiful, begging question, he could not ask it.

'Guy, why do you say that?'

'I just want to know, that's all!'

She pressed him back so they would be out of the traffic of the path. 'Guy, *has* someone accused you?'

'No!' he protested. He felt awkward and vexed. 'But if someone did, if someone tried to make out a strong case against me –'

She looked at him with that flash of disappointment, of surprise and mistrust that he had seen before when he said or did something out of anger, or out of a resentment, that Anne did not approve, did not understand. 'Do you expect someone to?' she asked.

'I just want to know!' He was in a hurry and it seemed so simple!

'At times like this,' she said quietly, 'you make me feel we're complete strangers.'

'I'm sorry,' he murmured. He felt she had cut an invisible bond between them.

'I don't think you're sorry, or you wouldn't keep on doing this!' She looked straight at him, keeping her voice low though her eyes had filled with tears. 'It's like that day in Mexico when you indulged yourself in that tirade against Miriam. I don't care – I don't like it, I'm not that kind of person! You make me feel I don't know you at all!'

Don't love you, Guy thought. It seemed she gave him up then, gave up trying to know him or to love him. Desperate, slipping, Guy stood there unable to make a move or say a word.

'Yes, since you ask me,' Anne said, 'I think it would make a difference if someone accused you. I'd want to ask why you expected it. Why do you?'

'I don't!'

She turned away from him, walked to the blind end of the lane, and stood with her head bent.

Guy came after her. 'Anne you do know me. You know me better than anyone in the world knows me. I don't want any secrets from you. It came to my mind and I asked you!' He felt he made a confession, and with the relief that followed it, he felt suddenly sure – as sure as he had been before that Bruno had written the letter – that Bruno hadn't and wouldn't.

She brushed a tear from the corner of her eye quickly, indifferently. 'Just one thing, Guy. Will you stop expecting the worst – about everything?'

'Yes,' he said. 'God, yes.'

'Let's go back to the car.'

He spent the day with Anne, and they had dinner that evening at her house. There was no letter from Bruno. Guy put the possibility from his mind, as if he had passed a crisis.

On Monday evening at about 8, Mrs McCausland called him to the telephone. It was Anne.

'Darling – I guess I'm a little upset.'

'What's the matter?' He knew what was the matter.

'I got a letter. In this morning's mail. About what you were talking about Saturday.'

'What is it, Anne?'

'About Miriam – typewritten. And it's not signed.'

'What does it say? Read it to me.'

Anne read shakily, but in her distinct speech, ' "Dear Miss Faulkner. It may interest you to know that Guy Haines had more to do with his wife's murder than the law thinks at present. But the truth will out. I think you should know in case you have any plans for marrying such a dual personality. Apart from that, this writer knows that Guy Haines will not remain a free man much longer." Signed, "A friend." '

Guy closed his eyes. 'God !'

'Guy, do you know who it could be? – Guy? Hello?'

'Yes,' he said.

'Who?'

He knew from her voice she was merely frightened, that she believed in him, was afraid only for him. 'I don't know, Anne.'

'Is that true, Guy?' she asked anxiously. 'You should know. Something should be done.'

'I don't know,' Guy repeated, frowning. His mind seemed tied in an inextricable knot.

'You must know. *Think*, Guy. Someone you might call an enemy?'

'What's the postmark?'

'Grand Central. It's perfectly plain paper. You can't tell a thing from that.'

'Save it for me.'

'Of course, Guy. And I won't tell anyone. The family, I mean.' A pause. 'There *must* be someone, Guy. You suspected someone Saturday – didn't you?'

'I didn't.' His throat closed up. 'Sometimes these things happen, you know, after a trial.' And he was aware of a desire to cover Bruno as carefully as if Bruno had been himself, and he guilty. 'When can I see you, Anne? Can I come out tonight?'

'Well, I'm – sort of expected to go with Mother and Dad to a benefit thing. I can mail you the letter. Special delivery, you'll get it tomorrow morning.'

So it came the next morning, along with another of Bruno's plans, and an affectionate but exhorting last paragraph in which he mentioned the letter to Anne and promised more.

22

Guy sat up on the edge of his bed, covered his face in his hands, then deliberately brought his hands down. It was the night that took up the body of his thoughts and distorted it, he felt, the night and the darkness and the sleeplessness. Yet the night had its truth also. In the night, one approached truth merely at a certain slant, but all truth was the same. If he told Anne the story, wouldn't she consider he had been partially guilty? Marry him? How could she? What sort of beast was he that he could sit in a room where a bottom drawer held plans for a murder and the gun to do it with?

In the frail pre-dawn light, he studied his face in the mirror. The mouth slanted downward to the left, unlike his. The full underlip was thinner with tension. He tried to hold his eyes to an absolute steadiness. They stared back above pallid semi-circles, like a part of him that had hardened with accusation, as if they gazed at their torturer.

Should he dress and go out for a walk or try to sleep? His step on the carpet was light, unconsciously avoiding the spot by the armchair where the floor squeaked. *You would skip these squeaking steps just for safety*, Bruno's letters said. *My father's door is just to the right as you know. I have gone over everything and there is no room for a hitch anywhere. See on map where the butler's (Herbert's) room is. This is the closest you'll come to anyone. The hall floor squeaks there where I marked X* . . . He flung himself on the bed. *You should not try to get rid of the Luger no matter what happens between the house and the RR station.* He knew it all by heart, knew the sound of the kitchen door and the colour of the hall carpet.

If Bruno should get someone else to kill his father, he would have ample evidence in these letters to convict Bruno. He could avenge himself for what Bruno had done to him. Yet Bruno would merely counter with his lies that would convict him of planning Miriam's murder. No, it would be only a matter of time until Bruno got someone. If he could weather Bruno's threats only a while longer, it would all be over and he could sleep. If he did it, he thought, he wouldn't use the big Luger, he would use the little revolver –

Guy pulled himself up from the bed, aching, angry, and frightened by the words that had just passed through his mind. 'The Shaw Building,' he said to himself, as if announcing a new scene, as if he could derail himself from the night's tracks and set himself on the day's. *The Shaw Building. The ground is all grass covered to the steps in back, except for gravel you won't have to touch ... Skip four, skip three, step wide at the top. You can remember it, it's got a syncopated rhythm.*

'*Mr Haines!*'

Guy started, and cut himself. He laid his razor down and went to the door.

'Hello, Guy. Are you ready yet?' asked the voice on the telephone, lewd in the early morning, ugly with the complexities of night. 'Want some more?'

'You don't bother me.'

Bruno laughed.

Guy hung up, trembling.

The shock lingered through the day, tremulous and traumatic. He wanted desperately to see Anne that evening, wanted desperately that instant of glimpsing her from some spot where he had promised to wait. But he wanted also to deprive himself of her. He took a long walk up Riverside Drive to tire himself, but slept badly nevertheless, and had a series of unpleasant dreams. It would be different, Guy thought, once the Shaw contract was signed, once he could go ahead on his work.

Douglas Frear of the Shaw Realty Company called the next morning as he had promised. 'Mr Haines,' said his slow, hoarse voice, 'we've received a most peculiar letter concerning you.'

'What? What kind of a letter?'

'Concerning your wife. I didn't know – Shall I read it to you?'

'Please.'

' "To Whom It May Concern: No doubt it will interest you to learn that Guy Daniel Haines, whose wife was murdered last June, had more of a role in the deed than the courts know. This is from one who knows, and who knows also that there will be a retrial soon which will show his real part in the crime." – I trust it's a crank letter, Mr Haines. I just thought you should know about it.'

'Of course.' In the corner, Myers worked over his drawing-board as calmly as on any other morning of the week.

'I think I heard about – uh – the tragedy last year. There's no question of a retrial, is there?'

'Certainly not. That is, I've heard nothing about it.' Guy cursed his confusion. Mr Frear wanted only to know if he would be free to work.

'Sorry we haven't quite made up our minds on that contract, Mr Haines.'

The Shaw Realty Company waited until the following morning to tell him they weren't entirely satisfied with his drawings. In fact, they were interested in the work of another architect.

How had Bruno found out about the building, Guy wondered. But there were any number of ways. It might have been mentioned in the papers – Bruno kept himself well informed on architectural news – or Bruno might have called when he knew he was out of the office, casually got the information from Myers. Guy looked at Myers again, and wondered if he had ever spoken on the telephone with Bruno. The possibility had a flavour of the unearthly.

Now that the building was gone, he began to see it in terms of what it would not mean. He would not have the extra money he had counted on by summer. Nor the prestige, the prestige with the Faulkner family. It did not once occur to him – as much at the root of his anguish as any of the other reasons – that he had suffered frustration in seeing a creation come to nothing.

It would be only a matter of time until Bruno informed the next client, and the next. This was his threat to ruin his career. And his life with Anne? Guy thought of her with a flash of pain. It seemed to him that he was forgetting for long intervals that he loved her. Something was happening between them, he could not say what. He felt Bruno was destroying his courage to love. Every slightest thing deepened his anxiety, from the fact he had lost his best pair of shoes by forgetting what repair shop he had taken them to, to the house at Alton, which already seemed more than they should have taken on, which he doubted they could fill.

In the office, Myers worked on his routine, drafting agency jobs, and Guy's telephone never rang. Once Guy thought, even Bruno doesn't call because he wants it to build up and build up, so his voice will be welcome when it comes. And disgusted with himself, Guy went down in the middle of the day and drank martinis in a Madison Avenue bar. He was to have had lunch with Anne, but she had called and broken the appointment, he could not remember why. She had not sounded precisely cool, but he thought she had not given any real reason for not lunching with him. She certainly hadn't said she was going shopping for something for the house, or he would have remembered it. Or would he have? Or was she retaliating for his breaking his promise to come out to dinner with her family last Sunday? He had been too tired and too depressed to see anyone last Sunday. A quiet, unacknowledged quarrel seemed to be going on between himself and Anne. Lately, he felt too miserable to inflict himself on her, and she pretended to be too busy to see him when he asked to see her. She was busy planning for the house, and busy quarrelling with him. It did not make sense. Nothing in the world made sense except to escape from Bruno. There was no way of doing that that made sense. What would happen in a court would not make sense.

He lighted a cigarette, then noticed he already had one. Hunched over the shiny black table, he smoked them both. His arms and hands with the cigarettes seemed mirrored. What was he doing here at 1.15 in the afternoon, growing swimmy on his third martini, making himself incapable of work, assuming he had any? Guy Haines who loved Anne, who had built the Palmyra? He hadn't even the courage to throw his martini glass into the corner. Quicksand. Suppose he sank completely. Suppose he did kill for Bruno. It would be so simple, as Bruno said, when the house was empty except for his father and the butler, and Guy knew the house more exactly than his home in Metcalf. He could leave clues against Bruno, too, leave the Luger in the room. This thought became a single point of concreteness. His fists closed reflexively against Bruno, then the impotence of his clenched hands before him on the table shamed him. He must not let his mind go there again. That was exactly what Bruno wanted his mind to do.

He wet his handkerchief in the glass of water and daubed his face. A shaving cut began to sting. He looked at it in the mirror beside him. It had started to bleed, a tiny red mark just to one side of the faint cleft in his chin. He wanted to throw his fist at the chin in the mirror. He jerked himself up and went to pay his bill.

But having been there once, it was easy for his mind to go there again. In the nights when he could not sleep, he enacted the murder, and it soothed him like a drug. It was not murder but an act he performed to rid himself of Bruno, the slice of a knife that cut away a malignant growth. In the night, Bruno's father was not a person but an object, as he himself was not a person but a force. To enact it, leaving the Luger in the room, to follow Bruno's progress to conviction and death, was a catharsis.

Bruno sent him an alligator billfold with gold corners and his initials G.D.H. inside. 'I thought this looked like you, Guy,' said the note inside. 'Please don't make things tough. I am very fond of you. As ever, Bruno.' Guy's arm moved to fling it into a trash-basket on the street, then he slipped it into his pocket. He hated to throw away a beautiful thing. He would think of something else to do with it.

That same morning, Guy declined an invitation to speak on a radio panel. He was in no condition to work and he knew it. Why did he even keep coming to the office? He would have been delighted to stay drunk all day, and especially all night. He watched his hand turning and turning the folded compass on his desk top. Someone had once told him that he had hands like a Capuchin monk. Tim O'Flaherty in Chicago. Once when they had sat eating spaghetti in Tim's basement apartment, talking of Le Corbusier and the verbal eloquence that seemed innate in architects, a natural concomitant of the profession, and how fortunate it was, because generally you had to talk your way. But it had all been possible then, even with Miriam draining him, merely a clean invigorating fight ahead, and somehow right with all its difficulties. He turned the compass over and over, sliding his fingers down it and turning it, until he thought the noise might be bothering Myers and stopped.

'Pull out of it, Guy,' Myers said amiably.

'It isn't anything one snaps out of. One either cracks up or doesn't,' Guy retorted with a dead calm in his voice, and then, unable to stop himself, 'I don't want advice, Myers. Thanks.'

'Listen, Guy –' Myers stood up, smiling, lanky, tranquil. But he did not come beyond the corner of his desk.

Guy got his coat from the tree by the door. 'I'm sorry. Let's forget it.'

'I know what's the matter. Pre-wedding nerves. I had them, too. What do you say we go down and have a drink?'

Myers' familiarity piqued a certain sense of dignity that Guy was never aware of until it was affronted. He could not bear to look at Myers' untroubled, empty face, his smug banality. 'Thanks,' he said, 'I really don't feel like it.' He closed the door softly behind him.

23

Guy glanced again at the row of brownstones across the street, sure he had seen Bruno. His eyes smarted and swam, fighting the dusk. He *had* seen him, there by the black iron gate, where he was not. Guy turned and ran up his steps. He had tickets to a Verdi opera tonight. Anne was going to meet him at the theatre at 8.30. He didn't feel like seeing Anne tonight, didn't want Anne's kind of cheering, didn't want to exhaust himself pretending he felt better than he did. She was worried about his not sleeping. Not that she said much, but that little annoyed him. Above all, he didn't want to hear Verdi. Whatever had possessed him to buy tickets to Verdi? He had wanted to do something to please Anne, but at best she wouldn't like it very much, and wasn't there something insane about buying tickets for something neither of them liked?

Mrs McCausland gave him a number he was supposed to call. He thought it looked like the number of one of Anne's aunts. He hoped Anne might be busy tonight.

'Guy, I don't see how I can make it,' Anne said. 'These two people Aunt Julie wanted me to meet aren't coming until after dinner.'

'All right.'

'And I can't duck out on it.'

'It's perfectly all right.'

'I am sorry though. Do you know I haven't seen you since Saturday?'

Guy bit the end of his tongue. An actual repulsion against her clinging, her concern, even her clear, gentle voice that had before been like an embrace itself – all this seemed a revelation he no longer loved her.

'Why don't you take Mrs McCausland tonight? I think it'd be nice if you did.'

'Anne, I don't care at all.'

'There haven't been any more letters, Guy?'

'No.' The third time she had asked him!

'I do love you. You won't forget, will you?'

'No, Anne.'

He fled upstairs to his room, hung up his coat and washed, combed his hair, and immediately there was nothing to do, and he wanted Anne. He wanted her terribly. Why had he been so mad as to think he didn't want to see her? He searched his pockets for Mrs McCausland's note with the telephone number, then ran downstairs and looked for it on the hall floor. It had vanished – as if someone had deliberately snatched it away to thwart him. He peered through the etched glass of the front door. Bruno, he thought, Bruno had taken it.

The Faulkners would know her aunt's number. He would see her, spend the evening with her, even if it meant spending the evening with her Aunt Julie. The telephone in Long Island rang and rang and nobody answered. He tried again to think of her aunt's last name, and couldn't.

His room seemed filled with palpable, suspenseful silence. He glanced at the low bookshelves he had built around the walls, at the ivy Mrs McCausland had given him in the wall brackets, at the empty red plush chair by the reading lamp, at his sketch in black and white over his bed entitled 'Imaginary Zoo', at the monk's cloth curtains that concealed his kitchenette. Almost boredly he went and moved the curtains aside and looked behind them. He had a definite feeling someone was waiting for him in the room, though he was not in the least frightened. He picked up the newspaper and started to read.

A few moments later, he was in a bar drinking a second martini. He had to sleep, he reasoned, even if it meant drinking alone, which he despised. He walked down to Times Square, got a haircut, and on the way home bought a quart of milk and a couple of tabloids. After he wrote a letter to his mother, he thought, he would drink some milk, read the papers, and go to bed. Or there might even be Anne's telephone number on the floor when he came in. But there wasn't.

At about 2 in the morning, he got up from bed and wandered about the room, hungry and unwilling to eat. Yet one night last week, he remembered, he had opened a can of sardines and devoured them on the blade of a knife. The night was a time for bestial affinities, for drawing closer to oneself. He plucked a notebook from the bookshelf and turned through it hastily. It was his first New York notebook, when he was about twenty-two. He had sketched indiscriminately – the Chrysler Building, the Payne Whitney Psychiatric Clinic, barges on the East River, workmen leaning on electric drills that bit horizontally into rock. There was a series on the Radio City building, with notes on space, on the opposite page the same building with the amendations he would make, or perhaps an entirely new building of his own conception. He closed the book quickly because it was good, and he doubted if he could do as well now. The Palmyra seemed the last spurt of that generous, happy energy of his youth. The sob he had been suppressing contracted his chest with a sickening, familiar pain – familiar from the years after Miriam. He lay down on his bed in order to stop the next.

Guy awakened to Bruno's presence in the dark, though he heard nothing. After the first small start at the suddenness, he felt no surprise at all. As he had imagined, in nights before this,

he was quite happy that Bruno had come. *Really* Bruno? Yes.
Guy saw the end of his cigarette now, over by the bureau.

'Bruno?'

'Hi,' Bruno said softly. 'I got in on a pass key. You're ready
now, aren't you?' Bruno sounded calm and tired.

Guy raised himself to one elbow. Of course Bruno was there.
The orangey end of his cigarette was there. 'Yes,' Guy said, and
felt the yes absorbed by the darkness, not like the other nights
when the yes had been silent, not even going out from him. It
undid the knot in his head so suddenly that it hurt him. It was
what he had been waiting to say, what the silence in the room
had been waiting to hear. And the beasts beyond the walls.

Bruno sat down on the side of the bed and gripped both his
arms above the elbows. 'Guy, I'll never see you again.'

'No.' Bruno smelled abominably of cigarettes and sweet bril-
liantine, of the sourness of drink, but Guy did not draw back
from him. His head was still at its delicious business of untying.

'I tried to be nice to him these last couple days,' Bruno said.
'Not nice, just decent. He said something tonight to my mother,
just before we went out –'

'I don't want to hear it!' Guy said. Time and again he had
stopped Bruno because he didn't want to know what his father
had said, what he looked like, anything about him.

They were both silent for several seconds, Guy because he
would not explain, and Bruno because he had been silenced.

Bruno snuffled with a disgusting rattle. 'We're going to Maine
tomorrow, starting by noon positively. My mother and me and
the chauffeur. Tomorrow night is a good night but any night
except Thursday night is just the same. Any time after 11 ...'

He kept talking, repeating what Guy knew already, and Guy
did not stop him, because he knew he was going to enter the
house and it would all come true.

'I broke the lock on the back door two days ago, slamming
it when I was tight. They won't get it fixed, they're too busy.
But if they do –' He pressed a key into Guy's hand. 'And I
brought you these.'

'What is it?'

'Gloves. Ladies' gloves, but they'll stretch.' Bruno laughed.

Guy felt the thin cotton gloves.

'You got the gun, huh? Where is it?'

'In the bottom drawer.'

Guy heard him stumble against the bureau and heard the drawer pull out. The lampshade crackled, the light came on, and Bruno stood there huge and tall in a new polo coat so pale it was nearly white, in black trousers with a thin white stripe in them. A white silk muffler hung long around his neck. Guy examined him from his small brown shoes to his stringy oiled hair, as if from his physical appearance he could discover what had caused his change of feeling, or even what the feeling was. It was familiarity and something more, something brotherly. Bruno clicked the gun shut and turned to him. His face was heavier than the last time Guy had seen it, flushed and more alive than he remembered ever having seen it. His grey eyes looked bigger with his tears and rather golden. He looked at Guy as if he tried to find words, or as if he pled with Guy to find them. Then he moistened the thin parted lips, shook his head, and reached an arm out towards the lamp. The light went out.

When he was gone, it hardly seemed he was gone. There were just the two of them in the room still, and sleep.

A grey glaring light filled the room when Guy awakened. The clock said 3.25. He imagined more than remembered that he had got up to go to the telephone that morning, that Myers had called to ask why he had not come in, and that he had said he didn't feel well. The devil with Myers. He lay there blinking his dullness away, letting it seep into the thinking part of his brain that tonight he was going to do it, and after tonight it would all be over. Then he got up and slowly went about his routine of shaving, showering, and dressing, aware that nothing he did mattered at all until the hour between 11 and midnight, the hour there was neither hurry nor delay about, that was coming just as it should. He felt he moved on certain definite tracks now, and that he could not have stopped himself or got off them if he had wanted to.

In the middle of his late breakfast in a coffee shop down the street, an eerie sensation came over him that the last time he had seen Anne he had told her everything that he was going to do, and that she had listened placidly, knowing she must for his sake, because he absolutely had to do what he was going to do. It seemed so natural and inevitable, he felt everyone in the world must know it, the man sitting beside him unconcernedly eating, Mrs McCausland, sweeping her hall as he went out, who had given him an especially maternal smile and asked if he was feeling well. March 12 FRIDAY, said the day-by-day calendar on the coffee-shop wall. Guy stared at it a moment, then finished his meal.

He wanted to keep moving. He decided by the time he walked up Madison Avenue, then Fifth to the end of Central Park, down Central Park West to Pennsylvania Station, it would be time to catch the train to Great Neck. He began to think of his course of action for tonight, but it bored him like something in school he had already studied too much, and he stopped. The brass barometers in a Madison Avenue window had a special appeal now, as if he were soon to have a holiday and possess them and play with them. Anne's sailboat, he thought, didn't have a barometer as handsome as any of these or he would have noticed it. He must get one before they sailed south on their honeymoon. He thought of his love, like a rich possession. He had reached the north end of Central Park, when it occurred to him he didn't have the gun with him. Or the gloves. And it was a quarter to 8. A fine, stupid beginning! He hailed a cab and hurried the driver back to his house.

There was plenty of time after all, so much that he wandered about his room absently for a while. Should he bother to wear crêpe-soled shoes? Should he wear a hat? He got the Luger out of the bottom drawer and laid it on the bureau. There was a single plan of Bruno's under the gun and he opened it, but immediately every word was so familiar, he threw it into the waste-basket. Momentum smoothed his movements again. He got the purple cotton gloves from the table by his bed. A small yellow card fluttered from them. It was a ticket to Great Neck.

He stared at the black Luger which more than before struck him as outrageously large. Idiotic of *someone* to have made a gun so big! He got his own little revolver from the top drawer.

Its pearl handle gleamed with a discreet beauty. Its short slender barrel looked inquisitive, willing, strong with a reserved and gallant strength. Still, he mustn't forget he'd been going to leave the Luger in the bedroom, because it was Bruno's gun. But it didn't seem worth it now, to carry the heavy gun just for that. He really felt no enmity towards Bruno now, and that was the odd thing.

For a moment, he was utterly confused. Of course take the Luger, the Luger was in the plan! He put the Luger in his overcoat pocket. His hand moved for the gloves on the bureau top. The gloves were purple and the flannel bag of his revolver was lavender. Suddenly it seemed fitting he should take the small revolver, because of the similar colours, so he put the Luger back in the bottom drawer and dropped the little revolver into his pocket. He did not check to see if anything else should be done, because he could simply feel, having gone over Bruno's plans so often, that he had done everything. At last he got a glass of water and poured it into the ivy in the wall brackets. A cup of coffee might make him more alert, he thought. He would get one at the Great Neck station.

There was a moment on the train, when a man bumped his shoulder, when his nerves seemed to go quivering up and up to a pitch at which he thought something *must* happen, and a flurry of words rushed to his mind, almost to his tongue: *It's not really a gun in my pocket. I've never thought of it as a gun. I didn't buy it because it was a gun.* And immediately he felt easier, because he knew he was going to kill with it. He was like Bruno. Hadn't he sensed it time and time again, and like a coward never admitted it? Hadn't he known Bruno was like himself? Or why had he liked Bruno? He loved Bruno. Bruno had prepared every inch of the way for him, and everything would go well because everything always went well for Bruno. The world was geared for people like Bruno.

It was drizzling in a fine, directionless mist as he stepped off the train. Guy walked straight to the row of buses Bruno had described. The air through the open window was colder than New York's, and fresh with open country. The bus moved out of the lighted community centre and into a darker road with houses along both sides. He remembered he hadn't stopped for coffee in the station. The omission threw him into a state of irritation just short of making him get off the bus and go back for it. A cup of coffee might make all the difference in the world. Yes, his life! But at the Grant Street stop, he stood up automatically, and the feeling of moving on established tracks returned to comfort him.

His step had a moist elastic sound on the dirt road. Ahead of him, a young girl ran up some steps, along a front walk, and the closing of the door behind her sounded peaceful and neighbourly. There was the vacant lot with the solitary tree, and off to the left, darkness and the woods. The street lamp Bruno had put in all his maps wore an oily blue and gold halo. A car approached slowly, its headlights rolling like wild eyes with the road's bumps, and passed him.

He came upon it suddenly, and it was as if a curtain had lifted on a stage scene he knew already: the long seven-foot high wall of white plaster in the foreground, darkened here and there by a cherry tree that overhung it, and beyond, the triangle of white housetop. The Doghouse. He crossed the street. From up the road came the grit of slow steps. He waited against the darker north side of the wall until the figure came into view. It was a policeman, strolling with hands and stick behind him. Guy felt no alarm whatever, less if possible than if the man hadn't been a policeman, he thought. When the policeman had passed, Guy walked fifteen paces beside the wall, sprang up and gripped its cornice across the top, and scrambled astride it. Almost directly below him, he saw the pale form of the milk crate Bruno had said he had flung near the wall. He bent to peer through the cherry tree branches at the house. He could see two of the five big windows on the first floor, and part of the rectangle of the swimming pond projecting towards him. There was no light. He jumped down.

Now he could see the start of the six white-sided steps at the back, and the misty frill of blossomless dogwood trees that surrounded the whole house. As he had suspected from Bruno's drawings, the house was too small for its ten double gables, obviously built because the client wanted gables and that was that. He moved along the inner side of the wall until crackling twigs frightened him. *Cut cattycornered across the lawn*, Bruno had said, and the twigs were why.

When he moved towards the house, a limb took his hat off. He rammed the hat in the front of his overcoat, and put his hand back in the pocket where the key was. When had he put the gloves on? He took a breath and moved across the lawn in a gait between running and walking, light and quick as a cat. I have done this many times before, he thought, this is only one of the times. He hesitated at the edge of the grass, glanced at the familiar garage towards which the gravel road curved, then went up the six back steps. The back door opened, heavy and smooth, and he caught the knob on the other side. But the second door with the Yale lock resisted, and a flush of something like embarrassment passed over him before he pushed harder and it yielded. He heard a clock on the kitchen table to his left. He knew it was a table, though he could see only blackness with less black forms of things, the big white stove, the servants' table and chairs left, the cabinets. He moved diagonally towards the back stairs, counting off his steps. *I would have you use the main stairway but the whole stairway creaks*. He walked slowly and stiffly, stretching his eyes, skirting the vegetable bins he did not really see. A sudden thought that he must resemble an insane somnambulist brought a start of panic.

Twelve steps up first, skip seven. Then two little flights after the turn ... Skip four, skip three, step wide at the top. You can remember it, it's got a syncopated rhythm. He skipped the fourth step in the first little flight. There was a round window just at the turn before the last flight. Guy remembered from some essay, *As a house is built so the pattern of activity of those will be who live in it ... Shall the child pause at the window for the view before he climbs fifteen steps to his playroom?* Ten feet ahead on his left was the butler's door. *This is the closest you'll come to anyone*, said Bruno in a crescendo as he passed the door's dark column.

The floor gave the tiniest wail of complaint, and Guy resiliently withdrew his foot, waited, and stepped around the spot. Delicately his hand closed on the knob of the hall door. As he opened it, the clock's tick on the landing of the main stairway came louder, and he realized he had been hearing it for several seconds. He heard a sigh.

A sigh on the main stairs!

A chime rang out. The knob rattled, and he squeezed it hard enough to break it, he thought. *Three. Four.* Close the door before the butler hears it! Was this why Bruno had said between 11 and midnight? Damn him! And now he didn't have the Luger! Guy closed the door with a *bump-bump*. While he sweated, feeling heat rise from his overcoat collar into his face, the clock kept on and on. And a last one.

Then he listened, and there was nothing but the deaf and blind *tick-tock* again, and he opened the door and went into the main hall. *My father's door is just to the right.* The tracks were back under him again. And surely he had been here before, in the empty hall that he could feel as he stared at Bruno's father's door, with the grey carpet, the panelled creamy walls, the marble table at the head of the stairs. The hall had a smell and even the smell was familiar. A sharp tickling sensation came at his temples. Suddenly he was sure the old man stood just the other side of the door, holding his breath just as he did, awaiting him. Guy held his own breath so long the old man must have died if he too had not breathed. Nonsense! Open the door!

He took the knob in his left hand, and his right moved automatically to the gun in his pocket. He felt like a machine, beyond danger and invulnerable. He had been here many, many times before, had killed him many times before, and this was only one of the times. He stared at the inch-wide crack in the door, sensing an infinite space opening out beyond, waiting until a feeling of vertigo passed. Suppose he couldn't *see* him when he got inside? Suppose the old man saw him first? *The night light on the front porch lights the room a little bit*, but the bed was over in the opposite corner. He opened the door wider, listened, and stepped too hastily in. But the room was still, the bed a big vague thing in the dark corner, with a lighter strip at the head. He closed the door, *the wind might blow the door*, then faced the corner.

The gun was in his hand already, aimed at the bed that looked empty however he peered at it.

He glanced at the window over his right shoulder. It was open only about a foot, and Bruno had said it would be open *all the way*. Because of the drizzle. He frowned at the bed, and then with a terrible thrill made out the form of the head lying rather near the wall side, tipped sideways as if it regarded him with a kind of gay disdain. The face was darker than the hair which blended with the pillow. The gun was looking straight at it as he was.

One should shoot the chest. Obediently the gun looked at the chest. Guy slid his feet nearer the bed and glanced again at the window behind him. There was no sound of breathing. One would really not think he were alive. That was what he had told himself he must think, that the figure was merely a target. And that, because he did not know the target, it was like killing in war. Now?

'Ha-ha-ha-a !' from the window.

Guy trembled and the gun trembled.

The laugh had come from a distance, a girl's laugh, distant but clear and straight as a shot. Guy wet his lips. The aliveness of the laugh had swept away everything of the scene for a moment, left nothing in its place, and now slowly the vacuum was filling with his standing here about to kill. It had happened in the time of a heartbeat. Life. The young girl walking in the street. With a young man, perhaps. And the man asleep in the bed, living. *No, don't think! You do it for Anne, remember? For Anne and for yourself! It is like killing in war, like killing –*

He pulled the trigger. It made a mere click. He pulled again and it clicked. It was a trick ! It was all false and didn't even exist ! Not even his standing here ! He pulled the trigger again.

The room tore up with a roar. His fingers tightened in terror. The roar came again, as if the crust of the world burst.

'Kagh !' said the figure on the bed. The grey face moved upward, showing the line of head and shoulders.

Guy was on the porch roof, falling. The sensation awakened him like the fall at the end of a nightmare. By a miracle an awning bar slid into one of his hands, and he fell downward again, on to hands and knees. He jumped off the porch edge, ran along the side of the house, then cut across the lawn, straight for the place where the milk crate was. He awakened to the clinging earth, to the hopelessness of his pumping arms that tried to hurry his race against the lawn. This is how it feels, how it is, he thought – *life*, like the laugh upstairs. The truth was that it is like a nightmare when one is paralysed, against impossible odds.

'Hey!' a voice called.

The butler was after him, just as he had anticipated. He felt the butler was right behind him. The nightmare!

'Hey! Hey, there!'

Guy turned under the cherry trees and stood with his fist drawn back. The butler was not just behind him. He was a long way off, but he had seen him. The crazily running figure in white pyjamas wavered like leaping smoke, then curved towards him. Guy stood, paralysed, waiting.

'Hey!'

Guy's fist shot out for the oncoming chin, and the white wraith collapsed.

Guy jumped for the wall.

Darkness ran up higher and higher about him. He dodged a little tree, leapt what looked like a ditch, and ran on. Then suddenly he was lying face down and pain was spreading from the middle of him in all directions, rooting him to the ground. His body trembled violently, and he thought he must gather up the trembling and use it to run, that this wasn't where Bruno had said to go at all, but he could not move. *You just take the little dirt road (no lights there) eastward off Newhope south of the house and keep going across two bigger streets to Columbia Street and walk south (right)* ... To the bus line that went to another railroad station. All very well for Bruno to write his damned instructions on paper. Damn him! He knew where he was now, in the field west of the house that never in any of the plans was to be used! He looked behind him. Which way was north now? What had happened to the street light? Maybe he wouldn't be able to find the little road in the dark. He didn't know whether the house lay behind him or to his left. A mysterious pain throbbed the length of his right forearm so sharp he thought it should have glowed in the dark.

He felt as if he had been shattered apart with the explosion of the gun, that he could never gather the energy to move again, and that he really didn't care. He remembered his being hit in the football game in high school, when he had lain face down like this, speechless with pain. He remembered the supper, the very supper and the hot-water bottle his mother had brought to him in bed, and the touch of her hands adjusting the covers under his chin. His trembling hand was sawing itself raw on a half-buried rock. He bit his lip and kept thinking vacuously, as one thinks when only half awake on an exhausted morning, that he must get up in the next moment regardless of the agony because he wasn't safe. He was still so close to the house. And suddenly his arms and legs scrambled under him as if statics had built up a charge abruptly released, and he was running again across the field.

A strange sound made him stop – a low musical moan that seemed to come from all sides.

Police sirens, of course. And like an idiot he had thought first of an airplane! He ran on, knowing he was only running blindly and directly away from the sirens that were over his left shoulder now, and that he should veer left to find the little road. He must have run far beyond the long plaster wall. He started to cut left to cross the main road that surely lay in that direction, when he realized the sirens were coming up the road. He would either have to wait – He couldn't wait. He ran on, parallel to the cars. Then something caught his foot, and cursing, he fell again. He lay in a kind of ditch with his arms outspread, the right bent up on higher ground. Frustration maddened him to a petulant sob. His left hand felt odd. It was in water up to the wrist. It'll wet my wristwatch, he thought. But the more he intended to pull it out the more impossible it seemed to move it. He felt two forces, one that would move the arm and another that would not, balancing themselves so perfectly his arm was not even tense. Incredibly, he felt he might have slept now. *The police will surround me*, he thought out of nowhere, and was up again, running.

Close on his right, a siren shrieked in triumph as if it had found him.

A rectangle of light sprang up in front of him, and he turned and fled it. A window. He had nearly run into a house. The whole world was awake! And he *had* to cross the road!

The police car passed thirty feet before him on the road, with a blink of headlights through bushes. Another siren moaned to his left, where the house must be, and droned away to silence. Stooping, Guy crossed the road not far behind the car and entered deeper darkness. No matter where the little road was now, he could run farther from the house in this direction. *There's sort of unlighted woods all around to the south, easy to hide in in case you have to get off the little road ... Do not try to get rid of the Luger no matter what happens between my house and the RR station.* His hand moved to his pocket and felt the cold of the little revolver through the holes in his gloves. He didn't remember putting the gun back in his pocket. It might have been lying on the blue carpet for all he knew! And suppose he had dropped it? A fine time to think of it!

Something had caught him and was holding him. He fought it automatically with his fists, and found it was bushes, twigs, briars, and kept fighting and hurling his body through it, because the sirens were still behind him and this was the only direction to go. He concentrated on the enemy ahead of him, and on both sides and even behind him, that caught at him with thousands of sharp tiny hands whose crackling began to drown out even the sirens. He spent his strength joyfully against them, relishing their clean, straight battle against him.

He awakened at the edge of a woods, face down on a downward sloping hill. Had he awakened, or had he fallen only a moment ago? But there was greyness in the sky in front of him, the beginning of dawn, and when he stood up, his flickering vision told him he had been unconscious. His fingers moved directly to the mass of hair and wetness that stood out from the side of his head. Maybe my head is broken, he thought in terror, and stood for a moment dully, expecting himself to drop dead.

Below, the sparse lights of a little town glowed like stars at dusk. Mechanically, Guy got out a handkerchief and wrapped it tight around the base of his thumb where a cut had oozed black-looking blood. He moved towards a tree and leaned against it. His eyes searched the town and the road below. There was not a moving thing. Was this he? Standing against the tree with the memory of the gun's explosion, the sirens, the fight against the woods? He wanted water. On the dirt road that edged the town, he saw a filling station. He made his way down towards it.

There was an old-fashioned pump beside the filling station. He held his head under it. His face stung like a mask of cuts. Slowly his mind grew clearer. He couldn't be more than two miles from Great Neck. He removed his right glove that hung by one finger and the wrist, and put it in his pocket. Where was the other? Had he left it in the woods where he tied his thumb? A rush of panic comforted him with its familiarity. He'd have to go back for it. He searched his overcoat pockets, opened his overcoat and searched his trousers pockets. His hat fell at his feet. He had forgotten about the hat, and suppose he had dropped that somewhere? Then he found the glove inside his left sleeve, no more than the seam of the top that still circled his wrist, and a tatter, and pocketed it with an abstract relief like happiness. He turned up a trousers cuff that had been torn down. He decided to walk in the direction he knew was southward, catch any bus farther southward, and ride until he came to a railroad station.

As soon as he realized his objective, pain set in. How could he walk the length of this road with these knees? Yet he kept walking, holding his head high to urge himself along. It was a time of dubious balance between night and day, still dark, though a low iridescence lay everywhere. The dark might still overcome the light, it seemed, because the dark was bigger. If the night could only hold this much until he got home and locked his door!

Then daylight made a sudden thrust at the night, and cracked the whole horizon on his left. A silver line ran around the top of a hill, and the hill became mauve and green and tan, as if it were opening its eyes. A little yellow house stood under a tree on the hill. On his right, a dark field had become high grass of green and tan, gently moving like a sea. As he looked, a bird flew out of the grass with a cry and wrote a fast, jagged, exuberant message with its sharp-pointed wings across the sky. Guy stopped and watched it until it disappeared.

24

For the hundredth time, he examined his face in the bathroom mirror, patiently touched every scratch with the styptic pencil, and repowdered them. He ministered to his face and hands objectively, as if they were not a part of himself. When his eyes met the staring eyes in the mirror, they slipped away as they must have slipped away, Guy thought, that first afternoon on the train, when he had tried to avoid Bruno's eyes.

He went back and fell down on his bed. There was the rest of today, and tomorrow, Sunday. He needn't see anyone. He could go to Chicago for a couple of weeks and say he was away on a job. But it might seem suspicious if he left town the day after. *Yesterday. Last night.* Except for his scratched hands, he might have believed it one of his dreams that he had done it. Because he had not wanted to do it, he thought. It had not been his will. It had been Bruno's will, working through him. He wanted to curse Bruno, curse him aloud, but he simply had not the energy now. The curious thing was that he felt no guilt, and it seemed to him now that the fact Bruno's will had motivated him was the explanation. But what was this thing, guilt, that he had felt more after Miriam's death than now? Now he was merely tired, and unconcerned about anything. Or was this how anyone would feel after killing? He tried to sleep, and his mind retraced the moments on the Long Island bus, the two workmen who had stared at him, his pretence of sleep with the newspaper over his face. He had felt more shame with the workmen ...

His knees buckled on the front steps and he almost fell. He did not look to see if he were being observed. It seemed an ordinary thing he did, to go down and buy a paper. But he knew also he hadn't the strength to look to see if he were being observed, the strength even to care, and he dreaded the time when the strength would come, as a sick or wounded man dreads the next inevitable operation.

The *Journal-American* had the longest account, with a silhouette of the murderer, composed from the butler's description, of a man six feet one, weighing about one hundred and seventy to eighty pounds, wearing a dark overcoat and hat. Guy read it with mild surprise, as if it might not have been about him: he was only five nine and weighed about a hundred and forty. And he had not been wearing a hat. He skipped the part of the story that told who Samuel Bruno was, and read with greatest interest the speculation about the murderer's flight. North along Newhope Road, it said, where it was believed he lost himself in the town of Great Neck, perhaps taking the 12.18 a.m. train out. Actually, he had gone south-east. He felt suddenly relieved, safe. It was an illusion, he warned himself, safety. He stood up, for the first time as panicked as he had been when he floundered in the lot beside the house. The paper was several hours old. They could have found their mistake by now. They could be coming for him, right outside his door, by now. He waited, and there was no sound anywhere, and feeling tired again, he sat down. He forced himself to concentrate on the rest of the long column. The coolness of the murderer was stressed, and the fact it seemed to be an inside job. No fingerprints, no clue except some shoe prints, size nine and a half, and the smudge of a black shoe on the white plaster wall. His clothes, he thought, he must get rid of his clothes and immediately, but when would he find the energy to do it? It was odd they overestimated his shoe size, Guy thought, with the ground so wet. '... an unusually small calibre of bullet,' the paper said. He must get rid of his revolver, too. He felt a little wrench of grief. He would hate that, how he would hate the instant he parted from his revolver! He pulled himself up and went to get more ice for the towel he was holding against his head.

Anne telephoned him in the late afternoon to ask him to go to a party with her Sunday night in Manhattan.

'Helen Heyburn's party. You know, I told you about it.'

'Yes,' Guy said, not remembering at all. His voice came evenly, 'I guess I don't quite feel like a party, Anne.'

For the last hour or so, he had felt numb. It made Anne's words distant, irrelevant. He listened to himself saying the right things, not even anticipating, or perhaps not even caring, that Anne might notice any difference. Anne said she might get Chris Nelson to go with her, and Guy said all right, and thought how happy Nelson would be to go with her because Nelson, who had used to see a great deal of Anne before she met Guy, was still in love with her, Guy thought.

'Why don't I bring in some delicatessen Sunday evening,' Anne said, 'and we'll have a snack together? I could have Chris meet me later.'

'I thought I might go out Sunday, Anne. Sketching.'

'Oh. I'm sorry. I had something to tell you.'

'What?'

'Something I think you'll like. Well – some other time.'

Guy crept up the stairs, alert for Mrs McCausland. Anne was cool to him, he thought monotonously, Anne was cool. The next time she saw him, she would know and she would hate him. Anne was through, Anne was through. He kept chanting it until he fell asleep.

He slept until the following noon, then lay in bed the rest of the day in a torpor that made it agony even to cross the room to refill his towel with ice. He felt he would never sleep enough to get back his strength. Retracing, he thought. His body and mind retracing the long road they had travelled. Coming back to what? He lay rigid and afraid, sweating and shivering with fear. Then he had to get up to go to the bathroom. He had a slight case of diarrhoea. From fear, he thought. As on a battle-field.

He dreamt in half-sleep that he crossed the lawn towards the house. The house was soft and white and unresisting as a cloud. And he stood there unwilling to shoot, determined to fight it to prove he could conquer it. The gunshot awakened him. He opened his eyes to the dawn in his room. He saw himself standing by his work table, exactly as he stood in the dream, pointing the gun at a bed in the corner, where Samuel Bruno struggled to sit up. The gun roared again. Guy screamed.

He sprang out of bed, staggering. The figure vanished. At

his window was the same struggling light he had seen that dawn, the same mingling of life and death. The same light would come every dawn that he lived, would always reveal that room, and the room would grow more distinct with repetition, his horror sharper. Suppose he awakened every dawn that he lived?

The doorbell rang in the kitchenette.

The police are downstairs, he thought. This was just the time they *would* catch him, at dawn. And he didn't care, didn't care at all. He would make a complete confession. He would blurt it all out at once!

He leaned on the release button, then went to his door and listened.

Light quick steps ran up. Anne's steps. Rather the police than Anne! He turned completely around, stupidly drew his shade. He thrust his hair back with both hands and felt the knot on his head.

'Me,' Anne whispered as she slipped in. 'I walked over from Helen's. It's a wonderful morning!' She saw his bandage, and the elation left her face. 'What happened to your hand?'

He stepped back in the shadow near his bureau. 'I got into a fight.'

'When? Last night? And your face, Guy!'

'Yes.' He had to have her, had to keep her with him, he thought. He would perish without her. He started to put his arms around her, but she pushed him back, peering at him in the half light.

'Where, Guy? Who was it?'

'A man I don't even know,' he said tonelessly, hardly realizing even that he lied, because it was so desperately necessary that he keep her with him. 'In a bar. Don't turn on the light,' he said quickly. 'Please, Anne.'

'In a bar?'

'I don't know how it happened. Suddenly.'

'Someone you'd never seen before?'

'Yes.'

'I don't believe you.'

She spoke slowly, and Guy was all at once terrified, realizing she was a separate person from himself, a person with a different mind, different reactions.

'How can I?' she went on. 'And why should I believe you about the letter, about not knowing who sent it?'

'Because it's true.'

'Or the man you fought with on the lawn. Was it the same one?'

'No.'

'You're keeping something from me, Guy.' Then she softened, but each simple word seemed to attack him: 'What is it, darling? You know I want to help you. But you've got to tell me.'

'I've told you,' he said, and set his teeth. Behind him, the light was changing already. If he could keep Anne now, he thought, he could survive every dawn. He looked at the straight, pale curtain of her hair, and put out his hand to touch it, but she drew back.

'I don't see how we can go on like this, Guy. We can't.'

'It won't go on. It's over. I swear to you, Anne. Please believe me.' The moment seemed a test, as if it were now or never again. He should take her in his arms, he thought, hold her fiercely until she stopped struggling against him. But he could not make himself move.

'How do you know?'

He hesitated. 'Because it was a state of mind.'

'That letter was a state of mind?'

'The letter contributed to it. I felt tied in a knot. It was my work, Anne!' He bowed his head. Nailing his sins to his work!

'You once said I made you happy,' she said slowly, 'or that I could in spite of anything. I don't see it any more.'

Certainly he did not make her happy, she meant to say. But if she could still love him now, how he would try to make her happy! How he would worship and serve her! 'You do, Anne. I have nothing else.' He bent lower with sudden sobs, shameless, wracking sobs that did not cease the long moment before Anne touched his shoulder. And though he was grateful, he felt like twisting away from the touch, too, because he felt it was only pity, only humanity that made her touch him at all.

'Shall I fix you some breakfast?'

Even in the note of exasperated patience he heard in her voice, there was a hint of forgiveness that meant total forgiveness, he knew. For fighting in a bar: Never, he thought, would she penetrate to Friday night, because it was already buried too deep for her or for any other person to go.

25

'I don't give a damn what you think!' Bruno said, his foot planted in his chair. His thin blond eyebrows almost met with his frown, and rose up at the ends like the whiskers of a cat. He looked at Gerard like a golden, thin-haired tiger driven to madness.

'Didn't say I thought anything,' Gerard replied with a shrug of hunched shoulders, 'did I?'

'You implied.'

'I did not imply.' The round shoulders shook twice with his laugh. 'You mistake me, Charles. I didn't mean you told anyone on purpose you were leaving. You let it drop by accident.'

Bruno stared at him. Gerard had just implied that if it was an inside job, Bruno and his mother must have had something to do with it, and it certainly was an inside job. Gerard knew that he and his mother had decided only Thursday afternoon to leave Friday. The idea of getting him all the way down here in Wall Street to tell him that! Gerard didn't have anything, and he couldn't fool him by pretending that he had. It was another perfect murder.

'Mind if I shove off?' Bruno asked. Gerard was fooling around with papers on his desk as if he had something else to keep him here for.

'In a minute. Have a drink.' Gerard nodded towards the bottle of bourbon on the shelf across the office.

'No, thanks.' Bruno was dying for a drink, but not from Gerard.

'How's your mother?'

'You asked me that.' His mother wasn't well, wasn't sleeping, and that was the main reason he wanted to get home. A hot resentment came over him again at Gerard's friend-of-the-family attitude. A friend of his father's maybe! 'By the way, we're not hiring you for this, you know.'

Gerard looked up with a smile on his round, faintly pink-and-purple mottled face. 'I'd work on this case for nothing, Charles. That's how interesting I think it is.' He lighted another of the cigars that were shaped something like his fat fingers, and Bruno noticed once more, with disgust, the gravy stains on the lapels of his fuzzy, light-brown suit and the ghastly marble-patterned tie. Every single thing about Gerard annoyed Bruno. His slow speech annoyed him. Memories of the only other times he had seen Gerard, with his father, annoyed him. Arthur Gerard didn't even look like the kind of a detective who was not supposed to look like a detective. In spite of his record, Bruno found it impossible to believe that Gerard was a top-notch detective. 'Your father was a very fine man, Charles. A pity you didn't know him better.'

'I knew him well,' said Bruno.

Gerard's small, speckled tan eyes looked at him gravely. 'I think he knew you better than you knew him. He left me several letters concerning you, your character, what he hoped to make of you.'

'He didn't know me at all.' Bruno reached for a cigarette. 'I don't know why we're talking about this. It's beside the point and it's morbid.' He sat down coolly.

'You hated your father, didn't you?'

'He hated me.'

'But he didn't. That's where you didn't know him.'

Bruno pushed his hand off the chair arm and it squeaked with sweat. 'Are we getting anywhere or what're you keeping me here for? My mother's not feeling well and I want to get home.'

'I hope she'll be feeling better soon, because I want to ask her some questions. Maybe tomorrow.'

Heat rose up the sides of Bruno's neck. The next few weeks would be terrible on his mother, and Gerard would make it worse because he was an enemy of both of them. Bruno stood up and tossed his raincoat over one arm.

'Now I want you to try to think once more,' Gerard wagged a finger at him as casually as if he still sat in the chair, 'just where you went and whom you saw Thursday night. You left your mother and Mr Templeton and Mr Russo in front of the Blue Angel at 2.45 that morning. Where did you go?'

'Hamburger Hearth,' Bruno sighed.

'Didn't see anyone you knew there?'

'Who should I know there, the cat?'

'Then where'd you go?' Gerard checked on his notes.

'Clarke's on Third Avenue.'

'See anyone there?'

'Sure, the bartender.'

'The bartender said he didn't see you,' Gerard smiled.

Bruno frowned. Gerard hadn't said that a half an hour ago. 'So what? The place was crowded. Maybe I didn't see the bartender either.'

'All the barmen know you in there. They said you weren't in Thursday night. Furthermore, the place wasn't crowded. Thursday night? Three or 3.30? — I'm just trying to help you remember, Charles.'

Bruno compressed his lips in exasperation. 'Maybe I wasn't in Clarke's. I usually go over for a nightcap, but maybe I didn't. Maybe I went straight home, I don't know. What about all the people my mother and I talked to Friday morning? We called up a lot of people to say good-bye.'

'Oh, we're covering those. But seriously, Charles –' Gerard leaned back, crossed a stubby leg, and concentrated on puffing his cigar to life – 'you wouldn't leave your mother and her friends just to get a hamburger and go straight home by yourself, would you?'

'Maybe. Maybe it sobered me up.'

'Why're you so vague?' Gerard's Iowan accent made his 'r' a snarl.

'So what if I'm vague? I've got a right to be vague if I was tight!'

'The point is – and of course it doesn't matter whether you were at Clarke's or some other place – *who* you ran into and told you were leaving for Maine the next day. You must think yourself it's funny your father was killed the night of the same day you left.'

'I didn't see anyone. I invite you to check up on everyone I know and ask them.'

'You just wandered around by yourself until after 5 in the morning.'

'Who said I got home after 5?'

'Herbert. Herbert said so yesterday.'

Bruno sighed. 'Why didn't he remember all that Saturday?'

'Well, as I say, that's how the memory works. Gone – and then it comes. Yours'll come, too. Meanwhile, I'll be around. Yes, you can go now, Charles.' Gerard made a careless gesture.

Bruno lingered a moment, trying to think of something to say, and not being able to, went out and tried to slam the door but the air pressure retarded it. He walked back through the shabby, depressing corridor of the Confidential Detective Bureau, where the typewriter that had been pecking thoughtfully throughout the interview came louder – 'We,' Gerard was always saying, and here they all were, grubbing away back of the doors – nodded good-bye to Miss Graham, the receptionist-secretary who had expressed her sympathies to him an hour ago when he had come in. How gaily he had come in an hour ago, determined not to let Gerard rile him, and now – He could never control his temper when Gerard made cracks about him and his mother, and he might as well admit it. So what? So what did they have on him? So what clues did they have on the murderer? Wrong ones.

Guy! Bruno smiled going down in the elevator. Not once had Guy crossed his mind in Gerard's office! Not one flicker even when Gerard had hammered at him about where he went Thursday night! Guy! Guy and himself! Who else was like them? Who else was their equal? He longed for Guy to be with him now. He would clasp Guy's hand, and to hell with the rest of the world! Their feats were unparalleled! Like a sweep across the sky! Like two streaks of red fire that came and disappeared so fast, everybody stood wondering if they really had seen them. He remembered a poem he had read once that said something of what he meant. He thought he still had it in a pocket of his address case. He hurried into a bar off Wall Street, ordered a drink, and pulled the tiny paper out of the address-book pocket. It was torn out of a poetry book he had had in college.

THE LEADEN-EYED
by *Vachel Lindsay*

> Let not young souls be
>   smothered out before
> They do quaint deeds and fully
>   flaunt their pride.
> It is the world's one crime its
>   babes grow dull,
> Its poor are ox-like, limp and leaden-eyed.
>
> Not that they starve, but starve
>   so dreamlessly,
> Not that they sow, but that they
>   seldom reap,
> Not that they serve, but have no
>   gods to serve,
> Not that they die, but that they
>   die like sheep.

He and Guy were not leaden-eyed. He and Guy would not die like sheep now. He and Guy would reap. He would give Guy money, too, if he would take it.

26

At about the same time the next day, Bruno was sitting in a beach chair on the terrace of his house in Great Neck, in a mood of complaisance and halcyon content quite new and pleasant to him. Gerard had been prowling around that morning, but Bruno had been very calm and courteous, had seen that he and his little stooge got some lunch, and now Gerard was gone and he felt very proud of his behaviour. He must never let Gerard get him down again like yesterday, because that was the way to get rattled and make mistakes. Gerard, of course, was the dumb one.

If he'd just been nicer yesterday, he might have co-operated. Co-operated? Bruno laughed out loud. What did he mean co-operated? What was he doing, kidding himself?

Overhead a bird kept singing, 'Tweedledee?' and answering itself, 'Tweedle*dum*!' Bruno cocked his head. His mother would know what kind of a bird it was. He gazed off at the russet-tinged lawn, the white plaster wall, the dogwoods that were beginning to bud. This afternoon, he found himself quite interested in nature. This afternoon, a cheque had arrived for twenty thousand for his mother. There would be a lot more when the insurance people stopped yapping and the lawyers got all the red tape cut. At lunch, he and his mother had talked about going to Capri, talked sketchily, but he knew they would go. And tonight, they were going out to dinner for the first time, at a little *intime* place that was their favourite restaurant, off the highway not far from Great Neck. No wonder he hadn't liked nature before. Now that he owned the grass and the trees, it meant something.

Casually, he turnel the pages of the address book in his lap. He had found it this morning, couldn't remember if he had had it with him in Santa Fe or not, and wanted to make sure there wasn't anything about Guy in it before Gerard found it. There certainly were a lot of people he wanted to look up again, now that he had the wherewithal. An idea came to him, and he took a pencil from his pocket. Under the P's he wrote:

Tommy Pandini
232 W. 76 Street

and under the S's:

'Slitch'
Life Guard Station
Hell Gate Bridge

Give Gerard a few mysterious people to look up.

Dan 8.15 Hotel Astor, he found in the memos at the back of the book. He didn't even remember Dan. *Get $ from Capt. by June 1*. The next page sent a little chill down him: *Item for Guy $25*. He tore the perforated page out. That Santa Fe belt for Guy. Why had he even put it down? In some dull moment –

Gerard's big black car purred into the driveway.

Bruno forced himself to sit there and finish checking the memos. Then he slipped the address book in his pocket, and poked the torn-out page into his mouth.

Gerard strolled on to the flagstones with a cigar in his mouth and his arms hanging.

'Anything new?' Bruno asked.

'Few things.' Gerard let his eyes sweep from the corner of the house diagonally across the lawn to the plaster wall, as though he reappraised the distance the murderer had run.

Bruno's jaw moved casually on the little wad of paper, as if he chewed gum. 'Such as what?' he asked. Past Gerard's shoulder he saw his little stooge sitting in the driver's seat of the car, staring at them fixedly from under a grey hatbrim. Of all the sinister-looking guys, Bruno thought.

'Such as the fact the murderer didn't cut back to town. He kept going in this general direction.' Gerard gestured like a country-store proprietor pointing out a road, bringing his whole arm down. 'Cut through those woods over there and must have had a pretty rough time. We found these.'

Bruno got up and looked at a piece of the purple gloves and a shred of dark blue material, like Guy's overcoat. 'Gosh. You sure they're off the murderer?'

'Reasonably sure. One's off an overcoat. The other – probably a glove.'

'Or a muffler.'

'No, there's a little seam.' Gerard poked it with a fat freckled forefinger.

'Pretty fancy gloves.'

'Ladies' gloves.' Gerard looked up with a twinkle.

Bruno gave an amused smirk, and stopped contritely.

'I first thought he was a professional killer,' Gerard said with a sigh. 'He certainly knew the house. But I don't think a professional killer would have lost his head and tried to get through those woods at the point he did.'

'Hm-m,' said Bruno with interest.

'He knew the right road to take, too. The right road was only ten yards away.'

'How do you know that?'

'Because this whole thing was carefully planned, Charles. The broken lock on the back door, the milk crate out there by the wall –'

Bruno was silent. Herbert had told Gerard that he, Bruno, broke the lock. Herbert had probably also told him he put the milk crate there.

'Purple gloves!' Gerard chuckled, as gaily as Bruno had ever heard him chuckle. 'What does the colour matter as long as they keep fingerprints off things, eh?'

'Yeah,' Bruno said.

Gerard entered the house through the terrace door.

Bruno followed him after a moment. Gerard went back to the kitchen, and Bruno climbed the stairs. He tossed the address book on his bed, then went down the hall. The open door of his father's room gave him a funny feeling, as if he were just realizing his father were dead. It was the door's hanging open that made him feel it, he thought, like a shirt-tail hanging out, like a guard let down, that never would have been if the Captain were alive. Bruno frowned, then went and closed the door quickly on the carpet scuffled by detectives' feet, by Guy's feet, on the desk with the looted pigeon-holes and the cheque-book that lay open as if awaiting his father's signatures. He opened his mother's door carefully. She was lying on her bed with the pink satin comforter drawn up to her chin, her head turned towards the inside of the room and her eyes open, as she had lain since Saturday night.

'You didn't sleep, Mom?'

'No.'

'Gerard's here again.'

'I know.'

'If you don't want to be disturbed, I'll tell him.'

'Darling, don't be silly.'

Bruno sat down on the bed and bent close to her. 'I wish you could sleep, Mom.' She had purple wrinkled shadows under her eyes, and she held her mouth in a way he had never seen before, that drew its corners long and thin.

'Darling, are you sure Sam never mentioned anything to you – never mentioned anyone?'

'Can you imagine him saying anything like that to me?' Bruno wandered about the room. Gerard's presence in the house irked him. It was Gerard's manner that was so obnoxious, as if he had something up his sleeve against everyone, even Herbert who he knew had idolized his father, who was saying everything against him short of plain accusation. But Herbert hadn't seen him measuring the grounds, Bruno knew, or Gerard would have let him know by now. He had wandered all over the grounds, and the house while his mother was sick, and anyone seeing him wouldn't have known when he was counting his paces or not. He wanted to sound off about Gerard now, but his mother wouldn't understand. She insisted on their continuing to hire him, because he was supposed to be the best. They were not working together, his mother and he. His mother might say something else to Gerard – like the fact they'd decided only Thursday to leave Friday – of terrible importance and not mention it to him at all!

'You know you're getting fat, Charley?' his mother said with a smile.

Bruno smiled, too, she sounded so like herself. She was putting on her shower cap at her dressing-table now. 'Appetite's not bad,' he said. But his appetite was worse and so was his digestion. He was getting fatter anyway.

Gerard knocked just after his mother had closed the bathroom door.

'She'll be quite a long time,' Bruno told him.

'Tell her I'll be in the hall, will you?'

Bruno knocked on the bathroom door and told her, then went down to his own room. He could tell by the position of the address book on his bed that Gerard had found it and looked at it. Slowly Bruno mixed himself a short highball, drank it, then went softly down the hall and heard Gerard already talking to his mother.

'– didn't seem in high or low spirits, eh?'

'He's a very moody boy, you know. I doubt if I'd have noticed,' his mother said.

'Oh – people pick up psychic feelings sometimes. Don't you agree, Elsie?'

His mother did not answer.

'– too bad, because I'd like more co-operation from him.'

'Do you think he's withholding anything?'

'I don't know,' with his disgusting smile, and Bruno could tell from his tone that Gerard expected him to be listening, too. 'Do you?'

'Of course, I don't think he is. What're you getting at, Arthur?'

She was standing up to him. She wouldn't think so much of Gerard after this, Bruno thought. He was being dumb again, a dumb Iowan.

'You want me to get at the truth, don't you, Elsie?' Gerard asked, like a radio detective. 'He's hazy about what he did Thursday night after leaving you. He's got some pretty shady acquaintances. One might have been a hireling of a business enemy's of Sam's, a spy or something like that. And Charles could have mentioned that you and he were leaving the next day –'

'What're you getting at, Arthur, that Charles knows something about this?'

'Elsie, I wouldn't be surprised. Would you, really?'

'Damn him!' Bruno murmured. Damn him for saying that to his *mother*!

'I'll certainly tell you everything he tells me.'

Bruno drifted towards the stairway. Her submissiveness shocked him. Suppose she began to suspect? Murder was something she wouldn't be able to take. Hadn't he realized it in Santa Fe? And if she remembered Guy, remembered that he had talked about him in Los Angeles? If Gerard found Guy in the next two weeks, he might have scratches on him from getting through those woods, or a bruise or a cut that might raise suspicion. Bruno heard Herbert's soft tread in the downstairs hall, saw him come into view with his mother's afternoon drink on a tray, and retreated up the stairs again. His heart beat as if he were in a battle, a strange many-sided battle. He hurried back to his own room, took a big drink, then lay down and tried to fall asleep.

He awakened with a jerk and rolled from under Gerard's hand on his shoulder.

'Bye-bye,' Gerard said, his smile showing his tobacco-stained lower teeth. 'Just leaving and thought I'd say good-bye.'

'Is it worth waking somebody up for?' Bruno said.

Gerard chuckled and waddled from the room before Bruno could think of some mitigating phrase he really wanted to say. He plunged back on the pillow and tried to resume his nap, but when he closed his eyes, he saw Gerard's stocky figure in the light-brown suit going down the halls, slipping wraithlike through closed doors, bending to look into drawers, to read letters, to make notes, turning to point a finger at him, tormenting his mother so it was impossible not to fight back.

27

'What else can you make of it? He's accusing me!' Bruno shouted across the table.

'Darling, he's not. He's attending to his business.'

Bruno pushed his hair back. 'Want to dance, Mom?'

'You're in no condition to dance.'

He wasn't and he knew it. 'Then I want another drink.'

'Darling, the food's coming right away.'

Her patience with it all, the purple circles under her eyes, pained him so he could not look in front of him. Bruno glanced around for a waiter. The place was so crowded tonight, it was hard to tell a waiter from any other guy. His eyes stopped on a man at a table across the dance floor who looked like Gerard. He couldn't see the man he was with, but he certainly looked like Gerard, the bald head and light brown hair, except this man wore a black jacket. Bruno closed one eye to stop the rhythmic splitting of the image.

'Charley, do sit down. The waiter's coming.'

It *was* Gerard, and he was laughing now, as if the other fellow had told him he was watching them. For one suspended, furious second, Bruno wondered whether to tell his mother. Then he sat down and said with vehemence: 'Gerard's over there!'

'Is he? Where?'

'Over left of the orchestra. Under the blue lamp.'

'I don't see him.' His mother stretched up. 'Darling, you're imagining.'

'I am not imagining!' Bruno shouted and threw his napkin in his roast beef au jus.

'I see the one you mean, and it's not Gerard,' she said patiently.

'You can't see him as good as I can! It's him and I don't feel like eating in the same room with him!'

'Charles,' she sighed. 'Do you want another drink? Have another drink. Here's a waiter.'

'I don't even feel like drinkin' with him! Want me to prove it's him?'

'What does it matter? He's not going to bother us. He's guarding us probably.'

'You admit it's him! He's spying on us and he's in a dark suit so he can follow us anywhere else we go!'

'It's not Arthur anyway,' she said quietly, squeezing lemon over her broiled fish. 'You're having hallucinations.'

Bruno stared at her with his mouth open. 'What do you *mean* saying things like that to me, Mom?' His voice cracked.

'Sweetie, everybody's looking at us.'

'I don't care!'

'Darling, let me tell you something. You're making too much out of this.' She interrupted him. 'You are, because you want to. You want excitement. I've seen it before.'

Bruno was absolutely speechless. His mother was turning against him. He had seen her look at the Captain the way she looked at him now.

'You've probably said something to Gerard,' she went on, 'in anger, and he thinks you're behaving most peculiarly. Well, you are.'

'Is that any reason for him to tail me day and night?'

'Darling, I don't think that's Gerard,' she said firmly.

Bruno pushed himself up and staggered away towards the table where Gerard sat. He'd prove to her it was Gerard, and prove to Gerard he wasn't afraid of him. A couple of tables blocked him at the edge of the dance floor, but he could see it was Gerard now.

Gerard looked up at him and waved a hand familiarly, and his little stooge stared at him. And *he*, he and his mother were paying for it! Bruno opened his mouth, not knowing exactly what he wanted to say, then teetered around. He knew what he wanted to do, call up Guy. Right here and now. Right in the same room with Gerard. He struggled across the dance floor towards the telephone booth by the bar. The slow, crazily revolving figures pressed him back like a sea wave, baffling him. The wave floated towards him again, buoyant but insuperable, sweeping him yet farther back, and a similar moment at a party in his house when he was a little boy, when he tried to get through the dancing couples to his mother across the living-room, came back to him.

Bruno woke up early in the morning, in bed, and lay perfectly still, retracing the last moments he could remember. He knew he had passed out. Had he called Guy before he passed out? If he had, could Gerard trace it? He surely hadn't talked to Guy or he'd remember it, but maybe he'd called his house. He got up to go ask his mother if he had passed out in the telephone booth. Then the shakes came on and he went into the bathroom. The Scotch and water splashed up in his face when he lifted the glass. He braced himself against the bathroom door. It was getting him at both ends now, the shakes, early and late, waking him earlier and earlier, and he had to take more and more at night to get to sleep.

And in between was Gerard.

28

Momentarily, and faintly, as one re-experiences a remembered sensation, Guy felt secure and self-sufficient as he sat down at his work table where he had his hospital books and notes carefully arranged.

In the last month, he had washed and repainted all his book-shelves, had his carpet and curtains cleaned, and had scrubbed his kitchenette until its porcelain and aluminium gleamed. All guilt, he had thought as he poured the pans of dirty water down the sink, but since he could sleep no more than two or three hours a night, and then only after physical exercise, he reasoned that cleaning one's house was a more profitable manner of tiring oneself than walking the streets of the city.

He looked at the unopened newspaper on his bed, then got up and glanced through all its pages. But the papers had stopped mentioning the murder six weeks ago. He had taken care of every clue – the purple gloves cut up and flushed down the toilet, the overcoat (a good overcoat, and he had thought of giving it to a beggar, but who would be so base as to give even a beggar a murderer's overcoat?) and the trousers torn in pieces and disposed of gradually in the garbage. And the Luger dropped off the Manhattan Bridge. And his shoes off another. The only thing he had not disposed of was the little revolver.

He went to his bureau to look at it. Its hardness under his fingertips soothed him. The one clue he had not disposed of, and all the clue they needed if they found him. He knew exactly why he kept the revolver : it was *his*, a part of himself, the third hand that had done the murder. It was himself at fifteen when he had bought it, himself when he had loved Miriam and had kept it in their room in Chicago, looking at it now and then in his most contented, most inward moments. The best of himself, with its mechanical, absolute logic. Like him, he thought now, in its power to kill.

If Bruno dared to contact him again, he would kill him, too. Guy was sure that he could. Bruno would know it, too. Bruno had always been able to read him. The silence from Bruno now brought more relief than the silence from the police. In fact, he was not anxious at all lest the police find him, had never been. The anxiety had always been within himself, a battle of himself against himself, so torturous he might have welcomed the law's intervention. Society's law was lax compared to the law of conscience. He might go to the law and confess, but confession seemed a minor point, a mere gesture, even an easy way out, an avoidance of truth. If the law executed him, it would be a mere gesture.

'I have no great respect for the law,' he remembered he had said to Peter Wriggs in Metcalf two years ago. Why should he have respect for a statute that called him and Miriam man and wife? 'I have no great respect for the church,' he had said sophomorishly to Peter at fifteen. Then, of course, he had meant the Metcalf Baptists. At seventeen, he had discovered God by himself. He had discovered God through his own awakening talents, and through a sense of unity of all the arts, and then of nature, finally of science – of all the creating and ordering forces in the world. He believed he could not have done his work without a belief in God. And where had his belief been when he murdered?

Awkwardly, he turned and faced his work table. A gasp hissed between his teeth, and nervously, impatiently, he passed his hand hard across his mouth. And yet, he felt, there was *something* still to come, still to be grasped, some severer punishment, some bitterer realization.

'I don't suffer enough!' burst from him suddenly in a whisper. But why had he whispered? Was he ashamed? 'I don't suffer enough,' he said in a normal voice, glancing about him as if he expected some ear to hear him. And he would have shouted it, if he had not felt some element of pleading in it, and considered himself unworthy of pleading for anything, from anyone.

His new books, for instance, the beautiful new books he had bought today – he could still think about them, love them. Yet he felt he had left them there long ago on his work table, like his own youth. He must go immediately and work, he thought. He had been commissioned to plan a hospital. He frowned at the little stack of notes he had already taken, spotlighted under his gooseneck lamp. Somehow it did not seem real that he had been commissioned. He would awaken soon and find that all these weeks had been a fantasy, a wishful dream. A hospital. Wasn't a hospital more fitting than even a prison? He frowned puzzledly, knowing his mind had strayed wildly, that two weeks ago when he had begun the hospital interior he had not thought once of death, that the positive requisites of health and healing alone had occupied him. He hadn't told Anne about the hospital, he remembered suddenly, that was why it seemed unreal. She was his glass of reality, not his work. But on the other hand, why hadn't he told her?

He must go immediately and work, but he could feel in his

legs now that frenzied energy that came every evening, that sent him out in the streets finally in a vain effort to spend it. The energy frightened him because he could find no task that would absorb it, and because he felt at times that the task might be his suicide. Yet very deep inside him, and very much against his own will, his roots still clung to life.

He thought of his mother, and felt he could never let her embrace him again. He remembered her telling him that all men were equally good, because all men had souls and the soul was entirely good. Evil, she said, always came from externals. And so he had believed even months after Miriam, when he had wanted to murder her lover Steve. So he had believed even on the train, reading his Plato. In himself, the second horse of the charioteer had always been obedient as the first. But love and hate, he thought now, good and evil, lived side by side in the human heart, and not merely in differing proportions in one man and the next, but all good and all evil. One had merely to look for a little of either to find it all, one had merely to scratch the surface. All things had opposites close by, every decision a reason against it, every animal an animal that destroys it, the male the female, the positive the negative. The splitting of the atom was the only true destruction, the breaking of the universal law of oneness. Nothing could be without its opposite that was bound up with it. Could space exist in a building without objects that stopped it? Could energy exist without matter, or matter without energy? Matter and energy, the inert and the active, once considered opposites, were now known to be one.

And Bruno, he and Bruno. Each was what the other had not chosen to be, the cast-off self, what he thought he hated but perhaps in reality loved.

For a moment, he felt as if he might be mad. He thought, madness and genius often overlapped, too. But what mediocre lives most people lived ! In middle waters, like most fish !

No, there was that duality permeating nature down to the tiny proton and electron within the tiniest atom. Science was now at work trying to split the electron, and perhaps it couldn't because perhaps only an idea was behind it: the one and only truth, that the opposite is always present. Who knew whether an electron was matter or energy? Perhaps God and the Devil danced hand in hand around every single electron!

He threw his cigarette at the waste-basket and missed.

When he put out the stub in the basket, he saw a crumpled page on which he had written last night one of his guilt-crazed confessions. It dragged him up sickeningly to a present that assaulted him from all sides – Bruno, Anne, this room, this night, the conference with the Department of Hospitals tomorrow.

Towards midnight, when he felt drowsy, he left his work table and lay down carefully on his bed, not daring to undress lest he awaken himself again.

He dreamed that he woke up in the night to the sound of the slow, watchful breathing that he heard every night in his room as he tried to fall asleep. It came from outside his window now. Someone was climbing the house. A tall figure in a great cape like a bat's wing sprang suddenly into the room.

'I'm here,' said the figure matter-of-factly.

Guy jumped from his bed to fight him. 'Who are you?' He saw it was Bruno.

Bruno resisted him rather than fought back. If Guy used his utmost strength, he could just pin Bruno's shoulders to the floor, and always in the recurrent dream, Guy had to use his utmost strength. Guy held Bruno to the floor with his knees and strangled him, but Bruno kept grinning up at him as if he felt nothing.

'You,' Bruno answered finally.

Guy awakened heavy-headed and perspiring. He sat up higher, vigilantly guarding his empty room. There were slimily wet sounds in the room now, as of a snake crawling through the cement court below, slapping its moist coils against the walls. Then suddenly he recognized the sound as that of rain, a gentle, silvery summer rain, and sank back again on his pillow. He began to cry softly. He thought of the rain, rushing at a slant to the earth. It seemed to say: Where are the spring plants to water? Where is the new life that depends on me? *Where is the green vine, Anne, as we saw love in our youth?* he had written last night on the crumpled paper. The rain would find the new life awaiting it, depending on it. What fell in his court was only its excess. *Where is the green vine, Anne . . .*

He lay with his eyes open until the dawn eased its fingertips on to the sill, like the stranger who had sprung in. Like Bruno. Then he got up and turned on his lights, drew the shades, and went back to his work.

29

Guy slammed his foot on the brake pedal, but the car leapt, screaming towards the child. There was a tinny clatter of the bicycle falling. Guy got out and ran around the car, banged his knee excruciatingly on the front bumper, and dragged the child up by his shoulders.

'I'm okay,' the little boy said.

'Is he all right, Guy?' Anne ran up, white as the child.

'I think so.' Guy gripped the bicycle's front wheel with his knees and straightened the handlebars, feeling the child's curious eyes on his own violently trembling hands.

'Thanks,' said the boy.

Guy watched him mount the bicycle and pedal off as if he watched a miracle. He looked at Anne and said quietly, with a shuddering sigh, 'I can't drive any more today.'

'All right,' she replied, as quietly as he, but there was a suspicion in her eyes, Guy knew, as she turned to go around to the driver's seat.

Guy apologized to the Faulkners as he got back into the car, and they murmured something about such things happening to every driver now and then. But Guy felt their real silence behind him, a silence of shock and horror. He had seen the boy coming down the side road. The boy had stopped for him, but Guy had swerved the car towards him as if he had intended to hit him. Had he? Tremulously, he lighted a cigarette. Nothing but bad co-ordination, he told himself, he had seen it a hundred times in the past two weeks – collisions with revolving doors, his inability even to hold a pen against a ruler, and so often the feeling he wasn't *here*, doing what he was doing. Grimly he reestablished what he was doing now, driving in Anne's car up to Alton to see the new house. The house was done. Anne and her mother had put the drapes up last week. It was Sunday, nearly noon. Anne had told him she had got a nice letter from his mother yesterday, and his mother had sent her three crocheted aprons and a lot of home-made preserves to start their kitchen shelves. Could he remember all that? All he seemed to remember was the sketch of the Bronx hospital in his pocket, that he hadn't told Anne about yet. He wished he could go away somewhere and do nothing but work, see no one, not even Anne. He stole a glance at her, at her coolly lifted face with the faint arch in the bridge of the nose. Her thin strong hands swung the wheel expertly into a curve and out. Suddenly he was sure she loved her car more than she loved him.

'If anybody's hungry, speak up now,' Anne said. 'This little store's the last place for miles.'

But no one was hungry.

'I expect to be asked for dinner at least once a year, Anne,' her father said. 'Maybe a brace of ducks or some quail. I hear there's some good hunting around here. Any good with a gun, Guy?'

Anne turned the car into the road that led to the house.

'Fair, sir,' Guy said finally, stammering twice. His heart was flogging him to run, he could still it only by running, he was sure.

'Guy!' Anne smiled at him. Stopping the car, she whispered to him, 'Have a nip when you get in the house. There's a bottle of brandy in the kitchen.' She touched his wrist, and Guy jerked his hand back, involuntarily.

He must, he thought, have a brandy or something. But he knew also that he would not take anything.

Mrs Faulkner walked beside him across the new lawn. 'It's simply beautiful, Guy. I hope you're proud of it.'

Guy nodded. It was finished, he didn't have to imagine it any more as he had in the brown bureau of the hotel room in Mexico. Anne had wanted Mexican tiles in the kitchen. So many things she wore from time to time were Mexican. A belt, a handbag, huarachas. The long embroidered skirt that showed now below her tweed coat was Mexican. He felt he must have chosen the Hotel Montecarlo so that dismal pink-and-brown room and Bruno's face in the brown bureau would haunt him the rest of his life.

It was only a month until their marriage now. Four more Friday nights, and Anne would sit in the big square green chair by the fireplace, her voice would call to him from the Mexican kitchen, they would work together in the studio upstairs. What right had he to imprison her with himself? He stood staring at their bedroom, vaguely aware that it seemed cluttered, because Anne had said she wanted their bedroom 'not modern'.

'Don't forget to thank Mother for the furniture, will you?' she whispered to him. 'Mother gave it to us, you know.'

The cherry bedroom set, of course. He remembered her telling him that morning at breakfast, remembered his bandaged hand, and Anne in the black dress she had worn to Helen's party. But when he should have said something about the furniture, he didn't, and then it seemed too late. They must know something is the matter, he felt. Everyone in the world must know. He was only somehow being reprieved, being saved for some weight to fall upon him and annihilate him.

'Thinking about a new job, Guy?' Mr Faulkner asked, offering him a cigarette.

Guy had not seen his figure there when he stepped on to the side porch. With a sense of justifying himself, he pulled the folded paper from his pocket and showed it to him, explained it to him. Mr Faulkner's bushy, grey and brown eyebrows came down thoughtfully. But he's not listening to me at all, Guy thought. He's bending closer only to see my guilt that is like a circle of darkness about me.

'Funny Anne didn't say anything to me about it,' Mr Faulkner said.

'I'm saving it.'

'Oh,' Mr Faulkner chuckled. 'A wedding present?'

Later, the Faulkners took the car and went back for sandwiches from the little store. Guy was tired of the house. He wanted Anne to walk with him up the rock hill.

'In a minute,' she said. 'Come here.' She stood in front of the tall stone fireplace. She put her hands on his shoulders and looked into his face, a little apprehensive, but still glowing with her pride in their new house. 'Those are getting deeper, you know,' she told him drawing her fingertips down the hollow in his cheek. 'I'm going to make you eat.'

'Maybe need a little sleep,' he murmured. He had told her that lately his work demanded long hours. He had told her, of all things, that he was doing some agency jobs, hack jobs, as Myers did, in order to earn some money.

'Darling, we're – we're well off. What on earth's troubling you?'

And she had asked him half a dozen times if it was the wedding, if he wanted not to marry her. If she asked him again, he might say yes, but he knew she would not ask it now, in front of their fireplace. 'Nothing's troubling me,' he said quickly.

'Then will you please not work so hard?' she begged him, then spontaneously, out of her own joy and anticipation, hugged him to her.

Automatically – as if it were nothing at all, he thought – he kissed her, because he knew she expected him to. She will notice, he thought, she always notices the slightest difference in a kiss, and it had been so long since he had kissed her. When she said nothing, it seemed to him only that the change in him was simply too enormous to mention.

30

Guy crossed the kitchen and turned at the back door. 'Awfully thoughtless of me to invite myself on the cook's night out.'

'What's thoughtless about it? You'll just fare as we do on Thursday nights, that's all.' Mrs Faulkner brought him a piece of the celery she was washing at the sink. 'But Hazel's going to be disappointed she wasn't here to make the shortcake herself. You'll have to do with Anne's tonight.'

Guy went out. The afternoon was still bright with sun, though the picket fence cast long oblique bars of shadow over the crocus and iris beds. He could just see Anne's tied-back hair and the pale green of her sweater beyond a crest in the rolling sea of lawn. Many times he had gathered mint and watercress there with Anne, from the stream that flowed out of the woods where he had fought Bruno. Bruno is past, he reminded himself, gone, vanished. Whatever method Gerard had used, he had made Bruno afraid to contact him.

He watched Mr Faulkner's neat black car enter the driveway and roll slowly into the open garage. What was he doing here, he asked himself suddenly, where he deceived everyone, even the coloured cook who liked to make shortcake for him because, once perhaps, he had praised her dessert? He moved into the shelter of the pear tree, where neither Anne nor her father would easily see him. If he should step out of Anne's life, he thought, what difference would it make to her? She had not given up all her old friends, hers and Teddy's set, the eligible young men, the handsome young men who played at polo and, rather harmlessly, at the night clubs before they entered their father's business and married one of the beautiful young girls who decorated their country clubs. Anne was different, of course, or she wouldn't have been attracted to him in the first place. She was not one of the beautiful young girls who worked at a career for a couple of years just to say they had done it, before they married one of the eligible young men. But wouldn't she have been just the same herself, without him? She had often told him he was her inspiration, he and his own ambition, but she had had the same talent, the same drive the day he met her, and wouldn't she have gone on? And wouldn't another man, like himself but worthy of her, have found her? He began to walk towards her.

'I'm almost done,' she called to him. 'Why didn't you come sooner?'

'I hurried,' he said awkwardly.

'You've been leaning against the house ten minutes.'

A sprig of watercress was floating away on the stream, and he sprang to rescue it. He felt like a possum, scooping it up. 'I think I'll take a job soon, Anne.'

She looked up, astoundedly. 'A job? You mean with a firm?'

It was a phrase to be used about other architects, 'a job with a firm'. He nodded, not looking at her. 'I feel like it. Something steady with a good salary.'

'Steady?' She laughed a little. 'With a year's work ahead of you at the hospital?'

'I won't need to be in the drafting room all the time.'

She stood up. 'Is it because of money? Because you're not taking the hospital money?'

He turned away from her and took a big step up the moist bank. 'Not exactly,' he said through his teeth. 'Maybe partly.' He had decided weeks ago to give his fee back to the Department of Hospitals after he paid his staff.

'But you said it wouldn't matter, Guy. We both agreed we – you could afford it.'

The world seemed silent all at once, listening. He watched her push a strand of her hair back and leave a smudge of wet earth on her forehead. 'It won't be for long. Maybe six months, maybe a lot less.'

'But why at all?'

'I feel like it!'

'Why do you feel like it? Why do you want to be a martyr, Guy?'

He said nothing.

The setting sun dropped free of the trees and poured on to them suddenly. Guy frowned deeper, shading his eye with the brow that bore the white scar from the woods – the scar that would always show, he thought. He kicked at a stone in the ground, without being able to dislodge it. Let her think the job was still part of his depression after the Palmyra. Let her think anything.

'Guy, I'm sorry,' she said.

Guy looked at her. 'Sorry?'

She came closer to him. 'Sorry. I think I know what it is.'

He still kept his hands in his pockets. 'What do you mean?'

She waited a long while. 'I thought all this, all your uneasiness after the Palmyra – even without your knowing it, I mean – goes back to Miriam.'

He twisted away abruptly. 'No. No, that's not it at all!' He said it so honestly, yet it sounded so like a lie! He thrust his fingers in his hair and shoved it back.

'Listen, Guy,' Anne said softly and clearly, 'maybe you don't want the wedding as much as you think you do. If you think that's part of it, say it, because I can take that a lot easier than this job idea. If you want to wait – still – or if you want to break it off entirely, I can bear it.'

Her mind was made up, and had been for a long while. He could feel it at the very centre of her calmness. He could give her up at this moment. The pain of that would cancel out the pain of guilt.

'Hey, there, Anne!' her father called from the back door. 'Coming in soon? I need that mint!'

'Minute, Dad!' she shouted back. 'What do you say, Guy?'

His tongue pressed the top of his mouth. He thought, she is the sun in my dark forest. But he couldn't say it. He could only say, 'I can't say –'

'Well – I want you now more than ever, because you need me now more than ever.' She pressed the mint and watercress into his hand. 'Do you want to take this to Dad? And have a drink with him. I have to change my clothes.' She turned and went off towards the house, not fast, but much too fast for Guy to try to follow her.

Guy drank several of the mint juleps. Anne's father made them the old-fashioned way, letting the sugar and bourbon and mint stand in a dozen glasses all day, getting colder and more frosted, and he liked to ask Guy if he had ever tasted better ones anywhere. Guy could feel the precise degree to which his tension lessened, but it was impossible for him to become drunk. He had tried a few times and made himself sick, without becoming drunk.

There was a moment after dusk, on the terrace with Anne, when he imagined he might not have known her any better than he had the first evening he visited her, when he suddenly felt a tremendous, joyous longing to make her love him. Then he remembered the house in Alton awaiting them after the wedding Sunday, and all the happiness he had known already with Anne rushed back to him. He wanted to protect her, to achieve some impossible goal, which would please her. It seeme   most positive, the happiest ambition he had ever known. There was a way out, then, if he could feel like this. It was only a part of himself he had to cope with, not his whole self, not Bruno, or his work. He had merely to crush the other part of himself, and live in the self he was now.

31

But there were too many points at which the other self could invade the self he wanted to preserve, and there were too many forms of invasion: certain words, sounds, lights, actions his hands or feet performed, and if he did nothing at all, heard and saw nothing, the shouting of some triumphant inner voice that shocked him and cowed him. The wedding so elaborately prepared for, so festive, so pure with white lace and linen, so happily awaited by everyone, seemed the worst act of treachery he could commit, and the closer it drew, the more frantically and vainly he debated cancelling it. Up to the last hour, he wanted simply to flee.

Robert Treacher, the friend of his Chicago days, telephoned his good wishes and asked if he might come to the wedding. Guy put him off with some feeble excuse. It was the Faulkners' affair, he felt, their friends, their family church, and the presence of a friend would put a hole in his armour. He had invited only Myers, who didn't matter – since the hospital commission, he no longer shared an office with him – Tim O'Flaherty, who couldn't come, and two or three architects from the Deems Academy, who knew his work better than they knew him. But half an hour after Treacher's call from Montreal, Guy telephoned back and asked Bob if he would be his best man.

Guy realized he had not even thought of Treacher in nearly a year, had not answered his last letter. He had not thought of Peter Wriggs, or Vic De Poyster and Gunther Hall. He had used to call on Vic and his wife in their Bleecker Street apartment, had once taken Anne there. Vic was a painter, and had sent him an invitation to his exhibit last winter, Guy remembered. He hadn't even answered. Vaguely now, he remembered that Tim had been in New York and had called him to have lunch during the period when Bruno had been haunting him by telephone, and that he had refused. The Theological Germanica, Guy recalled, said that the ancient Germans had judged an accused man innocent or guilty by the number of friends who came forth to vouch for his character. How many would vouch for him now? He had never given a great deal of time to his friends, because they were not the kind of people who expected it, but now he felt his friends were shunning him in turn, as if they sensed without seeing him that he had become unworthy of friendship.

The Sunday morning of the wedding, walking in slow circles around Bob Treacher in the vestry of the church, Guy clung to his memory of the hospital drawings as to a single last shred of hope, the single proof that he still existed. He had done an excellent job. Bob Treacher, his friend, had praised him. He had proven to himself that he could still create.

Bob had given up trying to make conversation with him. He sat with his arms folded, with a pleasant but rather absent expression on his chubby face. Bob thought he was simply nervous. Bob didn't know how he felt, Guy knew, because however much he thought it showed, it didn't. And that was the hell, that one's life could so easily be total hypocrisy. This was the essence, his wedding and his friend, Bob Treacher, who no longer knew him. And the little stone vestry with the high grilled window, like a prison cell. And the murmur of voices outside, like the self-righteous murmurings of a mob impatient to storm the prison and wreak justice.

'You didn't by any chance bring a bottle.'

Bob jumped up. 'I certainly did. It's weighing me down and I completely forgot it.' He set the bottle on the table and waited for Guy to take it. Bob was about forty-five, a man of modest but sanguine temperament, with an indelible stamp of contented bachelorhood and of complete absorption and authority in his profession. 'After you,' he prompted Guy. 'I want to drink a private toast to Anne. She's very beautiful, Guy.' He added softly, with a smile, 'As beautiful as a white bridge.'

Guy stood looking at the opened pint bottle. The hubbub out the window seemed to poke fun at him now, at him and Anne. The bottle on the table was part of it, the jaded, half-humorous concomitant of the traditional wedding. He had drunk whisky at his wedding with Miriam. Guy hurled the bottle into the corner. Its solid crack and spatter ended the hooting horns, the voices, the silly tremolo of the organ only for a second, and they began to seep back again.

'Sorry, Bob. I'm very sorry.'

Bob had not taken his eyes from him. 'I don't blame you a bit,' he smiled.

'But I blame myself!'

'Listen, old man –'

Guy could see that Bob did not know whether to laugh or be serious.

'Wait,' Treacher said. 'I'll get us some more.'

The door opened just as Bob reached for it, and Peter Wriggs' thin figure slipped in. Guy introduced him to Treacher. Peter had come all the way up from New Orleans to be at his wedding. He wouldn't have come to his wedding with Miriam, Guy thought. Peter had hated Miriam. There was grey at Peter's temples now, though his lean face still grinned like a sixteen-year-old's. Guy returned his quick embrace, feeling that he moved automatically now, on rails as he had the Friday night.

'It's time, Guy,' Bob said, opening the door.

Guy walked beside him. It was twelve steps to the altar. The accusing faces, Guy thought. They were silent with horror, as the Faulkners had been in the back of the car. When were they going to interfere and stop it all? How much longer was everyone going to wait?

'Guy!' somebody whispered.

Six, Guy counted, seven.

'Guy!' faint and direct, from among the faces, and Guy glanced left, followed the gaze of two women who looked over their shoulders, and saw Bruno's face and no other.

Guy looked straight again. Was it Bruno or a vision? The

face had been smiling eagerly, the grey eyes sharp as pins. Ten, eleven, he counted. *Twelve steps up, skip seven. ... You can remember it. it's got a syncopated rhythm.* His scalp tingled. Wasn't that a proof it was a vision and not Bruno? He prayed, Lord, don't let me faint. Better you fainted than married, the inner voice shouted back.

He was standing beside Anne, and Bruno was here with them, not an event, not a moment, but a condition, something that had always been and always would be. Bruno, himself, Anne. And the moving on the tracks. And the lifetime of moving on the tracks until death do us part, for that was the punishment. What more punishment was he looking for?

Faces bobbed and smiled all around him, and Guy felt himself aping them like an idiot. It was the Sail and Racquet Club. There was a buffet breakfast, and everyone had a champagne glass, even himself. And Bruno was not here. There was really no one here but wrinkled, harmless, perfumed old women in hats. Then Mrs Faulkner put an arm around his neck and kissed his cheek, and over her shoulder he saw Bruno thrusting himself through the door with the same smile, the same pinlike eyes that had already found him. Bruno came straight towards him and stopped, rocking on his feet.

'My best – best wishes, Guy. You didn't mind if I looked in, did you? It's a happy occasion!'

'Get out. Get out of here fast.'

Bruno's smile faded hesitantly. 'I just got back from Capri,' he said in the same hoarse voice. He wore a new dark royal-blue gabardine suit with lapels broad as an evening suit's lapels. 'How've you been, Guy?'

An aunt of Anne's babbled a perfumed message into Guy's ear, and he murmured something back. Turning, Guy started to move off.

'I just wanted to wish you well,' Bruno declared. 'There it is.'

'Get out,' Guy said. 'The door's behind you.' But he mustn't say any more, he thought. He would lose control.

'Call a truce, Guy. I want to meet the bride.'

Guy let himself be drawn away by two middle-aged women,

one on either arm. Though he did not see him, he knew that Bruno had retreated, with a hurt, impatient smile, to the buffet table.

'Bearing up, Guy?' Mr Faulkner took his half-empty glass from his hand. 'Let's get something better at the bar.'

Guy had half a glassful of Scotch. He talked without knowing what he was saying. He was sure he had said, Stop it all, tell everyone to go. But he hadn't, or Mr Faulkner wouldn't be roaring with laughter. Or would he?

Bruno watched from down the table as they cut the cake, watched Anne mostly, Guy noticed. Bruno's mouth was a thin, insanely smiling line, his eyes glinted like the diamond pin on his dark blue tie, and in his face Guy saw that same combination of wistfulness, awe, determination, and humour that he had seen the first moment he met him.

Bruno came up to Anne. 'I think I met you somewhere before. Are you any relation to Teddy Faulkner?'

Guy watched their hands meet. He had thought he wouldn't be able to bear it, but he was bearing it, without making a move.

'He's my cousin,' Anne said with her easy smile, the same smile she had given someone a moment before.

Bruno nodded. 'I played golf with him a couple of times.' Guy felt a hand on his shoulder.

'Got a minute, Guy? I'd –' It was Peter Wriggs.

'I haven't.' Guy started after Bruno and Anne. He closed his fingers around Anne's left hand.

Bruno sauntered on the other side of her, very erect, very much at ease, bearing his untouched piece of wedding cake on a plate in front of him. 'I'm an old friend of Guy's. An old acquaintance.' Bruno winked at him behind Anne's head.

'Really? Where'd you two know each other?'

'In school. Old school friends.' Bruno grinned. 'You know, you're the most beautiful bride I've seen in years, Mrs Haines. I'm certainly glad to have met you,' he said, not with finality but an emphatic conviction that made Anne smile again.

'Very glad to have met you,' she replied.

'I hope I'll be seeing you both. Where're you going to live?'

'In Connecticut,' Anne said.

'Nice state, Connecticut,' Bruno said with another wink at Guy, and left them with a graceful bow.

'He's a friend of Teddy's?' Guy asked Anne. 'Did Teddy invite him?'

'Don't look so worried, darling!' Anne laughed at him. 'We'll leave soon.'

'Where is Teddy?' But what was the use finding Teddy, what was the sense in making an issue of it, he asked himself at the same time.

'I saw him two minutes ago up at the head of the table,' Anne told him. 'There's Chris. I've got to say hello to him.'

Guy turned, looking for Bruno, and saw him helping himself to shirred eggs, talking gaily to two young men who smiled at him as if under the spell of a devil.

The ironic thing, Guy thought bitterly in the car a few moments later, the ironic thing was that Anne had never had time to know him. When they first met, he had been melancholic. Now his efforts, because he so rarely made efforts, had come to seem real. There had been, perhaps, those few days in Mexico City when he had been himself.

'Did the man in the blue suit go to Deems?' Anne asked.

They were driving out to Montauk Point. One of Anne's relatives had lent them her cottage for their three-day honeymoon. The honeymoon was only three days, because he had pledged to start work at Horton, Horton and Keese, Architects, in less than a month, and he would have to work on the double to get the detailed drawings for the hospital under way before he began. 'No, the Institute. For a while.' But why did he fall in with Bruno's lie?

'Interesting face he has,' Anne said, straightening her dress about her ankles before she put her feet on the jump seat.

'Interesting?' Guy asked.

'I don't mean attractive. Just intense.'

Guy set his teeth. Intense? Couldn't she see he was insane? Morbidly insane? Couldn't anyone see it?

32

The receptionist at Horton, Horton and Keese, Architects, handed him a message that Charles Bruno had called and left his number. It was the Great Neck number.

'Thank you,' Guy said, and went on across the lobby.

Suppose the firm kept records of telephone messages. They didn't, but suppose they did. Suppose Bruno dropped in one day. But Horton, Horton and Keese were so rotten themselves, Bruno wouldn't make much of a contrast. And wasn't that exactly why he was here, steeping himself in it, under some illusion that revulsion was atonement and that he would begin to feel better here?

Guy went into the big skylighted, leather-upholstered lounge, and lighted a cigarette. Mainwaring and Williams, two of the firm's first-string architects, sat in big leather armchairs, reading company reports. Guy felt their eyes on him as he stared out the window. They were always watching him, because he was supposed to be something special, a genius, the junior Horton had assured everybody, so what was he doing here? He might be broker than everybody thought, of course, and he had just got married, but quite apart from that and from the Bronx hospital, he was obviously nervous, had lost his grip. The best lost their grip sometimes, they would say to themselves, so why should they scruple about taking a comfortable job? Guy gazed down on to the dirty jumble of Manhattan roofs and streets that looked like a floor model of how a city should not be built. When he turned around, Mainwaring dropped his eyes like a schoolboy.

He spent the morning dawdling over a job that he had been on for several days. Take your time, they told him. All he had to do was give the client what he wanted and sign his name to it. Now, this job was a department store for an opulent little community in Westchester, and the client wanted something like an old mansion, in keeping with the town, only sort of modern, too, see? And he had asked especially for Guy Daniel Haines.

By adjusting his brain to the level of the trick, the cartoon, Guy could have tossed it off, but the fact it was really going to be a department store kept intruding certain functional demands. He erased and sharpened pencils all morning, and figured it would take him four or five more days, well into next week, until he got anything down as even a rough idea to show the client.

'Charley Bruno's coming tonight, too,' Anne called that evening from the kitchen.

'What?' Guy came around the partition.

'Isn't that his name? The young man we saw at the wedding.' Anne was cutting chives on a wooden board.

'You invited him?'

'He seems to have heard about it, so he called up and sort of invited himself,' Anne replied so casually that a wild suspicion she might be testing him sent a faint chill up his spine. 'Hazel – not milk, Angel, there's plenty of cream in the refrigerator.'

Guy watched Hazel set the cream container down by the bowl of crumbled gorgonzola cheese.

'Do you mind his coming, Guy?' Anne asked him.

'Not at all, but he's no friend of mine, you know.' He moved awkwardly towards the cabinets and got out the shoe-polish box. How could he stop him? There had to be a way, yet even as he racked his brain, he knew that the way would elude him.

'You do mind,' Anne said, with a smile.

'I think he's sort of a bounder, that's all.'

'It's bad luck to turn anyone away from a housewarming. Don't you know that?'

Bruno was pink-eyed when he arrived. Everyone else had made some comment about the new house, but Bruno stepped down into the brick-red and forest-green living-room as if he had been here a hundred times before. Or as if he lived here, Guy thought as he introduced Bruno around the room. Bruno focused a grinning, excited attention on Guy and Anne, hardly acknowledging the greetings of the others – two or three looked as if they knew him, Guy thought – except for that of a Mrs Chester Boltinoff of Muncey Park, Long Island, whose hand Bruno shook in both his as if he had found an ally. And Guy watched with horror as Mrs Boltinoff looked up at Bruno with a wide, friendly smile.

'How's every little thing?' Bruno asked Guy after he had got himself a drink.

'Fine. Very fine.' Guy was determined to be calm, even if he had to anaesthetize himself. He had already had two or three straight shots in the kitchen. But he found himself walking away, retreating, towards the perpendicular spiral stairway in the corner of the living-room. Just for a moment, he thought, just to get his bearings. He ran upstairs and into the bedroom, laid his cold hand against his forehead, and brought it slowly down his face.

'Pardon me, I'm still exploring,' said a voice from the other side of the room. 'It's such a terrific house, Guy, I had to retreat to the nineteenth century for a while.'

Helen Heyburn, Anne's friend from the Bermuda schooldays, was standing by the bureau. Where the little revolver was, Guy thought.

'Make yourself at home. I just came up for a handkerchief. How's your drink holding up?' Guy slid out the right top drawer where lay both the gun he didn't want and the handkerchief he didn't need.

'Well – better than I am.'

Helen was in another 'manic' period, Guy supposed. She was a commercial artist, a good one, Anne thought, but she worked only when her quarterly allowance gave out and she slipped into a depressive period. And she didn't like him, he felt, since the Sunday evening when he hadn't gone with Anne to her party. She was suspicious of him. What was she doing now in their bedroom, pretending to feel her drinks more than she did?

'Are you always so serious, Guy? You know what I said to Anne when she told me she was going to marry you?'

'You told her she was insane.'

'I said, "But he's so serious. Very attractive and maybe a genius, but he's so serious, how can you stand it?"' She lifted her squarish, pretty blonde face. 'You don't even defend yourself. I'll bet you're too serious to kiss me, aren't you?'

He forced himself towards her, and kissed her.

'That's no kiss.'

'But I deliberately wasn't being serious.'

He went out. She would tell Anne, he thought, she would tell her that she had found him in the bedroom looking pained at 10 o'clock. She might look into the drawer and find the gun, too. But he didn't believe any of it. Helen was silly, and he hadn't the slightest idea why Anne liked her, but she wasn't a trouble-maker. And she wasn't a snooper any more than Anne was. My God, hadn't he left the revolver there in the drawer next to Anne's all the time they had been living here? He was no more afraid Anne would investigate his half of the bureau than he was that she would open his mail.

Bruno and Anne were on the right-angled sofa by the fireplace when he came down. The glass Bruno wobbled casually on the sofa back had made dark green splotches on the cloth.

'He's telling me all about the new Capri, Guy,' Anne looked up at him. 'I've always wanted us to go there.'

'The thing to do is to take a whole house,' Bruno went on, ignoring Guy, 'take a castle, the bigger the better. My mother and I lived in a castle so big we never walked to the other end of it until one night I couldn't find the right door. There was a whole Italian family having dinner at the other end of the veranda, and the same night they all come over, about twelve of them, and ask if they can work for us for nothing, just if we let them stay there. So of course we did.'

'And you never learned any Italian?'

'No need to!' Bruno shrugged, his voice hoarse again, exactly as Guy always heard it in his mind.

Guy busied himself with a cigarette, feeling Bruno's avid, shyly flirtatious gaze at Anne boring into his back, deeper than the numbing tingle of the alcohol. No doubt Bruno had already complimented the dress she was wearing, his favourite dress of grey taffeta with the tiny blue pattern like peacocks' eyes. Bruno always noticed women's clothes.

'Guy and I,' Bruno's voice said distinctly behind him as if he had turned his head, 'Guy and I once talked about travelling.'

Guy jabbed his cigarette into an ashtray, put out every spark, then went towards the sofa. 'How about seeing our game room upstairs?' he said to Bruno.

'Sure.' Bruno got up. 'What kind of games you play?'

Guy pushed him into a small room lined with red, and closed the door behind them. 'How far are you going?'

'Guy! You're tight!'

'What's the idea of telling everyone we're old friends?'

'Didn't tell everyone. I told Anne.'

'What's the idea of telling her or anyone? What's the idea of coming here?'

'Quiet, Guy! Sh – sh – sh-h-h!' Bruno swung his drink casually in one hand.

'The police are still watching your friends, aren't they?'

'Not enough to worry me.'

'Get out. Get out now.' His voice shook with his effort to control it. And why should he control himself? The revolver with the one bullet was just across the hall.

Bruno looked at him boredly and sighed. The breath against his upper lip was like the breathing Guy heard in his room at night.

Guy staggered slightly, and the stagger enraged him.

'I think Anne's beautiful,' Bruno remarked pleasantly.

'If I see you talking with her again, I'll kill you.'

Bruno's smile went slack, then came back even broader. 'Is that a threat, Guy?'

'That's a promise.'

Half an hour later, Bruno passed out back of the sofa where he and Anne had been sitting. He looked extremely long on the floor, and his head tiny on the big hearthstone. Three men picked him up, then didn't know what to do with him.

'Take him – I suppose to the guest room,' Anne said.

'That's a good omen, Anne,' Helen laughed. 'Somebody's supposed to stay overnight at every housewarming, you know. First guest?'

Christopher Nelson came over to Guy. 'Where'd you dig him up? He used to pass out so often at the Great Neck Club, he can't get in any more.'

Guy had checked with Teddy after the wedding. Teddy hadn't invited Bruno, didn't know anything about him, except that he didn't like him.

Guy climbed the steps to the studio, and closed the door. On his work table lay the unfinished sketch of the cockeyed department store that conscience had made him take home to complete this week-end. The familiar lines, blurred now with drinking, almost made him sick. He took a blank sheet of paper and began to draw the building they wanted. He knew exactly what they wanted. He hoped he could finish before he became sick, and after he finished be as sick as a dog. But he wasn't sick when he finished. He only sat back in his chair, and finally went and opened a window.

33

The department store was accepted and highly praised, first by the Hortons and then by the client, Mr Howard Wyndham of New Rochelle, who came into the office early Monday afternoon to see the drawing. Guy rewarded himself by spending the rest of the day smoking in his office and thumbing through a morocco-bound copy of *Religio Medici* he had just bought at Brentano's to give Anne on her birthday. What assignment would they give him next, he wondered. He skipped through the book, remembering the passages he and Peter had used to like ... *the man without a navel yet lives in me* ... What atrocity would he be asked to do next? He had already fulfilled an assignment. Hadn't he done enough? Another thing like the department store would be unbearable. It wasn't self-pity, only *life*. He was still alive, if he wanted to blame himself for that. He got up from the drawing-table, went to his typewriter, and began his letter of resignation.

Anne insisted they go out and celebrate that evening. She was so glad, so overflowing with gladness, Guy felt his own spirits lifting a little, uncertainly, as a kite tries to lift itself from the ground on a still day. He watched her quick, slender fingers draw her hair tight back at the sides and close the bar pin over it in back.

'And, Guy, can't we make the cruise now?' she asked as they came down into the living-room.

Anne still had her heart set on the cruise down the coast in the *India*, the honeymoon trip they had put off. Guy had intended to give all his time to the drafting rooms that were doing his hospital drawings, but he couldn't refuse Anne now.

'How soon do you think we can leave? Five days? A week?'

'Maybe five days.'

'Oh, I just remember,' she sighed. 'I've got to stay till the twenty-third. There's a man coming in from California who's interested in all our cotton stuff.'

'And isn't there a fashion show the end of this month?'

'Oh, Lillian can take care of that.' She smiled. 'How wonderful of you to remember!'

He waited while she pulled the hood of her leopard coat up about her head, amused at the thought of her driving a hard bargain with the man from California next week. She wouldn't leave that to Lillian. Anne was the business half of the shop. He saw the long-stemmed orange flowers on the coffee table for the first time. 'Where'd these come from?' he asked.

'Charley Bruno. With a note apologizing for passing out Friday night.' She laughed. 'I think it's rather sweet.'

Guy stared at them. 'What kind are they?'

'African daisies.' She held the front door open for him, and they went on out to the car.

She was flattered by the flowers, Guy thought. But her opinion of Bruno, he also knew, had gone down since the night of the party. Guy thought again of how bound up they were now, he and Bruno, by the score of people at the party. The police might investigate him any day. They *would* investigate him, he warned himself. And why wasn't he more concerned? What state of mind was he in that he could no longer say even what state it it was? Resignation? Suicide? Or simply a torpor of stupidity?

During the next idle days he was compelled to spend at Horton, Horton and Keese to launch the drawings of the department store interior, he even asked himself whether he could be mentally deranged, if some subtle madness had not taken possession of him. He remembered the week or so after the Friday night, when his safety, his existence, had seemed to hang in a delicate balance that a failure of nerve might upset in a second. Now he felt none of that. Yet he still dreamt of Bruno invading his room. If he woke at dawn, he could still see himself standing in the room with the gun. He still felt that he must, and very soon, find some atonement for what he had done, some atonement for which no service or sacrifice he could yet envisage sufficed. He felt rather like two people, one of whom could create and feel in harmony with God when he created, and the other who could murder. 'Any kind of person can murder,' Bruno had said on the train. The man who had explained the cantilever principle to Bobbie Cartwright two years ago in Metcalf? No, nor the man who had designed the hospital, or even the department store, or debated half an hour with himself over the colour he would paint a metal chair on the back lawn last week, but the man who had glanced into the mirror just last night and had seen for one instant the murderer, like a secret brother.

And how could he sit at his desk thinking of murder, when in less than ten days he would be with Anne on a white ship? Why had he been given Anne, or the power to love her? And had he agreed so readily to the cruise only because he wanted to be free of Bruno for three weeks? Bruno, if he wanted to, could take Anne from him. He had always admitted that to himself, always tried to face it. But he realized that since he had seen them together, since the day of the wedding, the possibility had become a specific terror.

He got up and put on his hat to go out to lunch. He heard the switchboard buzz as he crossed the lobby. Then the girl called to him.

'Take it from here if you like, Mr Haines.'

Guy picked up the telephone, knowing it was Bruno, knowing he would agree to Bruno's seeing him some time today. Bruno asked him to have lunch, and Guy promised to meet him at Mario's Villa d'Este in ten minutes.

There were pink and white patterned drapes in the restaurant's window. Guy had a feeling that Bruno had laid a trap, that detectives would be behind the pink and white curtain, but not Bruno. And he didn't care, he felt, didn't care at all.

Bruno spotted him from the bar and slid off his stool with a grin. Guy walking around with his head in the air again, he thought, walking right by him. Bruno laid his hand on Guy's shoulder.

'Hi, Guy. I've got a table the end of this row.'

Bruno was wearing his old rust-brown suit. Guy thought of the first time he had followed the long legs, down the swaying train to the compartment, but the memory brought no remorse now. He felt, in fact, well-disposed towards Bruno, as he sometimes did by night, but never until now by day. He did not even resent Bruno's evident gratification that he had come to lunch with him.

Bruno ordered the cocktails and the lunch. He ordered broiled liver for himself, because of his new diet, he said, and eggs Benedict for Guy, because he knew Guy liked them. Guy was inspecting the table nearest them. He felt a puzzled suspicion of the four smartly dressed, fortyish women, all of whom were smiling with their eyes almost closed, all of whom lifted cocktail glasses. Beyond them, a well-fed, European-looking man hurled a smile across the table at his invisible companion. Waiters scurried zealously. Could it all be a show created and enacted by madmen, he and Bruno the main characters, and the maddest of all? For every movement he saw, every word he heard, seemed wrapped in the heroic gloom of predestination.

'Like 'em?' Bruno was saying. 'I got 'em at Clyde's this morning. Best selection in town. For summer anyway.'

Guy looked down at the four tie boxes Bruno had opened in their laps. There were knitted, silk and linen ties, and a pale lavender bow-tie of heavy linen. There was a shantung silk tie of aqua, like a dress of Anne's.

Bruno was disappointed. Guy didn't seem to like them. 'Too loud? They're summer ties.'

'They're nice,' Guy said.

'This is my favourite. I never saw anything like this.' Bruno held up the white knitted tie with the thin red stripe down the centre. 'Started to get one for myself, but I wanted you to have it. Just you, I mean. They're for you, Guy.'

'Thanks.' Guy felt an unpleasant twitch in his upper lip. He might have been Bruno's lover, he thought suddenly, to whom Bruno had brought a present, a peace offering.

'Here's to the trip,' Bruno said, lifting his glass.

Bruno had spoken to Anne this morning on the telephone, and Anne had mentioned the cruise, he said. Bruno kept telling him, wistfully, how wonderful he thought Anne was.

'She's so pure-looking. You certainly don't see a – a *kind*-looking girl like that very often. You must be awfully happy, Guy.' He hoped Guy might say something, a phrase or a word, that would somehow explain just why he was happy. But Guy didn't say anything, and Bruno felt rebuffed, felt the choking lump travelling from his chest up to his throat. What could Guy take offence at about that? Bruno wanted very much to put his hand over Guy's fist, that rested lightly on the edge of the table, just for a moment as a brother might, but he restrained himself. 'Did she like you right away or did you have to know her a long time? Guy?'

Guy heard him repeat the question. It seemed ages old. 'How can you ask me about time? It's a fact.' He glanced at Bruno's narrow, plumpening face, at the cowlick that still gave his forehead a tentative expression, but Bruno's eyes were vastly more confident than when he had seen them first, and less sensitive. Because he had his money now, Guy thought.

'Yeah. I know what you mean.' But Bruno didn't quite. Guy was happy with Anne even though the murder still haunted him. Guy would be happy with her even if he were broke. Bruno winced now for even having thought once that he might offer Guy money. He could hear the way Guy would say 'No,' with that look of drawing back in his eyes, of being miles away from him in a second. Bruno knew he would never have the things Guy had no matter how much money he had or what he did with it. Having his mother to himself was no guarantee of happiness, he had found out. Bruno made himself smile. 'You think Anne likes me all right?'

'All right.'

'What does she like to do outside of designing? Does she like to cook? Things like that?' Bruno watched Guy pick up his martini and drain it in three swallows. 'You know. I just like to know the kind of things you do together. Like take walks or work crossword puzzles.'

'We do things like that.'

'What do you do in the evenings?'

'Anne sometimes works in the evenings.' His mind slid easily, as it never had before with Bruno, to the upstairs studio where he and Anne often worked in the evenings, Anne talking to him from time to time, or holding something up for him to comment on, as if her work were effortless. When she dabbled her paint-brush fast in a glass of water, the sound was like laughter.

'I saw her picture in *Harper's Bazaar* a couple of months ago with some other designers. She's pretty good, isn't she?'

'Very good.'

'I –' Bruno laid his forearms one above the other on the table. 'I sure am glad you're happy with her.'

Of course he was. Guy felt his shoulders relax, and his breathing grow easier. Yet at this moment, it was hard to believe she was his. She was like a goddess who descended to pluck him from battles that would certainly have killed him, like the god-desses in mythology who saved the heroes, yet introduced an element at the end of the stories that had always struck him, when he read them as a child, as extraneous and unfair. In the nights when he could not sleep, when he stole out of the house and walked up the rock hill in pyjamas and overcoat, in the un-challenging, indifferent summer nights, he did not permit him-self to think of Anne. '*Dea ex machina*,' Guy murmured.

'What?'

Why was he sitting here with Bruno, eating at the same table with him? He wanted to fight Bruno and he wanted to weep. But all at once he felt his curses dissolve in a flood of pity. Bruno did not know how to love, and that was all he needed. Bruno was too lost, too blind to love or to inspire love. It seemed all at once tragic.

'You've never even been in love, Bruno?' Guy watched a restive, unfamiliar expression come into Bruno's eyes.

Bruno signalled for another drink. 'No, not really in love, I guess.' He moistened his lips. Not only hadn't he ever fallen in love, but he didn't care too much about sleeping with women. He had never been able to stop thinking it was a silly business, that he was standing off somewhere and watching himself. Once, one terrible time, he had started giggling. Bruno squirmed. That was the most painful difference he felt separating him and Guy, that Guy could forget himself in women, had practically killed himself for Miriam.

Guy looked at Bruno, and Bruno lowered his eyes. Bruno was waiting, as if for him to tell him how to fall in love. 'Do you know the greatest wisdom in the world, Bruno?'

'I know a lot of wisdoms,' Bruno smirked. 'Which one do you mean?'

'That everything has its opposite close beside it.'

'Opposites attract?'

'That's too simple. I mean – you give me ties. But it also occurred to me you might have the police waiting for me here.'

'F' Christ's sake, Guy, you're my *friend* !' Bruno said quickly, suddenly frantic. 'I like you !'

I like you, I don't hate you, Guy thought. But Bruno wouldn't say that, because he did hate him. Just as he would never say to Bruno, I like you, but instead, I hate you, because he did like him. Guy set his jaw, and rubbed his fingers back and forth across his forehead. He could foresee a balance of positive and negative will that would paralyse every action before he began it. Such as that, for instance, that kept him sitting here. He jumped up, and the new drinks splashed on the cloth.

Bruno stared at him in terrified surprise. 'Guy, what's the matter?' Bruno followed him. 'Guy, wait ! You don't think I'd do a thing like that, do you? I wouldn't in a million years !'

'Don't touch me !'

'*Guy!*' Bruno was almost crying. Why did people do these things to him? *Why?* He shouted on the sidewalk : 'Not in a million years ! Not for a million dollars ! Trust me, Guy !'

Guy pushed his hand into Bruno's chest and closed the taxi

door. Bruno would not in a million years betray him, he knew. But if everything were as ambiguous as he believed, how could he really be sure?

34

'What's your connection with Mrs Guy Haines?'

Bruno had expected it. Gerard had his latest charge accounts, and this was the flowers he had sent Anne. 'Friend. Friend of her husband.'

'Oh. Friend?'

'Acquaintance.' Bruno shrugged, knowing Gerard would think he was trying to brag because Guy was famous.

'Known him long?'

'Not long.' From his horizontal slump in his easy chair, Bruno reached for his lighter.

'How'd you happen to send flowers?'

'Feeling good, I guess. I was going to a party there that night.'

'Do you know him that well?'

Bruno shrugged again. 'Ordinary party. He was one of the architects we thought of when we were talking about building a house.' That had just popped out, and it was rather good, Bruno thought.

'Matt Levine. Let's get back to him.'

Bruno sighed. Skipping Guy, maybe because he was out of town, maybe just skipping him. Now Matt Levine – they didn't come any shadier, and without realizing it might be useful, he had seen a lot of Matt before the murder. 'What about him?'

'How is it you saw him the twenty-fourth, twenty-eighth, and thirtieth of April, the second, fifth, sixth, seventh of March, and two days before the murder?'

'Did I?' he smiled. Gerard had had only three dates the last time. Matt didn't like him either. Matt had probably said the worst. 'He was interested in buying my car.'

'And you were interested in selling it? Why, because you thought you'd get a new one soon?'

'Wanted to sell it to get a little car,' Bruno said obliviously. 'The one in the garage now. Crosley.'

Gerard smiled. 'How long have you known Mark Lev?'

'Since he was Mark Levitski,' Bruno retorted. 'Go back a little farther and you'll find he killed his own father in Russia.' Bruno glared at Gerard. The 'own' sounded funny, he shouldn't have said it, but Gerard trying to be smart with the aliases!

'Matt doesn't care for you either. What's the matter, couldn't you two come to terms?'

'About the car?'

'Charles,' Gerard said patiently.

'I'm not saying anything.' Bruno looked at his bitten nails, and thought again how well Matt matched Herbert's description of the murderer.

'You haven't seen Ernie Schroeder much lately.'

Bruno opened his mouth boredly to answer.

35

Barefoot, in white duck trousers, Guy sat cross-legged on the *India*'s forward deck. Long Island had just come in sight but he did not want to look at it yet. The gently rolling movement of the ship rocked him pleasantly and familiarly, like something he had always known. The day he had last seen Bruno, in the restaurant, seemed a day of madness. Surely he had been going insane. Surely Anne must have seen it.

He flexed his arm and pinched up the thin brown skin that covered its muscles. He was brown as Eagon, the half-Portuguese ship's boy they had hired from the Long Island dock at the start of the cruise. Only the little scar in his right eyebrow remained white.

The three weeks at sea had given him a peace and resignation he had never known before, and that a month ago he would have declared foreign to him. He had come to feel that his atonement, whatever it might be, was a part of his destiny, and like the rest of his destiny would find him without his seeking. He had always trusted his sense of destiny. As a boy with Peter, he had known that he would not merely dream, as he had somehow known, too, that Peter would do nothing but dream, that he would create famous buildings, that his name would take its proper place in architecture, and finally – it had always seemed to him the crowning achievement – that he would build a bridge. It would be a white bridge with a span like an angel's wing, he had thought as a boy, like the curving white bridge of Robert Maillart in his architecture books. It was a kind of arrogance, perhaps, to believe so in one's destiny. But, on the other hand, who could be more genuinely humble than one who felt compelled to obey the laws of his own fate? The murder that had seemed an outrageous departure, a sin against himself, he believed now might have been a part of his destiny, too. It was impossible to think otherwise. And if it were so, he would be given a way to make his atonement, and given the strength to make it. And if death by law overtook him first, he would be given the strength to meet that also, and strength besides sufficient for Anne to meet it. In a strange way, he felt humbler than the smallest minnows of the sea, and stronger than the greatest mountain on earth. But he was not arrogant. His arrogance had been a defence, reaching its height at the time of the break with Miriam. And hadn't he known even then, obsessed by her, wretchedly poor, that he would find another woman whom he could love and who would love him always? And what better proof did he need that all this was so than that he and Anne had never been closer, their lives never more like one harmonious life, than during these three weeks at sea?

He turned himself with a movement of his feet, so he could see her as she leaned against the mainmast. There was a faint smile on her lips as she gazed down at him, a half-repressed, prideful smile like that of a mother, Guy thought, who had brought her child safely through an illness, and smiling back at her, Guy marvelled that he could put such trust in her infallibility and rightness and that she could still be merely a human being. Most of all, he marvelled that she could be his. Then he looked down at his locked hands and thought of the work he would begin tomorrow on the hospital, of all the work to come, and the events of his destiny that lay ahead.

Bruno telephoned a few evenings later. He was in the neighbourhood, he said, and wanted to come by. He sounded very sober, and a little dejected.

Guy told him no. He told him calmly and firmly that neither he nor Anne wanted to see him again, but even as he spoke, he felt the sands of his patience running out fast, and the sanity of the past weeks crumbling under the madness of their conversing at all.

Bruno knew that Gerard had not spoken to Guy yet. He did not think Gerard would question Guy more than a few minutes. But Guy sounded so cold, Bruno could not bring himself to tell him now that Gerard had got his name, that he might be interviewed, or that he intended to see Guy strictly secretly from now on – no more parties or even lunches – if Guy would only let him.

'Okay,' Bruno said mutedly, and hung up.

Then the telephone rang again. Frowning, Guy put out the cigarette he had just lighted relievedly, and answered it.

'Hello. This is Arthur Gerard of the Confidential Detective Bureau . . .' Gerard asked if he could come over.

Guy turned around, glacing warily over the living-room, trying to reason away a feeling that Gerard had just heard his and Bruno's conversation over tapped wires, that Gerard had just captured Bruno. He went upstairs to tell Anne.

'A private detective?' Anne asked, surprised. 'What's it about?'

Guy hesitated an instant. There were so many, many places where he might hesitate too long! Damn Bruno! Damn him for dogging him! 'I don't know.'

Gerard arrived promptly. He fairly bowed over Anne's hand, and after apologizing for intruding on their evening, made polite conversation about the house and the strip of garden in front. Guy stared at him in some astonishment. Gerard looked dull, tired, and vaguely untidy. Perhaps Bruno wasn't entirely wrong about him. Even his absent air, heightened by his slow speech, did not suggest the absent-mindedness of a brilliant detective. Then as Gerard settled himself with a cigar and a highball, Guy caught the shrewdness in the light hazel eyes and the energy in the chunky hands. Guy felt uneasy then. Gerard looked unpredictable.

'You're a friend of Charles Bruno, Mr Haines?'

'Yes. I know him.'

'His father was murdered last March as you probably know, and the murderer has not been found.'

'I didn't know that !' Anne said.

Gerard's eyes moved slowly from her back to Guy.

'I didn't know either,' said Guy.

'You don't know him that well?'

'I know him very slightly.'

'When and where did you meet?'

'At –' Guy glanced at Anne – 'the Parker Art Institute, I think around last December.' Guy felt he had walked into a trap. He had repeated Bruno's flippant reply at the wedding, simply because Anne had heard Bruno say it, and Anne had probably forgotten. Gerard regarded him, Guy thought, as if he didn't believe a word of it. Why hadn't Bruno warned him about Gerard? Why hadn't they *settled* on the story Bruno had once proposed about their having met at the rail of a certain midtown bar?

'And when did you see him again?' Gerard asked finally.

'Well – not until my wedding in June.' He felt himself assuming the puzzled expression of a man who does not yet know his inquisitor's object. Fortunately, he thought, fortunately, he had already assured Anne that Bruno's assertion they were old friends was only Bruno's style of humour. 'We didn't invite him,' Guy added.

'He just came?' Gerard looked as if he understood. 'But you did invite him to the party you gave in July?' He glanced at Anne also.

'He called up,' Anne told him, 'and asked if he could come, so – I said yes.'

Gerard then asked if Bruno knew about the party through any friends of his who were coming, and Guy said possibly, and gave the name of the blonde woman who had smiled so horrifically at Bruno that evening. Guy had no other names to give. He had never seen Bruno with anyone.

Gerard leaned back. 'Do you like him?' he smiled.

'Well enough,' Anne replied finally, politely.

'All right,' Guy said, because Gerard was waiting. 'He seems a bit pushing.' The right side of his face was in shadow. Guy wondered if Gerard were scanning his face now for scars.

'A hero-worshipper. Power-worshipper, in a sense.' Gerard smiled, but the smile no longer looked genuine, or perhaps it never had. 'Sorry to bother you with these questions, Mr Haines.'

Five minutes later, he was gone.

'What does it mean?' Anne asked. 'Does he suspect Charles Bruno?'

Guy bolted the door, then came back. 'He probably suspects one of his acquaintances. He might think Charles knows something, because he hated his father so. Or so Charles told me.'

'Do you think Charles might know?'

'There's no telling. Is there?' Guy took a cigarette.

'Good Lord.' Anne stood looking at the corner of the sofa, as if she still saw Bruno where he had sat the night of the party. She whispered, 'Amazing what goes on in people's lives!'

36

'Listen,' Guy said tensely into the receiver. 'Listen, Bruno!' Bruno was drunker than Guy had ever heard him, but he was determined to penetrate to the muddled brain. Then he thought suddenly that Gerard might be with him, and his voice grew even softer, cowardly with caution. He found out Bruno was in a telephone booth, alone. 'Did you tell Gerard we met at the Art Institute?'

Bruno said he had. It came through the drunken mumblings that he had. Bruno wanted to come over. Guy couldn't make it register that Gerard had already come to question him. Guy banged the telephone down, and tore open his collar. Bruno calling him now! Gerard had externalized his danger. Guy felt it was more imperative to break completely with Bruno even than to arrange a story with him that would tally. What annoyed him most was that he couldn't tell from Bruno's drivelling what had happened to him, or even what kind of mood he was in.

Guy was upstairs in the studio with Anne when the door chime rang.

He opened the door only slightly, but Bruno bumped it wide, stumbled across the living-room, and collapsed on the sofa. Guy stopped short in front of him, speechless first with anger, then disgust. Bruno's fat, flushed neck bulged over his collar. He seemed more bloated than drunk, as if an oedema of death had inflated his entire body, filling even the deep eye-sockets so the red-grey eyes were thrust unnaturally forward. Bruno stared up at him. Guy went to the telephone to call a taxi.

'Guy, who it is?' Anne whispered down the stairway.

'Charles Bruno. He's drunk.'

'Not drunk!' Bruno protested suddenly.

Anne came halfway down the stairs, and saw him. 'Shouldn't we just put him upstairs?'

'I don't want him here.' Guy was looking in the telephone book, trying to find a taxi company's number.

'Yess-s!' Bruno hissed, like a deflating tyre.

Guy turned. Bruno was staring at him out of one eye, the eye the only living point in the sprawled, corpse-like body. He was muttering something, rhythmically.

'What's he saying?' Anne stood closer to Guy.

Guy went to Bruno and caught him by the shirt-front. The muttered, imbecile chant infuriated him. Bruno drooled on to his hand as he tried to pull him upright. 'Get up and get out!' Then he heard it:

'I'll *tell* her, I'll *tell* her – I'll *tell* her, I'll *tell* her,' Bruno chanted, and the wild red eye stared up. 'Don't send me away, I'll tell her – I'll –'

Guy released him in abhorrence.

'What's the matter, Guy? What's he saying?'

'I'll put him upstairs,' Guy said.

Guy tried with all his strength to get Bruno over his shoulder, but the flaccid, dead weight defeated him. Finally, Guy stretched him out across the sofa. He went to the front window. There was no car outside. Bruno might have dropped out of the sky. Bruno slept noiselessly, and Guy sat up watching him, smoking.

Bruno awakened about 3 in the morning, and had a couple of drinks to steady himself. After a few moments, except for the bloatedness, he looked almost normal. He was very happy at finding himself in Guy's house, and had no recollection of arriving. 'I had another round with Gerard,' he smiled. 'Three days. Been seeing the papers?'

'No.'

'You're a fine one, don't even look at the papers!' Bruno said softly. 'Gerard's hot on a bum scent. This crook friend of mine, Matt Levine. He doesn't have an alibi for that night. Herbert thinks it could be him. I been talking with all three of them for three days. Matt might get it.'

'Might die for it?'

Bruno hesitated, still smiling. 'Not die, just take the rap. He's got two or three killings on him now. The cops're glad to have him.' Bruno shuddered, and drank the rest in his glass.

Guy wanted to pick up the big ashtray in front of him and smash Bruno's bloated head, burn out the tension he felt would grow and grow until he did kill Bruno, or himself. He caught Bruno's shoulders hard in both hands. 'Will you get out? I swear this is the last time!'

'No,' Bruno said quietly, without any movement of resistance, and Guy saw the old indifference to pain, to death, that he had seen when he had fought him in the woods.

Guy put his hands over his own face, and felt its contortion against his palms. 'If this Matt gets blamed,' he whispered, 'I'll tell them the whole story.'

'Oh, he won't. They won't have enough. It's a joke, son!' Bruno grinned. 'Matt's the right character with the wrong evidence. You'd be the wrong character with the right evidence. You're an important guy, f' Christ's sake!' He pulled something out of his pocket and handed it to Guy. 'I found this last week. Very nice, Guy.'

Guy looked at the photograph of 'The Pittsburgh Store',

funereally backgrounded by black. It was a booklet from the Modern Museum. He read: 'Guy Daniel Haines, hardly thirty, follows the Wright tradition. He has achieved a distinctive, uncompromising style noted for a rigorous simplicity without starkness, for the grace he calls "singingness" ...' Guy closed it nervously, disgusted by the last word that was an invention of the Museum's.

Bruno repocketed the booklet. 'You're one of the tops. If you kept your nerve up, they could turn you inside out and never suspect.'

Guy looked down at him. 'That's still no reason for you to see me. Why do you do it?' But he knew. Because his life with Anne fascinated Bruno. Because he himself derived something from seeing Bruno, some torture that perversely eased.

Bruno watched him as if he knew everything that passed through his mind. 'I like you, Guy, but remember – they've got a lot more against you than against me. I could wriggle out if you turned me in, but you couldn't. There's the fact Herbert might remember you. And Anne might remember you were acting funny around that time. And the scratches and the scar. And all the little clues they'd shove in front of you, like the revolver, and glove pieces –' Bruno recited them slowly and fondly, like old memories. 'With me against you you'd crack up. I bet.'

37

Guy knew as soon as Anne called to him that she had seen the dent. He had meant to get it fixed, and had forgotten. He said first that he didn't know how it got there, then that he did. He had taken the boat out last week, he said, and it had bumped a buoy.

'Don't be terribly sorry,' she mocked him, 'it isn't worth it.' She took his hand as she stood up. 'Egon said you had the boat out one afternoon. Is that why you didn't say anything about it?'

'I suppose.'

'Did you take it out by yourself?' Anne smiled a little, because he wasn't a good-enough sailor to take the boat out by himself.

Bruno had called up and insisted they go out for a sail. Gerard had come to a new dead-end with Matt Levine, dead-ends everywhere, and Bruno had insisted that they celebrate. 'I took it out with Charles Bruno one afternoon,' he said. And he had brought the revolver with him that day, too.

'It's all right, Guy. Only why'd you see him again? I thought you disliked him so.'

'A whim,' he murmured. 'It was the two days I was doing that work at home.' It wasn't all right, Guy knew. Anne kept the *India*'s brass and white-painted wood gleaming and spotless, like something of chryselephantine. And Bruno! She mistrusted Bruno now.

'Guy he's not the man we saw that night in front of your apartment, is he? The one who spoke to us in the snow?'

'Yes. He's the same one.' Guy's fingers, supporting the weight of the revolver in his pocket, tightened helplessly.

'What's his interest in you?' Anne followed him casually down the deck. 'He isn't interested in architecture particularly. I talked with him the night of the party.'

'He's got no interest in me. Just doesn't know what to do with himself.' When he got rid of the revolver, he thought, he could talk.

'You met him at school?'

'Yes. He was wandering around a corridor.' How easy it was to lie when one *had* to lie! But it was wrapping tendrils around his feet, his body, his brain. He would say the wrong thing one day. He was doomed to lose Anne. Perhaps he had already lost her, at this moment when he lighted a cigarette and she stood leaning against the mainmast, watching him. The revolver seemed to weight him to the spot, and determinedly he turned and walked towards the prow. Behind him, he heard Anne's step on to the deck, and her soft tread in her tennis shoes, going back towards the cockpit.

It was a sullen day, promising rain. The *India* rocked slowly on the choppy surface, and seemed no farther from the grey shore than it had been an hour ago. Guy leaned on the bowsprit and looked down at his white-clad legs, the blue gilt-buttoned jacket he had taken from the *India*'s locker, that perhaps had belonged to Anne's father. He might have been a sailor instead of an architect, he thought. He had been wild to go to sea at fourteen. What had stopped him? How different his life might have been without – what? Without Miriam, of course. He straightened impatiently and pulled the revolver from the pocket of the jacket.

He held the gun in both hands over the water, his elbow on the bowsprit. How intelligent a jewel, he thought, and how innocent it looked now. Himself – He let it drop. The gun turned once head-over, in perfect balance, with its familiar look of willingness, and disappeared.

'What was that?'

Guy turned and saw her standing on the deck near the cabin. He measured the ten or twelve feet between them. He could think of nothing, absolutely nothing to say to her.

38

Bruno hesitated about the drink. The bathroom walls had that look of breaking up in little pieces, as if the walls might not really have been there, or he might not really have been here.

'Ma!' But the frightened bleat shamed him, and he drank his drink.

He tiptoed into his mother's room and awakened her with a press of the button by her bed, which signalled to Herbert in the kitchen that she was ready for her breakfast.

'Oh-h,' she yawned, then smiled. 'And how are you?' She patted his arm, slid up from the covers, and went into the bathroom to wash.

Bruno sat quietly on her bed until she came out and got back under the cover again.

'We're supposed to see that trip man this afternoon. What's his name, Saunders? You'd better feel like going in with me.'

Bruno nodded. It was about their trip to Europe, that they

might make into a round-the-world trip. It didn't have any charm this morning. He might like to go around the world with Guy. Bruno stood up, wondering whether to go get another drink.

'How're you feeling?'

His mother always asked him at the wrong times. 'Okay,' he said, sitting down again.

There was a knock on the door, and Herbert came in. 'Good morning, madam. Good morning, sir,' Herbert said without looking at either of them.

With his chin in his hand, Bruno frowned down at Herbert's silent, polished, turned-out shoes. Herbert's insolence lately was intolerable! Gerard had made him think he was the key to the whole case, if they just produced the right man. Everyone said how brave he was to have chased the murderer. And his father had left him twenty thousand in his will. Herbert *might* take a vacation!

'Does madam know if there'll be six or seven for dinner?'

As Herbert spoke, Bruno looked up at his pink, pointed chin and thought, Guy whammed him there and knocked him right out.

'Oh, dear, I haven't called yet, Herbert, but I think seven.'

'Very good, madam.'

Rutledge Overbeck II, Bruno thought. He had known his mother would end up having him, though she pretended to be doubtful because he would make an odd number. Rutledge Overbeck was madly in love with his mother, or pretending to be. Bruno wanted to tell his mother Herbert hadn't sent his clothes to be pressed in six weeks, but he felt too sickish to begin.

'You know, I'm dying to see Australia,' she said through a bite of toast. She had propped a map up against her coffee pot.

A tingling, naked sensation spread over his buttocks. He stood up. 'Ma, I don't feel so hot.'

She frowned at him concernedly, which frightened him more, because he realized there was nothing in the world she could do to help him. 'What's the matter, darling? What do you want?'

He hurried from the room, feeling he might have to be sick. The bathroom went black. He staggered out, and let the still corked Scotch bottle topple on to his bed.

'What, Charley? What is it?'

'I wanna lie down.' He flopped down, but that wasn't it. He motioned his mother away so he could get up, but when he sat up he wanted to lie down again, so he stood up. 'Feel like I'm dying!'

'Lie down, darling. How about some – some hot tea?'

Bruno tore off his smoking jacket, then his pyjama top. He was suffocating. He had to pant to breathe. He *did* feel like he was dying!

She hurried to him with a wet towel. 'What is it, your stomach?'

'Everything.' He kicked off his slippers. He went to the window to open it, but it was already open. He turned, sweating. 'Ma, maybe I'm dying. You think I'm dying?'

'I'll get you a drink!'

'No, get the doctor!' he shrieked. 'Get me a drink, too!' Feebly he pulled his pyjama string and let the pants drop. What was it? Not just the shakes. He was too weak to shake. Even his hands were weak and tingly. He held up his hands. The fingers were curved inward. He couldn't open them. 'Ma, somp'n's the matter with my hands! Look, Ma, what is it, what is it?'

'Drink this!'

He heard the bottle chatter on the rim of the glass. He couldn't wait for it. He trotted into the hall, stooped with terror, staring at his limp, curling hands. It was the two middle fingers on each hand. They were curving in, almost touching the palm.

'Darling, put your robe on!' she whispered.

'*Get the doctor!*' A robe! She talked about a robe! What did it matter if he was stark naked? 'Ma, but don't let 'em take me away!' He plucked at her as she stood at the telephone. 'Lock all the doors! You know what they do?' He spoke fast and confidentially, because the numbness was working up and he knew what was the matter now. He was a case! He was going to be like this all his life! 'Know what they do, Ma, they put you in a strait-jacket without a drop and it'll kill me!'

'Dr Packer? This is Mrs Bruno. Could you recommend a doctor in the neighbourhood?'

Bruno screamed. How would a doctor get out here in the

Connecticut sticks? 'Massom –' He gasped. He couldn't talk, couldn't move his tongue. It had gone into his vocal chords! 'Aaaaagh!' He wriggled from under the smoking jacket his mother was trying to throw over him. Let Herbert stand there gaping at him if he wanted to!

'Charles!'

He gestured towards his mouth with his crazy hands. He trotted to the closet mirror. His face was white, flat around the mouth as if someone had hit him with a board, his lips drawn horribly back from his teeth. And his hands! He wouldn't be able to hold a glass any more, or light a cigarette. He wouldn't be able to drive a car. He wouldn't even be able to go to the john by himself!

'*Drink* this!'

Yes, liquor, liquor. He tried to catch it all in his stiff lips. It burnt his face and ran down his chest. He motioned for more. He tried to remind her to lock the doors. Oh, Christ, if it went away, he would be grateful all his life! He let Herbert and his mother push him on to the bed.

'Tehmeh!' he choked. He twisted his mother's dressing-gown and nearly pulled her down on top of him. But at least he could hold to something now. 'Dome tehmeh way!' he said with his breath, and she assured him she wouldn't. She told him she would lock all the doors.

Gerard, he thought, Gerard was still working against him, and he would keep on and on and on. Not only Gerard but a whole army of people, checking and snooping and visiting people, hammering typewriters, running out and running back with more pieces, pieces from Santa Fe now, and one day Gerard might put them together right. One day Gerard might come in and find him like this morning, and ask him and he would tell everything. He had killed someone. They killed *you* for killing someone. Maybe he couldn't cope. He stared up at the light fixture in the centre of the ceiling. It reminded him of the round chromium drainstop in the basin at his grandmother's house in Los Angeles. Why did he think of that?

The cruel jab of the hypodermic needle shocked him to sharper consciousness.

The young, jumpy-looking doctor was talking to his mother in a corner of the darkened room. But he felt b They wouldn't take him away now. It was okay now. He had just been panicky. Cautiously, just under the top of the sheet, he watched his fingers flex. 'Guy,' he whispered. His tongue was still thick, but he could talk. Then he saw the doctor go out.

'Ma, I don't want to go to Europe!' he said in a monotone as his mother came over.

'All right, darling, we won't go.' She sat down gently on the side of the bed, and he felt immediately better.

'The doctor didn't say I couldn't go, did he?' As if he wouldn't go if he wanted to! What was he afraid of? Not even of another attack like this! He touched the puffed shoulder of his mother's dressing-gown, but he thought of Rutledge Overbeck at dinner tonight, and let his hand drop. He was sure his mother was having an affair with him. She went to see him too much at his studio in Silver Springs, and she stayed too long. He didn't want to admit it, but why shouldn't he when it was under his nose? It was the first affair, and his father was dead so why shouldn't she, but why did she have to pick such a jerk? Her eyes looked darker now, in the shaded room. She hadn't improved since the days after his father's death. She was going to be like this, Bruno realized now, stay like this, never be young again the way he liked her. 'Don't look so sad, Mom.'

'Darling, will you promise me you'll cut down? The doctor said this is the beginning of the end. This morning was a warning, don't you see? Nature's warning.' She moistened her lips, and the sudden softness of the rouged, lined underlip so close to him was more than Bruno could bear.

He closed his eyes tight shut. If he promised, he would be lying. 'Hell, I didn't get the D.T.s, did I? I never had 'em.'

'But this is worse. I talked with the doctor. It's destroying your nerve tissues, he said, and it can kill you. Doesn't that mean anything to you?'

'Yes, Ma.'

'Promise me?' She watched his eyelids flutter shut again, and heard him sigh. The tragedy was not this morning, she thought, but years ago when he had taken his first drink by himself. The tragedy was not even the first drink, because the first drink was not the first resort but the last. There'd had to be first the failure of everything else – of her and Sam, of his friends, of his hope, of his interests, really. And hard as she tried, she could never discover why or where it might have begun, because Charley had always been given everything, and both she and Sam had done their best to encourage him in everything and anything he had ever shown interest in. If she could only discover the place in the past where it might have begun – She got up, needing a drink herself.

Bruno opened his eyes tentatively. He felt deliciously heavy with sleep. He saw himself halfway across the room, as if he watched himself on a screen. He was in his red-brown suit. It was the island in Metcalf. He saw his younger, slimmer body arc towards Miriam and fling her to the earth, those few short moments separate from time before and time after. He felt he had made special movements, thought special brilliant thoughts in those moments, and that such an interval would never come again. Like Guy had talked about himself, the other day on the boat, when he built the Palmyra. Bruno was glad those special moments for both of them had come so near the same time. Sometimes he thought he could die without regrets, because what else could he ever do that would measure up to the night in Metcalf? What else wouldn't be an anticlimax? Sometimes, like now, he felt his energy might be winding down, and something, maybe his curiosity, dying down. But he didn't mind, because he felt so wise now somehow, and really so content. Only yesterday he wanted to go around the world. And why? To say he had been? To say to whom? Last month he had written to William Beebe, volunteering to go down in the new super-bathysphere that they were testing first without a man inside. Why? Everything was silly compared to the night in Metcalf. Every person he knew was silly compared to Guy. Silliest of all to think he'd wanted to see a lot of European women! Maybe the Captain's whores had soured him, so what? Lots of people thought sex was overrated. No love lasts forever, the psychologists said. But he really shouldn't say that about Guy and

Anne. He had a feeling theirs might last, but just why he didn't know. It wasn't only that Guy was so wrapped up in her he was blind to all the rest. It wasn't just that Guy had enough money now. It was something invisible that he hadn't even thought of yet. Sometimes he felt he was right on the brink of thinking of it. No, he didn't want the answer for himself. Purely in the spirit of scientific inquiry.

He turned on his side, smiling, clicking and unclicking the top of his gold Dunhill lighter. That trip man wouldn't see them today or any other day. Home was a hell of a lot more comfortable than Europe. And Guy was here.

39

Gerard was chasing him through a forest, waving all the clues at him – the glove scraps, the shred of overcoat, even the revolver, because Gerard already had Guy. Guy was tied up back in the forest, and his right hand was bleeding fast. If he couldn't circle around and get to him, Guy would bleed to death. Gerard giggled as he ran, as if it were a good joke, a good trick they'd played, but he'd guessed it after all. In a minute, Gerard would touch him with those ugly hands!

'Guy!' But his voice sounded feeble. And Gerard was almost touching him. That was the game, when Gerard *touched* him!

With all his power, Bruno struggled to sit up. The nightmare slid from his brain like heavy slabs of rock.

Gerard! There he was!

'What's the matter? Bad dream?'

The pink-purply hands touched him, and Bruno whirled himself off the bed on to the floor.

'Woke you just in time, eh?' Gerard laughed.

Bruno set his teeth hard enough to break them. He bolted to the bathroom and took a drink with the door wide open. In the mirror, his face looked like a battlefield in hell.

'Sorry to intrude, but I found something new,' Gerard said in the tense, high-pitched voice that meant he had scored a little victory. 'About your friend Guy Haines. The one you were just dreaming about, weren't you?'

The glass cracked in Bruno's hand, and meticulously he gathered up the pieces from the basin and put them in the jagged bottom of the glass. He staggered boredly back to his bed.

'When did you meet him, Charles? Not last December.' Gerard leaned against the chest of drawers, lighting a cigar. 'Did you meet him about a year and a half ago? Did you go with him on the train down to Santa Fe?' Gerard waited. He pulled something from under his arm and tossed it on the bed. 'Remember that?'

It was Guy's Plato book from Santa Fe, still wrapped and with its address half rubbed off. 'Sure, I remember it.' Bruno pushed it away. 'I lost it going to the post office.'

'Hotel La Fonda had it right on the shelf. How'd you happen to borrow a book of Plato?'

'I found it on the train.' Bruno looked up. 'It had Guy's address in it, so I meant to mail it. Found it in the dining-car, matter of fact.' He looked straight at Gerard, who was watching him with his sharp, steady little eyes that didn't always have anything behind them.

'When did you meet him, Charley?' Gerard asked again, with the patient air of one questioning a child he knows is lying.

'In December.'

'You know about his wife's murder, of course.'

'Sure, I read about it. Then I read about him building the Palmyra Club.'

'And you thought, how interesting, because you had found a book six months before that belonged to him.'

Bruno hesitated. 'Yeah.'

Gerard grunted, and looked down with a little smile of disgust.

Bruno felt odd, uncomfortable. When had he seen it before, a smile like that after a grunt? Once when he had lied to his father about something, very obviously lied and clung to it, and his father's grunt, the disbelief in the smile, had shamed him. Bruno realized that his eyes pled with Gerard to forgive him, so he deliberately looked off at the window.

'And you made all those calls to Metcalf not even knowing Guy Haines.' Gerard picked up the book.

'What calls?'

'Several calls.'

'Maybe one when I was tight.'

'Several. About what?'

'About the damned book!' If Gerard knew him so well, he should know that was exactly the kind of thing he would do. 'Maybe I called when I heard his wife got murdered.'

Gerard shook his head. 'You called before she was murdered.'

'So what? Maybe I did.'

'So what? I'll have to ask Mr Haines. Considering your interest in murder, it's remarkable you didn't call him after the murder, isn't it?'

'I'm sick of murder!' Bruno shouted.

'Oh, I believe it, Charley, I believe it!' Gerard sauntered out, and down the hall towards his mother's room.

Bruno showered and dressed with slow care. Gerard had been much, much more excited about Matt Levine, he remembered. As far as he knew, he had made only two calls to Metcalf from Hotel La Fonda where Gerard must have picked up the bills. He could say Guy's mother was mistaken about the others, that it hadn't been he.

'What'd Gerard want?' Bruno asked his mother.

'Nothing much. Wanted to know if I knew a friend of yours. Guy Haines.' She was brushing her hair with upward strokes, so it stood out wildly around the calm, tired face. 'He's an architect, isn't he?'

'Uh-huh. I don't know him very well.' He strolled along the floor behind her. She had forgotten the clippings in Los Angeles, just as he had thought she would. Thank Christ, he hadn't reminded her he knew Guy when all the Palmyra pictures came out! The back of his mind must have known he was going to get Guy to do it.

'Gerard was talking about your calling him last summer. What was all that?'

'Oh, Mom, I get so damn sick of Gerard's dumb steers!'

40

A few moments later that morning, Guy stepped out of the director's office at Hanson and Knapp Drafters, happier than he had felt in weeks. The firm was copying the last of the hospital drawings, the most complex Guy had ever supervised, the last okays had come through on the building materials, and he had got a telegram early that morning from Bob Treacher that made Guy rejoice for his old friend. Bob had been appointed to an advisory committee of engineers for the new Alberta Dam in Canada, a job he had been looking forward to for the last five years.

Here and there at one of the long tables that fanned out on either side of him, a draftsman looked up and watched him as he walked towards the outer door. Guy nodded a greeting to a smiling foreman. He detected the smallest glow of self-esteem. Or maybe it was nothing but his new suit, he thought, only the third suit in his life he had ever had made for him. Anne had chosen the grey-blue glen plaid material. Anne had chosen the tomato-coloured woollen tie this morning to go with it, an old tie but one that he liked. He tightened its knot in the mirror between the elevators. There was a wild grey hair sticking up from one black, heavy eyebrow. The brows went up a little in surprise. He smoothed the hair down. It was the first grey hair he had ever noticed on himself.

A draftsman opened the office door. 'Mr Haines? Lucky I caught you. There's a telephone call.'

Guy went back, hoping it wouldn't be long, because he was to meet Anne for lunch in ten minutes. He took the call in an empty office off the drafting room.

'Hello, Guy? Listen, Gerard found that Plato book ... Yeah, in Santa Fe. Now, listen, it doesn't change anything ...'

Five minutes had passed before Guy was back at the elevators. He had always known the Plato might be found. Not a chance, Bruno had said. Bruno could be wrong. Bruno could be caught, therefore. Guy scowled as if it were incredible, the idea Bruno could be caught. And somehow it had been incredible, until now.

Momentarily, as he came out into the sunlight, he was conscious again of the new suit, and he clenched his fist in frustrated anger with himself. 'I found the book on the train, see?' Bruno had said. 'If I called you in Metcalf, it was on account of the book. But I didn't meet you until December ...' The voice more clipped and anxious than Guy had ever heard it before, so alert, so harried, it hardly seemed Bruno's voice. Guy went over the fabrication Bruno had just given him as if it were something that didn't belong to him, as if it were a swatch of material he indifferently considered for a suit, he thought. No, there were no holes in it, but it wouldn't necessarily wear. Not if someone remembered seeing them on the train. The waiter, for instance, who had served them in Bruno's compartment.

He tried to slow his breathing, tried to slow his pace. He looked up at the small disc of the winter sun. His black brows with the grey hair, with the white scar, his brows that were growing shaggier lately, Anne said, broke the glare into particles and protected him. If one looks directly into the sun for fifteen seconds, one can burn through the cornea, he remembered from somewhere. Anne protected him, too. His work protected him. *The new suit, the stupid new suit.* He felt suddenly inadequate and dull-witted, helpless. Death had insinuated itself into his brain. It enwrapped him. He had breathed its air so long, perhaps, he had grown quite used to it. Well, then, he was not afraid. He squared his shoulders superfluously.

Anne had not arrived when he got to the restaurant. Then he remembered she had said she was going to pick up the snapshots they had made Sunday at the house. Guy pulled Bob Treacher's telegram from his pocket and read it again and again:

JUST APPOINTED TO ALBERTA COMMITTEE. HAVE RECOMMENDED YOU. THIS IS A BRIDGE, GUY. GET FREE SOON AS POSSIBLE. ACCEPTANCE GUARANTEED. LETTER COMING.

Acceptance guaranteed. Regardless of how he engineered his

life, his ability to engineer a bridge was beyond question. Guy sipped his martini thoughtfully, holding the surface perfectly steady.

41

'I've wandered into another case,' Gerard murmured pleasantly, gazing at the typewritten report on his desk. He had not looked at Bruno since the young man had come in. 'Murder of Guy Haines' first wife. Never been solved.'

'Yeah, I know.'

'I thought you'd know quite a lot about it. Now tell me everything you know.' Gerard settled himself.

Bruno could tell he had gone all the way into it since Monday when he had the Plato book. 'Nothing,' Bruno said. 'Nobody knows. Do they?'

'What do you think? You must have talked a great deal with Guy about it.'

'Not particularly. Not at all. Why?'

'Because murder interests you so much.'

'What do you mean, murder interests me so much?'

'Oh, come, Charles, if I didn't know from you, I'd know that much from your father!' Gerard said in a rare burst of impatience.

Bruno started to reach for a cigarette and stopped. 'I talked with him about it,' he said quietly, respectfully. 'He doesn't know anything. He didn't even know his wife very well then.'

'Who do you think did it? Did you ever think Mr Haines might have arranged it? Were you interested maybe in how he'd done it and got away with it?' At his ease again, Gerard leaned back with his hands behind his head, as if they were talking about the good weather that day.

'Of course I don't think he arranged it,' Bruno replied. 'You don't seem to realize the calibre of the person you're talking about.'

'The only calibre ever worth considering is the gun's, Charles.'

Gerard picked up his telephone. 'As you'd be the first to tell me probably. – Have Mr Haines come in, will you?'

Bruno jumped a little, and Gerard saw it. Gerard watched him in silence as they listened to Guy's footsteps coming closer in the hall. He had expected Gerard would do this, Bruno told himself. So what, so what, so what?

Guy looked nervous, Bruno thought, but his usual air of being nervous and in a hurry covered it. He spoke to Gerard, and nodded to Bruno.

Gerard offered him his remaining chair, a straight one. 'My whole purpose in asking you to come down here, Mr Haines, is to ask you a very simple question. What does Charles talk with you about most of the time?' Gerard offered Guy a cigarette from a pack that must have been years old, Bruno thought, and Guy took it.

Bruno saw Guy's eyebrows draw together with the look of irritation that was exactly appropriate. 'He's talked to me now and then about the Palmyra Club,' Guy replied.

'And what else?'

Guy looked at Bruno. Bruno was nibbling, so casually the action seemed nonchalant, at a fingernail of the hand that propped his cheek. 'Can't really say,' Guy answered.

'Talked to you about your wife's murder?'

'Yes.'

'How does he talk to you about the murder?' Gerard asked kindly. 'I mean your wife's murder.'

Guy felt his face flush. He glanced again at Bruno, as anybody might, he thought, as anybody might in the presence of a discussed party who is being ignored. 'He often asked me if I knew who might have done it.'

'And do you?'

'No.'

'Do you like Charles?' Gerard's fat fingers trembled slightly, incongruously. They began playing with a match cover on his desk blotter.

Guy thought of Bruno's fingers on the train, playing with the match cover, dropping it on to the steak. 'Yes, I like him,' Guy answered puzzledly.

'Hasn't he annoyed you? Hasn't he thrust himself on you many times?'

'I don't think so,' Guy said.

'Were you annoyed when he came to your wedding?'

'No.'

'Did Charles ever tell you that he hated his father?'

'Yes, he did.'

'Did he ever tell you he'd like to kill him?'

'No,' he replied in the same matter-of-fact tone.

Gerard got the brown paper-wrapped book from a drawer in his desk. 'Here's the book Charles meant to mail you. Sorry I can't let you have it just now, because I may need it. How did Charles happen to have your book?'

'He told me he found it on the train.' Guy studied Gerard's sleepy, enigmatic smile. He had seen a trace of it the night Gerard called at the house, but not like this. This smile was calculated to inspire dislike. This smile was a professional weapon. What it must be, Guy thought, facing that smile day after day. Involuntarily, he looked over at Bruno.

'And you didn't see each other on the train?' Gerard looked from Guy to Bruno.

'No,' said Guy.

'I spoke with the waiter who served you two dinner in Charles' compartment.'

Guy kept his eyes on Gerard. This naked shame, he thought, was more annihilating than guilt. This was annihilation he was feeling, even as he sat upright, looking straight at Gerard.

'So what?' Bruno said shrilly.

'So I'm interested in why you two take such elaborate trouble.' Gerard wagged his head amusedly, 'to say you met months later.' He waited, letting the passing seconds eat at them. 'You won't tell me the answer. Well, the answer is obvious. That is, one answer, as a speculation.'

All three of them were thinking of the answer, Guy thought. It was visible in the air now, linking him and Bruno, Bruno and Gerard, Gerard and himself. The answer Bruno had declared beyond thought, the eternally missing ingredient.

'Will you tell me, Charles, you who read so many detective stories?'

'I don't know what you're getting at.'

'Within a few days, your wife was killed, Mr Haines. Within a few months, Charles' father. My obvious and first speculation is that you both knew those murders were going to happen –'

'Oh, crap!' Bruno said.

'– and discussed them. Pure speculation, of course. That's assuming you met on the train. Where did you meet?' Gerard smiled. 'Mr Haines?'

'Yes,' Guy said, 'we met on the train.'

'And why've you been so afraid of admitting it?' Gerard jabbed one of his freckled fingers at him, and again Guy felt in Gerard's prosaicness his power to terrify.

'I don't know,' Guy said.

'Wasn't it because Charles told you he would like to have his father killed? And you were uneasy then, Mr Haines, because you knew?'

Was that Gerard's trump? Guy said slowly, 'Charles said nothing about killing his father.'

Gerard's eyes slid over in time to catch Bruno's tight smirk of satisfaction. 'Pure speculation, of course,' Gerard said.

Guy and Bruno left the building together. Gerard had dismissed them together, and they walked together down the long block towards the little park where the subways were, and the taxicabs. Bruno looked back at the tall narrow building they had left.

'All right, he still hasn't anything,' Bruno said. 'Any way you look at it, he hasn't anything.'

Bruno was sullen, but calm. Suddenly Guy realized how cool Bruno had been under Gerard's attack. Guy was continually imagining Bruno hysterical under pressure. He glanced quickly at Bruno's tall hunched figure beside him, feeling that wild, reckless comradeship of the day in the restaurant. But he had nothing to say. Surely, he thought, Bruno must know that Gerard wasn't going to tell them everything he had discovered.

'You know, the funny thing,' Bruno continued, 'Gerard's not looking for us, he's looking for other people.'

42

Gerard poked a finger between the bars and waggled it at the little bird that fluttered in terror against the opposite side of the cage. Gerard whistled a single soft note.

From the centre of the room, Anne watched him uneasily. She didn't like his having just told her Guy had been lying, then his strolling off to frighten the canary. She hadn't liked Gerard for the last quarter hour, and because she had thought she did like him on his first visit, her misjudgement annoyed her.

'What's his name?' Gerard asked.

'Sweetie,' Anne replied. She ducked her head a little, embarrassedly, and swung half around. Her new alligator pumps made her feel very tall and graceful, and she had thought, when she bought them that afternoon, that Guy would like them, that they would coax a smile from him as they sat having a cocktail before dinner. But Gerard's arrival had spoilt that.

'Do you have any idea why your husband didn't want to say he met Charles June before last?'

The month Miriam was murdered, Anne thought again. June before last meant nothing else to her. 'It was a difficult month for him,' she said. 'It was the month his wife died. He might have forgotten almost anything that happened that month.' She frowned, feeling Gerard was making too much of his little discovery, that it couldn't matter so very much, since Guy hadn't even seen Charles in the six months afterwards.

'Not in this case,' Gerard said casually, reseating himself. 'No, I think Charles talked with your husband on the train about his father, told him he wanted him dead, maybe even told him how he intended to go about —'

'I can't imagine Guy listening to that,' Anne interrupted him.

'I don't know,' Gerard went on blandly, 'I don't know, but I strongly suspect Charles knew about his father's murder and that he may have confided to your husband that night on the train. Charles is that kind of a young man. And I think the kind of man your husband is would have kept quiet about it, tried to avoid Charles from then on. Don't you?'

It would explain a great deal, Anne thought. But it would also make Guy a kind of accomplice. Gerard seemed to want to make Guy an accomplice. 'I'm sure my husband wouldn't have tolerated Charles even to this extent,' she said firmly, 'If Charles had told him anything like that.'

'A very good point. However –' Gerard stopped vaguely, as if lost in his own slow thoughts.

Anne did not like to look at the top of his bald freckled head, so she stared at the tile cigarette box on the coffee table, and finally took a cigarette.

'Do you think your husband has any suspicion who murdered his wife, Mrs Haines?'

Anne blew her smoke out defiantly. 'I certainly do not.'

'You see, if that night on the train, Charles went into the subject of murder, he went into it thoroughly. And if your husband did have some reason to think his wife's life was in danger, and if he mentioned it to Charles – why then they have a sort of mutual secret, a mutual peril even. It's only a speculation,' he hurried to add, 'but investigators always have to speculate.'

'I know my husband couldn't have said anything about his wife's being in danger. I was with him in Mexico City when the news came, and with him days before in New York.'

'How about March of this year?' Gerard asked in the same even tone. He reached for his empty highball glass, and submitted to Anne's taking it to refill.

Anne stood at the bar with her back to Gerard, remembering March, the month Charles' father was killed, remembering Guy's nervousness then. Had that fight been in February or March? And *hadn't* he fought with Charles Bruno?

'Do you think your husband could have been seeing Charles now and then around the month of March without your knowing about it?'

Of course, she thought, that might explain it: that Guy had known Charles intended to kill his father, and had tried to stop him, had fought with him, in a bar. 'He could have, I suppose,' she said uncertainly. 'I don't know.'

'How did your husband seem around the month of March, if you can remember, Mrs Haines?'

'He was nervous. I think I know the things he was nervous about.'

'What things?'

'His work –' Somehow she couldn't grant him a word more than that about Guy. Everything she said, she felt Gerard would incorporate in the misty picture he was composing, in which he was trying to see Guy. She waited, and Gerard waited, as if he vied with her not to break the silence first.

Finally, he tapped out his cigar and said, 'If anything does occur to you about that time in regard to Charles, will you be sure and tell me? Call me any time during the day or night. There'll be somebody there to take messages.' He wrote another name on his business card, and handed it to Anne.

Anne turned from the door and went directly to the coffee table to remove his glass. Through the front window, she saw him sitting in his car with his head bent forward, like a man asleep, while, she supposed, he made his notes. Then with a little stab, she thought of his writing that Guy might have seen Charles in March without her knowing about it. Why had she said it? She did know about it. Guy said he hadn't seen Charles, between December and the wedding.

When Guy came in about an hour later, Anne was in the kitchen, tending the casserole that was nearly done in the oven. She saw Guy put his head up, sniffing the air.

'Shrimp casserole,' Anne told him. 'I guess I should open a vent.'

'Was Gerard here?'

'Yes. You knew he was coming?'

'Cigars,' he said laconically. Gerard had told her about the meeting on the train, of course. 'What did he want this time?' he asked.

'He wanted to know more about Charles Bruno.' Anne glanced at him quickly from the front window. 'If you'd said anything to me about suspecting him of anything. And he wanted to know about March.'

'About March?' He stepped on to the raised portion of the floor where Anne stood.

He stopped in front of her, and Anne saw the pupils of his eyes contract suddenly. She could see a few of the hair-fine scars over his cheek-bone from that night in March, or February. 'Wanted to know if you suspected Charles was going to have his father killed that month.' But Guy only stared at her with his mouth in a familiar straight line, without alarm, and without guilt. She stepped aside, and went down into the living-room. 'It's terrible, isn't it,' she said, 'murder?'

Guy tapped a fresh cigarette on his watch face. It tortured him to hear her say 'murder'. He wished he could erase every memory of Bruno from her brain.

'You didn't know, did you, Guy – in March?'

'No, Anne. What did you tell Gerard?'

'Do you believe Charles had his father killed?'

'I don't know. I think it's possible. But it doesn't concern us.' And he did not realize for seconds that it was even a lie.

'That's right. It doesn't concern us.' She looked at him again. 'Gerard also said you met Charles June before last on the train.'

'Yes, I did.'

'Well – what does it matter?'

'I don't know.'

'Was it because of something Charles said on the train? Is that why you dislike him?'

Guy shoved his hands deeper in his jacket pockets. He wanted a brandy suddenly. He knew he showed what he felt, that he could not hide it from Anne now: 'Listen, Anne,' he said quickly. 'Bruno told me on the train he wished his father were dead. He didn't mention any plans, he didn't mention any names. I didn't like the way he said it, and after that I didn't like him. I refuse to tell Gerard all that, because I don't know if Bruno had his father killed or not. That's for the police to find out. Innocent men have been hanged because people reported their saying something like that.'

But whether she believed him or not, he thought, he was finished. It seemed the basest lie he had ever told, the basest thing he had ever done – the transferring of his guilt to another man. Even Bruno wouldn't have lied like this, wouldn't have lied against him like this. He felt himself totally false, totally a lie. He flung his cigarette into the fireplace and put his hands over his face.

'Guy, I do believe you're doing what you should,' Anne's voice said gently.

His face was a lie, his level eyes, the firm mouth, the sensitive hands. He whipped his hands down and put them in his pockets. 'I could use a brandy.'

'Wasn't it Charles you fought with in March?' she asked as she stood at the bar.

There was no reason not to lie about this also, but he could not. 'No, Anne.' He knew from the quick sidelong glance she gave him that she didn't believe him. She probably thought he had fought with Bruno to stop him. She was probably proud of him! Must there always be this protection, that he didn't even want? Must everything always be so easy for him? But Anne would not be satisfied with this. She would come back to it and back to it until he told her, he knew.

That evening, Guy lighted the first fire of the year, the first fire in their new house. Anne lay on the long hearthstone with her head on a sofa pillow. The thin nostalgic chill of autumn was in the air, filling Guy with melancholy and a restless energy. The energy was not buoyant as autumnal energy had been in his youth, but underlaid with frenzy and despair, as if his life were winding down and this might be his last spurt. What better proof did he need that his life was winding down than that he had no dread of what lay ahead? Couldn't Gerard guess it now, knowing that he and Bruno had met on the train? Wouldn't it dawn on him one day, one night, one instant as his fat fingers lifted a cigar to his mouth? What were they waiting for, Gerard and the police? He had sometimes the feeling that Gerard wanted to gather every tiniest contributing fact, every gramme of evidence against them both, then let it fall suddenly upon them and demolish them. But however they demolished him, Guy thought, they would not demolish his buildings. And he felt again the strange and lonely isolation of his spirit from his flesh, even from his mind.

But suppose his secret with Bruno were never found out? There were still those moments of mingled horror at what he had done, and of absolute despondency, when he felt that secret bore a charmed inviolability. Perhaps, he thought, that was why he was not afraid of Gerard or the police, because he still believed in its inviolability. If no one had guessed it so far, after all their carelessness, after all Bruno's hints, wasn't there something making it impregnable?

Anne had fallen asleep. He stared at the smooth curve of her forehead, paled to silver by the fire's light. Then he lowered his lips to her forehead and kissed her, so gently she would not awaken. The ache inside him translated itself into words: 'I forgive you.' He wanted Anne to say it, no one but Anne.

In his mind, the side of the scale that bore his guilt was hopelessly weighted, beyond the scale's measure, yet into the other side he continually threw the equally hopeless featherweight of self-defence. He had committed the crime in self-defence, he reasoned. But he vacillated in completely believing this. If he believed in the full complement of evil in himself, he had to believe also in a natural compulsion to express it. He found himself wondering, therefore, from time to time, if he might have enjoyed his crime in some way, derived some primal satisfaction from it – how else could one really explain in mankind the continued toleration of wars, the perennial enthusiasm for wars when they came, if not for some primal pleasure in killing? – and because the capacity to wonder came so often, he accepted it as true that he had.

43

District Attorney Phil Howland, immaculate and gaunt, as sharp of outline as Gerard was fuzzy, smiled tolerantly through his cigarette smoke. 'Why don't you let the kid alone? It was an angle at first, I grant you. We combed through his friends, too. There's nothing, Gerard. And you can't arrest a man on his personality.'

Gerard recrossed his legs and allowed himself a complaisant smile. This was his hour. His satisfaction was heightened by the fact that he sat here smiling in the same way during other less momentous interviews.

Howland pushed a typewritten sheet with his fingertips to the edge of the desk. 'Twelve new names here, if you're interested. Friends of the late Mr Samuel furnished us by the insurance companies,' Howland said in his calm, bored voice, and Gerard knew he pretended especial boredom now, because as District Attorney he had so many hundreds of men at his disposal, could throw so much finer nets so much farther.

'You can tear them up,' Gerard said.

Howland hid his surprise with a smile, but he couldn't hide the sudden curiosity in his dark, wide eyes. 'I suppose you've already got your man. Charles Bruno, of course.'

'Of course,' Gerard chuckled. 'Only I've got him for another murder.'

'Only one? You always said he was good for four or five.'

'I never said,' Gerard denied quietly. He was smoothing out a number of papers, folded in thirds like letters, on his knees.

'Who?'

'Curious? Don't you know?' Gerard smiled with his cigar between his teeth. He pulled a straight chair closer to him, and proceded to cover its seat with his papers. He never used Howland's desk, however many papers he had, and Howland knew now not to bother offering it. Howland disliked him personally as well as professionally, Gerard knew. Howland accused him of not being co-operative with the police. The police had never been in the least co-operative with him, but with all their hindrance, Gerard in the last decade had solved an impressive number of cases the police hadn't even been warm on.

Howland got up and strolled slowly towards Gerard on his long thin legs, then hung back, leaning against the front of his desk. 'But does all this shed any light on the *case*?'

'The trouble with the police force is that it has a single-track mind,' Gerard announced. 'This case, like many others, took a double-track mind. Simply couldn't have been solved without a double-track mind.'

'Who and when?' Howland sighed.

'Ever hear of Guy Haines?'

'Certainly. We questioned him last week.'

'His wife. June eleventh of last year in Metcalf, Texas. Strangulation, remember? The police never solved it.'

'Charles Bruno?' Howland frowned.

'Did you know that Charles Bruno and Guy Haines were on the same train going South on June first? Ten days before the murder of Haines's wife. Now, what do you deduce from that?'

'You mean they knew each other before last June?'

'No, I mean they met each other on that train. Can you put the rest together? I'm giving you the missing link.'

The District Attorney smiled faintly. 'You're saying Charles Bruno killed Guy Haines' wife?'

'I certainly am.' Gerard looked up from his papers, finished. 'The next question is, what's my proof? There it is. All you want.' He gestured towards the papers that overlapped in a long row, like cards in a game of solitaire. 'Read from the bottom up.'

While Howland read, Gerard drew a cup of water from the tank in the corner and lighted another cigar from the one he had been smoking. The last statement from Charles' taxi-driver in Metcalf, had come in this morning. He hadn't even had a drink on it yet, but he was going to have three or four as soon as he left Howland, in the lounge car of an Iowa-bound train.

The papers were signed statements from Hotel La Fonda bellhops, from one Edward Wilson who had seen Charles leaving the Santa Fe station on an eastbound train the day of Miriam Haines' murder, from the Metcalf taxi-driver who had driven Charles to the Kingdom of Fun Amusement Park at Lake Metcalf, from the barman in the roadhouse where Charles had tried to get hard liquor, plus telephone bills of long-distance calls to Metcalf.

'But no doubt you know that already,' Gerard remarked.

'Most of it, yes,' Howland answered calmly, still reading.

'You knew he made a twenty-four-hour trip to Metcalf that day, too, did you?' Gerard asked, but he was really in too good spirits for sarcasm. 'That taxi-driver was certainly hard to find. Had to trace him all the way up to Seattle, but once we found him, it didn't take any jostling for him to remember. People don't forget a young man like Charles Bruno.'

'So you're saying Charles Bruno is so fond of murder,' Howland remarked amusedly, 'that he murders the wife of a man he meets on a train the week before? A woman he's never even seen? Or had he seen her?'

Gerard chuckled again. 'Of course he hadn't. My Charles had a plan.' The 'my' slipped out, but Gerard didn't care. 'Can't you see it? Plain as the nose on your face? And this is only half.'

'Sit down, Gerard, you'll work yourself into a heart attack.'

'You can't see it. Because you didn't know and don't know Charles' personality. You weren't interested in the fact he spends most of his time planning perfect crimes of various sorts.'

'All right, what's the rest of your theory?'

'That Guy Haines killed Samuel Bruno.'

'Ow!' Howland groaned.

Gerard smiled back at the first grin Howland had given him since he, Gerard, had made a mistake in a certain case years ago. 'I haven't finished checking on Guy Haines yet,' Gerard said with deliberate ingenuousness, puffing away at the cigar. 'I want to take it easy, and that's the only reason I'm here, to get you to to take it easy with me. I didn't know but what you'd grab Charles, you see, with all your information against him.'

Howland smoothed his black moustache. 'Everything you say confirms my belief you should have retired about fifteen years ago.'

'Oh, I've solved a few cases in the last fifteen years.'

'A man like Guy Haines?' Howland laughed again.

'Against a fellow like Charles? Mind you, I don't say Guy Haines did it of his own free will. He was made to do it for Charles' unsolicited favour of freeing him of his wife. Charles hates women,' he remarked in a parenthesis. 'That was Charles' plan. Exchange. No clues, you see. No motives. Oh, I can just hear him! But even Charles is human. He was too interested in Guy Haines to leave him alone afterwards. And Guy Haines was too frightened to do anything about it. Yes –' Gerard jerked his head for emphasis, and his jowls shook – 'Haines was coerced. How terribly probably no one will ever know.'

Howland's smile went away momentarily at Gerard's earnestness. The story had the barest possibility, but still a possibility. 'Hmm-m.'

'Unless he tells us,' Gerard added.

'And how do you propose to make him tell us?'

'Oh, he may yet confess. It's wearing him down. But otherwise, confront him with the facts. Which my men are busy gathering. One thing, Howland –' Gerard jabbed a finger at his papers on the chair seat. 'When you and your – your army of oxes go out checking these statements, don't question Guy Haines' mother. I don't want Haines forewarned.'

'Oh. Cat-and-mouse technique for Mr Haines,' Howland smiled. He turned to make a telephone call about an inconsequential matter, and Gerard waited, resenting that he had to turn his information over to Howland, that he had to leave the Charles-Guy Haines spectacle. 'Well–' Howland let his breath out in a long sigh – 'what do you want me to do, work over your little boy with this stuff? Think he'll break down and tell all about his brilliant plan with Guy Haines, architect?'

'No, I don't want him worked over. I like clean jobs. I want a few days more or maybe weeks to finish checking on Haines, then I'll confront them both. I'm giving you this on Charles, because from now on I'm out of the case personally, so far as they're to know. I'm going to Iowa for a vacation, I really am, and I'm going to let Charles know it.' Gerard's face lighted with a big smile.

'It's going to be hard to hold the boys back,' Howland said regretfully, 'especially for all the time it'll take you to get evidence against Guy Haines.'

'Incidentally –' Gerard picked up his hat and shook it at Howland. 'You couldn't crack Charles with all that, but I could crack Guy Haines with what I've got this minute.'

'Oh, you mean *we* couldn't crack Guy Haines?'

Gerard looked at him with elaborate contempt. 'But you're not interested in cracking him, are you? You don't think he's the man.'

'Take that vacation, Gerard!'

Methodically, Gerard gathered his papers and started to pocket them.

'I thought you were going to leave those.'

'Oh, if you think you'll need them.' Gerard presented the papers courteously, and turned towards the door.

'Mind telling me what you've got that'll crack Guy Haines?'

Gerard made a disdainful sound in his throat. 'The man is tortured with guilt,' he said, and went out.

44

'You know, in the whole world,' Bruno said, and tears started in his eyes so he had to look down at the long hearthstone under his feet, 'I wouldn't want to be anywhere else but here tonight, Anne.' He leaned his elbow jauntily on the high mantel.

'Very nice of you to say,' Anne smiled, and set the plate of melted cheese and anchovy canapés on the sawbuck table. 'Have one of these while they're hot.'

Bruno took one, though he knew he wouldn't be able to get it down. The table looked beautiful, set for two with grey linen and big grey plates. Gerard was off on a vacation. They had beaten him, Guy and he, and the lid was off his brains! He might have tried to kiss Anne, he thought, if she didn't belong to Guy. Bruno stood taller and adjusted his cuffs. He took great pride in being a perfect gentleman with Anne. 'So Guy thinks he's going to like it up there?' Bruno asked. Guy was in Canada now, working on the big Alberta dam. 'I'm glad all this dumb questioning is over, so he won't have to worry about it when he's working. You can imagine how I feel. Like celebrating!' He laughed, mainly at his understatement.

Anne stared at his tall restless figure by the mantel, and wondered if Guy, despite his hatred, felt the same fascination she did. She still didn't know, though, whether Charles Bruno would have been capable of arranging his father's murder, and she had spent the whole day with him in order to make up her mind. He slid away from certain questions with joking answers, he was serious and careful about answering others. He hated Miriam as if he had known her. It rather surprised Anne that Guy had told him so much about Miriam.

'Why didn't you want to tell anyone you'd met Guy on the train?' Anne asked.

'I didn't mind. I just made the mistake of kidding around about it first, said we'd met in school. Then all those questions came up, and Gerard started making a lot out of it. I guess because it looked bad, frankly. Miriam killed so soon after, you know. I think it was quite nice of Guy at the inquest on Miriam not to drag in anybody he'd just met by accident.' He laughed, a single loud clap, and dropped into the armchair. 'Not that I'm a suspicious character, by any means!'

'But that didn't have anything to do with the questioning about your father's death.'

'Of course not. But Gerard doesn't pay any attention to logic. He should have been an inventor!'

Anne frowned. She couldn't believe that Guy would have fallen in with Charles' story simply because telling the truth would have looked bad, or even because Charles had told him on the train that he hated his father. She must ask Guy again. There was a great deal she had to ask him. About Charles' hostility to Miriam, for instance, though he had never seen her. Anne went into the kitchen.

Bruno strolled to the front window with his drink, and watched a plane alternating its red and green lights in the black sky. It looked like a person exercising, he thought, touching fingertips to shoulders and stretching arms out again. He wished Guy might be on that plane, coming home. He looked at the dusky pink face of his new wrist-watch, thinking again, before he read the time on its tall gold numerals, that Guy would probably like a watch like this, because of its modern design. In just three hours more, he would have been with Anne twenty-four hours, a whole day. He had driven by last evening instead of telephoning, and it had got so late, Anne had invited him to spend the night. He had slept up in the guest room where they had put him the night of the party, and Anne had brought him some hot bouillon before he went to sleep. Anne was terribly sweet to him, and he really loved her! He spun around on his heel, and saw her coming in from the kitchen with their plates.

'Guy's very fond of you, you know,' Anne said during the dinner.

Bruno looked at her, having already forgotten what they had been talking about. 'There's *nothing* I wouldn't do for him! I feel a tremendous tie with him, like a brother. I guess because everything started happening to him just after we met each other on the train.' And though he had started out to be gay, even funny, the seriousness of his real feeling for Guy got the better of him. He fingered the rack of Guy's pipes near him on an end table. His heart was pounding. The stuffed potato was beautiful, but he didn't dare eat another mouthful. Nor the red wine. He had an impulse to try to spend the night again. Couldn't he manage to stay again tonight, if he didn't feel well? On the other hand, the new house was closer than Anne thought. Saturday he was giving a big party. 'You're sure Guy'll be back this week-end?' he asked.

'So he said.' Anne ate her green salad thoughtfully. 'I don't know whether he'll feel like a party, though. When he's been working, he usually doesn't like anything more distracting than a sail.'

'I'd like a sail. If you wouldn't mind company.'

'Come along.' Then she remembered, Charles had already been out on the *India*, had invited himself with Guy, had dented the gunwhale, and suddenly she felt puzzled, tricked, as if something had prevented her remembering until now. And she found herself thinking, Charles could probably do anything, atrocious things, and fool everyone with the same ingratiating naïveté, the same shy smile. Except Gerard. Yes, he could have arranged his father's murder. Gerard wouldn't be speculating in that direction if it weren't possible. She might be sitting opposite a murderer. She felt a little pluck of terror as she got up, a bit too abruptly as if she were fleeing, and removed the dinner plates. And his grim, merciless pleasure in talking of his loathing for Miriam. He would have enjoyed killing her, Anne thought. A fragile suspicion that he might have killed her crossed her mind like a dry leaf blown by the wind.

'So you went on to Santa Fe after you met Guy?' she almost stammered, from the kitchen.

'Uh-huh.' Bruno was deep in the big green armchair again.

Anne dropped a demitasse spoon and it made an outrageous clatter on the tiles. The odd thing, she thought, was that it didn't seem to matter what one said to Charles or asked him. Nothing would shock him. But instead of making it simpler to talk to him, this was the very quality that she felt rattling her and throwing her off.

'Have you ever been to Metcalf?' she heard her own voice call around the partition.

'No,' Bruno replied. 'No, I always wanted to. Have you?'

Bruno sipped his coffee at the mantel. Anne was on the sofa, her head tipped back so the curve of her throat above the tiny ruffled collar of her dress was the lightest thing about her. *Anne is like light to me,* Bruno remembered Guy once saying. If he could strangle Anne, too, then Guy and he could really be together. Bruno frowned at himself, then laughed and shifted on his feet.

'What's funny?'

'Just thinking,' he smiled. 'I was thinking of what Guy always says, about the doubleness of everything. You know, the positive and negative, side by side. Every decision has a reason against it.' He noticed suddenly he was breathing hard.

'You mean two sides to everything?'

'Oh, no, that's too simple!' Women were really so crude sometimes! 'People, feelings, everything! Double! Two people in each person. There's also a person exactly the opposite of you, like the unseen part of you, somewhere in the world, and he waits in ambush.' It thrilled him to say Guy's words, though he hadn't liked hearing them, he remembered, because Guy had said the two people were mortal enemies, too, and Guy had meant him and himself.

Anne brought her head up slowly from the sofa back. It sounded so like Guy, yet he had never said it to her. Anne thought of the unsigned letter last spring. Charles must have written it. Guy must have meant Charles when he talked of ambush. There was no one else besides Charles to whom Guy reacted so violently. Surely it was Charles who alternated hatred with devotion.

'It's not all good and evil either, but that's how it shows itself best, in action,' Bruno went on cheerfully. 'By the way, I mustn't forget to tell Guy about giving the thousand dollars to a beggar. I always said when I had my own money, I'd give a thousand to a beggar. Well, I did, but you think he thanked me? It took me twenty minutes to prove to him the money was real! I had to take a hundred in a bank and break it for him! Then he acted as if he thought I was crazy!' Bruno looked down and shook his head. He had counted on its being a memorable experience, and then to have the bastard look practically *sore* at him the next time he saw him – still begging on the same street corner, too – because he hadn't brought him *another* thousand! 'As I was saying anyway –'

'About good and evil,' Anne said. She loathed him. She knew all that Guy felt now about him. But she didn't yet know why Guy tolerated him.

'Oh. Well, these things come out in actions. But for instance, murderers. Punishing them in the law courts won't make them any better, Guy says. Every man is his own law court and punishes himself enough. In fact, every man is just about every-thing to Guy!' He laughed. He was so tight, he could hardly see her face now, but he wanted to tell her everything that he and Guy had ever talked about, right up to the last little secret that he couldn't tell her.

'People without consciences don't punish themselves, do they?' Anne asked.

Bruno looked at the ceiling. 'That's true. Some people are too dumb to have consciences, other people too evil. Generally the dumb ones get caught. But take the two murderers of Guy's wife and my father.' Bruno tried to look serious. 'Both of them must have been pretty brilliant people, don't you think.'

'So they have consciences and don't deserve to get caught?'

'Oh, I don't say that. Of course not! But don't think they aren't suffering a little. In their fashion!' He laughed again, be-cause he was really too tight to know just where he was going. 'They weren't just madmen, like they said the murderer of Guy's wife was. Shows how little the authorities know about real criminology. A crime like that took planning.' Out of the blue, he remembered he hadn't planned that one at all, but he certainly had planned his father's, which illustrated his point well enough. 'What's the matter?'

Anne laid her cold fingers against her forehead. 'Nothing.'

Bruno fixed her a highball at the bar Guy had built into the side of the fireplace. Bruno wanted a bar just like it for his own house.

'Where did Guy get those scratches on his face last March?'

'What scratches?' Bruno turned to her. Guy had told him she didn't know about the scratches.

'More than scratches. Cuts. And a bruise on his head.'

'I didn't see them.'

'He fought with you, didn't he?' Charles stared at her with a strange pinkish glint in his eyes. She was not deceitful enough to smile now. She was sure. She felt Charles was about to rush across the room and strike her, but she kept her eyes fixed on his. If she told Gerard, she thought, the fight would be proof of Charles' knowledge of the murder. Then she saw Charles' smile waver back.

'No!' he laughed. He sat down. 'Where did he say he got the scratches? I didn't see him anyway in March. I was out of town then.' He stood up. He suddenly didn't feel well in the stomach, and it wasn't the questions, it was his stomach. Suppose he was in for another attack now. Or tomorrow morning. He mustn't pass out, mustn't let Anne see *that* in the morning! 'I'd better go soon,' he murmured.

'What's the matter? You're not feeling well? You're a little pale.'

She wasn't sympathetic. He could tell by her voice. What woman ever was, except his mother? 'Thank you very much, Anne, for – for all day.'

She handed him his coat, and he stumbled out the door, gritting his teeth as he started the long walk towards his car at the kerb.

The house was dark when Guy came home a few hours later. He prowled the living-room, saw the cigarette stub ground on the hearth, the pipe rack askew on the end table, the depression in a small pillow on the sofa. There was a peculiar disorder that couldn't have been created by Anne and Teddy, or by Chris, or by Helen Heyburn. Hadn't he known?

He ran up to the guest room. Bruno wasn't there, but he saw a tortured roll of newspaper on the bed table and a dime and two pennies domestically beside it. At the window, the dawn was coming in like that dawn. He turned his back on the window, and his held breath came out like a sob. What did Anne mean by doing this to him? Now of all times when it was intolerable - when half of himself was in Canada and the other half here, caught in the tightening grip of Bruno, Bruno with the police off his trail. The police had given him a little insulation ! But he had overreached now. There was no enduring much longer.

He went into the bedroom and knelt beside Anne and kissed her awake, frightenedly, harshly, until he felt her arms close around him. He buried his face in the soft muss of the sheets over her breast. It seemed there was a rocking, roaring storm all around him, all around both of them, and that Anne was the only point of stillness, at its centre, and the rhythm of her breathing the only sign of a normal pulse in a sane world. He got his clothes off with his eyes shut.

'I've missed you,' were the first words Anne said.

Guy stood near the foot of the bed with his hands in the pockets of his robe, clenched. The tension was still in him, and all the storm seemed gathered in his own core now. 'I'll be here three days. Have you missed me?'

Anne slid up a few inches in the bed. 'Why do you look at me like that?'

Guy did not answer.

'I've seen him only once, Guy.'

'Why did you see him at all?'

'Because –' Her cheeks flushed as pink as the spot on her shoulder, Guy noticed. His beard had scratched her shoulder. He had never spoken to her like this before. And the fact she was going to answer him reasonably seemed only to give more reason to his anger. 'Because he came by –'

'He always comes by. He always telephones.'

'Why?'

'He slept here!' Guy burst out, then he saw Anne's recoil in the subtle lift of her head, the flicker of her lashes.

'Yes. Night before last,' her steady voice challenged him. 'He came by late, and I asked him to stay over.'

It had crossed his mind in Canada that Bruno might make advances to Anne, simply because she belonged to him, and that Anne might encourage him, simply because she wanted to know what he had not told her. Not that Bruno would go very far, but the touch of his hand on Anne's, the thought of Anne permitting it, and the reason for which she would permit it, tormented him. 'And he was here last evening?'

'Why does it bother you so?'

'Because he's dangerous. He's half insane.'

'I don't think that's the reason he bothers you,' Anne said in the same slow steady voice. 'I don't know why you defend him, Guy. I don't know why you don't admit he's the one who wrote that letter to me and the one who almost drove you insane in March.'

Guy stiffened with guilty defensiveness. Defence of Bruno, he thought, always defence of Bruno! Bruno hadn't admitted sending the letter to Anne, he knew. It was just that Anne, like Gerard, with different facts, was putting pieces together. Gerard had quit, but Ann would never quit. Anne worked with the intangible pieces, and the intangible pieces were the ones that would make the picture. But she didn't have the picture yet. It would take time, a little more time, and a little more time to torture him! He turned to the window with a tired leaden movement, too dead even to cover his face or bow his head. He did not care to ask Anne what she and Bruno had talked of yesterday. Somehow he could *feel* exactly what they had said, exactly how much more Anne had learned. There was some allotted period of time, he felt suddenly, in this agony of postponement. It had gone on beyond all logical expectation, as life sometimes did against a fatal disease, that was all.

'Tell me, Guy,' Anne said quietly, not pleading with him now, her voice merely like the tolling of a bell that marked another length of time. 'Tell me, will you?'

'I shall tell you,' he replied, still looking at the window, but hearing himself say it now, believing himself, such a lightness filled him, he was sure Anne must see it in the half of his face, in his whole being, and his first thought was to share it with her, though for a moment he could not take his eyes from the sunlight on the window-sill. *Lightness*, he thought, both a lifting of darkness and of weight, weightlessness. He would tell Anne.

'Guy, come here.' She held up her arms for him, and he sat beside her, slipped his arms around her, and held her tight against him. 'There's going to be a baby,' she said. 'Let's be happy. Will you be happy, Guy?'

He looked at her, feeling suddenly like laughing for happiness, for surprise, for her shyness. 'A baby !' he whispered.

'What'll we do these days you're here?'

'When, Anne?'

'Oh – not for ages. I guess in May. What'll we do tomorrow?'

'We'll definitely go out on the boat. If it's not too rough.' And the foolish, conspiratorial note in his voice made him laugh out loud now.

'Oh, Guy !'

'Crying?'

'It's so good to hear you laugh !'

45

Bruno telephoned Saturday morning to congratulate Guy on his appointment to the Alberta Committee, and to ask if he and Anne would come to his party that evening. Bruno's desperate, elated voice exhorted him to celebrate. 'Talking over my own private wires, Guy. Gerard's gone back to Iowa. Come on, I want you to see my new house.' Then, 'Let me talk to Anne.'

'Anne's out right now.'

Guy knew the investigations were over. The police had notified him and so had Gerard, with thanks.

Guy went back into the living-room where he and Bob Treacher were finishing their late breakfast. Bob had flown down to New York a day ahead of him, and Guy had invited him for the week-end. They were talking of Alberta and the men they worked with on the Committee, of the terrain, the trout fishing, and of whatever came into their heads. Guy laughed at a joke Bob told in French-Canadian dialect. It was a fresh, sunny November morning, and when Anne got back from her marketing, they were going to take the car to Long Island and go for a sail. Guy felt a boyish, holiday delight in having Bob with him. Bob symbolized Canada and the work there, the project in which Guy felt he had entered another vaster chamber of himself where Bruno could not follow. And the secret of the coming child gave him a sense of impartial benevolence, of magical advantage.

Just as Anne came in the door, the telephone rang again. Guy stood up, but Anne answered it. Vaguely, he thought, Bruno always knows exactly when to call. Then he listened, incredulously, to the conversation drifting towards the sail that afternoon.

'Come along then,' Anne said. 'Oh, I suppose some beer would be nice if you must bring something.'

Guy saw Bob staring at him quizzically.

'What's up?' Bob asked.

'Nothing.' Guy sat down again.

'That was Charles. You don't mind too much if he comes, do you, Guy?' Anne walked briskly across the room with her bag of groceries. 'He said Thursday he'd like to come sailing if we went, and I practically invited him.'

'I don't mind,' Guy said, still looking at her. She was in a gay, euphoric mood this morning, in which it would have been difficult to imagine her refusing anybody anything, but there was more than that, Guy knew, in her inviting Bruno. She wanted to see them together again. She couldn't wait, even today. Guy felt a rise of resentment, and said quickly to himself, she doesn't realize, she can't realize, and it's all your own fault anyway for the hopeless muddle you've made. So he put the resentment down, refused even to admit the odium Bruno would inspire that afternoon. He determined to keep himself under the same control all day.

'You could do worse than watch your nerves a bit, old man,' Bob told him. He lifted his coffee cup and drained it, contentedly. 'Well, at least you're not the coffee fiend you used to be. What was it, ten cups a day?'

'Something like that.' No, he had cut out coffee entirely, trying to sleep, and now he hated it.

They stopped for Helen Heyburn in Manhattan, then crossed the Triboro Bridge to Long Island. The winter sunlight had a frozen clarity at the shore, lay thin on the pale beach, and sparkled nervously on the choppy water. The *India* was like an iceberg at anchor, Guy thought, remembering when its whiteness had been the essence of summer. Automatically, as he rounded the corner of the parking lot, his eye fell on Bruno's long, bright blue convertible. The merry-go-round horse Bruno had ridden on, Guy remembered Bruno saying, had been royal blue, and that was why he had bought the car. He saw Bruno standing under the shed of the dockhouse, saw everything of him except his head, the long black overcoat and the small shoes, the arms with the hands in the pockets, the familiar anxiety of his waiting figure.

Bruno picked up the sack of beer and strolled towards the car with a shy smile, but even at a distance, Guy could see the pent elation, ready to explode. He wore a royal-blue muffler, the same colour as his car. 'Hello. Hello, Guy. Thought I'd try and see you while I could.' He glanced at Anne for help.

'Nice to see you!' Anne said. 'This is Mr Treacher. Mr Bruno.'

Bruno greeted him. 'You couldn't possibly make it to the party tonight, Guy? It's quite a big party. All of you?' His hopeful smile included Helen and Bob.

Helen said she was busy or she would love to. Glancing at her as he locked the car, Guy saw her leaning on Bruno's arm, changing into her moccasins. Bruno handed Anne the sack of beer with an air of departure.

Helen's blonde eyebrows fluted troubledly. 'You're coming with us, aren't you?'

'Not exactly dressed,' Bruno protested feebly.

'Oh, there's lots of slickers on board,' Anne said.

They had to take a rowboat from the dock. Guy and Bruno

argued politely but stubbornly about who should row. until Helen suggested they both row. Guy pulled in long d rokes, and Bruno, beside him on the centre thwart, matched him carefully. Guy could feel Bruno's erratic excitement mounting as they drew near the *India*. Bruno's hat blew off twice, and at last he stood up and spun it spectacularly into the sea.

'I hate hats anyway!' he said with a glance at Guy.

Bruno refused to put on a slicker, though the spray dashed now and then over the cockpit. It was too gusty to raise sail. The *India* entered the Sound under engine power, with Bob steering.

'Here's to Guy!' Bruno shouted, but with the odd hitch of repression and inarticulateness Guy had noticed since he first spoke that morning. 'Congratulations, salutations!' He brought the beautiful, fruit-ornamented silver flask down suddenly and presented it to Anne. He was like some clumsy, powerful machine that could not catch its proper time beat to start. 'Napoleon brandy. Five-star.'

Anne declined, but Helen, who was already feeling the cold, drank some, and so did Bob. Under the tarpaulin, Guy held Anne's mittened hand and tried not to think about anything, not about Bruno, not about Alberta, not about the sea. He could not bear to look at Helen, who was encouraging Bruno, nor at Bob's polite, vaguely embarrassed smile as he faced front at the wheel.

'Anybody know "Foggy, Foggy Dew"?' Bruno asked, brushing spray fussily off a sleeve. His pull from the silver flask had pushed him over the line into drunkenness.

Bruno was nonplussed because no one wanted any more of his specially selected liquor, and because no one wanted to sing. It also crushed him that Helen said 'Foggy, Foggy Dew' was depressing. He loved 'Foggy, Foggy Dew'. He wanted to sing or shout or do *something*. When else would they all be together again like this? He and Guy. Anne. Helen. And Guy's friend. He twisted up in his corner seat and looked all around him, at the thin line of horizon that appeared and disappeared behind the swells of sea, at the diminishing land behind them. He tried to look at the pennant at the top of the mast, but the mast's swaying made him dizzy.

'Some day Guy and I are going to circle the world like an isinglass ball, and tie it up in a ribbon!' he announced, but no one paid any attention.

Helen was talking with Anne, making a gesture like a ball with her hands, and Guy was explaining something about the motor to Bob. Bruno noticed as Guy bent over that the creases in his forehead looked deeper, his eyes as sad as ever.

'Don't you realize anything!' Bruno shook Guy's arm. 'You have to be so serious *today*?'

Helen started to say something about Guy's always being serious, and Bruno roared her down, because she didn't know a damned thing about the way Guy was serious or why. Bruno returned Anne's smile gratefully, and produced the flask again.

But still Anne did not want any, and neither did Guy.

'I brought it specially for you, Guy. I thought you'd like it,' Bruno said, hurt.

'Have some, Guy,' Anne said.

Guy took it and drank a little.

'To Guy! Genius, friend, and partner!' Bruno said and drank after him. 'Guy *is* a genius. Do you all realize that?' He looked around at them, suddenly wanting to call them all a bunch of numbskulls.

'Certainly,' said Bob agreeably.

'As you're an old friend of Guy's,' Bruno raised his flask, 'I salute you also!'

'Thank you. A very old friend. One of the oldest.'

'How old?' Bruno challenged.

Bob glanced at Guy and smiled. 'Ten years or so.'

Bruno frowned. 'I've known Guy all his life,' he said softly, menacingly. 'Ask him.'

Guy felt Anne wriggle her hand from his tight hold. He saw Bob chuckling, not knowing what to make of it. Sweat made his forehead cold. Every shred of calm had left him, as it always did. Why did he always think he could endure Bruno, given one more chance?

'Go on and tell him I'm your closest friend, Guy.'

'Yes,' Guy said. He was conscious of Anne's small tense smile and of her silence. Didn't she know everything now? Wasn't she merely waiting for him and Bruno to put it into words in the next seconds? And suddenly it was like the moment in the coffee shop, the afternoon of the Friday night, when he felt he had already told Anne everything that he was going to do. He was going to tell her, he remembered. But the fact he hadn't quite yet told her, that Bruno was once more dancing around him, seemed the last good measure of excoriation for his delay.

'Sure I'm mad!' Bruno shouted to Helen, who was inching away from him on the seat. 'Mad enough to take on the whole world and whip it! Any man doesn't think I whipped it, I'll settle with him privately!' He laughed, and the laugh, he saw, only bewildered the blurred, stupid faces around him, tricked them into laughing with him. 'Monkeys!' he threw at them cheerfully.

'Who is he?' Bob whispered to Guy.

'Guy and I are superman!' Bruno said.

'You're a superman drinker,' Helen remarked.

'That's not true!' Bruno struggled on to one knee.

'Charles, calm *down*!' Anne told him, but she smiled, too, and Bruno only grinned back.

'I defy what she said about my drinking!'

'What's he talking about?' Helen demanded. 'Have you two made a killing on the stock market?'

'Stock market, cr—!' Bruno stopped, thinking of his father. 'Yee-hoo-oo! I'm a Texan! Ever ride the merry-go-round in Metcalf, Guy?'

Guy's feet jerked under him, but he did not get up and he did not look at Bruno.

'Awright, I'll sit down,' Bruno said to him. 'But you disappoint me. You disappoint me horribly!' Bruno shook his empty flask, then lobbed it overboard.

'He's crying,' Helen said.

Bruno stood up and stepped out of the cockpit on to the deck. He wanted to take a long walk away from all of them, even away from Guy.

'Where's he going?' Anne asked.

'Let him go,' Guy murmured, trying to light a cigarette.

Then there was a splash, and Guy knew Bruno had fallen overboard. Guy was out of the cockpit before any of them spoke.

Guy ran to the stern, trying to get his overcoat off. He felt his arms pinned behind him and, turning, hit Bob in the face with his fist and flung himself off the deck. Then the voices and the rolling stopped, and there was a moment of agonizing stillness before his body began to rise through the water. He shed the overcoat in slow motion, as if the water that was so cold it was merely a pain had frozen him already. He leapt high, and saw Bruno's head incredibly far away, like a mossy, half-submerged rock.

'You can't reach him!' Bob's voice blared, cut off by a burst of water against his ear.

'Guy!' Bruno called from the sea, a wail of dying.

Guy cursed. He could reach him. At the tenth stroke, he leapt up again. 'Bruno!' But he couldn't see him now.

'There, Guy!' Anne pointed from the stern of the *India*.

Guy couldn't see him, but he threshed towards the memory of his head, and went down at the place, groping with his arms wide, the farthest tips of his fingers searching. The water slowed him. As if he moved in a nightmare, he thought. As on the lawn. He came up under a wave and took a gasp of water. The *India* was in a different place, and turning. Why didn't they direct him? They didn't care, those others!

'Bruno!'

Perhaps behind one of the wallowing mountains. He threshed on, then realized he was directionless. A wave bashed the side of his head. He cursed the gigantic, ugly body of the sea. Where was his friend, his brother?

He went down again, deep as he could, spreading his ridiculous length as wide as he could. But now there seemed nothing but a silent grey vacuum filling all space, in which he was only a tiny point of consciousness. The swift, unbearable loneliness pressed him closer, threatening to swallow his own life. He stretched his eyes desperately. The greyness became a brown, ridged floor.

'Did you find him?' he blurted, raising himself up. 'What time is it?'

'Lie still, Guy,' Bob's voice said.

'He went down, Guy,' Anne said. 'We saw him.'

Guy closed his eyes and wept.

He was aware that, one by one, they all went out of the bunk-room and left him, even Anne.

46

Carefully, so as not to awaken Anne, Guy got out of bed and went downstairs to the living-room. He drew the drapes together and turned on the light, though he knew there was no shutting out the dawn that slithered now under the Venetian blinds, between the green drapes, like a silvery-mauve and amorphous fish. He had lain upstairs in the darkness awaiting it, knowing it would come for him finally over the foot of the bed, fearing more than ever the grip of the mechanism it set in motion, because he knew now that Bruno had borne half his guilt. If it had been almost unbearable before, how would he bear it now alone? He knew that he couldn't.

He envied Bruno for having died so suddenly, so quietly, so violently, and so young. And so easily, as Bruno had always done everything. A tremor passed through him. He sat rigidly in the armchair, his body under the thin pyjamas as hard and tense as in the first dawns. Then on the spasmic snap that always broke his tension, he got up and went upstairs to the studio before he actually knew what he intended to do. He looked at the big sleek-surfaced sheets of drawing paper on his work table, four or five lying as he had left them after sketching something for Bob. Then he sat down and began to write from the upper left-hand corner across, slowly at first, then more and more rapidly. He wrote of Miriam and of the train, the telephone calls, of Bruno in Metcalf, of the letters, the gun, and his dissolution, and of the Friday night. As if Bruno were still alive, he wrote every detail he knew that might contribute to an understanding of him. His writing blackened three of the big sheets. He folded the sheets, put them into an oversized envelope, and sealed it. For a long while he stared at the envelope, savouring its partial relief, wondering at its separateness now from himself. Many times before he had written passionate, scribbled admissions but, knowing no one would ever see them, they had never really left him. This was for Anne. Anne would touch this envelope. Her hands would hold the sheets of paper, and her eyes would read every word.

Guy put his palms up to his own hot, aching eyes. The hours of writing had tired him almost to a point of sleepiness. His thoughts drifted, resting on nothing, and the people he had been writing about – Bruno, Miriam, Owen Markman, Samuel Bruno, Arthur Gerard, Mrs McCausland, Anne – the people and the names danced around the edge of his mind. *Miriam*. Oddly, she was more a person to him now than ever before. He had tried to describe her to Anne, tried to evaluate her. It had forced him to evaluate her to himself. She was not worth a great deal as a person, he thought, by Anne's standards or by anyone's. But she had been a human being. Neither had Samuel Bruno been worth a great deal – a grim, greedy maker of money, hated by his son, unloved by his wife. Who had really loved him? Who had really been hurt by either Miriam's death or Samuel Bruno's? If there were someone who had been hurt – Miriam's family, perhaps? Guy remembered her brother on the witness stand at the inquest, the small eyes that had held nothing but malicious, brutal hatred, not grief. And her mother, vindictive, as vicious of spirit as ever, not caring where the blame fell as long as it fell on someone, unbroken, unsoftened by grief. Was there any purpose, even if he wanted to, in going to see them and giving them a target for their hatred? Would it make them feel any better? Or him? He couldn't see that it would. If anyone had really loved Miriam – Owen Markman.

Guy took his hands down from his eyes. The name had swum into his mind mechanically. He hadn't thought of Owen at all until he wrote the letter. Owen had been a dim figure in the background. Guy had held him of less value than Miriam. But Owen must have loved her. He had been going to marry her. She had been carrying his child. Suppose Owen had staked all his happiness on Miriam. Suppose he had known the grief in the months afterwards that Guy himself had known when Miriam died to him in Chicago. Guy tried to recall every detail of Owen Markman at the inquest. He remembered his hangdog manner, his calm, straightforward answers until his accusation of jealousy. Impossible to tell what really might have been going on in his head.

'Owen,' Guy said.

Slowly, he stood up. An idea was taking form in his mind even as he tried to weigh his memories of the long, dark face and tall, slouching figure that was Owen Markman. He would go and see Markman and talk with him, tell him everything. If he owed it to anyone, he owed it to Markman. Let Markman kill him if he would, call the police in, anything. But he would have told him, honestly, and face to face. Suddenly it was an urgent necessity. Of course. It was the only step and the next step. After that, after his personal debt, he would shoulder whatever the law put upon him. He would be ready then. He could catch a train today, after the questions they were supposed to answer about Bruno. The police had told him to be at the station with Anne this morning. He could even catch a plane this afternoon, if he was lucky. Where was it? Houston. If Owen was still there. He mustn't let Anne go with him to the airport. She must think he was going to Canada as he had planned. He didn't want Anne to know yet. The appointment with Owen was more urgent. It seemed to transform him. Or perhaps it was like the shedding of an old and worn-out coat. He felt naked now, but not afraid any longer.

47

Guy sat on a jumpseat in the aisle of a plane bound for Houston. He felt miserable and nervous, as out of place and wrong, somehow, as the little lump of the seat itself that clogged the aisle and spoilt the symmetry of the plane's interior. Wrong, unnecessary, and yet he was convinced that what he was doing was necessary. The difficulties he had hurdled in getting this far had put him in a mood of stubborn determination.

Gerard had been at the police station to hear the questioning on Bruno's death. He had flown over from Iowa, he said. It was too bad, Charles' end, but Charles had never been cautious about anything. It was too bad it had had to happen on Guy's boat. Guy had been able to answer the questions without any emotion whatever. It had seemed so insignificant, the details of the disappearance of his body. Guy had been more disturbed by Gerard's presence. He didn't want Gerard to follow him down to Texas. To be doubly safe, he had not even cancelled his ticket on the plane to Canada, which had left earlier in the afternoon. Then he had waited nearly four hours at the airport for this plane. But he was safe. Gerard had said he was going back to Iowa by train this afternoon.

Nevertheless, Guy took another look around him at the passengers, a slower and more careful look than he had dared take the first time. There was not one who seemed the least interested in him.

The thick letter in his inside pocket crackled as he bent over the papers in his lap. The papers were sectional reports of the Alberta work, which Bob had given him. Guy couldn't have read a magazine, he didn't want to look out the window, but he knew he could memorize, mechanically and efficiently, the items in the reports that had to be memorized. He found a page from an English architectural magazine torn out and stuck between the mimeographed sheets. Bob had circled a paragraph in red pencil:

Guy Daniel Haines is the most significant architect yet to emerge from the American South. With his first independent work at the age of twenty-seven, a simple, two-storey building which has become famous as 'The Pittsburgh Store', Haines set forth principles of grace and function to which he has steadfastly held, and through which his art has grown to its present stature. If we seek to define Haines' peculiar genius, we must depend chiefly upon that elusive and aery term, 'grace', which until Haines has never distinguished modern architecture. It is Haines' achievement to have made classic in our age his own concept of grace. His main building of the widely known Palmyra group in Palm Beach, Florida, has been called 'The American Parthenon' . . .

An asterisked paragraph at the bottom of the page said:

Since the writing of this article, Mr Haines has been appointed a member of the Advisory Committee of the Alberta Dam project in Canada. Bridges have always interested him, he says. He estimates that this work will occupy him happily for the next three years.

'Happily,' he said. How had they happened to use such a word?

A clock was striking 9 as Guy's taxi crossed the main street of Houston. Guy had found Owen Markman's name in a telephone book at the airport, had checked his bags and got into a taxi. It won't be so simple, he thought. You can't just arrive at 9 in the evening and find him at home, and alone, and willing to sit in a chair and listen to a stranger. He won't be home, or he won't be living there any more, or he won't even be in Houston any more. It might take days.

'Pull up at this hotel,' Guy said.

Guy got out and reserved a room. The trivial, provident gesture made him feel better.

Owen Markman was not living at the address in Cleburne Street. It was a small apartment building. The people in the hall downstairs, among them the superintendent, looked at him very suspiciously and gave him as little information as possible. No one knew where Owen Markman was.

'You're not the police, are you?' asked the superintendent finally.

Despite himself, he smiled. 'No.'

Guy was on his way out when a man stopped him on the steps and, with the same air of cautious reluctance, told him that he might be able to find Markman at a certain café in the centre of town.

Finally, Guy found him in a drugstore, sitting at the counter with two women whom he did not introduce. Owen Markman simply slid off his stool and stood up straight, his brown eyes a little wide. His long face looked heavier and less handsome than Guy remembered it. He slid his big hands warily into the slash pockets of his short leather jacket.

'You remember me,' Guy said.

'Reckon I do.'

'Would you mind if I had a talk with you? Just for a little while.' Guy looked around him. The best thing was to invite him to his hotel room, he supposed. 'I've got a room here at the Rice Hotel.'

Markman looked Guy slowly up and down once more, and after a long silence said, 'All right.'

Passing the cashier's desk, Guy saw the shelves of liquor bottles. It might be hospitable to offer Markman a drink. 'Do you like Scotch?'

Markman loosened up a bit as Guy bought it. 'Coke's fine, but it tastes better with a little something in it.'

Guy bought some bottles of Coca-Cola, too.

They rode to the hotel in silence, rode up in the elevator and entered the room in silence. How would he begin, Guy wondered. There were a dozen beginnings. Guy discarded them all.

Owen sat down in the armchair, and divided his time between eyeing Guy with insouciant suspicion, and savouring the long glass of Scotch and Coca-Cola.

Guy began stammeringly, 'What —'

'What?' asked Owen.

'What would you do if you knew who murdered Miriam?'

Markman's foot thudded down to the floor, and he sat up. His frowning brows made a black, intense line above his eyes. 'Did you?'

'No, but I know the man who did.'

'Who?'

What was he feeling as he sat there frowning, Guy wondered. Hatred? Resentment? Anger? 'I know, and so will the police very soon.' Guy hesitated. 'It was a man from New York whose name was Charles Bruno. He died yesterday. He was drowned.'

Owen sat back a little. He took a sip of his drink. 'How do you know? Confessed?'

'I know. I've known for some time. That's why I've felt it was my fault. For not betraying him.' He moistened his lips. It was difficult every syllable of the way. And why did he uncover himself so cautiously, inch by inch? Where were all his fantasies, the imagined pleasure and relief of blurting it all out? 'That's why I blame myself. I –' Owen's shrug stopped him. He watched Owen finish his glass, then automatically, Guy went and mixed another for him. 'That's why I blame myself,' he repeated. 'I have to tell you the circumstances. It was very complex. You see, I met Charles Bruno on a train, coming down to Metcalf. The train in June, just before she was killed. I was coming down to get my divorce.' He swallowed. There it was, the words he had never said to anyone before, said of his own will, and it felt so ordinary now, so ignominious evèn. He had a huskiness in his throat he could not get rid of. Guy studied Owen's long, dark attentive face. There was less of a frown now. Owen's leg was crossed again, and Guy remembered suddenly the grey buckskin work shoes Owen had worn at the inquest. These were plain brown shoes with elastic sidepieces. 'And –'

'Yeah,' Owen prompted.

'I told him Miriam's name. I told him I hated her. Bruno had an idea for a murder. A double murder.'

'Jesus !' Owen whispered.

The 'Jesus' reminded him of Bruno, and Guy had a horrible, an utterly horrible thought all at once, that he might ensnare Owen in the same trap that Bruno had used for him, that Owen in turn would capture another stranger who would capture another, and so on in infinite progression of the trapped and the hunted. Guy shuddered and clenched his hands. 'My mistake was in speaking to him. My mistake was in telling a stranger my private business.'

'He told you he was going to kill her?'

'No, of course not. It was an idea he had. He was insane. He was a psychopath. I told him to shut up and go to hell. I got rid of him !' He was back in the compartment. He was leaving it to go on to the platform. He heard the bang of the train's heavy door. Got rid of him, he had thought !

'You didn't tell him to do it.'

'No. He didn't say he was going to do it.'

'Why don't you have a straight shot? Why don't you sit down?' Owen's slow, rasping voice made the room steady again. His voice was like an ugly rock, solidly lodged in dry ground.

He didn't want to sit down, and he didn't want to drink. He

had drunk Scotch like this in Bruno's compartment. This was the end and he didn't want it to be like the beginning. He touched the glass of Scotch and water that he had fixed for himself only for politeness' sake. When he turned around, Owen was pouring more liquor into his glass, continued to pour it, as if to show Guy that he hadn't been trying to do it behind his back.

'Well,' Owen drawled, 'if the fellow was a nut like you say – That was the court's opinion finally, too, wasn't it, that it must have been a madman?'

'Yes.'

'I mean, sure I can understand how you felt afterwards, but if it was just a conversation like you say, I don't see where you should blame yourself so awful much.'

Guy was staring at him incredulously. Didn't it matter to Owen more than this? Maybe he didn't entirely understand. 'But you see –'

'When did you find out about it?' Owen's brown eyes looked slurry.

'About three months after it happened. But you see, if not for me, Miriam would be alive now.' Guy watched Owen lower his lips to the glass again. He could taste the sickening mess of Coca-Cola and Scotch sliding into Owen's wide mouth. What was Owen going to do? Leap up suddenly and fling the glass down, throttle him as Bruno had throttled Miriam? He couldn't imagine that Owen would continue to sit there, but the seconds went by and Owen did not move. 'You see, I had to tell you,' Guy persisted. 'I considered you the one person I might have hurt, the one person who suffered. Her child had been yours. You were going to marry her. You loved her. It was you –'

'Hell, I didn't love her.' Owen looked at Guy with no change whatever in his face.

Guy stared back at him. Didn't love her, didn't love her, Guy thought. His mind staggered back, trying to realign all the past equations that no longer balanced. 'Didn't love her?' he said.

'No. Well, not the way you seem to think. I certainly didn't want her to die – and understand, I'd have done anything to prevent it, but I was glad enough not to have to marry her. Getting married was her idea. That's why she had the child.

That's not a man's fault, I wouldn't say. Would you?' Owen was looking at him with a tipsy earnestness, waiting, his wide mouth the same firm, irregular line it had been on the witness stand, waiting for Guy to say something, to pass judgement on his conduct with Miriam.

Guy turned away with a vaguely impatient gesture. He couldn't make the equations balance. He couldn't make any sense to it, except an ironic sense. There was no reason for his being here now, except for an ironic reason. There was no reason for his sweating, painful self-torture in a hotel room for the benefit of a stranger who didn't care, except for an ironic reason.

'Do you think so?' Owen kept on, reaching for the bottle on the table beside him.

Guy couldn't have made himself say a word. A hot, inarticulate anger was rising inside him. He slid his tie down and opened his shirt collar, and glanced at the open windows for an air-conditioning apparatus.

Owen shrugged. He looked quite comfortable in his open-collared shirt and unzipped leather jacket. Guy had an absolutely unreasonable desire to ram something down Owen's throat, to beat him and crush him, above all to blast him out of his complacent comfort in the chair.

'Listen,' Guy began quietly, 'I am a –'

But Owen had begun to speak at the same instant, and he went on, droningly, not looking at Guy who stood in the middle of the floor with his mouth still open. '... the second time. Got married two months after my divorce, and there was trouble right away. Whether Miriam would of been any different, I don't know, but I'd say she'd of been worse. Louisa up and left two months ago after damn near setting the house on fire, a big apartment house.' He droned on, and poured more Scotch into his glass from the bottle at his elbow, and Guy felt a disrespect, a definite affront, directed against himself, in the way Owen helped himself. Guy remembered his own behaviour at the inquest, undistinguished behaviour, to say the least, for the husband of the victim. Why should Owen have respect for him? 'The awful thing is, the man gets the worst of it, because the women do more talking. Take Louisa, she can go back to that apartment house and they'll give her a welcome, but let me so much –'

'Listen!' Guy said, unable to stand it any longer. 'I – I killed someone, too! I'm a murderer, too!'

Owen's feet came down to the floor again, he sat up again, he even looked from Guy to the window and back again, as if he contemplated having to escape or having to defend himself, but the befuddled surprise and alarm on his face was so feeble, so half-hearted, that it seemed a mockery itself, seemed to mock Guy's seriousness. Owen started to set his glass on the table and then didn't. 'How's that?' he asked.

'Listen!' Guy shouted again. 'Listen, I'm a dead man. I'm as good as dead right now, because I'm going to give myself up. Immediately! Because I killed a man, do you understand? Don't look so unconcerned, and don't lean back in that chair again!'

'Why shouldn't I lean back in this chair?' Owen had both hands on his glass now, which he had just refilled with Coca-Cola and Scotch.

'Doesn't it mean anything to you that I am a murderer, and took a man's life, something no human being has a right to do?'

Owen might have nodded, or he might not have. At any rate, he drank again, slowly.

Guy stared at him. The words, unutterable tangles of thousands and thousands of words, seemed to congest even his blood, to cause waves of heat to sweep up his arms from his clenched hands. The words were curses against Owen, sentences and paragraphs of the confession he had written that morning, that were growing jumbled now because the drunken idiot in the armchair didn't want to hear them. The drunken idiot was determined to look indifferent. He didn't look like a murderer, he supposed, in his clean white shirt-sleeves and his silk tie and his dark blue trousers, and maybe even his strained face didn't look like a murderer's to anybody else. 'That's the mistake,' Guy said aloud, 'that nobody knows what a murderer looks like. A murderer looks like anybody!' He laid the back of his fist against his forehead and took it down again, because he had known the last words were coming, and had been unable to stop them. It was exactly like Bruno.

Abruptly Guy went and got himself a drink, a straight three-finger shot, and drank it off.

'Glad to see I've got a drinking companion,' Owen mumbled. Guy sat down on the neat, green-covered bed opposite Owen. Quite suddenly, he had felt tired. 'It doesn't mean anything,' he began again, 'it doesn't mean anything to you, does it?'

'You're not the first man I seen that killed another man. Or woman.' He chuckled. 'Seems to me there's more women that go free.'

'I'm not going free. I'm not free. I did this in cold blood. I had no reason. Don't you see that might be worse? I did it for –' He wanted to say he did it because there had been that measure of perversity within him sufficient to do it, that he had done it because of the worm in the wood, but he knew it would make no sense to Owen, because Owen was a practical man. Owen was so practical, he would not bother to hit him, or flee from him, or call the police, because it was more comfortable to sit in the chair.

Owen waggled his head as if he really did consider Guy's point. His lids were half dropped over his eyes. He twisted and reached for something in his hip pocket, a bag of tobacco. He got cigarette papers from the breast pocket of his shirt.

Guy watched his operations for what seemed like hours. 'Here,' Guy said, offering him his own cigarettes.

Owen looked at them dubiously. 'What kind are they?'

'Canadian. They're quite good. Try one.'

'Thanks, I –' Owen drew the bag closed with his teeth – 'prefer my own brand.' He spent at least three minutes rolling the cigarette.

'This was just as if I pulled a gun on someone in a public park and shot him,' Guy went on, determined to go on, though it was as if he talked to an inanimate thing like a dictaphone in the chair, with the difference that his words didn't seem to be penetrating in any way. Mightn't it dawn on Owen that he could pull a gun on him now in his hotel room? Guy said, 'I was driven to it. That's what I'll tell the police, but that won't make any difference, because the point is, I did it. You see, I have to tell you Bruno's idea.' At least Owen was looking at him now, but his face, far from being rapt, seemed actually to wear an expression of pleasant, polite drunken attention. Guy refused to let it stop him. 'Bruno's idea was that we should kill for each other, that he should kill Miriam and I should kill his father. Then he came to Texas and killed Miriam, behind my back. Without my knowledge or consent, do you see?' His choice of words was abominable, but at least Owen was listening. At least the words were coming out. 'I didn't know about it, and I didn't even suspect – not really. Until months later. And then he began to haunt me. He began to tell me he would pin the blame for Miriam's death on me, unless I went through with the rest of his damned plan, do you see? Which was to kill his father. The whole idea rested on the fact that there was no reason for the murders. No personal motives. So we couldn't be traced, individually. Provided we didn't see each other. But that's another point. The point is, I did kill him. I was broken down. Bruno broke me down with letters and blackmail and sleeplessness. He drove me insane, too. And listen, I believe any man can be broken down. I could break you down. Given the same circumstances, I could break you down and make you kill someone. It might take different methods from the ones Bruno used on me, but it could be done. What else do you think keeps the totalitarian states going? Or do you ever stop to wonder about things like that, Owen? Anyway, that's what I'll tell the police, but it won't matter, because they'll say I shouldn't have broken down. It won't matter, because they'll say I was weak. But I don't care now, do you see? I can face anyone now, do you see?' He bent to look into Owen's face, but Owen seemed scarcely to see him. Owen's head was sagged sideways, resting in his hand. Guy stood up straight. He couldn't make Owen see, he could feel that Owen wasn't understanding the main point at all, but that didn't matter either. 'I'll accept it, whatever they want to do to me. I'll say the same thing to the police tomorrow.'

'Can you prove it?' Owen asked.

'Prove what? What is there to prove about my killing a man?'

The bottle slipped out of Owen's fingers and fell on to the floor, but there was so little in it now that almost nothing spilled. 'You're an architect, aren't you?' Owen asked. 'I remember now.' He righted the bottle clumsily, leaving it on the floor.

'What does it matter?'

'I was wondering.'

'Wondering what?' Guy asked impatiently.

'Because you sound a little touched – if you want my honest opinion. Ain't saying you do.' And behind Owen's fogged expression now was a simple wariness lest Guy might walk over and hit him for his remark. When he saw that Guy didn't move, he sat back in his chair again, and slumped lower than before.

Guy groped for a concrete idea to present to Owen. He didn't want his audience to slip away, indifferent as it was. 'Listen, how do you feel about the men you know who've killed somebody? How do you treat them? How do you act with them? Do you pass the time of day with them the same as you'd do with anybody else?'

Under Guy's intense scrutiny, Owen did seem to try to think. Finally he said with a smile, blinking his eyes relaxedly, 'Live and let live.'

Anger seized him again. For an instant, it was like a hot vice, holding his body and brain. There were no words for what he felt. Or there were too many words to begin. The word formed itself and spat itself from between his teeth: *'Idiot!'*

Owen stirred slightly in his chair, but his unruffledness prevailed. He seemed undecided whether to smile or to frown. 'What business is it of mine?' he asked firmly.

'What business? Because you – you are a part of society!'

'Well, then it's society's business,' Owen replied with a lazy wave of his hand. He was looking at the Scotch bottle, in which only half an inch remained.

What business, Guy thought. Was that his real attitude, or was he drunk? It must be Owen's attitude. There was no reason for him to lie now. Then he remembered it had been his own attitude when he had suspected Bruno, before Bruno had begun to dog him. Was that most people's attitude? If so, who was society?

Guy turned his back on Owen. He knew well enough who society was. But the society he had been thinking about in regard to himself, he realized, was the law, was inexorable rules. Society was people like Owen, people like himself, people like – Brillhart, for instance, in Palm Beach. Would Brillhart have reported him?

No. He couldn't imagine Brillhart reporting him. Everyone would leave it for someone else, who would leave it for someone else, and no one would do it. Did he care about rules? Wasn't it a rule that had kept him tied to Miriam? Wasn't it a person who was murdered, and therefore people who mattered? If people from Owen to Brillhart didn't care sufficiently to betray him, should he care any further? Why did he think this morning that he had wanted to give himself up to the police? What masochism was it? He wouldn't give himself up. What, concretely, did he have on his conscience now? What human being would inform on him?

'Except a stool-pigeon,' Guy said. 'I suppose a stool-pigeon would inform.'

'That's right,' Owen agreed. 'A dirty, stinking stool-pigeon.' He gave a loud, relieving laugh.

Guy was staring into space, frowning. He was trying to find solid ground that would carry him to something he had just seen as if by a flash, far ahead of him. The law was not society, it began. Society was people like himself and Owen and Brillhart, who hadn't the right to take the life of another member of society. And yet the law did. 'And yet the law is supposed to be the will of society at least. It isn't even that. Or maybe it is collectively,' he added, aware that as always he was doubling back before he came to a point, making things as complex as possible in trying to make them certain.

'Hmm-m?' Owen murmured. His head was back against the chair, his black hair tousled over his forehead, and his eyes almost closed.

'No, people collectively might lynch a murderer, but that's exactly what the law is supposed to guard against.'

'Never hold with lynchings,' Owen said. ''S not true! Gives the whole South a bad name – unnec'sarily.'

'My point is, that if society hasn't the right to take another person's life, then the law hasn't either. I mean, considering that the law is a mass of regulations that have been handed down and that nobody can interfere with, no human being can touch. But it's human beings the law deals with, after all. I'm talking about people like you and me. My case in particular. At the moment,

I'm only talking about my case. But that's only logic. Do you know something, Owen? Logic doesn't always work out, so far as people go. It's all very well when you're building a building, because the material behaves then, but –' His argument went up in smoke. There was a wall that prevented him from saying another word, simply because he couldn't think any further. He had spoken loudly and distinctly, but he knew Owen hadn't been hearing, even if he was trying to listen. And yet Owen *had* been indifferent, five minutes ago, to the question of his guilt. 'What about a jury, I wonder,' Guy said.

'What jury?'

'Whether a jury is twelve human beings or a body of laws. It's an interesting point. I suppose it's always an interesting point.' He poured the rest of the bottle into his glass and drank it. 'But I don't suppose it's interesting to you, is it, Owen? What is interesting to you?'

Owen was silent and motionless.

'Nothing is interesting to you, is it?' Guy looked at Owen's big scuffed brown shoes extended limply on the carpet, the toes tipped inward towards each other, because they rested on their heels. Suddenly, their flaccid, shameless, massive stupidity seemed the essence of all human stupidity. It translated itself instantly into his old antagonism against the passive stupidity of those who stood in the way of the progress of his work, and before he knew how or why, he had kicked, viciously, the side of Owen's shoe. And still, Owen did not move. His work, Guy thought. Yes, there was his work to get back to. Think later, think it all out right later, but he had work to do.

He looked at his watch. Ten past 12. He didn't want to sleep here. He wondered if there was a plane tonight. There must be something out. Or a train.

He shook Owen. 'Owen, wake up. Owen!'

Owen mumbled a question.

'I think you'll sleep better at home.'

Owen sat up and said clearly, 'That I doubt.'

Guy picked up his topcoat from the bed. He looked around, but he hadn't left anything because he hadn't brought anything. It might be better to telephone the airport now, he thought.

'Where's the john?' Owen stood up. 'I don't feel so good.'

Guy couldn't find the telephone. There was a wire by the bed table, though. He traced the wire under the bed. The telephone was off the hook, on the floor, and he knew immediately it hadn't fallen, because both parts were dragged up near the foot of the bed, the hand piece eerily focused on the armchair where Owen had been sitting. Guy pulled the telephone slowly towards him.

'Hey, ain't there a john anywheres?' Owen was opening a closet door.

'It must be down the hall.' His voice was like a shudder. He was holding the telephone in a position for speaking, and now he brought it closer to his ear. He heard the intelligent silence of a live wire. 'Hello?' he said.

'Hello, Mr Haines.' The voice was rich, courteous, and just the least brusque.

Guy's hand tried unavailingly to crush the telephone, and then he surrendered without a word. It was like a fortress falling, like a great building falling apart in his mind, but it crumbled like powder and fell silently.

'There wasn't time for a dictaphone. But I heard most of it from just outside your door. May I come in?'

Gerard must have had his scouts at the airport in New York, Guy thought, must have followed in a chartered plane. It was possible. And here it was. And he had been stupid enough to sign the register in his own name. 'Come in,' Guy echoed. He put the telephone on the hook and stood up, rigidly, watching the door. His heart was pounding as it never had before, so fast and hard, he thought surely it must be a prelude to his dropping dead. Run, he thought. Leap, attack as soon as he comes in. This is your very last chance. But he didn't move. He was vaguely aware of Owen being sick in the basin in the corner behind him. Then there was a rap at the door, and he went towards it, thinking, wouldn't it have to be like this after all, by surprise, with someone, a stranger who didn't understand anything, throwing up in a basin in a corner of the room, without his thoughts ordered, and worse, having already uttered half of them in a muddle. Guy opened the door.

'Hello,' Gerard said, and he came in with his hat on and his arms hanging, just as he had always looked.

'Who is it?' Owen asked.

'Friend of Mr Haines,' Gerard said easily, and glancing at Guy with his round face as serious as before, he gave him a wink. 'I suppose you want to go to New York tonight, don't you?'

Guy was staring at Gerard's familiar face, at the big mole on his cheek, at the bright, living eye that had winked at him, undoubtedly had winked at him. Gerard was the law, too. Gerard was on his side, so far as any man could be, because Gerard knew Bruno. Guy knew it now, as if he had known it the whole time, yet it had never even occurred to him before. He knew, too, that he had to face Gerard. That was part of it all, and always had been. It was inevitable and ordained, like the turning of the earth, and there was no sophistry by which he could free himself from it.

'Eh?' Gerard said.

Guy tried to speak, and said something entirely different from what he had intended. 'Take me.'